Therapy

THERAPY

* A NOVEL *

David Lodge

VIKING

VIKING
Published by the Penguin Group
Penguin Books USA Inc., 375 Hudson Street, New York, New York 10014, U.S.A.
Penguin Books Ltd, 27 Wrights Lane, London W8 5TZ, England
Penguin Books Australia Ltd, Ringwood, Victoria, Australia
Penguin Books Canada Ltd, 10 Alcorn Avenue, Toronto, Ontario, Canada M4V 3B2
Penguin Books (N.Z.) Ltd, 182-190 Wairau Road, Auckland 10, New Zealand

Penguin Books Ltd, Registered Offices: Harmondsworth, Middlesex, England

First American edition
Published in 1995 by Viking Penguin,
a division of Penguin Books USA Inc.

3 5 7 9 10 8 6 4 2

PUBLISHER'S NOTE
This is a work of fiction. Names, characters, places, and incidents either are the product
of the author's imagination or are used fictitiously, and any resemblance to actual
persons, living or dead, events, or locales is entirely coincidental.

Grateful acknowledgment is made for permission to reprint excerpts from the following
copyrighted works: "Too Young," words by Sylvia Dee, music by Sid Lippman.
By permission of Aria Music Company. "Mr. Bleaney" from *Collected Poems* by
Philip Larkin. Copyright © 1988, 1989 by the Estate of Philip Larkin.
Reprinted by permission of Farrar, Straus & Giroux, Inc.

LIBRARY OF CONGRESS CATALOGING IN PUBLICATION DATA
Lodge, David, 1935-
Therapy: a novel/David Lodge.
p   cm.
ISBN 0-670-86358-0
I. Title.
PR6062.O36T48 1995
823' .914—dc20   95-16337

This book is printed on acid-free paper.

Printed in the United States of America
Set in Plantin

To Dad, with love

Many people have kindly helped me with the research for and composition of this novel, by answering my questions and/or by reading and commenting on the text. I am especially indebted to Marie Andrews, Bernard and Anne Bergonzi, Izak Winkel Holm, Michael Paul and Martin Shardlow.

The locations of events in this novel are the usual mixture of the real and the imaginary, but the characters and their actions are entirely fictitious, with the possible exception of the writer-presenter of a television documentary briefly mentioned in Part Four.

D.L.

Therapy. The treatment of physical, mental or social disorders or disease.

– Collins English Dictionary

"You know what, Søren? There's nothing the matter with you but your silly habit of holding yourself round-shouldered. Just straighten your back and stand up and your sickness will be over."

– Christian Lund,
uncle of Søren Kierkegaard.

"Writing is a form of therapy."

– Graham Greene

✳ ✳ ONE ✳ ✳

RIGHT, here goes.

Monday morning, 15th Feb., 1993. A mild February day has brought the squirrels out of hibernation. The leafless trees in the garden make a kind of adventure playground for them. I watched two playing tag in the chestnuts just outside my study window: spiralling up a trunk, dodging and feinting among the branches, then scampering along a bough and leaping to the next tree, then zooming down the side of its trunk headfirst, freezing halfway, claws sticking like Velcro to the corrugated bark, then streaking across the grass, one trying to shake off the other by jinking and swerving and turning on a sixpence till he reached the bole of a Canadian poplar and they both rocketed up its side into the thin elastic branches and balanced there, swaying gently and blinking contentedly at each other. Pure play – no question. They were just larking about, exercising their agility for the sheer fun of it. If there's such a thing as reincarnation, I wouldn't mind coming back as a squirrel. They must have knee-joints like tempered steel.

The first time I felt the pain was about a year ago. I was leaving the London flat, hurrying to catch the 18.10 from Euston, scuttling backwards and forwards between the four rooms, stuffing scripts and dirty socks into my briefcase, shutting windows, switching off lights, re-setting the central-heating timer, emptying milk cartons down the sink, sloshing Sanilav round the toilet bowl – in short, going through the Before You Leave The Flat hit-list that Sally had written out and stuck on the fridge door with magnetic yellow Smileys, when I felt it: a sharp, piercing pain, like a red-hot needle thrust into the inside of the right knee and then withdrawn, leaving a quickly fading afterburn. I uttered a sharp, surprised cry and keeled over on to the bed (I was in the bedroom at the time). "Christ!" I said, aloud, although I was alone. "What the fuck was that?"

Gingerly I got to my feet. (Should that be "gingerlyly"? No, I've just looked it up, adjective and adverb both have the same form.) Gingerly I got to my feet and tested my weight on the knee, took a few paces forward (funny word actually, nothing to do with ginger, I always thought it meant the way you taste ground ginger, very carefully, dipping a moistened finger into it, and then trying it on the tip of your tongue, but no, it's thought to come from Old French *genson*, dainty, or *gent*, of noble birth, neither of which applies to me). I took a few paces forward without any ill-effects, shrugged, and put it down to some freakish twitch of a nerve, like the sudden excruciating crick you can get in your neck sometimes, twisting round to get something from the back seat of a car. I left the flat, caught my train, and thought no more about it.

About a week later, when I was working in my study, I crossed my legs underneath the desk, and I felt it again, the sudden stab of pain on the inside of the right knee, which made me gasp, sucking in a lungful of air and then expelling it with a resounding "*Fuuuuckinell!*" From then onwards, I began to get the pain with increasing frequency, though there was nothing predictable about it. It rarely happened when I might have expected it, like when I was playing golf or tennis, but it could happen just *after* a game, in the club-house bar, or while driving home, or when I was sitting perfectly still in my study, or lying in bed. It would make me cry out in the middle of the night, so that Sally thought I was having a nightmare. In fact nightmares are about the only thing I don't have, in that line. I have depression, anxiety, panic attacks, night sweats, insomnia, but not nightmares. I never did dream much. Which simply means, I understand, that I don't remember my dreams, because we dream all the time we're asleep, so they say. It's as if there's an unwatched telly flickering all night long inside my head. The Dream Channel. I wish I could make a video recording of it. Maybe I would get a clue then to what's the

4

matter with me. I don't mean my knee. I mean my head. My mind. My soul.

I felt it was a bit hard that I should get a mysterious pain in the knee on top of all my other problems. Admittedly, there are worse things that can happen to you, physically. For instance: cancer, multiple sclerosis, motor neurone disease, emphysema, Alzheimer's and AIDS. Not to mention the things you can be born with, like muscular dystrophy, cerebral palsy, haemophilia and epilepsy. Not to mention war, pestilence and famine. Funny how knowing that doesn't make the pain in your knee any easier to bear.

Perhaps it's what they call "compassion fatigue", the idea that we get so much human suffering thrust in our faces every day from the media that we've become sort of numbed, we've used up all our reserves of pity, anger, outrage, and can only think of the pain in our own knee. I haven't got to that stage yet, not quite, but I know what they mean. I get a lot of charity appeals through the mail. I think they pass names and addresses to each other: you only have to make a donation to one organization and, before you know where you are, the envelopes are falling through the letterbox faster than you can pick them up. OXFAM, CAFOD, UNICEF, Save the Children, Royal Institute for the Blind, Red Cross, Imperial Cancer, Muscular Dystrophy, Shelter, etc. etc., all containing form letters and leaflets printed on recycled paper with smudgy b/w pictures of starving black babies with limbs like twigs and heads like old men, or young kids in wheelchairs, or stunned-looking refugees, or amputees on crutches. How is one supposed to stem this tide of human misery? Well, I'll tell you what I do. I subscribe a thousand pounds a year to an organization that gives you a special cheque book to make donations to the charities of your choice. They also recover the tax you've paid on the money, which bumps it up to £1400 in my case. So every year I dispense fourteen hundred quid in little parcels: £50 for the starving babies of Somalia, £30 for the rape victims in Bosnia, £45 towards a water pump in Bangladesh, £25 to a drug-abuse rehabilitation unit in Basildon, £30 for AIDS research, and so on, until the account is empty. It's rather like trying to mop up the oceans of the world with a box of Kleenex, but it keeps compassion fatigue at bay.

Of course, I could afford to give much more. I could afford *ten* thousand a year from my present income, without too much pain. I could give it all away, for that matter, it still wouldn't be more than a box of Kleenex. So I keep most of it and spend it on, among other things, private medical treatment for my knee.

I went to my GP first. He recommended physiotherapy. After a while, the physiotherapist recommended that I see a consultant. The consultant recommended an arthroscopy. That's a new kind of hi-tech microsurgery, all done by television and fibre-optics. The surgeon pumps water into your leg to create a kind of studio in there, and then sticks three needle-thin instruments into it. One has a camera on the end, another is a cutting tool and the third is a pump for sucking out the debris. They're so fine you can hardly tell the difference between them with the naked eye and the surgeon doesn't even have to put a stitch in the perforations afterwards. He sees what's wrong with your knee-joint by wiggling it about and watching it on a TV monitor, and then cuts away the torn cartilage or tissue or rough bit of bone or whatever it is that's causing the trouble. I'd heard that some patients have just a local anaesthetic and watch the whole operation on the monitor as it's being done, but I didn't fancy that, and said so. Nizar smiled reassuringly. (That's the name of my orthopaedic consultant, Mr Nizar. I call him Knees 'R Us. Not to his face, of course. He's from the Near East, Lebanon or Syria or one of those places, and well out of it from what I hear.) He said I would have a general anaesthetic, but he would give me a videotape of the op to take home. He wasn't joking, either. I knew people had their weddings and christenings and holidays videotaped nowadays instead of photographed, but I didn't know it had got as far as operations. I suppose you could make up a little compilation and invite your friends round to view it over wine and cheese. "*That's my appendectomy, had it done in 1984, or was it '85 . . . neat, eh? . . . And this is my open heart surgery, oops, a little bit of camera-jog there . . . Dorothy's womb-scrape is coming up next . . .*" [Memo: idea for *The People Next*

Door in this?] I said to Nizar, "You could probably run a little video-rental business on the side for folk who haven't had any operations of their own." He laughed. He was very confident about the arthroscopy. He claimed that there was a ninety-five per cent success rate. I suppose somebody's got to be in the unlucky five per cent.

I had the operation done at Rummidge General. Being a private patient I would normally have gone into the Abbey, the BUPA hospital near the cricket ground, but they had a bit of a bottleneck there at the time – they were refurbishing one of their operating theatres or something – and Nizar said he could fit me in quicker if I came into the General, where he works one day a week for the NHS. He promised I would have a room to myself, and as the op entailed staying in for only one night, I agreed. I wanted to get it over and done with as soon as possible.

As soon as I arrived at the General by taxi, at nine o'clock one winter morning, I began to wish I'd waited for a bed at the Abbey. The General is a huge, gloomy Victorian pile, blackened redbrick on the outside, slimy green and cream paint on the inside. The main reception area was already full of rows of people slumped in moulded plastic chairs, with that air of abandoned hope I always associate with NHS hospitals. One man had blood seeping through a bandage wrapped round his head. A baby was screaming its head off.

Nizar had given me a scrap of graph paper with his name scrawled on it, and the date and time of my appointment – a ludicrously inadequate document for admission to a hospital, I thought, but the receptionist seemed to recognize it, and directed me to a ward on the third floor. I took the lift and was told off by a sharp-faced nursing sister who stepped in at the first floor and pointed out that it was for the use of hospital staff only. "Where are you going?" she demanded. "Ward 3J," I said. "I'm having a minor operation. Mr Nizar." "Oh," she said with a slight sneer, "You're one of his private patients, are you?" I got the impression she disapproved of private patients being treated in NHS hospitals. "I'm only in for one night," I said, in mitigation. She gave a brief, barking laugh, which unsettled me. It turned out that she was in charge of Ward 3J. I wonder sometimes if she didn't deliberately engineer the harrowing ordeal of the next hour and a half.

There was a row of black plastic chairs up against the wall outside the ward where I sat for about twenty minutes before a thin, drawn-looking young Asian woman, in a house-doctor's white coat, came and wrote down my particulars. She asked me if I had any allergies and tied a dogtag with my name on it to my wrist. Then she led me to a small, two-bed room. There was a man in striped pyjamas lying on one of the beds, with his face to the wall. I was about to protest that I had been promised a private room, when he turned over to look at us and I saw that he was black, probably Caribbean. Not wishing to appear racist, I swallowed my complaint. The house-doctor ordered me to take off all my clothes and to put on one of those hospital nightgowns that open down the back, which was lying folded on top of the vacant bed. She told me to remove any false teeth, glass eyes, artificial limbs or other such accessories I might be secreting on my person, and then left me. I undressed and put on the gown, watched enviously by the Caribbean. He told me he had been admitted three days ago, for a hernia operation, and nobody had come near him since. He seemed to have dropped into some kind of black hole in the system.

I sat on the edge of the bed in my gown, feeling the draught up my legs. The Caribbean turned his face to the wall again and seemed to fall into a light sleep, groaning and whimpering to himself occasionally. The young Asian house-doctor came back into the room and checked the name on my dogtag against her notes as if she had never met me before. She asked me again if I had any allergies. I was rapidly losing faith in this hospital. "That man says he has been here three days and nobody has taken any notice of him," I said. "Well, at least he's had some sleep," said the house-doctor, "which is more than I've had for the last thirty-six hours." She left the room again. Time passed very slowly. A low winter sun shone through the dusty window. I watched the shadow of the window-frame inch its way across the linotiled floor. Then a nurse and a porter pushing a stretcher on wheels came to fetch me to the operating theatre. The porter was a young local man with a poker-player's pallid, impassive face, and the nurse a buxom Irish girl whose starched uniform seemed a size too small for her, giving her a slightly tarty look. The porter tossed me the usual local greeting – "A'right?" – and told me to hop on to the stretcher. I said, "I could walk, you know, in a dressing-gown. I'm not in any actual pain." In fact I hadn't felt a single twinge in the knee for over a week, which is pretty typical of all such ailments: as soon as you decide to have treatment, the symptoms disappear. "No, you've got to be wheeled," he said. "Regulations." Carefully holding the flaps of my gown together like an Edwardian lady adjusting her bustle, I mounted the stretcher and lay down. The nurse asked me if I was nervous. "Should I be?" I asked. She giggled but made no comment. The porter checked the name on my dogtag. "Passmore, yes. Right leg amputation, ennit?" "No!" I exclaimed, sitting up in alarm. "Just a minor knee operation." "He's only having you on," said the nurse. "Stop it, Tom." "Just pulling your leg," said Tom, deadpan. They covered me with a blanket and tucked it in, pinning my arms to my sides. "Stops you getting knocked as we go through the swing doors," Tom explained. The Caribbean woke up and raised himself on one elbow to watch me go. "So long," I said. I never saw him again.

You feel curiously helpless when you're lying on your back on a stretcher without a pillow under your head. You can't tell where you are or where you're going. All you can see is ceilings, and the ceilings of the General Hospital weren't a pretty sight: cracked plaster, flaking emulsion, cobwebs in corners and dead flies in the lighting fixtures. We seemed to be travelling through miles and miles of corridors. "Got to take the scenic route today," Tom remarked from behind my head. "Theatre lift's broke, ennit? Have to take you down to the basement by the utilities lift and then across to the other wing, then up the other lift and back over again." The utilities lift was industrial-size: cavernous, dimly lit and smelling faintly of boiled cabbage and laundry. As I was pushed over the threshold the wheels caught on something and I found myself staring up into the space between the lift and the shaft at the black greasy cables and grooved wheels of the ancient-looking machinery. It was like being in one of those arty-farty movies where everything is shot from unnatural angles.

Tom clashed the folding gate shut, the nurse pressed a button and the lift began to descend very slowly with much creaking and groaning. Its ceiling was even more depressing than the ceilings of the corridors. My companions conducted a desultory conversation out of my sight. "Got a smoke on you?" said the nurse. "No," said Tom, "I've given it up. Gave it up last Tuesday." "Why?" "Health." "What d'you do instead?" "Lots and lots of sex," said Tom levelly. The nurse giggled. "I'll tell you a secret, though," said Tom. "I hid cigarettes all over the hospital when I gave up, in case I get desperate. There's one in the basement." "What kind is it?" "Benson's. You can have it if you like." "Alright," said the nurse, "thanks." The lift stopped with a jolt.

The air in the basement was hot and dry from the central-heating plant, and I began to perspire under the blanket as Tom pushed me between walls of cartons and boxes and bins of hospital supplies. Cobwebs hung thickly from the vaulted ceiling like batshit. The wheels jolted over the stone-flagged floor, jarring my spine. Tom stopped for a minute to ferret for one of his hidden cigarettes. He and the nurse disappeared behind a mountainous bale of laundry, and I heard a little squeal and scuffle which suggested he had exacted a favour in return for the Benson and Hedges. I couldn't believe what was happening to me. How could a private patient be subjected to such indignities? It was as if I'd paid for Club Class and found myself in a broken seat at the back of the plane next to the toilet with smokers coughing in my face (metaphorically speaking – the nurse didn't have the nerve to actually light up). What made it worse was knowing that I'd get no sympathy from Sally when I told her the story: she disapproves of private medicine on principle and refused to join BUPA when I did.

We moved on again, twisting and turning through the labyrinth of stores, until we reached another, similar lift on the far side of the enormous basement, and rose slowly back into daylight. There was another long journey through more corridors – then suddenly everything changed. I passed through swing doors from the nineteenth century to the twentieth, from Victorian Gothic to hi-tech modern. It was like stepping on to a brightly lit, elegant studio set after stumbling about in the dark, cable-encumbered space at the back of a sound stage. Everything was white and silver, stainless and gleaming in the diffused light, and the medical staff welcomed me with kind smiles and soft, cultured voices. I was deftly lifted off the stretcher and onto another, more sophisticated mobile bed, on which I was wheeled into an anteroom where the anaesthetist was waiting. He asked me to flex my left hand, and warned me in soothing tones to expect a slight prick as he inserted a kind of plastic valve into a vein in my arm. Nizar sauntered into the room, swathed in pale blue theatre overalls and wearing a snood over his hair, looking like a plump pyjama-clad housewife who had just risen from her bed and hadn't taken her curlers out yet. " 'Morning, old bean," he greeted me. "Everything tickety-boo?" Nizar speaks immaculate English, but I think he must have read a lot of P. G. Wodehouse once. I was about to say, no, it hadn't been at all tickety-boo so far, but this didn't seem the right moment to complain about my reception. Besides, a warm drowsy feeling of well-being was beginning to come over me. Nizar was looking at X-rays of my knee, holding them up before a lighted screen. "Ah yes," he murmured to himself, as if vaguely recognizing a snapshot of some fleeting acquaintance from the past. He came over and stood at the side of the bed opposite the anaesthetist. They smiled down at me. "A hand-joiner," the anaesthetist commented. What was he implying, I wondered. My blanket had been removed, and not knowing what else to with my hands I had clasped them on my stomach. The anaesthetist patted my hands. "That's good, very good," he said reassuringly. "Some people clench their fists, bite their nails." Nizar lifted the hem of my gown and squeezed my knee. I sniggered and was about to make a joke about sexual harassment when I passed out.

When I came round, I was back in the two-bedded room but the Caribbean man had gone, nobody could tell me where. My right leg, swaddled in bandages, was as big as an elephant's. Sally, who visited me on her way home from work, thought it looked very funny. As I anticipated, I got no sympathy when I described my morning. "Serves you right for queue-jumping," she said. "My Auntie Emily has been waiting two years for a hip operation." Nizar came in later and asked me to lift my leg gently a few inches off the bed. I did it very gently – gingerly, you might say – without adverse effect, and he seemed satisfied. "Jolly good," he said, "spiffing."

After a few days on crutches, waiting for the swelling to subside, and several weeks of physiotherapy and controlled exercise to get the quadriceps back to strength, I started to get the same intermittent pain as before. *Fuuuuuuckinell!* I couldn't believe it. Nizar couldn't believe it either. He reckoned he'd identified the trouble – a bit of tissue called plica that was getting nipped in the knee joint – and cut it away. We watched the video of my operation together on the TV in his office. I hadn't been able to bring myself to watch it before. It was a brightly lit, coloured, circular image, like looking through the porthole of a submarine with a powerful searchlight. "There it is, you see!" cried Nizar. All I could see was what looked like a slim silvery eel biting chunks out of the soft underside of a shellfish. The little steel jaws snapped viciously and fragments of my knee floated off to be sucked out by the aspirator. I couldn't watch for long. I always was squeamish about violence on television.

"Well?" I said, when Nizar switched off the video. "Well, frankly old bean, I'm baffled," he said. "You saw for yourself the plica that was causing the trouble, and you saw me cut it away. There's no evidence of torn meniscus or arthritic degeneration of the joint. There's no bally reason why the knee should be giving you any more pain."

"But it is," I said.

"Yes, quite so. It's jolly annoying."

"Particularly for me," I said.

"It must be idiopathic patella chondromalacia," said Nizar. When I asked him to explain he said, "Patella chondromalacia, means pain in the knee, and idiopathic means it's peculiar to you, old boy." He smiled as if awarding me a prize.

I asked him what could be done about it, and he said, rather less confidently than before, that he could do another arthroscopy, to see if he had by any chance missed something in the first one, or I could try aspirins and physiotherapy. I said I would try aspirins and physiotherapy.

"Of course, I'd do it in the BUPA hospital next time," he said. He was aware that I had been less than enchanted with the standard of care at the General.

"Even so," I said. "I'm not rushing into another operation."

When I told Roland – that's the name of my physiotherapist – when I told Roland the substance of this consultation, he gave his sardonic lopsided smile and said, "You've got Internal Derangement of the Knee. That's what the orthopaedic surgeons call it amongst themselves. Internal Derangement of the Knee. I.D.K. I Don't Know."

Roland is blind, by the way. That's another thing that can happen to you that's worse than a pain in the knee. Blindness.

Tuesday afternoon, 16th Feb. Immediately after writing that last bit yesterday I thought I would try shutting my eyes for a bit, to give myself an idea of what it would be like to be blind, and remind myself how lucky I am compared to poor old Roland. I actually went so far as to blindfold myself, with a sleeping mask British Airways gave me once on a flight from Los Angeles. I thought I would see what it was like to do something quite simple and ordinary, like making a cup of tea, without being able to see. The experiment didn't last long. Trying to get out of the study and into the kitchen I cracked my knee, the right one needless to say, against the open drawer of a filing cabinet. I tore off the blindfold and hopped round the room cursing and blaspheming so terribly I finally shocked myself into silence. I was sure I'd done my knee in for good. But after a while the pain wore off, and this morning the joint doesn't seem to be any worse than it was before. No better, either, of course.

There's one advantage of having Internal Derangement of the Knee, and that is, when people ring you up, and ask you how you are, and you don't want to say, "terminally depressed," but don't feel like pretending that you're brimming over with happiness either, you can always complain about your knee. My agent, Jake Endicott, just called to confirm our lunch appointment tomorrow, and I gave him an earful about the knee first. He's having a meeting with the people at Heartland this afternoon to discuss whether they're going to commission another series of *The People Next Door*. I delivered the last script of the present series only a few weeks ago, but these things have to be decided long in advance, because the actors' contracts will be coming up for renewal soon. Jake is confident that Heartland will commission at least one more series, and probably two. "With audience figures like you're getting, they'd be crazy not to." He said he would tell me the upshot of his meeting at lunch tomorrow. He's taking me to Groucho's. He always does.

It's a year since my arthroscopy, and I'm still getting pain. Should I risk another operation? I Don't Know. I can't decide. I can't make a decision about anything these days. I couldn't decide what tie to wear this morning. If I can't make a decision about a little thing like a tie, how can I make my mind up about an operation? I hesitated so long over my tie-rack that I was in danger of being late for my appointment with Alexandra. I couldn't decide between a dark, conservative tie or a bright, splashy one. Eventually I narrowed the choice down to a plain navy knitted job from Marks and Sparks and an Italian silk number hand-painted in orange, brown and red. But then neither of them seemed to go with the shirt I was wearing, so I had to change that. Time was running out: I put the silk tie round my neck and stuffed the woollen one into my jacket pocket in case I had second thoughts on my way over to Alexandra's office. I did, too – changed over to the knitted tie at a red light. Alexandra is my shrink, my current shrink. Dr Alexandra Marbles. No, her real name is Marples. I call her Marbles for a joke. If she ever moves or retires, I'll be able to say I've lost my Marbles. She doesn't know I call her that, but she wouldn't mind if she did. She *would* mind if she knew I referred to her as my shrink, though. She doesn't describe herself as a psychiatrist, you see, but as a cognitive behaviour therapist.

I have a lot of therapy. On Mondays I see Roland for Physiotherapy, on Tuesdays I see Alexandra for Cognitive Behaviour Therapy, and on Fridays I have either aromatherapy or acupuncture. Wednesdays and Thursdays I'm usually in London, but then I see Amy, which is a sort of therapy too, I suppose.

What's the difference between a psychiatrist and a cognitive behaviour therapist? Well, as I understand it, a psychiatrist tries to uncover the hidden cause of your neurosis, whereas the cognitive behaviour therapist treats the symptoms that are making you miserable. For instance, you might suffer from claustrophobia in buses and trains, and a psychiatrist would try to discover some traumatic experience in your previous life that caused it. Say you were sexually assaulted as a child in a train when it went through a tunnel or something like that, by a man who was sitting next to you – say he interfered with you while it was dark in the compartment because of the tunnel and you were terrified and ashamed and didn't dare accuse the man when the train came out of the tunnel and never even told your parents or anyone about it afterwards but suppressed the memory completely. Then if the psychiatrist could get you to remember that experience and see that it wasn't your fault, you wouldn't suffer from the claustrophobia any more. That's the theory, anyway. The trouble is, as cognitive behaviour therapists point out, it can take for ever to discover the suppressed traumatic experience, even supposing there was one. Take Amy, for instance. She's been in analysis for three years, and she sees her shrink *every day*, Monday to Friday, nine to nine-fifty every morning on her way to work. Imagine how much it's costing her. I asked her once how she would know when she was cured. She said, "When I don't feel the need to see Karl any more." Karl is her shrink, Dr Karl Kiss. If you ask me, Karl is on to a good thing.

So a cognitive behaviour therapist would probably give you a programme for conditioning yourself to travelling by public transport, like going round the Inner Circle on the Tube, travelling for just one stop the first time, then two, then three, and so on, in the off-peak time for starters, then in the rush hour, rewarding yourself each time you increased the length of your journey with some kind of treat, a drink or a meal or a new tie, whatever turns you on – and you're so pleased with your own achievements and these little presents to yourself that you forget to be frightened and finally wake up to the fact that there is nothing to be frightened *of*. That's the theory, anyway. Amy wasn't impressed when I tried to explain it to her. She said, "But supposing one day you got raped on the Inner Circle?" She's rather literal-minded, Amy.

Mind you, people do get raped on the Inner Circle, these days. Even men.

It was my GP who referred me to Alexandra. "She's very good," he assured me. "She's very practical. Doesn't waste time poking around in your unconscious, asking you about potty training, or whether you saw your parents having it off together, that sort of thing." I was relieved to hear that. And Alexandra has certainly been a help. I mean the breathing exercises are quite effective, for about five minutes after I've done them. And I always feel calmer after I've seen her, for at least a couple of hours. She specializes in something called rational-emotive therapy, RET for short. The idea is to get the patient to see that his fears or phobias are based on an incorrect or unwarranted interpretation of the facts. In a way I know that already, but it helps to have Alexandra spell it out. There are times, though, when I hanker after a bit of old-fashioned Viennese analysis, when I almost envy Amy her daily Kiss. (The guy's name is actually pronounced "Kish", he's Hungarian, but I prefer to call him "Kiss".) The thing is, I wasn't always unhappy. I can remember a time when I was happy. Reasonably content anyway. Or at least, a time when I didn't think I was *un*happy, which is perhaps the same thing as being happy. Or reasonably content. But somewhere, sometime, I lost it, the knack of just living, without being anxious and depressed. How? I Don't Know.

"So how are you today?" Alexandra said, as she always does at the beginning of our sessions. We sit facing each other across ten feet of deep-pile pale grey carpet in two easy chairs, in her handsome, high-ceilinged office, which, apart from the antique desk by the window, and a tall functional filing cabinet in one corner, is furnished more like a drawing-room. The chairs are placed each side of a fireplace, where a gas fire made of imitation coals burns cheerfully throughout the winter months, and a vase of freshly cut flowers stands in the summer. Alexandra is tall and slim, and wears graceful, flowing clothes: silk shirts and pleated skirts of fine wool long enough to cover her knees demurely when she sits down. She has a narrow, fine-boned face on top of a very long, slender neck, and her hair is drawn back in a tight bun, or is it chignon? Imagine a rather beautiful, long-lashed female giraffe drawn by Walt Disney.

I began by telling her of my pathological indecision over the ties. "Pathological?" she said. "What makes you use that word?" She's always picking me up on negative words I use about myself.

"Well, I mean, a *tie*, for God's sake! I wasted half an hour of my life anguishing about . . . I mean, how trivial can you get?"

Alexandra asked me why I had found it so difficult to decide between the two ties.

"I thought, if I wore the plain dark blue one you would take it as a sign that I was depressed, or rather as a sign that I was *giving in* to my depression, instead of fighting it. But when I put on the bright one, I thought you would take it as a sign that I'd got over my depression, but I haven't. It seemed to me that whichever tie I wore would be a kind of lie." Alexandra smiled, and I experienced that deceptive lift of the spirits that often comes in therapy when you give a neat answer, like a clever kid in school.

"You could have dispensed with a tie altogether."

"I considered that. But I always wear a tie to these sessions. It's an old habit. It's how I was brought up: always dress properly when you're going to the doctor's. If I suddenly stopped wearing a tie you might think it signified something – disrespect, dissatisfaction – and I'm not dissatisfied. Well, only with myself."

A few weeks ago Alexandra got me to write a short description of myself. I found it quite an interesting exercise. I suppose it was what got me going on the idea of writing this . . . whatever it is. Journal. Diary. Confession. Up till now, I've always written exclusively in dramatic form – sketches, scripts, screenplays. Of course, there's a bit of description in every TV script – stage directions, notes on

17

characters for the casting director ("*JUDY is a good-looking bottle-blonde in her twenties*"), but nothing detailed, nothing analytical, apart from the lines. That's what TV is – all lines. The lines people speak and the lines of the cathode-ray tube that make up the picture. Everything's either in the picture, which tells you where you are, or in the dialogue, which tells you what the characters are thinking and feeling, and often you don't even need words for *that* – a shrug of the shoulders, a widening of the eyes will do it. Whereas if you're writing a book, you've got nothing but words for everything: behaviour, looks, thoughts, feelings, the whole boiling. I take my hat off to book writers, I do honestly.

✳ Laurence Passmore ✳

A SELF-DESCRIPTION

I AM FIFTY-EIGHT YEARS OLD, five feet nine-and-a-half inches tall and thirteen stone eight pounds in weight – which is two stone more than it should be according to the table in our dog-eared copy of *The Family Book of Health*. I didn't acquire the nickname "Tubby" until I was a National Serviceman in the Army, after which it stuck. But I was always a bit on the heavy side for my height, even when I played football as a youth, with a barrel-shaped torso that curved gently outwards from the chest to the point where shirt met shorts. My stomach was all muscle in those days, and useful for bustling opposing players off the ball, but as I got older, in spite of regular exercise, the muscle turned to flab and then spread to my hips and bum, so now I'm more pear-shaped than barrel-shaped. They say that inside every fat man there's a thin man struggling to get out, and I hear his stifled groans every time I look into the bathroom mirror. It's not just the shape of my torso that bothers me, either, and it's not just the torso, come to that. My chest is covered with what looks like a doormat-sized Brillo pad that grows right up to my Adam's apple: if I wear an open-necked shirt, wiry tendrils sprout from the top like some kind of fast-growing fungus from outer space in an old Nigel Kneale serial. And by a cruel twist of genetic fate I have practically no hair *above* the Adam's apple. My pate is as bald as an electric light bulb, like my father's, apart from a little fringe around the ears, and at the nape, which I wear very long, hanging down over my collar. It looks a bit tramp-like, but I can hardly bear to have it cut, each strand is so precious. I hate to see it falling on to the barber-shop floor – I feel they should put it in a paper bag for me to take home. I tried to grow a moustache once, but it turned out rather funny-looking, grey on one side and a sort of gingery-brown on the other, so I shaved it off quick. I considered growing a beard, but I was afraid it would look like a continuation of my chest. So there's nothing to disguise the ordinariness of my face: a pink, puffy oval, creased and wrinkled like a slowly deflating balloon, with pouchy cheeks, a fleshy, slightly bulbous nose and two rather sad-looking watery-blue eyes. My teeth are nothing to write home about, either, but they are my own, the ones you can see anyway (I have a bridge on the lower right-hand side where a few molars are missing). My neck is as thick as a tree-trunk, but my arms are rather short, making it difficult to buy shirts that fit. For most of my life I put up with shirts with cuffs that fell down over my hands as far as the knuckle unless restrained by a long-sleeved sweater or elastic bands round the elbows. Then I went to America where they have discovered that some men have arms shorter than average (in Britain for some reason you are only allowed to have arms that are longer than average) and bought a dozen shirts at Brooks Brothers with 32" sleeves. I top up my wardrobe from an American mail-order firm that started trading in England a few years ago. Of course, I could afford to have my shirts made to measure nowadays, but the snobby-looking shops around Piccadilly where they do it put me off and the striped poplins in the windows are too prim for my taste. In any case, I can't stand shopping. I'm an impatient bloke. At least, I am now. I used not to be. Queuing, for instance. When I was young, queuing was a way of life, I thought nothing of it. Queuing for buses, queuing for the pictures, queuing in shops. Nowadays I hardly ever ride on a bus, I watch most movies at home on video, and if I go into a shop and there are more than two people waiting to be served, more likely than not I'll turn round and walk straight out. I'd rather do without whatever I came for. I especially hate banks and post offices where they have those cordoned-off lanes like Airport Immigration where you have to shuffle slowly forward in line and when you get to the head of the queue you have to keep swivelling your head to see which counter is the first to be free, and more likely than not you don't spot it and some clever dick behind you nudges you in the kidneys and says, "Your turn, mate." I do as much of my banking as possible by a computerized phoneline system nowadays, and I send most of my letters by fax, or have Datapost call at the house if I have a script to mail, but occasionally I need some stamps and have to go and stand in one of those long Post Office queues with a lot of old biddies and single parents with snuffling infants in pushchairs waiting to collect their pensions and income support, and I can hardly restrain myself from shouting, "Isn't it about time we had a counter for people who just want to buy stamps? Who want to *post* things? After all, this *is* a Post Office, isn't it?" That's just a figure of speech, of course, I can restrain myself very easily, I wouldn't dream of shouting anything at all in a public place, but that's the way I feel. I never show my feelings much. Most people who know me would be surprised if I told them I was impatient. I have a reputation in the TV world for being rather placid, unflappable, for keeping my cool when all around are losing theirs. They'd be surprised to learn that I was unhappy with my physique, too. They think I like being called Tubby. I tried dropping a hint once or twice that I wouldn't mind being called Laz instead, but it didn't catch on. The only parts of my body that I'm reasonably pleased with are the extremities, the hands and feet. My feet are quite small, size seven, and narrow, with a high instep. They look good in the Italian shoes I buy more frequently than is strictly necessary. I was always light on my feet, considering the bulk they have to support, a nifty dribbler of a football and not a bad ballroom dancer. I move about the house very quietly, sometimes making my wife jump when she turns round and finds me right behind her. My hands are quite small too, but with long, shapely fingers like a pianist's, not that I can play any keyboard except an IBM one.

* * * * * * * * * * * * * * * * *

I gave this self-description to Alexandra and she glanced at it and said, "Is this all?" I said it was the longest piece of continuous prose I'd written in years. She said, "It hasn't any paragraphs, why is that?" and I explained that I was out of practice in writing paragraphs, I was used to writing lines, speeches, so my self-description had come out as a kind of monologue. I said: "I can only write as if I'm speaking to someone." (It's true. Take this journal for example – I've no intention of letting anybody else read it, but I can only write it as if it's addressed to a "you". I've no idea who "you" is. Just an imaginary, sympathetic ear.) Alexandra put my self-description away in a drawer to read later. At our next meeting she said it was interesting but very negative. "It's mostly about what's wrong with your body, or what you think is wrong with it, and even the two good points you mention, your hands and your feet, are undercut by the references to buying too many shoes and not being able to play the piano." Alexandra thinks I'm suffering from lack of self-esteem. She's probably right, though I read in the paper that there's a lot of it about. There's something like an epidemic of lack of self-esteem in Britain at the moment. Maybe it has something to do with the recession. Not in my case, though. I'm not in recession. I'm doing fine. I'm well-off. I'm almost rich. *The People Next Door*, which has been running for five years, is watched by thirteen million people every week, and there's an American adaptation which is just as successful, and other foreign-language versions all round the globe. Money from these sub-licences pours into my bank account like water from a running tap. So what's the matter with me? Why aren't I satisfied? I don't know.

Alexandra says it's because I'm a perfectionist. I demand impossibly high standards from myself, so I'm bound to be disappointed. There may be some truth in that. Most people in show business are perfectionists. They may be producing crap, acting in crap, writing crap, but they try and make it *perfect* crap. That's the essential difference between us and other people. If you go into the Post Office to buy stamps, the clerk doesn't aim to give you perfect service. Efficient, maybe, if you're lucky, but perfect – no. Why should he try? What's the point? There's no difference between one first-class stamp and another, and there's a very limited number of ways in which you can tear them off the sheets and shove them across the counter. He does the same transactions, day in, day out, year in, year out, he's trapped on a treadmill of repetition. But there's something special about every single episode of a sitcom, however trite and formulaic it may be, and that's for two reasons. The first is that nobody *needs* a sitcom, like they sooner or later need postage stamps, so its only justification for existing is that it gives pleasure, and it won't do that if it's exactly the same as last week's. The second reason is that everyone involved is aware of the first reason, and knows that they'd better make it as good as it possibly can be, or they'll be out of a job. You'd be surprised how much collective effort and thought goes into every line, every gesture, every reaction shot. In rehearsals, right up to recording, everybody's thinking: how can we sharpen this, improve that, get an extra laugh there . . . Then the critics slag you off with a couple of snide sentences. That's the one drawback of television as a medium: television critics. You see, although I'm lacking in self-esteem, that doesn't mean to say that I don't want to be esteemed by others. In fact I get pretty depressed if they don't esteem me. But I get depressed anyway, because I don't esteem myself. I want everybody to think I'm perfect, while not believing it myself. Why? I don't know. I.D.K.

Early on in my treatment, Alexandra told me to take a sheet of paper and write down a list of all the good things about my life in one column and all the bad things in another. Under the "Good" column I wrote:

1. Professionally successful
2. Well-off
3. Good health
4. Stable marriage
5. Kids successfully launched in adult life
6. Nice house
7. Great car
8. As many holidays as I want.

Under the "Bad" column I wrote just one thing:

1. Feel unhappy most of the time.

A few weeks later I added another item:

2. Pain in knee.

It's not so much the pain itself that gets me down as the way it limits my scope for physical exercise. Sport used to be my chief form of therapy, though I didn't call it that. I just enjoyed hitting and kicking and chasing balls about – always did, ever since I was a kid playing in a London backstreet. I suppose I got a charge from showing that I was better at it than people expected me to be – that my thick, ungainly body was capable of a surprising agility, and even grace, when it had a ball to play with. (There has to be a ball: without one I'm about as graceful as a hippopotamus.) Of course it's common knowledge that sport is a harmless way of discharging tension, sluicing adrenalin through the system. But best of all, it helps you sleep. I don't know anything like that glowing, aching tiredness you feel after a keen game of squash or eighteen holes of golf or five sets of tennis, the luxury of stretching out your limbs between the sheets when you go to bed, knowing you're just about to slide effortlessly into a long, deep sleep. Sex is nowhere near as effective. It will send you off for a couple of hours, but that's about all. Sally and I made love last night (at her suggestion, it usually is these days) and I fell asleep immediately afterwards, as if I'd been sandbagged, with her naked in my arms. But I woke at 2.30 feeling chilly and wide awake, with Sally breathing quietly beside me in one of the oversized T-shirts she uses for nighties, and although I went for a pee and put on my pyjamas, I couldn't get back to sleep. I just lay there with my mind spinning – spiralling, I should say, down and down into the dark. Bad thoughts. Gloomy thoughts. My knee was throbbing – I suppose the sex had set it off – and I began to wonder whether it wasn't the first sign of bone cancer and how I'd cope with having my leg amputated if this was how I coped with a mere Internal Derangement of the Knee.

That's the sort of thought that comes to you in the middle of the night. I hate these involuntary vigils, lying awake in the dark with Sally calmly asleep beside me, wondering whether I should turn on the bedside lamp and read for a while, or go downstairs and make a hot drink, or take a sleeping pill, buying a few hours' oblivion at the cost of feeling next day as if my bone marrow has been siphoned off in the night and replaced with lead. Alexandra says I should read till I'm sleepy again, but I don't like to turn on my bedside lamp in case it disturbs Sally and in any case Alexandra says you should get up and read in another room, but I can't face going downstairs into the silent, empty living space of the house, like an intruder in my own home. So usually I just lie there, as I did last night, hoping to drop off, twisting and turning in the effort to find a comfortable position. I snuggled up to Sally for a while, but she got too hot and pushed me away in her sleep. So then I tried hugging myself, with my arms crossed tightly over my chest, each hand grasping the opposite shoulder, like a man in a strait-jacket. That's what I ought to wear instead of pyjamas, if you ask me.

✳ ✳ ✳ ✳ ✳ ✳ ✳ ✳ ✳ ✳ ✳ ✳ ✳ ✳ ✳ ✳ ✳

Wednesday 17th Feb. 2.05 a.m. Tonight we didn't have sex and I woke even earlier: 1.40. I stared appalled at the red figures on the LCD of my alarm clock, which cast a hellish glow on the polished surface of the bedside cabinet. I decided to try getting up this time, and swung my feet to the floor and felt for my slippers before I had a chance to change my mind. Downstairs I pulled a jogging-suit over my pyjamas and made a pot of tea which I carried into my study. And here I am, sitting in front of the computer, tapping out this. Where was I yesterday? Oh, yes. Sport.

Roland says I shouldn't do any sport until the symptoms have disappeared, with or without another operation. I'm allowed to work out on some of the machines in the Club's multi-gym, the ones that don't involve the knee, and I can swim as long as I don't do the breast-stroke – the frog kick is bad for the knee-joint, apparently. But I never did like working out – it bears the same relation to real sport as masturbation does to real sex, if you ask me; and as for swimming, the breast-stroke happens to be the only one I can do properly. Squash is right out, for obvious reasons. Golf too, unfortunately: the lateral twist on the right knee at the follow-through of the swing is lethal. But I do play a bit of tennis still, wearing a kind of brace on the knee which keeps it more or less rigid. I have to sort of drag the right leg like Long John Silver when I hop around the court, but it's better than nothing.

They have indoor courts at the Club, and anyway you can play outdoors nearly all the year round with these mild winters we've been having – it seems to be one of the few beneficial effects of global warming.

I play with three other middle-aged cripples at the Club. There's Joe, he's got serious back trouble, wears a corset all the time and can barely manage to serve overarm; Rupert, who was in a bad car crash a few years ago and limps with both legs, if that's possible; and Humphrey, who has arthritis in his feet and a plastic hip-joint. We exploit each other's handicaps mercilessly. For instance, if Joe is playing against me up at the net I'll return high because I know he can't lift his racket above his head, and if I'm defending the baseline he'll keep switching the direction of his returns from one side of the court to the other because he knows I can't move very fast with my brace. It would bring tears to your eyes to watch us, of either laughter or pity.

Naturally I can't partner Sally in mixed doubles any more, which is a great shame because we used to do rather well in the Club veterans' tournaments. Sometimes she'll knock up with me, but she won't play a singles game because she says I'd do my knee in trying to win, and she's probably right. I usually beat her when I was fit, but now she's improving her game while I languish. I was down at the Club the other day with my physically-challenged peer group when she turned up, having come straight from work for a spot of coaching. It gave me quite a surprise, actually, when she walked along the back of the indoor court with Brett Sutton, the Club coach, because I wasn't expecting to see her there. I didn't know that she'd arranged the lesson, or more likely she'd told me and I hadn't taken it in. That's become a worrying habit of mine lately: people talk to me and I go through the motions of listening and responding, but when they finish I realize I haven't taken in a single word, because I've been following some train of thought of my own. It's another type of Internal Derangement. Sally gets pissed off when she twigs it – understandably – so when she waved casually to me through the netting, I waved back casually in case I was supposed to know that she had arranged to have coaching that afternoon. In fact there was a

26

second or two when I didn't recognize her – just registered her as a tall, attractive-looking blonde. She was wearing a shocking-pink and white shell suit I hadn't seen before, and I'm still not used to her new hair. One day just before Christmas she went out in the morning grey and came back in the afternoon gold. When I asked her why she hadn't warned me, she said she wanted to see my unrehearsed reaction. I said it looked terrific. If I didn't sound over the moon, it was sheer envy. (I've tried several treatments for baldness without success. The last one consisted of hanging upside down for minutes on end to make the blood rush to your head. It was called Inversion Therapy.) When I sussed it was her down at the tennis club, I felt a little glow of proprietorial pride in her lissome figure and bouncing golden locks. The other guys noticed her too.

"You want to watch your missus, Tubby," said Joe, as we changed ends between games. "By the time you're fit again, she'll be running rings round you."

"You reckon?" I said.

"Yeah, he's a good coach. Good at other things too, I've heard." Joe winked at the other two, and of course Humphrey backed him up.

"He's certainly got the tackle. I saw him in the showers the other day. It must be a ten-incher."

"How d'you measure up to that, Tubby?"

"You'll have to raise your game."

"You'll get yourself arrested one day, Humphrey," I said. "Ogling blokes in the showers." The others hooted with laughter.

This kind of joshing is standard between us four. No harm in it. Humphrey's a bachelor, lives with his mother and doesn't have a girlfriend, but nobody supposes for a moment that he's gay. If we did, we wouldn't wind him up about it. Likewise with the innuendo about Brett Sutton and Sally. It's a stock joke that all the women in the club wet their knickers at the sight of him – he's tall, dark, and handsome enough to wear his hair in a ponytail without looking like a ponce – but nobody believes any real hanky-panky goes on.

For some reason I remembered this conversation as we were going to bed tonight, and relayed it to Sally. She sniffed and said, "Isn't it a bit late in the day for you lot to be worrying about the size of your willies?''

I said that for a really dedicated worrier it was never too late.

One thing I've never worried about, though, is Sally's fidelity. We've had our ups and downs, of course, in nearly thirty years of marriage, but we've always been faithful to each other. Not for lack of opportunity, I may say, at least on my side, the entertainment world being what it is, and I daresay on hers too, though I can't believe that she's exposed to the same occupational temptations. Her colleagues at the Poly, or rather University as I must learn to call it now, don't look much of an erotic turn-on to me. But that's not the point. We've always been faithful to each other. How can I be sure? I just am. Sally was a virgin when I met her, nice girls usually were in those days, and I wasn't all that experienced myself. My sexual history was a very slim volume, consisting of isolated, opportunistic couplings with garrison slags in the Army, with drunken girls at drama-school parties, and with lonely landladies in seedy theatrical digs. I don't think I had sex with any of them more than twice, and it was always fairly quick and in the missionary position. To enjoy sex you need comfort – clean sheets, firm mattresses, warm bedrooms – and continuity. Sally and I learned about making love together, more or less from scratch. If she were to go with anyone else, something new in her behaviour, some unfamiliar adjustment of her limbs, some variation in her caresses, would tell me, I'm certain. I always have trouble with adultery stories, especially those where one partner has been betraying the other for years. How could you not know? Of course, Sally doesn't know about Amy. But then I'm not having an affair with Amy. What am I having with her? I don't know.

I met Amy six years ago when she was hired to help cast the first series of *The People Next Door*. Needless to say, she did a brilliant job. Some people in the business reckon that ninety per cent of the success of a sitcom is in the casting. As a writer I would question that, naturally, but it's true that the best script in the world won't work if the actors are all wrong. And the right ones are not always everybody's obvious

28

fiirst choice. It was Amy's idea, for instance, to cast Deborah Radcliffe as Priscilla, the middle-class mother – a classical actress who'd just been let go by the Royal Shakespeare, and had never done sitcom before in her life. Nobody except Amy would have thought of her for Priscilla, but she took to the part like a duck to water. Now she's a household name and can earn five grand for a thirty-second commercial.

It's a funny business, casting. It's a gift, like fortune-telling or water-divining, but you also need a trained memory. Amy has a mind like a Rolodex: when you ask her advice about casting a part she goes into a kind of trance, her eyes turn up to the ceiling, and you can almost hear the *fllick-flick-flick* inside her head as she spools through that mental card-index where the essence of every actor and actress she has ever seen is inscribed. When Amy goes to see a show, she's not just watching the actors perform their given roles, she's imagining them all the time in other roles, so that by the end of the evening she's assimilated not only their performance on the night, but also their potential for quite other performances. You might go with Amy to see *Macbeth* at the RSC and say to her on the way home, "Wasn't Deborah Radcliffe a great Lady Macbeth?" and she'd say, "Mmm, I'd love to see her do Judith Bliss in *Hay Fever*." I wonder sometimes whether this habit of mind doesn't prevent her from enjoying what's going on in front of her. Perhaps that's what we have in common – neither of us being able to live in the present, always hankering after some phantom of perfection elsewhere.

I put this to her once. "Balls, darling," she said. "With the greatest respect, complete *cojones*. You forget that every now and again I pull it off. I achieve the perfect fit between actor and role. *Then* I enjoy the show and nothing but the show. I live for those moments. So do you, for that matter. I mean when everything in an episode goes exactly right. You sit in front of the telly holding your breath thinking, they can't possibly keep this up, it's going to dip in a moment, but they do, and it doesn't – that's what it's all about, *n'est ce pas?*"

"I can't remember when I thought an episode was that good," I said.

"What about the fumigation one?"

"Yes, the fumigation one was good."

"It was bloody brilliant."

That's what I like about Amy – she's always pumping up my self-esteem. Sally's style is more bracing: stop moping and get on with your life. In fact in every way they're antithetical. Sally is a blonde, blue-eyed English rose, tall, supple, athletic. Amy is the Mediterranean type (her father was a Greek Cypriot): dark, short and buxom, with a head of frizzy black curls and eyes like raisins. She smokes, wears a lot of make-up, and never walks anywhere, let alone runs, if she can possibly avoid it. We had to run for a train once at Euston: I shot ahead and held the door open for her as she came waddling down the ramp on her high heels like a panicked duck, all her necklaces and earrings and scarves and bags and other female paraphernalia atremble, and I burst out laughing. I just couldn't help myself. Amy asked me what was so funny as she scrambled breathlessly aboard, and when I told her she refused to speak to me for the rest of the journey. (Incidentally, I just looked up "paraphernalia" in the dictionary because I wasn't sure I'd spelled it right, and discovered it comes from the Latin *paraphema*, meaning "a woman's personal property apart from her dowry." Interesting.)

It was one of our very few tiffs. We get on very well together as a rule, exchanging industry gossip, trading personal moans and reassurances, comparing therapies. Amy is divorced, with custody of her fourteen-year-old daughter, Zelda, who is just discovering boys and giving Amy a hard time about clothes, staying out late, going to dubious discos, etc. etc. Amy is terrified that Zelda's going to get into sex and drugs any minute now, and distrusts her ex-husband, Saul, a theatre manager who has the kid to stay one weekend every month and who, Amy says, has no morals, or, to quote her exactly, "wouldn't recognize a moral if it bit him on the nose." Nevertheless she feels riven with guilt about the break-up of the marriage, fearing that Zelda will go off the rails for lack of a father-figure in the home. Amy started analysis primarily to discover what went wrong between herself and Saul. In a sense she knew that already: it was sex. Saul wanted to do things that she didn't want to do, so eventually he found someone else to do them with. But she's still trying to work out whether this was his fault or hers, and doesn't seem to be any nearer a conclusion. Analysis has a way of unravelling the self: the longer you pull on the thread, the more flaws you find.

I see Amy nearly every week, when I go to London. Sometimes we go to a show, but more often than not we just spend a quiet evening together, at the flat, and/or have a bite to eat at one of the local restaurants. There's never been any question of sex in our relation-ship, because Amy doesn't really want it and I don't really need it. I get plenty of sex at home. Sally seems full of erotic appetite these days – I think it must be the hormone replacement therapy she's having for the menopause. Sometimes, to stimulate my own sluggish libido, I suggest something Saul wanted to do with Amy, and Sally hasn't turned me down yet. When she asks me where I get these ideas from, I tell her magazines and books, and she's quite satisfied. If it ever got back to Sally that I was seen out in London with Amy, it wouldn't bother her because I don't conceal the fact that we meet occasionally. Sally thinks it's for professional reasons, which in part it is.

So really you would say that I've got it made, wouldn't you? I've solved the monogamy problem, which is to say the monotony problem, without the guilt of infidelity. I have a sexy wife at home and a platonic mistress in London. What have I got to complain about? I don't know.

It's three-thirty. I think I'll go back to bed and see if I can get a few hours' kip before sparrowfart.

Wednesday 11 a.m. I did sleep for a few hours, but it wasn't a refreshing sleep. I woke feeling knackered, like I used to be after guard duty in National Service: two hours on, four hours off, all through the night, and all through the day too, if it was a weekend. Christ, just writing that down brings it all back: snatching sleep lying on a bunk fully dressed in ankle-bruising boots and neck-chafing battledress under the glare of a naked electric light bulb, and then being roughly woken to gulp down sweetened lukewarm tea, and maybe some cold congealed eggs and baked beans, before stumbling out yawning and shivering into the night, to loiter for two hours by the barrack gates, or circle the silent shuttered huts and stores, listening to your own footsteps, watching your own shadow lengthen and shorten under the arc-lamps. Let me just concentrate for a moment on that memory, close my eyes and try and squeeze the misery out of it, so that I will appreciate my present comforts.

Tried it. No good. Doesn't work.

I'm writing this on my laptop on the train to London. First class, naturally. Definition of a well-off man: somebody who pays for a first-class ticket out of his own pocket. It's tax-deductible of course, but still . . . Most of my fellow passengers in this carriage are on expenses. Businessmen with digital-lock briefcases and mobile phones, and businesswomen with wide-shouldered jackets and bulging filofaxes. The odd retired county type in tweeds. I'm wearing a suit myself today in honour of the Groucho, but sometimes, when I'm in jeans and leather jacket, with my tramp's haircut falling over the back of the collar, people glance suspiciously at me as if they think I'm in the wrong part of the train. Not the conductors, though – they know me. I travel up and down a lot on this line.

Don't get the idea that I'm an enthusiast for British Rail's Inter-City service to London. *Au contraire*, as Amy would say (she likes to pepper her conversation with foreign phrases). There are a lot of things I don't like about it. For instance: I don't like the smell of the bacon and tomato rolls that pollute the air of the carriage every time somebody brings one back from the buffet car and opens the little polystyrene box they micro-wave them in. I don't like the brake linings on the wheels of the Pullman rolling stock which when warm emit sulphurous-smelling fumes, allegedly harmless to health, that creep into the carriages and mingle with the smell of bacon and tomato rolls. I don't like the taste of the bacon and tomato rolls when I am foolish enough to buy one for myself, somehow suppressing the memory of how naff it was last time. I don't like the fact that if you ask at the buffet for a cup of coffee you will be given a giant-sized plastic beaker of the stuff unless you ask for a small (i.e., normal) size. I don't like the way the train rocks from side to side when it picks up any kind of speed, causing the coffee to slop over the sides of the plastic beaker as you raise it to your lips, scalding your fingers and dripping onto your lap. I don't like the fact that if the air-conditioning fails, as it not infrequently does, you can't ventilate the carriage because the windows are sealed. I don't like the way that, not infrequently, but never when the air-conditioning has failed, the automatic sliding doors at each end of the coach jam in the open position, and cannot be closed manually, or if they can be closed, slowly open again of their own accord, or are opened by passing passengers who leave them open assuming that they will close automatically, obliging you either to leap up every few minutes to close the doors or sit in a permanent draught. I don't like the catches in the WC compartments designed to hold the toilet seats in an upright position, which are spring-loaded, but often loose or broken, so that when you are in mid-pee, holding on to a grab handle with one hand and aiming your todger with the other, the seat, dislodged from the upright position by the violent motion of the train, will suddenly fall forwards, breaking the stream of urine and causing it to spatter your trousers. I don't like the way the train always races at top speed along the section of the track that runs beside the M1, overtaking all the cars and lorries in order to advertise the superiority of rail travel, and then a few minutes later comes to a halt in a field near Rugby because of a signalling failure.

Ow! Ouch! Yaroo! Sudden stab of pain in the knee, for no discernible reason.

Sally said the other day that it was my thorn in the flesh. I wondered where the phrase came from and went to look it up. (I do a lot of looking up – it's how I compensate for my lousy education. My study is full of reference books, I buy them compulsively.) I discovered that it was from Saint Paul's Second Epistle to the Corinthians: "*And lest I should be exalted above measure through the abundance of revelations, there was given to me a thorn in the flesh, the messenger of Satan to buffet me . . .*" I came back into the kitchen with the Bible, rather pleased with myself, and read the verse out to Sally. She stared at me and said, "But that's what I just told you," and I realized I'd had one of my absent-minded spells, and while I was wondering where the phrase came from she had been telling me. "Oh, yes, I know you said it was St Paul," I lied. "But what's the application to my knee? The text seems a bit obscure." "That's the point," she said. "Nobody knows what Paul's thorn in the flesh was. It's a mystery. Like your knee." She knows a lot about religion, does Sally, much more than I do. Her father was a vicar.

True to form, the train has stopped, for no apparent reason, amid empty fields. In the sudden hush the remarks of a man in shirtsleeves across the aisle speaking into his cellphone about a contract for warehouse shelving are annoyingly intrusive. I would really prefer to drive to London, but the traffic is impossible once you get off the M1, not to mention *on* the M1, and parking in the West End is such a hassle that it's really not worth the effort. So I drive the car to Rummidge Expo station, which is only fifteen minutes from home, and leave it in the car park there. I'm always a little bit apprehensive on the return journey in case I find somebody has scratched it, or even nicked it, though it has all the latest alarms and security systems. It's a wonderful vehicle, with a 24-valve three-litre V6 engine, automatic transmission, power steering, cruise control, air-conditioning, ABS brakes, six-speaker audio system, electric tilt-and-slide sunroof and every other gadget you can imagine. It goes like the wind, smooth and incredibly quiet. It's the silent effortless power that intoxicates me. I never was one for noisy *brrrm brmmm* sports cars, and I never did understand the British obsession with manual gear-changing. Is it a substitute for sex, I wonder, that endless fondling of the knob on the end of the gear lever, that perpetual pumping of the clutch pedal? They say that you don't get the same acceleration in the middle range with an automatic, but there's quite enough if your engine is as powerful as the one in my car. It's also incredibly, heartstoppingly beautiful.

I fell in love with it at first sight, parked outside the showroom, low and streamlined, sculpted out of what looked like mist with the sun shining through it, a very very pale silvery grey, with a pearly lustre. I kept finding reasons to drive past the showroom so that I could look at it again, and each time I felt a pang of desire. I daresay a lot of other people driving past felt the same way, but unlike them I knew I could walk into the showroom and buy the car without even having to think if I could afford it. But I hesitated and hung back. Why? Because, when I couldn't afford a car like that, I disapproved of cars like that: fast, flash, energy-wasteful – and Japanese. I always said I'd never buy a Japanese car, not so much out of economic patriotism (I used to drive Fords which usually turned out to have been made in Belgium or Germany) as for emotional reasons. I'm old enough to remember World War Two, and I had an uncle who died as a POW working on the Siamese railway. I thought something bad would happen to me if I bought this car, or that at the very least I would feel guilty and miserable driving it. And yet I coveted it. It became one of my "things" – things I can't decide, can't forget, can't leave alone. Things I wake up in the middle of the night worrying about.

I bought all the motoring magazines hoping that I would find some damning criticism of the car that would enable me to decide against it. No go. Some of the road-test reports were a bit condescending – "bland", "docile", even "inscrutable", were some of the epithets they used – but you could tell that nobody could find anything wrong with it. I hardly slept at all for a week, stewing it over. Can you believe it? While war raged in Yugoslavia, thousands died daily of AIDS in Africa, bombs exploded in Northern Ireland and the unemployment figures rose inexorably in Britain, I could think of nothing except whether or not to buy this car.

I began to get on Sally's nerves. "For God's sake, go and have a test drive, and if you like the car, buy it," she said. (She drives an Escort herself, changes it every three years after a two-minute telephone conversation with her dealer, and never gives another thought to the matter.) So I had a test-drive. And of course I liked the car. I loved the car. I was utterly seduced and enraptured by the car. But I told the salesman I would think about it. "What is there to think about?" Sally demanded, when I came home. "You like the car, you can afford the car, why not buy the car?" I said I would sleep on it. Which meant, of course, that I lay awake all night worrying about it. In the morning at breakfast I announced that I had reached a decision. "Oh yes?" said Sally, without raising her eyes from the newspaper. "What is it?"

"I've decided against," I said. "However irrational my scruples may be, I'll never be free from them, so I'd better not buy it." "OK," said Sally. "What will you buy instead?" "I don't really need to buy anything," I said. "My present car is good for another year or two." "Fine," said Sally. But she sounded disappointed. I began to worry again whether I'd made the right decision.

A couple of days later, I drove past the showroom and the car was missing. I went in and buttonholed the salesman. I practically dragged him from his seat by the lapels, like people do in movies. Someone else had bought my car! I couldn't believe it. I felt as if my bride had been abducted on our wedding eve. I said I wanted the car. *I had to have the car.* The salesman said he could get me another one in two or three weeks, but when he checked on his computer there wasn't an exactly similar model in the same colour in the country. It's not one of those Japanese manufacturers that have set up factories in Britain – they import from Japan under the quota system. He said there was one in a container ship somewhere on the high seas, but delivery would take a couple of months. To cut a long story short, I ended up paying £1000 over the list price to gazump the chap who had just bought my car.

I've never regretted it. The car is a joy to drive. I'm only sorry that Mum and Dad aren't around any more, so I can't give them a spin in it. I feel the need for someone to reflect back to me my pride of ownership. Sally's no use for that – to her a car is just a functional machine. Amy has never even seen the vehicle, because I don't drive to London. My children, on their occasional visits, regard it with a mixture of mockery and disapproval – Jane refers to it as the "Richmobile" and Adam says it's a compensation for hair-loss. What I need is an appreciative passenger. Like Maureen Kavanagh, for instance, my first girlfriend. Neither of our families could afford to run a car in those far-off days. A ride in any kind of car was a rare treat, intensely packed with novel sensations. I remember Maureen going into kinks when my Uncle Bert took us to Brighton one bank holiday in his old pre-war Singer that smelled of petrol and leather and swayed on its springs like a pram. I imagine driving up to her house in my present streamlined supercar and glimpsing her face at the window all wonder; and then she bursts out of the front door and bounds down the steps and jumps in and wriggles about in her seat with excitement, trying all the gadgets, laughing and wrinkling up her nose in that way she had, and looking adoringly at me as I drive off. That's what Maureen used to do: look adoringly at me. Nobody ever did it since, not Sally, not Amy, not Louise or any of the other women who've occasionally made a pass at me. I haven't seen Maureen for nearly forty years – God knows where she is, or what she's doing, or what she looks like now. Sitting beside me in the car she's still sweet sixteen, dressed in her best summer frock, white with pink roses on it, though I'm as I am now, fat and bald and fifty-eight. It makes no kind of sense, but that's what fantasies are for, I suppose.

The train is approaching Euston. The conductor has apologized over the PA system for its late arrival, "which was due to a signalling failure near Tring". I used to be a closet supporter of privatizing British Rail, before the Transport Minister announced his plans to separate the company that maintains the track from the companies that run the trains. You can imagine how well that will work, and what wonderful alibis it will provide for late-running trains. Are they mad? Is this Internal Derangement of the Government?

Actually, I read somewhere that John Major has a dodgy knee. Had to give up cricket, apparently. Explains a lot, that.

Wednesday 10.15 p.m. Amy has just left. We came back to the flat from Gabrielli's to watch "News at Ten" on my little Sony, to keep abreast of the global gloom (atrocities in Bosnia, floods in Bangladesh, drought in Zimbabwe, imminent collapse of Russian economy, British trade deficit worst ever recorded), and then I put her in a cab back to St John's Wood. She doesn't like to be out late if she can help it, on account of Zelda, though her lodger, Miriam, a speech therapist with a conveniently quiet social life, keeps an eye on the girl when Amy is out in the evenings.

Now I'm alone in the flat, and possibly in the whole building. The other owners, like me, are only occasionally in residence – there's a long-haul air hostess, a Swiss businessman whose job requires him to shuttle between London and Zürich, accompanied by his secretary and/or mistress, and a gay American couple, academics of some kind, who only come here in university vacations. Two flats are still unsold, because of the recession. I haven't seen anybody in the lift or hall today, but I never feel lonely here, as I sometimes do at home during the day, when Sally is at work. It's so quiet in those suburban streets. Whereas here it is never quiet, even at night. The growl and throb of buses and taxis inching up the Charing Cross Road in low gear carry faintly through the double glazing, punctuated occasionally by the shrill ululation of a police car or ambulance. If I go to the window, I look down on pavements still thronged with people coming out of theatres, cinemas, restaurants and pubs, or standing about munching takeaway junk food or swigging beer and coke from the can, their breath condensing in the cold night air. Very rarely does anyone raise their eyes from the ground level of the building, which is occupied by a pizza & pasta restaurant, and notice that there are six luxury flats above it, with a man standing at one of the windows, pulling the curtain aside, looking down at them. It isn't a place where you would expect anybody to *live*, and indeed it wouldn't be much fun to do so three hundred and sixty-five days a year. It's too noisy and dirty. Noise not just from the traffic, but also from the high-pitched whine of restaurant ventilator fans at the back of the building that never seem to be turned off, and dirt not just in the air, which leaves a fine sediment of black dust on every surface though I keep the windows shut most of the time, but also on the ground, the pavement permanently covered with a slimy patina of mud and spittle and spilt milk and beer dregs and vomit, and scattered over with crushed burger boxes, crumpled drinks cans, discarded plastic wrappers and paper bags, soiled tissues and used bus tickets. The efforts of the Westminster Borough street-cleaners are simply swamped by the sheer numbers of litter-producing pedestrians in this bit of London. And the human detritus is just as visible: drunks, bums, loonies and criminal-looking types abound. Beggars accost you all the time, and by 10 p.m. every shop doorway has its sleeping occupant. *"Louche"* was Amy's verdict on the ambience (or, as she would say, *ambiance*) when I first brought her here, but I'm not sure that's the right word. (I looked it up, it means shifty and disreputable, from the French word for squint.) The porn and peepshow district is half a mile away. Here second-hand bookshops and famous theatres jostle with fastfood outlets and multicinemas. It's certainly not your conventional des. res. area, but as a metropolitan base for an out-of-towner like me, the situation is hard to beat. London is a midden anyway. If you have to live here you're better off perched on the steaming, gleaming pinnacle of the dunghill, instead of burrowing your way up and down through all the strata of compacted old shit every morning and evening. I know: I've been a London commuter in my time.

When we moved to Rummidge from London twelve years ago, because of Sally's job, all my friends regarded me with ill-concealed pity, as if I was being exiled to Siberia. I was a bit apprehensive myself, to be honest, never having lived north of Palmer's Green in my life (apart from Army Basic Training in Yorkshire, and touring when I was a young actor, neither of which really counts as "living") but I reckoned that it was only fair to let Sally take the chance of a career move from schoolteaching to higher education. She'd worked bloody hard, doing an M.Ed. part-time while being Deputy Head of a Junior School in Stoke Newington, and the advertisement for the lecture-ship in the Education Department at Rummidge Poly was bang on the nose of her research field, psycholinguistics and language acquisition (don't ask me to explain it). So she applied and got the job. Now she's Principal Lecturer. Maybe she'll be a Professor one day, now that the Poly has become a University. Professor Sally Passmore: it has a ring to it. Pity about the name of the University. They couldn't call it the University of Rummidge because there was one already, so they called it James Watt University, after the great local inventor. You can bet your life that this rather cumbersome title will soon be shortened to "Watt University", and imagine the conversational confusion *that* will cause. "What university did you go to?" "Watt University." "Yes, what university?" "*Watt* University." And so on.

Anyway, I was a bit apprehensive about the move at the time, we all were, the kids too, having always lived in the South-East. But the first thing we discovered was that the price we got for our scruffy inter-war semi in Palmer's Green would buy us a spacious five-bedroomed detached Edwardian villa in a pleasant part of Rummidge, so that I could have a study of my own for the first time in our married life, looking out on to a lawn screened by mature trees, instead of the bay window of our lounge with a view of an identical scruffy semi across the street; and the second thing we discovered was that Sally and the kids could get to their college and schools with half the hassle and in half the time they were used to in London; and the third thing we discovered was that people were still civil to each other outside London, that shop assistants said "lovely" when you gave them the right change, and that taxi-drivers looked pleasantly surprised when you tipped them, and that the workmen who came to repair your washing-machine or decorate your house or repair your roof were courteous and efficient and reliable. The superior quality of life in Britain outside London was still a well-kept secret in those days, and Sally and I could hardly contain our mirth at the thought of all our friends back in the capital pitying us as they sat in their traffic jams or hung from straps in crowded commuter trains or tried in vain to get a plumber to answer the phone at the weekend. Our luck changed in more ways than one with the move to Rummidge. Who knows whether *The People Next Door* would have ever seen the light of studio if I hadn't met Ollie Silver at a civic reception Sally had been invited to, just when Heartland were looking for a new idea for a sitcom . . .

When Jane and Adam left home to go to University we moved out to Hollywell, a semi-rural suburb on the southern outskirts of the city – the stockbroker belt I suppose it would be called in the South-East, only stockbrokers are rather thin on the ground in the Midlands. Our neighbours are mostly senior managers in industry, or accountants, doctors and lawyers. The houses are all modern detached, in different styles, set well back from the road and bristling with burglar alarms. It's green and leafy and quiet. On a weekday the loudest noise is the whine of the milk float delivering semi-skimmed milk and organic yoghurt and free-range eggs door-to-door. At the weekend you sometimes hear the hollow clop of ponies' hoofs or the rasp of Range-Rover tyres on the tarmac. The Country Club, with its eighteen-hole golf course, tennis courts, indoor and outdoor pools and spa, is just ten minutes away. That's the main reason we moved to Hollywell – that and the fact that it's conveniently close to Rummidge Expo station.

The station was built fairly recently to serve the International Exhibition Centre and the Airport. It's all very modern and hi-tech, apart from the main Gents. For some reason they seem to have lovingly reconstructed a vintage British Rail loo in the heart of all the marble and glass and chromium plate, complete with pee-up-against-the-wall zinc urinals, chipped white tiles, and even a rich pong of blocked drains. Apart from that, it's a great improvement on the City Centre station, and is twelve minutes nearer London for me. Because, of course, if you're in any branch of show business, you can't keep away from London entirely. Heartland record in their Rummidge studios as a condition of their franchise – bringing employment to the region and all that – but they have offices in London and rehearse most of their shows there because that's where most actors and directors live. So I'm always up and down to Euston on good old BR. I bought the flat three years ago, partly as an investment (though property prices have fallen since) but mainly to save myself the fatigue of a return journey in one day, or the alternative hassle of checking in and out of hotels. I suppose at the back of my mind also was the thought that it would be a private place to meet Amy.

Lately I've come to value the privacy, the anonymity of the place even more. Nobody on the pavement knows I'm up here in my cosy, centrally-heated, double-glazed eyrie. And if I go down into the street to get a newspaper or pick up a pint of milk from the 24-hour Asian grocery store on the corner, and mingle with the tourists and the bums and the young runaways and the kids up from the suburbs for an evening out and the office workers who stopped for a drink on the way home and decided to make a night of it, and the actors and catering workers and buskers and policemen and beggars and newspaper vendors – their gaze will slide over me without clicking into focus, nobody will recognize me, nobody will greet me or ask how I am, and I don't have to pretend to anyone that I'm happy.

Amy came to the flat straight from work and we had a couple of g & t's before going round the corner to Gabrielli's for a bite to eat. Sometimes, if she comes here from home, she brings one of her own dishes from her deep-freeze, *moussaka*, or beef with olives or *coq au vin*, and heats it up in my microwave, but usually we eat out. Very occasionally she invites me to dinner at her house and lays on a super spread, but it's always a dinner *party*, with other people present. Amy doesn't want Zelda to get the idea that there's anything special about her relationship with me, though I can't believe the kid doesn't suspect something, seeing her mother sometimes going out in the evening dressed to kill and carrying a container of home-made frozen food in one of her smartly gloved hands. "Because I hide it in my handbag, *stupido*," Amy said, when I raised this question once. And it's true that she carries an exceptionally large handbag, one of those soft Italian leather scrips, full of female paraphernalia (or should I just say paraphernalia?) – lipsticks and eyeliner, face-powder and perfume, cigarettes and lighters, pens and pencils, notebooks and diaries, aspirin and Elastoplast, Tampax and panti-liners, a veritable life-support system, in which a plastic container of frozen *moussaka* could be concealed without much difficulty.

I was replacing a phutted lightbulb when Amy buzzed the entryphone, so I was slow to push the button that brought her comically distorted face, all mouth and nose and eyes, swimming into view on the videoscreen in my microscopic hall. "Hurry up, Lorenzo," she said, "I'm dying for a pee and a drink, in that order." One of the things I like about Amy is that she never calls me Tubby. She calls me by a lot of other familiar names, but never that one. I pushed the button to open the front door, and moments later admitted her to the flat. Her cheek was cold against mine as we embraced, and I inhaled a heady whiff of her favourite perfume, Givenchy, eddying round her throat and ears. I hung up her coat and fiixed drinks while she went to the bathroom. She emerged a few minutes later, lips gleaming with freshly applied lipstick, sank into an armchair, crossed her fat little legs, lit a cigarette, took her drink and said, "Cheers, darling. How's the knee?"

I told her it had given me one bad twinge today, in the train.

"And how's the *Angst*?"

"What's that?"

"Oh, come, sweetheart! Don't pretend you don't know what *Angst* is. German for anxiety. Or is it anguish?"

"Don't ask me," I said. "You know I'm hopeless at languages."

"Well anyway, how have you been? Apart from the knee."

"Pretty bad." I described my state of mind over the last few days in some detail.

"It's because you're not writing." She meant script-writing.

"But I am writing," I said. "I'm writing a journal."

Amy's black eyes blinked with surprise. "What on earth for?"

I shrugged. "I don't know. It started with something I did for Alexandra."

"You should write something that will take you out of yourself, not deeper in. Is there going to be another series?"

"I'll tell you later," I said. "I had lunch about it with Jake. How was your day?"

"Oh awful, awful," she said grimacing. Amy's days are invariably awful. I don't think she'd be really happy if they weren't. "I had a row with Zelda at breakfast about the pigsty state of her room. Well, *c'est normal*. But then Karl's secretary called to say he couldn't see me today because of a sore throat, though why he should cancel just because of a sore throat I don't know, because sometimes he doesn't say anything by choice, but his secretary said he had a temperature too. So of course I've been on edge all day like a junkie needing a fix. And Michael Hinchcliffe, whose agent told me he was 'technically available' for that BBC spy serial, and would have been wonderful in the part, has taken a film offer instead, the sod. Not to mention Harriet's latest clanger." Harriet is Amy's partner in the casting agency. Her long-standing relationship with a man called Norman has just broken up and she is consequently unable to think straight

43

and is apt to weep uncontrollably when speaking to clients on the phone. Amy said she would tell me about Harriet's latest clanger when I had told her about my lunch with Jake, so we went out and settled ourselves at our usual table in Gabrielli's first.

Jake Endicott is the only agent I ever had. He wrote to me when he heard a sketch of mine on the radio, yonks ago, and offered to take me on. For years nothing much happened, but then I struck oil with *The People Next Door* and I wouldn't be surprised if I was his number one client now. He had booked a table in the back room at Groucho's, under the glass roof. It's his kind of place. Everybody is there to see and be seen without letting on that that's what they're there for. There's a special kind of glance that habitués have perfected I call the Groucho Fast Pan, which consists of sweeping the room with your eyes very rapidly under half-lowered lids, checking for the presence of celebrities, while laughing like a drain at something your companion has just said, whether it's funny or not. I had imagined it was just going to be a social lunch, a bit of gossip, a bit of mutual congratulation, but it turned out that Jake had something significant to report.

When we had ordered (I chose smoked duck's breast on a warm salad of rocket and lollo rosso, followed by sausage and mash at a price that would have given my poor old Mum and Dad a heart-attack apiece) Jake said, "Well, the good news is, Heartland want to commission another two series."

"And what's the bad news?" I asked.

"The bad news is that Debbie wants out." Jake looked anxiously at me, waiting for my reaction.

It wasn't exactly a bombshell. I knew that the present series was the last Debbie Radcliffe had contracted for, and I could well believe that she was getting tired of spending more than half of every year making *The People Next Door*. Sitcom is hard work for actors. It's the weekly rep of TV. The schedule for *The People Next Door* is: readthrough on Tuesday and rehearse Wednesday to Friday in London, travel up to Rummidge on Saturday, dress-rehearse and record there on Sunday, day off on Monday, and start again with the next script on Tuesday. It wipes out the actors' weekends, and if filming on location is required that sometimes takes up their day off. They're well paid, but it's a gruelling routine and they dare not get ill. More to the point: for an actress like Deborah Radcliffe, the character of Priscilla Springfield must have ceased to be a challenge some time ago. True, she's free to do live theatre for about four months a year, between series, but that's not quite long enough for a West End production and anyway Sod's Law would ensure that the parts she wanted didn't come up when she was available. So I wasn't surprised to learn that she wanted her freedom. Jake, needless to say, didn't see it that way. "The ingratitude of people in this profession . . ." he sighed, shaking his head and twisting a sliver of gravlax on the end of his fork in a puddle of dill sauce. "Who ever heard of Deborah Radcliffe before *The People Next Door,* apart from a few people on the RSC mailing list? We made her a star, and now she's just turning her back on us. Whatever happened to loyalty?"

"Come off it, Jake," I said. "We're lucky that we've had her this long."

"Thank me for that, my boy," said Jake. (He's actually ten years younger than me, but he likes to play the father in our relationship.) "*I* pressured Heartland into writing a four-year retainer into her renewal contract, after the first series. They would have settled for three."

"I know, Jake, you did well," I said. "I suppose this isn't just a ploy by her agent to up her fee?"

"That was my first thought, naturally, but she says she wouldn't do it for double."

"How can we have another series without Debbie?" I said. "We can't cast another actress. The audience wouldn't accept it. Debbie *is* Priscilla, as far as they're concerned."

Jake allowed the waiter to refill our wine glasses, then leaned forward and lowered his voice. "I spoke to the people at Heartland about that. David Treece, Mel Spacks and Ollie. Incidentally, this is *completely* confidential, Tubby. Are you going to rehearsal tomorrow? Then don't breathe a *word.* The rest of the cast know nothing about

Debbie leaving. Heartland want you to do a rewrite on the last script."

"What's wrong with it?"

"There's nothing wrong with it. But you're going to have to write Debbie out of the series."

"You mean, kill off Priscilla?"

"Good God, no. This is a *comedy* series, for Chrissake, not drama. No, Priscilla's got to leave Edward."

"Leave him? Why?"

"Well, that's your department, old son. Perhaps she meets another fella."

"Don't be daft, Jake. Priscilla would never desert Edward. It's just not in her nature."

"Well, women do funny things. Look at Margaret. She left me."

"That's because you were having an affair with Rhoda."

"Well, maybe Edward could have an affair with someone to provoke Priscilla into divorcing him. There's your new character!"

"It's not in Edward's nature either. He and Priscilla are the archetypal monogamous couple. They're about as likely to split up as Sally and me."

We argued for a while. I pointed out that the Springfields, in spite of their trendy liberal opinions and cultural sophistication, are really deeply conventional at heart, whereas the next-door Davises, for all their vulgarity and philistinism, are much more tolerant and liberated. Jake knew this already, of course.

"All right," he said at last. "What do you suggest?"

"Perhaps we should call it a day," I said, without premeditation. Jake nearly choked on his sautéd sweetbreads and polenta.

"You mean, kill the show at the end of this series?"

"Perhaps it's reached the end of its natural life." I wasn't sure whether I believed this, but I discovered to my surprise that I wasn't unduly bothered by the prospect.

Jake, though, was very bothered. He dabbed his mouth with his napkin. "Tubby, don't do this to me. Tell me you're joking. *The People Next Door* could run for another three series. There are a lot of golden eggs still to come out of that goose. You'd be cutting your own throat."

"He's right, you know," Amy said, when I related this conversation to her over supper (in the light of the Groucho lunch, I confined myself virtuously to one dish, spinach canelloni, but poached from Amy's dessert, a voluptuous tiramisu). "Unless you've got an idea for another series?"

"I haven't," I admitted. "But I could live quite comfortably on the money I've already earned from *The People Next Door*."

"You mean, *retire*? You'd go mad."

"I'm going mad anyway," I said.

"No, you're not," said Amy. "You don't know what mad means."

When we had thoroughly discussed the ins and outs and pros and cons of trying to go on with *The People Next Door* without Deborah Radcliffe, it was Amy's turn to tell me about her day in more detail. But I'm ashamed to say that now I come to try and record that part of our conversation, I can't remember much about it. I know that Harriet's latest clanger was sending the wrong actress to an interview at the BBC, causing great offence and embarrassment all round, but I'm afraid my mind wandered fairly early on in the relation of this story, and I failed to register the surname of the actress, so that when I came to again, and Amy was saying how furious Joanna had been, I didn't know which Joanna she was talking about and it was too late to ask without revealing that I hadn't been listening. So I had to confine myself to nodding and shaking my head knowingly and making sympathetic noises and uttering vague generalizations, but Amy didn't seem to notice, or if she noticed, not to mind. Then she talked about Zelda, and I don't remember a word of that, though I could make it up fairly confidently, since Amy's complaints about Zelda are always much the same.

I didn't tell Amy the whole of my conversation with Jake. At the end of the meal, while we were waiting for the waiter to come back with the receipted bill and Jake's platinum credit card, he said casually, fast-panning round the room and waving discreetly to Stephen Fry, who was just leaving, "Any chance of borrowing your flat next week,

Tubby?" I assumed he had some foreign client arriving whom he wanted to put up, until he added, "Just for an afternoon. Any day that suits you." He caught my eye and grinned slyly. "We'll bring our own sheets."

I was shocked. It's less than two years since Jake's marriage to Margaret ended in an acrimonious divorce and he married his then secretary, Rhoda. Margaret had become a kind of friend, or at least a familiar fixture, over the years, and I've only recently got used to Jake going to functions or staying for the occasional weekend accompanied by Rhoda instead. He could see from my expression that I was disturbed.

"Of course, if it's inconvenient, just say so . . ."

"It's not a matter of convenience or inconvenience, Jake," I said. "It's just that I'd never be able to look Rhoda straight in the eye again."

"This doesn't affect Rhoda, believe me," he said earnestly. "It's not an affair. We're both happily married. We just have a common interest in recreational sex."

"I'd rather not be involved," I said.

"No problem," he said, with a dismissive wave of his hand. "Forget I ever asked." He added, with a trace of anxiety, "You won't mention it to Sally?"

"No, I won't. But isn't it about time you packed it in, this lark?"

"It keeps me feeling young," he said complacently. He does look young, too, for his age, not to say immature. He's got one of those faces sometimes described as "boyish": chubby cheeks, slightly protuberant eyes, snub nose, a mischievous grin. You wouldn't call him good-looking. It's hard to understand how he manages to pull the birds. Perhaps it's the eager, puppyish, tail-wagging energy he seems to have such endless reserves of. "You should try it, Tubby," he said. "You've been looking peaky lately."

When we sat on the sofa together to watch *News at Ten*, I put my arm round Amy's back and she leaned her head against my shoulder. It's the furthest we ever go in physical intimacy, except that our goodbye kiss is always on the lips; it seems safe to go that far when we're parting. We don't neck while we're sitting on the sofa, nor have I ever attempted any squeezing or stroking below the neckline. I admit that I sometimes wonder what Amy would look like naked. The image that comes into my mind is a slightly overweight version of that famous nude by whatsisname, the Spanish bloke, old master, he did two paintings of the same woman reclining on a couch, one clothed, one naked, I must look it up. Amy is always so *dressed*, so thoroughly buttoned and zipped and sheathed in her layers of carefully co-ordinated clothing that it's hard to imagine her ever being completely naked except in the bath, and even then I bet she covers herself with foam. Divesting Amy of her clothes would be a slow and exciting business, like unpacking an expensively and intricately wrapped parcel, rustling with layers of fragrant tissue paper, in the dark. (It would have to be in the dark – she told me one of her problems with Saul was his insistence on making love with the lights on.) Whereas Sally's clothes are loose and casual, and so few and functional that she can strip in about ten seconds flat, which she frequently does after coming home from work, walking around upstairs stark naked while doing humdrum domestic tasks like changing the sheets or sorting the laundry.

This train of thought is proving rather arousing, but unprofitably so, since Sally is not here to slake my lust and Amy wouldn't even if she were. Why do I only seem to get horny these days in London, where my girlfriend is contentedly chaste, and almost never at home in Rummidge, where I have a partner of tireless sexual appetite? I don't know.

"You should try it, Tubby." How does Jake know I haven't tried it? It must show in my body language, somehow. Or my face, my eyes. Jake's eyes light up like an infra-red security scanner every time a pretty girl comes within range.

I suppose the nearest I came to trying it in recent memory was with Louise, in L.A., three or four years ago, when I went out for a month to advise on the American version of *The People Next Door*. She was a "creative executive" in the American production company, a Vice-President in fact, which isn't quite as impressive as it sounds to a

British ear, but pretty good all the same for a woman in her early thirties. She was my minder and intermediary with the scriptwriting team. There were eight writers working on the pilot. Eight. They sat round a long table drinking coffee and Diet Coke, anxiously trying out gags on each other. As the company had bought the rights they could do anything they liked with my scripts, and they did, throwing out most of the original storylines and dialogue and retaining only the basic concept of incompatible neighbours. It seemed to me that I was being paid thousands of dollars for almost nothing, but I wasn't complaining. At first I used to attend the script conferences and brainstorming sessions dutifully, but after a while I begin to think my presence was only an embarrassment and a distraction to these people, who seemed engaged in some desperately competitive contest from which I was happily excluded, and my participation became more and more a matter of stretching out on a lounger beside the pool of the Beverly Wilshire and reading the draft scripts which Louise Lightfoot brought to me in her smart, leather-trimmed canvas script satchel. She used to come back at the end of the day in her little Japanese sports coupé to collect my notes, and drink a cocktail, and more often than not we would eat together. She had recently split up with a partner and "wasn't seeing anybody" and I, marooned in Beverly Hills, was very glad of her company. She took me to the "in" Hollywood restaurants and pointed out the important producers and agents. She took me to movie previews and premières. She took me to art galleries and little theatres and, on the grounds that it would help me understand American television, to more plebeian places of resort: drive-in Burger Kings and Donut Delites, ten-pin bowling alleys, and on one occasion a baseball game.

Louise was small but shapely in build. Straight bobbed brown hair which always shone and swung as if it had been freshly washed, which it invariably had been. Perfect teeth. Is there anybody in Hollywood who hasn't got perfect teeth? But Louise needed them, because she laughed a lot. It was a resonant, full-bodied laugh, rather a surprise given her petite figure and general style of poised professional career woman; and when she laughed she threw back her head and shook it from side to side, making her hair fan out. I seemed to be able to produce this effect very easily. My wry little British digs at Hollywood manners and Californiaspeak tickled Louise. Naturally, for a script-writer there is nothing more gratifying than having an attractive and intelligent young woman helpless with laughter at your jokes.

One warm evening towards the end of my stay, we drove down to Venice to eat at one of the shoreside fish places they have there. We ate outside on the restaurant's deck to watch the sun set on the Pacific in a vulgar blaze of Technicolor glory, and sat on in the gloaming over coffee and a second bottle of Napa Valley Chardonnay, with just a small oil-lamp flickering between us on the table. For once I wasn't trying to make her laugh, but talking seriously about my writing career, and the thrill of making the breakthrough with *The People Next Door*. I paused to ask if I should order some more coffee and she smiled and said, "No, what I'd like to do now is take you back to my place and fuck your brains out."

"Would you really?" I stalled, grateful for the semi-darkness as I struggled to arrange my thoughts.

"Yep, how does that grab you, Mr Passmore?" The "Mr Passmore" was a joke, of course – we had been on first-name terms since Day One. But that was how she always referred to me when speaking to other people in the company. I had heard her doing it on the phone. *"Mr Passmore thinks it's a mistake to make the Davises a Latino family, but he will defer to our judgement. Mr Passmore thinks the scene beginning page thirty-two of the twelfth draft is overly sentimental."* Louise said it was a mark of respect in the industry.

"It's very sweet of you, Louise," I said, "and don't think that I wouldn't like to go to bed with you, because I would. But, to coin a phrase, I love my wife."

"She would never know," said Louise. "How could it hurt her?"

"I'd feel so guilty it would probably show," I said. "Or I'd blurt it out one day." I sighed miserably. "I'm sorry."

"Hey, it's no big deal, Tubby, I'm not in love with you or anything. Why don't you get the check?"

Driving me back to my hotel she said suddenly, "Am I the only girl you've had these scruples about?" and I said I'd always had them, and she said, "Well, that makes me feel better."

I didn't sleep much that night, tossing and turning in my vast bed at the Beverly Wilshire, wondering whether to call Louise and ask if I could have second thoughts, but I didn't; and although we saw each other again on several occasions it was never quite the same, she was gradually backing away instead of coming closer. She drove me to the airport at the end of my stay and kissed me on the cheek and said, " 'Bye, Tubby, it's been great." I agreed enthusiastically, but I spent most of the flight home wondering what I'd missed.

Time to go to bed. I wonder what they'll be showing on the Dream Channel tonight. Blue movies, I shouldn't wonder.

❊ ❊ ❊ ❊ ❊ ❊ ❊ ❊ ❊ ❊ ❊ ❊ ❊ ❊ ❊ ❊ ❊

Thursday morning, 18th Feb. The video entryphone in the flat is connected to a camera in the porch which gives you a choice of two shots: a close-up of the face of the person ringing your bell, and a wide shot of the porch, with the street in the background. Sometimes in idle moments I press the button for the wide shot to have a look at the people passing or pausing on the pavement. It gives me ideas for characters – you see all types – and I suppose there's a certain childish, voyeuristic pleasure in using the gadget. It's like an inverted periscope. From my cosy cabin high above the ground I scan life on the scruffy surface: tourists frowning over their street-maps, young girls too vain to cover their skimpy going-out gear with topcoats clutching themselves against the cold, young bucks in leather jackets scuffling and nudging each other, infatuated couples stopping in mid-stride to kiss, bumped by impatient men with briefcases hurrying to catch a train at Charing Cross.

Last night, for no particular reason, I pressed the button as I was going to bed, and blow me if there wasn't someone kipping down for the night in the porch. I suppose it's surprising it hasn't happened before, but it's a very small square space not big enough for a grown man to lie down in without his feet sticking out onto the pavement. This bloke was sitting up inside his sleeping-bag, with his back against one wall and his feet against the other, and his head sunk on his chest. He looked young, with a pointed, foxy face and long, lank hair falling down over his eyes.

I felt quite shocked to see him there, then angry. What a nerve! He was taking up the whole porch. It would be impossible to go in or out without stepping over him. Not that I wanted to go in or out any more that night, but one of the other residents might turn up, and in any case it lowered the tone of the property to have him camped there. I thought about going downstairs and telling him to push off, but I was already in pyjamas and I didn't fancy confronting him in dressing-gown and slippers or alternatively going to the trouble of dressing myself again. I thought of phoning the police and asking them to move him on, but there's so much serious crime in this part of London that I doubted whether they would be bothered to respond, and anyway they would want to know if I had already requested him to move on myself. I stood there, staring at the fuzzy black and white image, wishing that sound as well as vision could be activated from inside the flat on the entryphone, so that I could bark, *"Hey, you! Piss off!"* through the loudspeaker, and watch his reaction on the video screen. I smiled at the thought, then felt a bit of a bastard for smiling.

These young people who beg and sleep rough on the streets of London, they bother me. They're not like the tramps and winos who have always been with us, filthy and smelly and dressed in rags. The new vagrants are usually quite nicely clothed, in new-looking anoraks and jeans and Doc Martens, and they have thickly quilted sleeping bags that wouldn't disgrace an Outward Bound course. And whereas the tramps skulk like insects in dark neglected places like under railway arches or beside rubbish tips, these youngsters choose shop doorways in brightly lit West End streets, or the staircases and passages of the Underground, so that you can't avoid them. Their presence is like an accusation – but what are they accusing us of? Did we drive them onto the streets? They look so normal, so presentable, they ask you so politely if you have any change, that it's hard to believe they couldn't find shelter, and even work, if they really tried. Not in the West End, perhaps, but who says they have a right to a home in the West End? I have one, but I had to work for it.

Thus and so went my self-justificatory interior monologue, as I went to bed and, eventually, to sleep. I woke at four and went for a pee. On my way back to bed I pressed the video button on the entryphone, and he was still there, curled up inside his sleeping-bag on the tiled floor of the porch, like a dog in its basket. A police car flashed past in the background, and I heard the strident blare of its siren through the double-glazed windows of the living-room, but the youth didn't stir. When I looked again at half past seven this morning, he had gone.

✳ ✳ ✳ ✳ ✳ ✳ ✳ ✳ ✳ ✳ ✳ ✳ ✳ ✳ ✳ ✳ ✳

Thursday afternoon. I'm writing this on the 5.10 from Euston. I meant to catch the 4.40, but my taxi got trapped in a huge traffic jam caused by a bomb alert in Centre Point. The police had cordoned off the intersection of Tottenham Court Road and Oxford Street, and the traffic was backed up in all directions. I said to the cab-driver, "Who's trying to blow up the building – the IRA or Prince Charles?" But he didn't get the joke – or, more likely, he wasn't amused. These bomb scares keep the tourists away and hurt his business.

I dropped in on a rehearsal this morning, as is my usual practice on Thursdays. When *The People Next Door* was new and still finding its feet I used to attend rehearsals practically every day, but now it runs like a train (or like a train *should* run – this one has suddenly slowed to a crawl for some reason, and we haven't even got to Watford Junction) and I just put in an appearance once a week to check that everything's going smoothly, and maybe do a little fine-tuning on the script. Rehearsals are held in a converted church hall near Pimlico tube station, its floor marked out with lines corresponding to the studio set in Rummidge. Walking in there on a winter's day would disabuse you of any illusion that television light entertainment is a glamorous profession. (I think that's the first time I've ever used the word "disabuse". I like it – it has a touch of class.) The brick walls are painted an institutional slime green and curdled cream, like Rummidge General Hospital, and the windows are barred and glazed with grimy frosted glass. There's the usual job-lot of miscellaneous furniture pushed against the walls or arranged in the various "rooms": splay-legged Formica-topped tables, plastic stacking chairs, collapsing three-piece suites, and beds with unsavoury-looking mattresses. Apart from the trestle table in one corner with a coffee machine, soft drinks, fruit and snacks laid out on it, the place could be a Salvation Army refuge or a depository for second-hand furniture. The actors wear old, comfortable clothes – all except Debbie, who always looks as if she's on her way to be photographed for *Vogue* – and when they aren't required for a scene they sit slumped in the broken-down chairs, reading newspapers and paperback novels, doing crosswords, knitting or, in Debbie's case, embroidering.

But they all look up and give me a cheerful smile and greeting as I come in. *"Hi, Tubby! How're you? How goes it?"* Actors are always very punctilious that way. Most producers and directors secretly despise writers, regarding them as mere drudges whose job it is to provide the raw material for the exercise of their own creativity, necessary evils who must be kept firmly in their place. Actors, however, regard writers with respect, even a certain awe. They know that the Writer is the ultimate source of the lines without which they themselves are impotent; and they know that, in the case of a long-running series, it is in his power to enhance or reduce the importance of their roles in episodes as yet unwritten. So they usually go out of their way to be nice to him.

This week they're doing Episode Seven of the present series, due to be transmitted in five weeks' time. Do they, I wonder, have any inkling that this may be the last series? No, I detect no signs of anxiety in their eyes or body language as we exchange greetings. Only between Debbie and myself does a message flash briefly, as I stoop to kiss her cheek where she sits in an old armchair, doing her eternal embroidery, and our eyes meet: she knows that I know that she wants out. Otherwise the secret seems to be safe for the time being. Not even Hal Lipkin, the director, knows yet. He bustles over to me as soon as I come in, frowning and biting his ballpen, but it's a query about the script that's on his mind.

Sitcom is pure television, a combination of continuity and novelty. The continuity comes from the basic "situation" – in our case, two

55

families with radically different lifestyles living next door to each other: the happy-go-lucky, welfare-sponging Davises, having unexpectedly inherited a house in a gentrified inner-city street, decide to move into it instead of selling it, to the ill-concealed dismay of their next-door neighbours, the cultured, middle-class, *Guardian*-reading Springfields. The viewers quickly become familiar with the characters and look forward to watching them behave in exactly the same way, every week, like their own relatives. The novelty comes from the story each episode tells. The art of sitcom is finding new stories to tell, week after week, within the familiar framework. It can't be a very complicated story, because you've only got twenty-five minutes to tell it in and, for both budgetary and technical reasons, most of the action must take place in the same studio set.

I was looking forward to seeing this week's episode in production, because it's one of those cases where we approach the territory of serious drama. Basically sitcom is light, family entertainment, which aims to amuse and divert the viewers, not to disturb and upset them. But if it doesn't occasionally touch on the deeper, darker side of life, however glancingly, then the audience won't believe in the characters and will lose interest in their fortunes. This week's episode centres on the Springfields' teenage daughter, Alice, who's about sixteen. When the series started five years ago, she was about fifteen. Phoebe Osborne, who plays her, was fourteen when she started and is now nineteen, but fortunately she hasn't grown much in that time and it's amazing what make-up and hairstyling can do. Adult characters in long-running sitcoms lead enchanted lives, they never age, but with the juveniles you have to allow for a certain amount of growth in the actors, and build it into the script. When young Mark Harrington's voice broke, for instance (he plays the Springfields' youngest, Robert) I made it a running joke for a whole series.

Anyway, this week's episode centres on Edward and Priscilla's fear that Alice may be pregnant, because she keeps throwing up. Cindy Davis next door is a teenage unmarried mother, her Mum looks after the baby while she's at school, and the dramatic point of the episode is that while the Springfields have been terribly liberal-minded about Cindy, they're horrorstruck at the thought of the same thing happening to their own daughter, especially as the likely father is young Terry Davis, whom Alice has been dating with their teeth-gritting consent. Needless to say, Alice isn't pregnant or even at risk since she won't allow Terry any liberties at all. She keeps throwing up because the sexually frustrated Terry is spiking the goats' milk which is delivered exclusively for Alice's use (she's allergic to cows' milk) with an alleged aphrodisiac (in fact a mild emetic) with the collusion of his mate, Rodge, the milkman's assistant. This is eventually revealed when Priscilla accidentally helps herself to Alice's special milk and is violently sick. ("EDWARD (*aghast*): Don't tell me you're pregnant too?") But before that a good deal of comedy is generated by the elaborately circuitous ways in which Edward and Priscilla try to check out their dreadful suspicion, and the contrast between their public tolerance and private disapproval of single-parent families.

"It's running a bit long, Tubby," Hal said, indistinctly because he was gripping a ballpen between his teeth as he riffled through his copy of the script. Another ballpen protruded from his wiry thatch of hair just above his right ear – parked there some time earlier and forgotten. (*I* should be so lucky.) "I was wondering if we could cut a few lines here," he mumbled. I knew exactly which lines he was going to point to before he found the page:

EDWARD: Well, if she *is* pregnant, she'll have to have a termination.

PRISCILLA *(angrily)*:   I suppose you think that will solve everything?

EDWARD: Hang on! I thought you were all in favour of a woman's right to choose?

PRISCILLA: She's not a woman, she's a child. Anyway, suppose she chooses to have the baby?

PAUSE, AS EDWARD FACES UP TO THIS POSSIBILITY.

EDWARD *(quietly but firmly)*:

Then of course we shall support her.

PRISCILLA *(softening)*:   Yes, of course.

PRISCILLA *REACHES OUT AND SQUEEZES* EDWARD′S *HAND.*

I'd already had a run-in about these lines with Ollie Silvers, my producer, when I first delivered the script. Actually he's much more than my producer nowadays, he's Head of Series and Serials at Heartland, no less; but since *The People Next Door* was in a sense his baby, and still gets better ratings than anything else Heartland does, he couldn't bear to hand it over to a line producer when he was promoted, and still finds time somehow to poke his nose into the detail of every episode. He said you couldn't have references to abortion in a sitcom, even one that goes out after the nine-o'clock watershed when young viewers are supposed to be tucked up in bed, because it's too controversial, and too upsetting. I said it was unrealistic to suppose that an educated middle-class couple would discuss the possible pregnancy of their schoolgirl daughter without mentioning the subject. Ollie said that audiences accepted the conventions of sitcom, that some things simply weren't mentioned, and they liked it that way. I said that all kinds of things that used to be taboo in sitcom were acceptable now. Ollie said, not abortion. I said, there's always a first time. He said, why on our show? I said, why not? He gave in, or so I thought. I might have known he'd find a way to get rid of the lines.

When I asked Hal if the cut was Ollie's idea, Hal looked a bit embarrassed. "Ollie was in yesterday," he admitted. "He did suggest the lines aren't absolutely essential to the story."

"Not absolutely essential," I said. "Just a little moment of truth."

Hal looked unhappy and said we could discuss the matter further with Ollie, who was coming in after lunch, but I said it was too late in the day to have a knock-down-drag-out argument on a matter of principle. The cast would pick up the vibrations and get anxious and uptight about the scene. Hal looked relieved, and hurried off to tell Suzie, his production assistant, to amend the script. I left before Ollie arrived. Now I wonder why I didn't put up more of a fight.

The senior conductor has just announced that we are approaching Rugby. "Rugby will be the next station stop." BR has taken to using this cumbersome phrase, "station stop" lately, presumably to distinguish scheduled stops at stations from unscheduled ones in the middle of fields, concerned perhaps that passengers disoriented by the fumes of bacon and tomato rolls and overheated brake linings in carriages with defective air-conditioning might otherwise stumble out on to the track by mistake and get killed.

Thursday evening. I got home at about 7.30. The train was only twelve minutes late in the end, and I found my car, unscathed by thieves or vandals, waiting for me where I had left it, like a faithful pet. I roused it with the remote button on my keyring as I approached and it blinked its indicator lights at me and cheeped three times, as the doorlocks clicked open. These remote-control gadgets give me an inexhaustible childish pleasure. Our garage door is operated by one, and it amuses me to start it opening as I turn the corner at the end of the road so that I can drive straight in without pausing. As the door yawned open this evening I saw that Sally's car wasn't parked inside, and when I let myself into the house I found a note in the kitchen to say that she'd gone down to the Club for a swim and sauna. I felt unreasonably disappointed, because I was all primed to tell her about the crisis over Debbie Radcliffe and the argument about the cut in this week's episode. Not that she would be dying to hear about either topic. *Au contraire.*

In my experience there are two kinds of writers' wives. One kind is a combination of nanny, secretary and fan-club president. She reads the writer's work in progress and always praises it; she watches his programmes at transmission and laughs at every joke; she winces at a bad review and rejoices at a good one as feelingly as he does; she keeps an anxious eye on his mood and workrate, brings him cups of tea and coffee at regular intervals, tiptoeing in and out of his study without disturbing his concentration; she answers the telephone and replies to letters, protecting him from tiresome and unprofitable invitations, requests and propositions; she keeps a note of his appointments and reminds him of them in good time, drives him to the station or airport and meets him again when he returns, and gives cocktail parties and dinner parties for his professional friends and patrons. The other kind is like Sally, who does none of these things, and has a career of her own which she considers just as important as her spouse's, if not more so.

Actually, Sally is the only writer's wife of this kind that I've met, though I suppose there must be others.

So it wasn't that I was hoping for sympathetic advice and knowledgeable counsel when I got home, just an opportunity to get some oppressive thoughts off my chest. Driving from the station, I felt a growing conviction that I had made a mistake in giving in so easily to cutting the reference to abortion in this week's script, and began to torment myself by wondering whether or not to re-open discussion of the matter by phoning Ollie and Hal at their respective homes – knowing that I would be in a very weak position, having agreed to the cut this morning, and that I would create bad feeling all round by trying to revoke that decision, without actually achieving anything in the end anyway because it was probably too late to change the script again. Probably, but not *necessarily*. The actors rehearsed the cut version this afternoon, but could if required restore the missing lines at tomorrow's rehearsal.

I paced restlessly around the empty house, picked up the telephone a couple of times, and put it down again without dialling. I made myself a ham sandwich, but the meat was too cold from the fridge to have any flavour, and drank a can of beer that filled my stomach with gas. I turned on the telly at random and found myself watching a rival sitcom on BBC1 which seemed much wittier and sharper than *The People Next Door*, and switched it off again after ten minutes. I went into my study and sat down at the computer.

I feel self-esteem leaking out of me like water from an old bucket. I despise myself both for my weakness in accepting the cut and for my vacillation over whether to do anything about it. My knee has begun to throb, like a rheumatic joint sensitive to the approach of bad weather. I sense a storm of depression flickering on the horizon, and a tidal wave of despair gathering itself to swamp me.

Thank God. Sally has just come in. I just heard the door slam behind her, and her cheerful call from the front hall.

Friday morning 19th Feb. There was appeal from MIND in my mail this morning. First time I've had one from them, I think. They must have got my address from one of the other charities. Inside the envelope was a letter and a blue balloon. There was an instruction at the top of the letter: *"Please blow up the balloon before you read any further, but don't tie a knot in it."* So I blew up the balloon, and on it, drawn in white lines, appeared the profile of a man's head, looking a bit like me actually, with a thick neck and no visible hair; and packed inside the cranium, one on top of the other, like thoughts, were the words: BEREAVED, UNEMPLOYED, MONEY, SEPARATED, MORTGAGE, DIVORCED, HEALTH. *"To you,"* said the letter, *"the words on the balloon may seem just that – words. But the events they describe are at the heart of someone's nervous breakdown."*

Just then, the doorbell rang. Sally had left for work, so I went to the front door, still holding the balloon by its tail, pinched between thumb and index finger to stop the air from escaping. I felt a vaguely superstitious compulsion to obey the instructions in the letter, like a character in a fairy tale.

It was the milkman, wanting to be paid. He looked at the balloon and grinned. "Having a party?" he said. It was half past nine in the morning. "Your birthday, is it?" he said. "Many happy returns."

"It just came in the post," I said, gesturing lamely with the balloon. "How much do we owe you?" I fiddled a ten-pound note out of my wallet one-handed.

"Cracking programme the other night," said the milkman as he gave me my change. "When Pop Davis hid all those cigarettes around the house before he gave up smoking . . . very funny."

"Thanks, glad you enjoyed it," I said. All the local tradesmen know I write the scripts for *The People Next Door*. I can do instant audience research on my own doorstep.

I took the balloon back into my study and picked up the letter from MIND. *"Just as the words grow larger with the balloon, so somebody's problems can seem greater as the pressure on them increases,"* it said.

I looked again at the words packed inside the head. I'm not bereaved (or not very recently – Mum died four years ago, and Dad seven), I'm not unemployed, I have plenty of money, I'm not separated or divorced, and I could pay off my mortgage tomorrow if I wanted to, but my accountant advised me against because of the tax relief. The only way I qualify for a nervous breakdown is under Health, though I suspect MIND was thinking of something more life-threatening than Internal Derangement of the Knee.

I skimmed through the rest of the letter: *"Suicide . . . psychosis . . . halfway house . . . helpline . . . "* After the final appeal for money, there was a PS: *"You can let the air out of the balloon now. And as you do so, please think about how quickly the pressure of someone's problems can be released with the time, care, and special understanding your gift will give today."* I let the balloon go and it rocketed round the room like a madly farting bluebottle for a few seconds before hitting a window pane and collapsing to the floor. I got out my charity chequebook and sent MIND £36 to provide somebody with a specially trained mental health nurse for a morning.

I could do with one myself today.

Last night, after Sally came in, we talked in the kitchen as she made herself a cup of hot chocolate, and I had a scotch. Or rather I talked, and she listened, rather abstractedly. She was feeling languorously euphoric from her sauna and seemed to have more than usual difficulty in focusing on my professional problems. When I announced that the lines about abortion had been cut from this week's script, she said, "Oh, good," and although she saw from my expression that this was the wrong response, she typically proceeded to defend it, saying that *The People Next Door* was too light-hearted a show to accommodate such a heavy subject – exactly Ollie's argument. Then, when I told her that the future of the show was threatened by Debbie's intention of leaving at the end of the present series, Sally said, "Well, that will suit you, won't it? You can do something new with another producer prepared to take more risks than Ollie." Which was quite logical, but not particularly helpful, since I don't have an idea for a new show, and am unlikely to get one in my present state.

Sally ran her finger round the inside of her cup and licked it. "When are you going to bed?" she said, which is her usual way of suggesting that we have sex, so we did, and I couldn't come. I had an erection, but no climax. Perhaps it was the scotch, on top of the beer, I don't know, but it was worrying, like working a pump handle and getting nothing out of the spout. Sally came – at least I think she did. I saw a programme on television the other night in which a lot of women were sitting round talking about sex and every one of them had faked orgasm on occasion, either to reassure their partners or to bring an unsatisfactory experience to a conclusion. Perhaps Sally does too. I don't know. She went off to sleep happily enough. I heard her breathing settle into a deep, slow rhythm before I dropped off myself. I woke again at 2.35 with the collar of my pyjama jacket damp with sweat. I felt a great sense of foreboding, as if there was something unpleasant I had forgotten and had to remember. Then I remembered: now I had Internal Derangement of the Gonads on top of all my other problems. I contemplated a life without sex, without tennis, without a TV show. I felt myself spiralling down into the dark. I always think of despair as a downward spiral movement – like an aeroplane that loses a wing and falls through the air like a leaf, twisting and turning as the pilot struggles helplessly with the controls, the engine note rising to a high-pitched scream, the altimeter needle spinning round and round the dial towards zero.

Reading through that last entry reminded me of Amy's odd question, "How's your *Angst?*" and I looked the word up. I was slightly surprised to find it in my English dictionary: "**1.** *An acute but unspecific sense of anxiety or remorse.* **2.** *(In Existentialist philosophy) the dread caused by man's awareness that his future is not determined, but must be freely chosen."* I didn't fully understand the second definition – philosophy is one of the bigger blank spots in my education. But I felt a little shiver of recognition at the word "dread". It sounds more like what I suffer than "anxiety". Anxiety sounds trivial, somehow. You can feel anxious about catching a train, or missing the post. I suppose that's why we've borrowed the German word. *Angst* has a sombre resonance to it, and you make a kind of grimace of pain as you pronounce it. But "Dread" is good. Dread is what I feel when I wake in the small hours in a cold sweat. Acute but unspecific Dread. Of course I soon think of specific things to attach it to. Impotence, for instance.

It has to happen sometime, of course, to every man. Fifty-eight seems a bit premature, but I suppose it's not impossible. Sooner or later, anyway, there has to be a last time. The trouble is, you'll only know when you discover that you can't do it any more. It's not like your last cigarette before you quit smoking, or your last game of football before you hang up your boots. You can't make a special occasion of your last fuck because you won't know it is your last one while you're having it; and by the time you find out you probably won't be able to remember what it was like.

I just looked up Existentialism in a paperback dictionary of modern thought. *"A body of philosophical doctrine that dramatically emphasizes the contrast between human existence and the kind of existence possessed by natural objects. Men, endowed with will and consciousness, find themselves in an alien world of objects which have neither."* That didn't seem much of a discovery to me. I thought I knew that already. *"Existentialism was inaugurated by Kierkegaard in a violent reaction against the all-encompassing absolute Idealism of Hegel."* Oh, it was, was it? I looked up Kierkegaard. *"Kierkegaard, Søren. Danish philosopher, 1813–55. See under EXISTENTIALISM."*

I looked up Kierkegaard in another book, a biographical dictionary. He was the son of a self-made merchant and inherited a considerable fortune from his father. He spent it all on studying philosophy and religion. He was engaged to a girl called Regine but broke it off because he decided he wasn't suited to marriage. He trained to be a minister but never took orders and at the end of his life wrote some controversial essays attacking conventional Christianity. Apart from a couple of spells in Berlin, he never left Copenhagen. His life sounded as dull as it was short. But the article listed some of his books at the end. I can't describe how I felt as I read the titles. If the hairs on the back of my neck were shorter, they would have lifted.

Fear and Trembling, The Sickness Unto Death, The Concept of Dread –
they didn't sound like titles of philosophy books, they seemed to
name my condition like arrows thudding into a target. Even the ones I
couldn't understand, or guess at the contents of, like *Either/Or* and
Repetition, seemed pregnant with hidden meaning designed especially for me. And, what do you know, Kierkegaard wrote a Journal. I
must get hold of it, and some of the other books.

* * * * * * * * * * * * * * * * *

Friday evening. Acupuncture at the Wellbeing Clinic this afternoon.
Miss Wu began, as she always does, by taking my pulse, holding my
wrist between her cool damp fingers as delicately as if it were the stem
of a fragile and precious flower, and asked me how I was. I was
tempted to tell her about my ejaculation problem last night, but
chickened out. Miss Wu, who was born in Hong Kong but brought
up in Rummidge, is very shy and demure. She always leaves the room
while I strip to my underpants and climb on to the high padded couch
and cover myself with a cellular blanket; and she always knocks on the
door to check that I'm ready before she comes back in. I thought she
might be embarrassed if I mentioned my seminal no-show, and to tell
you the truth I didn't fancy the idea of needles being stuck in my
scrotum. Not that she normally puts the needles where you might
expect, but you never know. So I just mentioned my usual symptoms
and she put the needles in my hands and feet, as she usually does.
They look a bit like the pins with coloured plastic heads that are used
on wall-maps and notice-boards. You feel a kind of tingling jolt when
she hits the right spot, sometimes it can be as powerful as a low-
voltage electric shock. There's definitely something to this acupuncture business, though whether it does you any lasting good, I don't
know. I went to Miss Wu originally for my Internal Derangement of
the Knee, but she told me frankly that she didn't think she could do
much about it except to assist the healing process by improving my
general physical and mental health, so I settled for that. I feel better
afterwards for the rest of the day, and maybe the next morning, but
after that the effect seems to wear off. There's a slightly penitential

aspect to it – the needles do hurt a little, and you're not allowed to drink alcohol on the day of the treatment, which is probably why I feel better for it – but I find Miss Wu's infinitely gentle manner comforting. She always apologizes if a particularly strong reaction to the needle makes me jump; and when (very rarely) she can't find the spot, and has to have several tries, she gets quite distressed. When she accidentally drew blood one day, I thought she would die of shame.

While the treatment is going on we chat, usually about my family. She takes a keen interest in the lives of Adam and Jane. Her questions, and my occasional difficulty in answering them, make me guiltily aware how little thought I give to my children these days, but they have their own lives now, independent and self-sufficient, and they know that if they are in serious need of money they only have to ask. Adam works for a computer software company in Cambridge, and his wife Rachel teaches Art History part-time at the University of Suffolk. They have a young baby so they're completely taken up with the complex logistics of their domestic and professional lives. Jane, who did a degree in archaeology, was lucky enough to get a job at the museum in Dorchester, and lives in Swanage with her boyfriend Gus, a stonemason. They lead a quiet, unambitious, vegetarian life in that dull little resort and seem happy enough in a New Age sort of way. We see them all together these days only at Christmas, when we have them to stay in Hollywell. A tiny shadow of a frown passed across Miss Wu's face when she realized from my remarks that Jane and Gus are not married – I guess that this would not be acceptable in her community. Well, I hope Jane will get married one day, preferably not to Gus, though she could probably do worse. Today I boldly asked Miss Wu if she expected to marry herself and she smiled and blushed and lowered her eyes, and said, "Marriage is a very serious responsibility." She took my pulse again and pronounced that it was much improved and wrote down something in her book. Then she left the room for me to get dressed.

I left her cheque in a plain brown envelope on the little table where she keeps her needles and other stuff. The first time she treated me I made the mistake of taking out my wallet and crassly thrusting banknotes into her hand. She was very embarrassed, and so was I when I perceived my *faux pas*. Paying therapists is always a bit tricky. Alexandra prefers to do it all by mail. Amy told me that on the last Friday of every month when she goes into Karl Kiss's consulting room there's a little envelope on the couch with her bill in it. She picks it up and silently secretes it in her handbag. It is never referred to by either of them. It's not surprising, really, this reticence. Healing shouldn't be a financial transaction – Jesus didn't charge for miracles. But therapists have to live. Miss Wu only charges fifteen quid for a one-hour session. I wrote her out a cheque for twenty, once, but this only caused more embarrassment because she ran after me in the car park and said I'd made a mistake.

When I was dressed she came back into the room and we made an appointment for two weeks' time. Next Friday I have aromatherapy. Miss Wu doesn't know that, though.

I'm game for almost any kind of therapy except chemotherapy. I mean tranquillizers, antidepressants, that sort of stuff. I tried it once. It was quite a long time ago, 1979. My first very own sitcom was in development with Estuary – *Role Over*, the one about a house-husband with a newly liberated, careerist wife. I was working on the pilot when Jake called me with an offer from BBC Light Entertainment to join the script-writing team for a new comedy series. It was a typical twist in the life of a freelance writer: after struggling for years to get my work produced, suddenly I was in demand from two different channels at once, I decided that I couldn't do both jobs in tandem. (Jake thought I could, but then all *he* had to do was draw up two contracts and hold out two hands for his commission.) So I turned down the Beeb, since *Role Over* was obviously the more important project. Instead of just telephoning Jake, I wrote him a long letter setting out my reasons in minutely argued detail, more for my own sake than for his (I doubt if he even bothered to read it through to the end). But the pilot was a disaster, so bad that Estuary wouldn't even expose it to the light of cathode tube, and it looked as if the series would never happen. Naturally I began to regret my decision about the BBC offer. Indeed "regret" is a ridiculously inadequate description of my state of mind. I was convinced that I had totally destroyed my career, committed professional suicide, passed up the best opportunity of my life etc. etc. I suppose, looking back, it was my first really bad attack of Internal Derangement. I couldn't think about anything else but my fateful decision. I couldn't work, I couldn't relax, I couldn't read, couldn't watch TV, couldn't converse with anybody on anything for more than a few minutes before my thought process, like the stylus arm of a haunted record deck, returned inexorably to the groove of futile brooding on The Decision. I developed Irritable Bowel Syndrome, and went about drained of energy by the peristaltic commotion in my gut, fell exhausted into bed at ten-thirty and woke two hours later soaked in sweat, to spend the rest of the night mentally rewriting my letter to Jake demonstrating with impeccable logic why I could perfectly well work for the BBC and Estuary at the same time, and constructing other scenarios which turned back the clock and allowed me to escape in fantasy the consequences of my decision: my letter to Jake was lost, or returned to me unopened because wrongly addressed, or the BBC came back pleading with me to have second thoughts, and so on. After a week of this, Sally made me go and see my GP, a taciturn Scot called Patterson, not the one I have now. I told him about my restless bowels and sleeplessness, and guardedly admitted to being under stress (I wasn't yet prepared to open the door on the raving madhouse of my mind to another person). Patterson listened, grunted, and wrote me out a prescription for Valium.

I was a Valium virgin – I suppose that was why the effect of the drug was so powerful. I couldn't believe it, the extraordinary peace and relaxation that enveloped me like a warm blanket within minutes. My fears and anxieties shrank and receded and disappeared, like gibbering ghosts in the light of day. That night I slept like a baby, for ten hours. The next morning I felt torpid and mildly depressed in an unfocused sort of way. I dimly sensed bad thoughts mustering below the horizon of consciousness, getting ready to return, but another little pale green tablet zapped that threat, and cocooned me in tranquillity again. I was all right – not exactly in scintillating form either creatively or socially, but perfectly all right – as long as I was taking the pills. But when I finished the course, my obsession

68

returned like a rabid Rottweiler freed from the leash. I was in an infinitely worse state than I had been before.

The addictive nature of Valium wasn't fully appreciated in those days, and of course I hadn't been taking it long enough to become addicted anyway, but I went through a kind of cold turkey as I struggled against the temptation to go back to Patterson and ask for another prescription. I knew that if I did so, I would become totally dependent. Not just that, but I was sure that I would never be able to write as long as I was on Valium. Of course I couldn't write while I was *off* it, either, at the time, but I had a kind of intuition that eventually the nightmare would pass of its own accord. And of course it did, ten seconds after Jake called me to say Estuary were going to re-cast and do another pilot. It got an encouraging response, and they commissioned a whole series, which was a modest success, my first, while the BBC show bombed. A year later I could hardly remember why I had ever doubted the wisdom of my original decision. But I remembered the withdrawal symptoms after the last Valium and vowed never to expose myself to that again.

Two spasms in the knee while I was writing this, one sharp enough to make me cry out.

✻ ✻ ✻ ✻ ✻ ✻ ✻ ✻ ✻ ✻ ✻ ✻ ✻ ✻ ✻ ✻ ✻

Saturday evening, 20th Feb. I heard a surprising and rather disturbing story from Rupert at the Club today. Sally and I went there after an early lunch to play tennis, outdoors. It was a lovely winter's day, dry and sunny, the air crisp but still. Sally played doubles with three other women, I with my crippled cronies. It takes us blokes a long time to get into our kit, we have to put on so many bandages, splints, supports, trusses and prostheses first – it's like mediaeval knights getting into their armour before a battle. So Sally and her pals were well into their first set as we walked, or rather limped, past their court on our way to ours. Rupert's wife Betty was partnering Sally, and just at that moment she played a particularly good backhand volley to win a point, and we all applauded. "Betty's been having some coaching too, has she, Rupert?" Joe remarked, with a grin. "Yes," said Rupert, rather abruptly. "Well, our Mr Sutton certainly does something for the ladies," said Joe. "I don't know what exactly, but . . ." "Oh, knock it off, Joe," said Rupert irritably, striding on ahead. Joe pulled a face and waggled his eyebrows at Humphrey and me, but said nothing more until we reached the court and picked partners.

I played with Humphrey, and we beat the other two in five sets, 6–2, 5–7, 6–4, 3–6, 7–5. It was a keenly contested match, even if to an observer it might have looked from the speed of our movements as if we were playing underwater. My backhand was working well for once, and I played a couple of cracking returns of service, low over the net, that took Rupert quite by surprise. There's nothing quite so satisfying as a sweetly hit backhand, it seems so effortless. I actually won the match with a mistimed volley off the frame of my racquet, which was more characteristic of our normal play. However, it was all very enjoyable. Joe wanted to switch partners and play the best of three sets, but my knee had tightened up ominously, and Rupert said his painkillers were beginning to wear off (he always takes a couple of tablets before a game), so we left the other two to play singles and went for a drink after we'd showered. We carried our pints to a nice quiet corner of the Club bar. In spite of the occasional twinge of pain in my knee, I felt good, glowing from the exercise, almost like the old days, and relished the cool bitter, but Rupert frowned into his jar as if there was something nasty at the bottom of it. "I wish Joe wouldn't keep on about Brett Sutton," he said. "It's embarrassing. It's worse than embarrassing, it's unpleasant. It's like watching somebody picking at a scab." I asked him what he meant. He said, lowering his voice, "Didn't you know about Jean?" "Jean who?" I said stupidly. "Oh, you weren't there, were you," Rupert said. "Joe's Jean. She had it off with young Ritchie at the New Year's Eve do."

Young Ritchie is Alistair, son of Sam Ritchie, the Club's golf pro. He looks after the shop when his father is out giving lessons, and does a bit of beginners' tuition himself. He can't be more than twenty-five. "You're not serious?" I said. "Cross my heart," Rupert said. "Jean got tight, and started complaining because Joe wouldn't dance, then she got young Ritchie to dance with her, giggling and hanging round

70

his neck she was, then some time later they both disappeared. Joe went looking for her, and found them together in the First Aid room, in a compromising position. It's not the first time it's been used for that purpose, I believe. They'd locked the door, but Joe had a key, being on the Committee." I asked Rupert how he knew all this. "Jean told Betty, and Betty told me." I shook my head incredulously. I wondered why Joe was making all these cracks about Brett Sutton being the club gigolo, if he himself had just been cuckolded by young Ritchie. "Diversionary tactics, I suppose," Rupert said. "He's trying to draw attention away from Ritchie and Jean." "What possessed young Ritchie?" I said. "Jean is old enough to be his mother." "Perhaps it was pity," Rupert suggested. "Jean told him she hadn't had it since Joe had his back operation." "Had what?" "*It*," said Rupert. "Sex. You're a bit slow on the uptake today, Tubby." "Sorry, I'm gobsmacked," I said. I was thinking of our conversation in the indoor courts last week: it was disturbing to realize that what I took to be Joe's harmless teasing had had this painful subtext. I recalled now that Rupert hadn't joined in the banter, though Humphrey had. "Does Humphrey know about this?" I asked. "I dunno. I don't think so. He hasn't got a wife to pass on the gossip, has he? I'm surprised Sally hasn't picked it up." Perhaps she has, I thought, and hasn't told me.

But when I asked her later if she'd heard any scandal about Jean Wellington, she said, no. "But then I wouldn't," she said. "It's a trade-off, that sort of gossip. You don't get any dirt if you don't dish some yourself." I thought she would ask me for more details, but she didn't. Sally has extraordinary self-control in that way. Or perhaps she just isn't curious about other people's private lives. She's very wrapped up in her work at the moment – not only her teaching and research, but admin. There's a lot of reorganization going on as a result of the change of status from Poly to University. They can make up their own degree programmes now, and Sally is chairing a new inter-Faculty postgraduate degree course in Applied Linguistics shared between Education and Humanities, as well as sitting on numerous committees, internal and external, with names like F-QUAC (Faculty Quality Assurance Committee) and C-CUE

71

(Council for College and University English), and organizing the in-service training of local junior-school teachers to implement the new National Curriculum. I think she's being exploited by her Head of Department, who gives her all the trickiest jobs because he knows she'll do them better than anyone else, but when I tell her this she just shrugs and says that it shows he's a good manager. She brings home piles of boring agendas and reports to work through in the evenings and at the weekends. We sit in silence on opposite sides of the fireplace, she with her committee papers, I connected to the muted television by the umbilical cord of my headphones.

Severe twinge in the knee while I was watching the news tonight. I suddenly shouted "Fuck!" Sally looked up from her papers enquiringly. I took off the headphones momentarily and said, "Knee." Sally nodded and went back to her reading. I went back to the news. The main story was a development in the James Bulger murder case, which has been dominating the media for days. Last week the little boy, only two years old, was enticed away from a butcher's shop in a shopping mall in Bootle by two older boys, while his mother's attention was distracted. Later he was found dead, with appalling injuries, beside a railway line. The abduction was recorded by a security video camera, and every newspaper and TV news programme has carried the almost unbearably poignant blurred still of the toddler being led away by the two older boys, trustingly holding the hand of one of them, like an advertisement for Startrite shoes. It appears that several adults saw the trio after that, and noticed that the little boy was crying and looking distressed, but nobody intervened. Tonight it was announced that two ten-year-old boys have been charged with murder. "The question is being asked," the TV reporter said, standing against the backdrop of the Bootle shopping mall, "What kind of society do we live in, in which such things can happen?" A pretty sick one, is the answer.

* * * * * * * * * * * * * * * * *

Sunday 21st Feb. 6·30 p.m. I'm writing this on my laptop in the break between the dress rehearsal and the recording of *The People Next Door*, sitting at a Formica table in the Heartland Studios canteen, surrounded by soiled plates and cups and glasses left over from an early dinner shared with the cast and production team, and not yet cleared away by the somewhat lackadaisical catering staff. Recording begins at 7.30, after a half-hour warm-up session for the audience. The actors have gone off to Make-Up for repairs, or are resting in their dressing-rooms. Hal is doing a last check on the camera script with his PA and vision mixer, Ollie is having a drink with David Treece, Heartland's Controller of Comedy (I love that title), and I have just managed to shake off the attentions of Mark Harrington's chaperone, Samantha, who lingered after the others had gone, so I have an hour to myself. Samantha Handy has a degree in Drama from Exeter University and is doing the job *faute de mieux*, as Amy would say. Looking after a twelve-year-old boy whose chief topic of conversation is computer games, and making sure he does his homework, is obviously not her natural vocation. She really wants to write for television and seems to think I can help her get a commission. She's a good-looking redhead, with amazing boobs, and I suppose another man, Jake Endicott for instance, might be tempted to encourage her in this illusion, but I told her frankly that she would do better to try and persuade Ollie to give her some scripts to report on as a first step. She pouted a little and said, "It's just that I have this fabulous idea for an offbeat soap, a kind of English *Twin Peaks*. Sooner or later somebody else is going to think of it, and I couldn't bear that." "What is it?" I said, averting my eyes from her own twin peaks; and then added hastily, "No, don't tell me. Tell Ollie. I don't want to be accused of pinching it one day." She smiled and said it wasn't my sort of thing, it was too kinky. "What's kinky?" said Mark, who was working his way through a second helping of Mississippi Mud Pie. "None of your business," said Samantha, flicking him lightly on the ear with a long, tapered fingernail. She asked me if I thought she should get an agent, and I said I thought that would be a good idea, but I didn't offer to introduce her to Jake Endicott. This was entirely for her own good, but naturally she didn't appreciate my chivalrous motives, and took her young charge off to Make-Up slightly miffed.

I never miss these Sunday recording sessions if I can help it. It's not that I can contribute much at this late stage, but there's always a kind of First Night excitement about the occasion, because of the studio audience. You never know who they're going to be or how they're going to react. The ones who write in for tickets are usually fans and can be relied upon to laugh in the right places, but there's always a risk that because the tickets are free people won't show up on the night. To be sure of filling the seats Heartland relies mostly on organized groups, like social clubs and staff associations looking for a cheap night out – bussing them in and out so they can't escape. Sometimes you get a party from an old people's home who are too gaga to follow the plot, or too deaf to hear the dialogue, or too short-sighted to see the monitors, and once we had a group of Japanese who didn't have a word of English between them and sat in baffled silence throughout, smiling politely. Other nights you get a crowd who really enjoy themselves, and the cast surf through the show on continuous waves of laughter. The unpredictability of the studio audience makes sitcom the nearest thing on television to live theatre, which is probably why I get such a buzz out of the recording sessions.

Heartland TV's Rummidge studios occupy a huge new building that looks a bit like an airport terminal from the outside, all cantilevered glass and tubular steel flying buttresses, erected three years ago on reclaimed derelict industrial land about a mile from the city centre, between a canal and a railway line. It was intended to be the hub of a vast Media Park, full of studios, galleries, printshops and advertising agencies, which never materialized because of the recession. There's nothing on the site except the gleaming Heartland monolith and its enormous landscaped car park. *The People Next Door* is recorded in Studio C, the biggest one, big enough to house an airship, with raked seating for three hundred and sixty running its entire length. On the floor, facing the seats, the permanent set is laid out – a particularly large and complex one, since there are two of everything: two living

74

rooms, two kitchens, two hallways and staircases, all separated by a party wall. *Party Wall* was my original working title, in fact, and the split-screen we use for some scenes, with action going on simultaneously in both households, is the visual trademark of the show, and frankly the only innovative thing about it. About a million lights sprout from the ceiling on metal stalks, like an inverted field of sunflowers, and the air-conditioning, designed to cope with all of them at once, is too cool for comfort. I always wear a thick sweater to dress rehearsals, even in summer. Hal Lipkin and most of the other production staff sport *The People Next Door* sweatshirts, navy blue with the title sloping in yellow cursive writing across the chest.

This is a long hard day for everyone, but especially for Hal. He's totally in command, totally responsible. When I arrived in the late morning he was down on the set talking to Ron Deakin, who was standing on top of a stepladder with a Black and Decker power tool. It's a "party wall" kitchen scene. Pop Davis is in the process of putting up some shelves under the sarcastic goading of Dolly Davis, while Priscilla and Edward next door are having a worried conversation about Alice, distracted by the whine of the drill. At the climax of the scene Pop Davis pushes his drill right through the wall, dislodging a saucepan that nearly falls on Edward's head – a tricky bit of business, which depends on pin-sharp timing. They've rehearsed it of course, but now they're having to do it for the first time with real props. The lead on Ron's Black and Decker is not long enough to reach the powerpoint, and there's a hiatus while the electrician goes to fetch an extension cord. The cameramen yawn and look at their watches to see how long it is to the next coffee-break. The actors stretch and pace about the set. Phoebe Osborne practises ballet steps in front of a mirror. Making television programmes consists very largely of waiting around.

The day's routine is slow and methodical. First Hal directs a scene from the edge of the set, stopping and starting to re-block the moves if necessary, until he's satisfied. Then he retires to the control room to see what it looks like from there. Five cameras are positioned at different angles to the set, focused on different characters or groups of characters, and each one is sending its pictures to a black-and-white monitor in the control room. A colour monitor in the middle of the bank of screens shows what will be recorded tonight on the master tape: a selection made by the production assistant, following a camera script prepared by Hal, in which every shot is numbered and allocated to a particular camera. She chants out the numbers to the vision mixer at her side as the action proceeds, and he presses the appropriate buttons. If you're sitting in the studio audience you can tell which camera is actually recording at any given moment because a little red bulb on the camera body lights up. From the gallery Hal speaks to his floor manager Isabel through her headset, and she relays his instructions to the cast. Sometimes he decides he needs to change a shot, or insert a new one, but it's striking how seldom he has to do this. He's already "seen" the entire show in his head, shot by shot.

Multicamera, as this technique is known in the trade, is peculiar to television. In the early days of the medium everything was done this way, even serious drama – and done *live* (imagine the tension and stress, with actors running round the back of the set to get into position for their next scene). Nowadays most drama and a good deal of sitcom is done on film or single-camera video. In other words, they're made like movies, every scene being shot several times from various angles and focal distances, in take after take, on location rather than in a studio, and then edited at the director's leisure. Directors prefer this method because it makes them feel like genuine *auteurs*. The younger ones sneer at multicamera and call it "joined-up television", but the fact is that most of them couldn't handle it, and would have their limitations cruelly exposed if they tried. With post-production editing you can always cover up your mistakes, but multicamera requires everything to be pretty well perfect on the night. It's a dying art, and Hal is one of the few masters of it still around.

Ollie came into the studio later and sat down beside me. He was wearing one of his Boss suits – he must own a wardrobeful. I think he buys them because of the name. As he sat down the wide shoulders of the jacket rode up and nudged his big red ears. Bracketing his broken nose, these make him look like an ex-boxer, and indeed it's rumoured that he started his career promoting fights in the East End of London.

"We must talk," he said. "About Debbie?" I asked. He looked alarmed and raised his finger to his lips. "Not so loud, walls have ears," he said, though we were alone in the raked seating and the nearest wall was fifty feet away. "Lunch? Dinner?" I suggested. "No, I want to involve Hal, and the cast will think it's funny if we get into a huddle on our own. Can you stay for a drink after the recording?" I said I could. At that moment I was surprised to hear Lewis Parker saying from the set, "*Well, if she is pregnant she'll have to have a termination,*" and Debbie replying, "*I suppose you think that will solve everything.*" I turned to Ollie. "I thought those lines had been cut." "We decided to respect your artistic integrity, Tubby," Ollie said, with a wolfish grin. When I asked Hal about it in a coffee break, he explained that they had saved some time by cutting a bit of business in a later scene so there had been no need to lose the lines after all. But I wonder if this isn't part of some plot to soften me up for the more serious matter of Priscilla's role.

It's five to seven. Time for me to take my seat in the studio. Wonder what kind of an audience we've got.

Monday morning, 22nd Feb. The audience turned out to be bloody awful. For starters we had a Moronic Laugher among them. That's always bad news: some idiot with a very loud, inane laugh, who goes on baying or cackling or shrieking at something long after everybody else has stopped, or starts up when nobody else is laughing, in the lull between two gags. It distracts the audience – after a while they start laughing at the Moronic Laugher instead of at the show – and it plays havoc with the actors' timing. Billy Barlow, our warm-up man, spotted the danger right away and tried to subdue the woman (for some reason, it's invariably a woman) with a few sarcastic asides, but Moronic Laughers are impervious to irony. "Did I say something funny?" he enquired as she cackled suddenly (she was a cackler) in the middle of his perfectly straight explanation of some technical term. "I think it must be in your mind, madam. This is a family show – no innuendos. You know what an innuendo is, don't you? Italian

77

for suppository." There was enough laughter to drown the cackler temporarily, though I've known Billy get a lot more with that joke on other occasions.

The warm-up man is essential to a successful recording. Not only does he have to get the audience in a receptive mood beforehand, he also has to bridge the gaps between scenes, as the cameras are moved from one part of the set to another, and fill in the pauses while the technicians check the tape after each take; and if a retake or pick-up is required he has to soothe the audience's impatience and appeal for their co-operation in laughing at the same lines the second time round. Billy is the best in the business, but there are limits to what even he can do. This audience was really sticky. They merely tittered at what should have been big laughs, and were silent when they should have tittered. As line after line fell flat the cast got anxious, and began to make mistakes or dry, requiring frequent re-takes, which made the audience still more unresponsive. Billy began to perspire, pacing up and down in front of the seats with his radio mike, frantically cracking jokes, his capped teeth exposed in a strained smile. I laughed like a drain, though I'd heard them all before, to encourage the people around me. I even forced a laugh at some of my own lines, something I never normally do. I began to think that it couldn't just be the audience's fault, there must be something wrong with the script. It had obviously been a bad idea to centre the plot on Alice's suspected pregnancy. Ollie and Sally had been right. The subject was making the audience uneasy. Then of course, when it came to the lines about termination, in the dramatic pause that followed Priscilla's question, "*Suppose she chooses to have the baby?*" the Moronic Laugher broke the silence with all the sensitive understanding of a mynah bird. I covered my face with my hands.

They wrapped the programme at five past nine, after more retakes than I could ever remember. Billy hypocritically thanked the audience for their support, and we all dispersed. The actors scurried from the set, giving me tired little waves and wan smiles of farewell. They're always in a hurry to get off on Sunday nights, to drive or catch the last train to London, and there was no temptation to linger tonight. I would have been glad to slope off home myself, if I hadn't had the confab with Ollie and Hal pending. I went to the control room, where Hal was running both hands through his birds' nest of wiry hair. "Jesus Christ, Tubby, who were those zombies out there tonight?" I shrugged my bafflement. "Maybe it was the script," I said miserably. Ollie came steaming into the room in time to hear this. "It wouldn't have made any difference if you were Shakespeare, Oscar Wilde and Groucho Marx rolled into one," he said, "those fuckers would have killed anybody's script. Where did we get them from – the local morgue?" Suzie the PA said she thought the largest contingent was a local factory's social club. "Well, the first thing I'm going to do tomorrow morning is find out who the hell they were and who invited them, and make sure they never come to a recording again. Let's go and have a drink. We need it."

Ollie is notoriously tight-fisted, and always wriggles out of standing his round if he possibly can. He's always the last to say, "Anybody for another one?" – by which time anyone who's driving has switched to fruit juice or stopped drinking altogether. When we go to the bar with him, Hal and I usually have a bit of fun trying to trick him into buying the first round – for instance, Hal will pretend to remember he's left something in the control room, and double back, shouting his order over his shoulder, and I'll suddenly veer into the Gents, doing the same. But yesterday evening neither of us had the heart for it, and Hal bought the first round without putting up any kind of fight. "Cheers," he said gloomily. We drank and sat in silence for a moment. "I've put Hal in the picture about Debbie," Ollie said. Hal nodded gravely. "It's a bitch," he said. But I knew I couldn't count on any real support from him. When push came to shove, he would side with Ollie. "Jake told you what we're suggesting, Tubby?" Ollie said.

At this moment Suzie came into the bar, and looked around until she spotted us. "Not a word about the Debbie thing," Ollie warned in a low voice, as she approached our table. I offered her a seat, but she shook her head. "I won't stop, thanks," she said. "I went outside and mingled with the audience while they were waiting for their buses. Most of them are from an electrical component factory in West Wallsbury. They heard on Friday that it's going to shut down at the end of next month. They all got redundancy notices with their payslips." We looked at each other. "Well, that explains a lot," I said. "Just our luck," said Hal. "Sodding management might have waited till tomorrow," said Ollie.

I was sorry for the workers, but the explanation couldn't have come at a better time as far as I was concerned. I'd been so demoralized by the way that evening's show had bombed that I would probably have agreed to anything Ollie and Hal proposed. Now, I no longer blamed myself. I was a bloody good scriptwriter after all – always had been and always would be. I was ready to do battle for my principles. "Jake gave me a rough idea of what you have in mind," I said to Ollie. "You want me to write Priscilla out of the story, is that it?" "What we have in mind," said Ollie, "is an amicable separation which removes Priscilla from the scene at the end of the current series, and sets up a new female interest in Edward's life for the next one." "*Amicable?*" I exploded. "They would be completely traumatized." "There would be a certain amount of pain, of course," said Ollie, "but Edward and Priscilla are mature modern people. They know that one in three marriages ends in divorce. So does our audience. You're always saying sitcom should deal with the serious things in life occasionally, Tubby." "As long as it's consistent with character," I said. "Why should Priscilla want to leave Edward?"

They had various bizarre suggestions: e.g., Priscilla decides she's a lesbian and goes off with a girlfriend; she gets oriental religion and goes off to an ashram to learn meditation; she is offered a wonderful job in California; or she just falls for a handsome foreigner. I asked them if they seriously thought any of these developments were (*a*) credible or (*b*) manageable in just one episode. "You might have to rewrite the last two or three, to prepare the ground," Ollie conceded, avoiding the first question. "I have an idea for the final episode," said Hal. "Let me run it by you." "This is a great idea, Tubby," Ollie assured me. Hal leaned forward. "After Priscilla walks out, Edward advertises for a housekeeper, and this stunning bird arrives at the door for an interview. Edward suddenly sees there may be a silver lining to his troubles. It's the very last shot of the series. Leaves the punters feeling better about the split, and interested in what will happen in the next series. What do you think?" "I think it stinks," I said. "Naturally you'd be paid handsomely for the extra work," said Ollie. "To be frank, you and Jake have us over a barrel on this one." He glanced slyly at me from under his hooded eyelids to see if he had awakened my greed by this admission. I said it wasn't money I was concerned about, but character and motivation. Hal asked me if I had any better ideas. I said: "The only plausible way to remove Priscilla from the show is to kill her." Ollie and Hal exchanged startled looks. "You mean, like have her murdered?" Hal faltered. I said, of course not, maybe a car crash or a swift fatal disease. Or a minor operation that goes wrong. "Tubby, I don't believe I'm hearing this," said Ollie. "We're talking sitcom here, not soap. You can't have one of your principal characters *die*. It's a no-no." I said there was always a first time. "That's what you said about tonight's episode," said Ollie, "and look what happened." "That was the audience's fault," I protested, "you said so yourself." "The best audience in the world is going to be stymied if they turn up expecting a comedy show and find that it's all about the mother of a family dying in the prime of life," said Ollie, and Hal sagely nodded his agreement. Then Ollie said something that really made me angry. "We appreciate how hard this is for you, Tubby. Perhaps we should think about getting another writer to work on it." "No way, José," I said. "It's commonplace in America," Ollie said. "They have whole teams of writers working on shows like ours." "I know," I said, "that's why the shows sound like a string of gags written by a committee. I'll tell you another thing about America. In New York they have street signs saying, 'DON'T even think of parking here.' That's how I feel about *The People Next Door*." I glowered at Ollie. "It's been a long day," said Hal nervously. "We're all tired." "Yeah, we'll talk again," said Ollie. "Not about other writers," I said. "I'd rather scuttle the ship than hand it over to somebody else." It seemed a good exit line, so I got to my feet and bade them both goodnight.

I just opened the dictionary to check the spelling of "glowered", and as I flipped the pages the headword "Dover's Powder" caught my eye. The definition said: *"a preparation of opium and ipecac, formerly used to relieve pain and check spasms. Named after Thomas Dover (1660–1742) English physician."* I wonder if you can still get it. Might be good for my knee.

It's amazing what you can learn from dictionaries by accident. That's one reason why I never use the Spellchecker on my computer. The other reason is that it has such a pathetically small vocabulary. If it doesn't recognize a word it suggests another one it thinks you might have meant to write. This can be quite funny sometimes. Like once I wrote "Freud" and the computer came back with the suggestion, "Fraud?" I told Amy, but she wasn't amused.

I called Jake this morning and reported my conversation with Ollie and Hal. He was sympathetic but not exactly supportive. "I think you should be as flexible as you can," he said. "Heartland are desperately keen for the series to continue. It's their comedy flagship." "Whose side are you on, Jake?" I asked him. "Yours, of course, Tubby." Of course. But at heart Jake believes in Ollie Silver's adage, "Art for art's sake but money for Christ's sake." I arranged to call in at his office on Thursday.

Had a restless night last night. Sally was already in bed and asleep when I got back from the recording. I snuggled up to her spoonwise and went off quite quickly, but was jerked awake at two-thirty by internal derangement of the knee. I lay awake for hours, replaying the events of yesterday in my head, and waiting for the next twinge. This morning I noticed a touch of tennis elbow, too, when I was shaving. Be great, wouldn't it, if I had another operation on my knee, only to find I had to give up tennis because of the elbow? Good job it's my day for physiotherapy.

Monday evening. I asked Roland if he'd ever heard of Dover's Powder, but he said it didn't ring a bell. He's a connoisseur of anti-inflammatory gels with names like Movelat and Traxam and Ibuleve (reminds me of the song, *"Ibuleve for every drop of rain that falls, a flower grows . . ."*) which he rubs into my knee after ultrasonic treatment. (*"Ibuleve for every stab of pain that galls, new tissue grows* . . .") Physiotherapy these days is largely automated. When I'm stripped down and ready on the couch, Roland wheels a big box of electronic tricks into the room and wires me up to it, or aims a dish or a lamp or a laser at the affected part. It's amazing how deftly he handles the equipment. There's just one gadget I have to operate myself. It gives electric shocks which stimulate the quadriceps, and I have to turn up the voltage to the maximum I can bear. It's like self-inflicted torture. Funny how much the pursuit of fitness has in common with the infliction of pain. From my couch, shackled with wires and electrodes, I gaze through the window and across a small courtyard at the glass wall of a gymnasium where men, grimacing with effort and glistening with sweat, are exercising on machines that, apart from their hi-tech finish, could be engines of torture straight out of a mediaeval dungeon: racks, pulleys, weights, and treadmills.

Roland asked me if I had heard about the trans-sexual trout. No, I said, tell me about the trans-sexual trout. He's a mine of information, is Roland. His wife reads interesting snippets out of the newspaper to him, and he remembers everything. Apparently male trout are suffering sex-changes because of the high level of female hormones getting into the sewage outfall from contraceptive pills and hormone replacement therapy. It's feared that all the male fish in the affected rivers will become hermaphrodites, and cease to reproduce. "Makes you think, doesn't it?" said Roland. "After all, we drink the same water eventually. Next thing you know, men will be growing breasts." I wondered if Roland was winding me up. I have a lot of fatty tissue on my chest, under the hair. Roland might have felt it one day, when he was giving me a massage.

Perhaps I couldn't come the other night because I'm turning into a hermaphrodite. Internal Derangement of the Hormones.

✾ ✾ ✾ ✾ ✾ ✾ ✾ ✾ ✾ ✾ ✾ ✾ ✾ ✾ ✾ ✾ ✾

Tuesday evening, 23rd Feb. I asked for Dover's Powder in the biggest Boots in Rummidge today, but the pharmacist said he'd never heard of it, and he couldn't find it in his book of patent medicines. I said, "I expect it was banned because of the opium," and he gave me a funny look. I left the shop before he could call the Drug Squad.

I went into the City Centre primarily to buy some books by Kierkegaard, but didn't have much joy. Waterstone's only had the Penguin edition of *Fear and Trembling*, so I bought that and went along to Dillons. When Dillons proved to have the same book and nothing else, I began to feel my usual symptoms of shopping syndrome, i.e. unreasonable rage and impatience. Low Frustration Tolerance, LFT, it's called, according to Alexandra. I'm afraid I was very scathing to a harmless assistant who thought "Kierkegaard" was two words and started searching on her microfiche under "Gaard." Fortunately the Central Library was better supplied. I was able to borrow *The Concept of Dread*, and a couple of the other titles that had intrigued me, *Either/Or* and *Repetition*. The *Journals* were out.

It's quite a while since I used the Library, and I hardly recognized it from the outside. It's a typical piece of sixties civic architecture, a brutalist construction in untreated concrete, said by the Prince of Wales to resemble a municipal incinerating plant. It's built in a hollow square around a central courtyard in which there was once a shallow pond and a seldom-functioning fountain, the repository for much unseemly garbage. This gloomy and draughty space was a public thoroughfare, though most people avoided it, especially at night. Recently, however, it's been converted into a glazed and tiled atrium, festooned with hanging greenery, adorned with neoclassical fibreglass statues, and designated "The Rialto" in pink neon lettering. The floor area is dedicated to a variety of boutiques, stalls and catering outlets of a vaguely Italianate character. Operatic muzak and Neapolitan pop songs ooze from hidden speakers. I sat down at a table "outside" Giuseppe's café-bar (outside still being indoors in this studio-like setting) and ordered a *cappuccino*, which seemed designed to be inhaled through the nose rather than drunk, since it consisted mostly of foam.

Much of the city centre has been given the same kind of face-lift, in a brave attempt to make it attractive to tourists and visiting businessmen. Resigned to the erosion of the region's traditional industrial base, the city fathers looked to service industries as an alternative source of employment. A vast conference centre and a state-of-the-art concert hall now face the Library from the other end of a tessellated piazza. Hotels, wine bars, nightclubs and restaurants have sprung up in the neighbourhood, almost overnight. The surrounding canals have been cleaned up and their towpaths paved for the exploration of industrial archeology. It was a typical project of the later Thatcher years, that brief flare of prosperity and optimism between the recession of the early eighties and the recession of the early nineties. Now the new buildings, with their stainless steel escalators and glass lifts and piped music, stand expectant and almost empty, like a theme park before opening day, or like some utopian capital city of a third-world country, built for ideological reasons in the middle of the jungle, an object of wonder to the natives but seldom visited by foreigners. The principal patrons of the Rialto in the daytime are unemployed youths, truanting schoolkids, and mothers with infant children, who are grateful for a warm and cheerful place in which to while away the winter afternoons. Plus the occasional privileged wanker like me.

I don't recall hearing the word "recession" until a few years ago. Where did it come from, and what does it mean exactly? For once the dictionary is not much help: *"a temporary depression in economic activity or prosperity."* How long does a recession have to last before it's called a depression? Even the Slump of the Thirties was "temporary", in the long run. Perhaps there's so much psychological depression about that somebody decided we needed a new word for the economic sort. Recession-depression, recession-depression. The words echo in my head, like the rhythm of a steam engine. They're connected, of course. People get depressed because they can't get a job, or their businesses collapse or their houses are repossessed. They lose hope. A Gallup poll published today said that nearly half the people in the country would like to emigrate if they could. Walking about the city centre this afternoon you'd have thought they already had.

My young brother Ken emigrated to Australia in the early seventies, when it was easier than it is now, and never made a better decision in his life. He's an electrician by trade. In London he worked for one of the big stores in the West End and never made enough money to buy a decent car or a house big enough for his growing family. Now he has his own contracting business in Adelaide, and a ranch-style house in the suburbs with a two-car garage and a swimming pool. Until *The People Next Door* took off, he was doing considerably better than me. Mind you, he was always happier than me, even when he was hard up. He has a naturally cheerful temperament. Funny how some people have, and some people haven't, even when their genes were dealt from the same deck.

I went to my appointment with Alexandra straight from the Rialto, and, as I was describing the scene to her, I let slip the phrase "privileged wanker". "Why do you call yourself that?" she demanded. "Wanker because I was sitting about drinking coffee in the middle of the day," I replied, "and privileged because it was a free choice, not because I had nothing better to do." "If I remember rightly," she said, "you told me that you work extremely hard when you're writing a television series, often up to twelve hours a day." I nodded. "Are you not entitled to relax at other times?" "Yes, of course," I said, "I meant I was struck by the contrast between my life and the lives of the no-hopers in the Rialto." "How do you know they have no hope?" I didn't, of course. "Did they look hopeless?" I had to admit they hadn't. In fact they probably looked more cheerful than me to an observing eye, swapping jokes and cigarettes, tapping their feet in time to the muzak. "But with the recession the way it is," I said, "I have this sense that I'm getting richer while everybody else around me is getting poorer. It makes me feel guilty." "Do you feel personally responsible for the recession?" "No, of course not." "In fact, I think you told me that your earnings from abroad are quite considerable?" "Yes." "So you're actually making a positive contribution to the nation's trading balance?" "You could look at it that way, I suppose." "Who *is* responsible for the recession, would you say?" I thought for a moment. "No individual, of course. It's a complex of factors, mostly outside anyone's control. But I think the Government could do more to alleviate its effects." "Did you vote for this Government?" "No,

I've always voted Labour," I said. "But . . ." I hesitated. Suddenly the stakes had become very high. "But what?" "But I felt secretly relieved when the Tories won."

I had never admitted this to anybody before, not even to myself. I was flooded with a mixture of shame and relief at having finally uncovered a genuine reason for my lack of self-esteem. I felt as I imagine Freud's patients felt when they broke down and admitted that they had always wanted to have sex with their mummies and daddies. "Why was that?" Alexandra enquired calmly. "Because it meant I wouldn't have to pay higher taxes," I said. "As I understand it," said Alexandra, "the Labour Party proposed to the electorate a rise in income tax, the electorate rejected it, and now the Labour Party has dropped it. Is that your understanding?" "Yes," I said. "So what are you feeling guilty about?" Alexandra said. "I don't know," I said.

I think Alexandra's talents are wasted on me. She should be working in the City of London convincing people that Greed is good.

I had a go at *The Concept of Dread* this evening – thought I'd start with the title that seemed most obviously relevant to me – but it was a great disappointment. The table of contents alone was enough to put me off:

Chap. I   Dread as the presupposition of original sin and as explaining it retrogressively by going back to its origin.
Chap. II   Dread as original sin progressively.
Chap. III   Dread as the consequence of that sin which is the default of the consciousness of sin.
Chap. IV   The dread in sin, or dread as the consequence of sin in the particular individual.
Chap. V   Dread as saving experience by means of faith.

I've never regarded myself as a religious person. I believe in God, I suppose. I mean I believe there's Something (rather than Somebody) beyond the horizons of our understanding, which explains, or would explain if we could interrogate it, why we're here and what it's all about. And I have a sort of faith that we survive after death to find out the answer to those questions, simply because it's intolerable to think that we never will, that our consciousness goes out at death like an electric light being switched off. Not much of a reason for believing, I admit, but there you are. I respect Jesus as an ethical thinker, not casting the first stone and turning the other cheek and so on, but I wouldn't call myself a Christian. My Mum and Dad sent me to Sunday school when I was a nipper – don't ask me why, because they never went to church themselves except for weddings and funerals. I liked going at first because we had a very pretty teacher called Miss Willow, with yellow curls and blue eyes and a lovely dimpled smile, who got us to act out stories from the Bible – I suppose that was my first experience of drama. But then she left and instead we had a severe-looking middle-aged lady called Mrs Turner, with hairs growing out of a big spot on her chin, who told us our souls were stained black with sin and had to be washed in the Blood of the Lamb. I had nightmares about being dunked in a bath full of blood by Mrs Turner, and after that my parents didn't make me go to Sunday School any more.

Much later, when I was a teenager, I used to attend a Catholic Youth Club, because Maureen Kavanagh was a Catholic and belonged to it; and occasionally I would get trapped or dragged in to some kind of service on Sunday evenings, a recitation of the rosary in the parish hall, or something they called Benediction in the church next door, a funny business with a lot of hymn-singing in Latin and clouds of incense and the priest on the altar holding up something like a gold football trophy. I always felt awkward and embarrassed on these occasions, not knowing what I was supposed to do next, sit or stand or kneel. I was never tempted to become a Catholic, though Maureen used to throw out the occasional wistful hint. There seemed to be far too much about sin in her religion, too. Most of the things I wanted to do with Maureen (and she wanted to do with me) turned out to be sins.

So all this stuff about sin in the chapter headings of *The Concept of Dread* was discouraging, and the actual book confirmed my misgivings. It was dead boring and very difficult to follow. He defines dread, for instance, as *"freedom's appearance before itself in possibility."* What the fuck does that mean? To tell you the truth I skimmed though the book, dipping here and there and hardly understanding a word. There was just one interesting bit at the very end:

> I would say that learning to know dread is an adventure which every man has to affront if he would not go to perdition either by not having known dread or by sinking under it. He therefore who has learned rightly to be in dread has learned the most important thing.

But what is learning rightly to be in dread, and how is it different from sinking under it? That's what I'd like to know.

Three spasms in the knee today, one while driving, two while sitting at my desk.

Wednesday 24th Feb, 11.30 p.m. Bobby Moore died today, of cancer. He was only fifty-one. People in the media must have known he was ill, because the BBC had a tribute all ready to slot into *Sportsnight* tonight. It included an interview with Bobby Charlton that must have been live, though, or recorded today, because he was crying. I was nearly crying myself, as a matter of fact.

The first I knew of it was when Amy and I came out of a cinema in Leicester Square at about eight. We'd been to an early-evening showing of *Reservoir Dogs*. A brilliant, horrible film. The scene where one of the gangsters tortures a helpless cop is the most sickening thing I've ever seen. Everybody in the film dies violently. I honestly believe that every character you see is shot to death – the police who shoot the Harvey Keitel character at the end are just voices off camera. Amy didn't seem disturbed by the mayhem. She was more bothered by the fact that she couldn't recall what she had seen one of the actors in before, and kept muttering to me, "Was it *House of Games*? No. Was it *Taxi-driver*? No. What was it?" until I had to beg her to shut up. As we came out of the cinema, she said triumphantly, "I remember now, it wasn't a movie at all, it was an episode of *Miami Vice*." Just at that moment I clocked a newspaper billboard, "BOBBY MOORE DIES." Suddenly the deaths in *Reservoir Dogs* seemed cartoon-thin. I hurried Amy through her supper so that I could get back to the flat to watch the telly, and she decided to go home straight from Gabrielli's. "I can see you want to be alone with your grief," she said sardonically, and she wasn't far wrong.

There were lots of clips of Bobby Moore in his prime as a player in *Sportsnight*, with of course a special emphasis on the World Cup Final of 1966, and that unforgettable image of Moore receiving the cup from the Queen, carefully wiping his hands on his shirt first, and then turning to face the crowd, holding the trophy high in the air for the whole of Wembley, and the whole country, to worship. What a day that was. England 4, Germany 2, after extra time. A story straight out of a boys' comic. Who believed at the start of the tournament that, after years of humiliation by South Americans and Slavs, we'd at last be world champions in the game we'd invented? What heroes they were, that team. I can still recite the names from memory. Banks, Wilson, Cohen, Moore (*capt.*), Stiles, Jack Charlton, Ball, Hurst, Hunt, Peters and Bobby Charlton. He cried on that occasion, too, I seem to remember. But not Bobby Moore, always the model captain, calm, confident, poised. He had immaculate timing as a player – it made up for his slowness on the turn. Seeing the clips brought it all back: the way his long leg would stretch out at the last possible moment and take the ball off an opponent's toe without fouling him. And then the way he would bring the ball out of defence and into attack, head up, back straight, like a captain leading a cavalry charge. He looked like a Greek god, with his clean-cut limbs and short golden curls. Bobby Moore. They don't make them like that any more. They make overpaid lager louts plastered with advertising logos, who spit all over the pitch and swear so much that lip-reading deaf viewers write to the BBC to complain.

(I make an exception of Ryan Giggs, the young Manchester United winger. He's a lovely player, thrilling to watch when he's running at a defence with the ball apparently tied to his feet, scattering them like sheep. And he still has his innocence, if you know what I mean. He hasn't yet been kicked into caution and cynicism, he hasn't been worn down by playing too many games too close together, he hasn't had his head turned by stardom. He still plays as if he enjoys the game, like a kid. I tell you what I like about him most: when he's done something really good, scored a goal, or dribbled past three players, or made a perfect cross, and he's trotting back towards the centre circle, and the crowd are going wild, he *frowns*. He looks terribly serious, like a little boy who's trying to seem ever so grown-up, as if it's the only way he can stop himself from turning cartwheels or beating his chest or screaming with excitement. I love that, the way he frowns when he's done something really brilliant.)

But back to Bobby Moore and that glorious June day of the 1966 World Cup Final. Even Sally, who was never a great soccer fan, got caught up in the excitement, put Jane to sleep in her pram and sat down to watch the telly with me and Adam – who was too young to really understand what it was all about, but sensed intuitively that it was important and sat patiently through the whole match with his thumb in his mouth and his blanket-comforter pressed to his cheek, watching me all the time instead of the screen. It was our first colour set. England wore red shirts instead of the usual all-white strip, strawberry-jam red. I suppose we tossed up with Germany for the privilege of wearing white, and lost, but we should have stuck with red ever after, it seemed to bring us luck. We were lucky to be awarded that third goal, which was why getting the fourth one was so deliriously satisfying. When the ball went in the net you could hear the cheering coming out of the neighbours' open windows; and when it was all over people went into their back gardens, or out into the street, grinning all over their faces, to babble about it to other people they'd never said more than "Good morning" to in their lives before.

It was a time of hope, a time when it was possible to feel patriotic without being typecast as a Tory blimp. The shame of Suez was behind us, and now we were beating the world in the things that really mattered to ordinary people, sport and pop music and fashion and television. Britain was the Beatles and mini-skirts and *That Was The Week That Was* and the victorious England team. I wonder if the Queen was watching the telly tonight, and what she felt seeing herself presenting the World Cup to Bobby Moore. A pang or two of nostalgia, I should think. *"Those were the days, Philip, eh?"* Those were the days when she could wake up in the morning confident of not having to read detailed accounts of the sexual misbehaviour of her family in the newspapers: Dianagate, Camillagate, Squidgey tapes, Charles's tampon fantasies, Fergie's toe-sucking. Internal Derangement of the Monarchy. I was never a great one for the Royal Family, but you can't help feeling sorry for the poor old Queen.

Which reminds me of an oddly disturbing experience I had this morning on my way to London. As I waited for the train at Rummidge Expo, I spotted Nizar further up the platform. I was just going up to greet him, my face already arranged into a suitable smile, when I saw that he was with a young woman. She wasn't young enough to be his daughter, and I knew she wasn't his wife, because I'd seen a silver-framed photo of the wife on his desk, a plump, rather severe-looking matron in a floral dress, flanked by three children, and she bore no resemblance to this tall slim young woman with glistening black hair falling to the shoulders of a smartly cut black woollen coat. Nizar was standing very close to her, talking animatedly and touching her, his surgeon's fingers fluttering over the collar of her coat and adjusting her hair and plucking at her sleeves, in a manner which was at once possessive and deferential, like a star's dresser. She was smiling complacently at whatever Nizar was murmuring into her ear, with her head bent because he was several inches shorter than herself, but she happened to look up just as I clocked what was going on. Fortunately she didn't know me from Adam. I wheeled round and retreated rapidly to the waiting room, where I sat down and hid my face behind the *Guardian* until the train arrived.

There seems to be an adultery epidemic going on: Jake, Jean Wellington, the Royal Family, and now Nizar. What I want to know is, why should *I* feel embarrassed, even guilty, at having surprised Nizar with his bimbo? Why did *I* run away? Why did *I* hide? I don't know.

Sally and I haven't made love since last Thursday. I've been going to bed at different times from her, or complaining of indigestion or of feeling a cold coming on, etc., to discourage the idea. I'm scared of fiinding that I can't come again. I suppose I could try masturbating, just to check there's nothing mechanically wrong.

✳ ✳ ✳ ✳ ✳ ✳ ✳ ✳ ✳ ✳ ✳ ✳ ✳ ✳ ✳ ✳ ✳

Thursday morning, 25th Feb. After I wrote that last bit, I undressed and lay on the bed with a towel handy and tried to jerk myself off. It's a long time since I did this, getting on for thirty-five years in fact, and I was out of practice. I couldn't find any Vaseline in the bathroom cabinet, and it so happened that I'd just run out of olive oil in the kitchen, so I lubricated my cock with Paul Newman's Own Salad Dressing, which was a mistake. First of all it was freezing cold from the fridge and had a shrivelling rather than a stimulating effect at first, secondly the vinegar and lemon juice in it stung like hell, and thirdly I began to smell like Gabrielli's *pollo alla cacciatora* as the herbs warmed up with the friction. But the main problem was that I couldn't summon up the appropriate thoughts. Instead of erotic imagery I kept thinking of Bobby Moore triumphantly holding aloft the Jules Rimet trophy, or Tim Roth lying in a pool of his own blood in *Reservoir Dogs*, with the red stain spreading up his shirt front till he looked as if he was wearing the England strip.

I thought of trying one of the telephone sex lines I'd heard so much about lately – but where would I get a number from? The Yellow Pages weren't any use, and I hardly thought I could consult Directory Enquiries. Then I remembered that there was an old listings magazine in the magazine rack, and sure enough I found columns of ads for phone sex in the back pages. I chose a number that promised *"Fast Instant Sex Relief, Hard Smutty Sex Talk"* with a footnote explaining that *"due to new EEC regulations we can now bring you European-strength action."* I listened for about ten minutes to a girl describing with much sighing and groaning the process of peeling and swallowing a banana, and began to wonder whether it was EEC agricultural regulations that were being invoked. It was a total con, and so were the other two lines I tried.

It occurred to me that I was only a few minutes' walk from the largest concentration of pornographic bookshops in the country, and although it was now well past midnight, some of them might still be open. It was a bind having to get dressed again to go out, but I was determined to bring my experiment to a conclusion. Then, just as I was about to leave the flat, it crossed my mind to check the front porch on the entryphone video screen – and, sure enough, there was my squatter of last week, curled up cosily inside his sleeping bag. I recognized his pointed nose and chin peeping out of the top of the bag, and the hank of hair over his eyes. I stared at the picture until the camera cut out automatically and I was left with my own faint grey reflection in the screen. I imagined myself going downstairs and opening the front door. Either I would have to wake him up and have an argument, or I would have to step over him as if he wasn't there – and not just once, but twice, since I would be returning after a short interval with a bundle of girlie magazines under my arm. Neither of these alternatives appealed to me. I undressed again and went back to bed, suffering acutely from Low Frustration Tolerance. It was as if this vagrant was holding me a moral prisoner in my own home.

Eventually I managed to produce a spurt of jism by sheer physical effort, so I know the plumbing is basically sound, but my cock is quite sore and it hasn't done my tennis elbow any good either.

Thursday afternoon. I'm sitting in the Pullman lounge, Euston station, waiting for the 5.10. I meant to catch the 4.40, but just missed it. The ticket-collector saw me running down the ramp and shut the barrier when I was ten yards short, at 4.39 precisely. The station is plastered with notices saying that platforms will be closed one minute before the advertised departure times of trains *"in the interests of punctuality and customer safety"*, but he could have let me through without endangering either. I had no luggage except the briefcase containing my laptop. The last coach of the train was only twenty yards away, with the guard standing at ease beside it, looking up the deserted platform, waiting for the OFF signal. I could have made it easily, as I vehemently pointed out, but the guy at the barrier, an officious, determined little Asian, wouldn't let me. I tried to push past him, but he pushed me back. We actually wrestled for a full minute, until the train finally pulled out, and I turned on my heel and walked furiously back up the ramp, uttering empty threats about making a complaint. He has better grounds for complaint than me (should that be "I"?) – indeed, he could probably have me for assault.

I'm still trembling a bit from the adrenalin rush, and I think I've pulled a small muscle in my back in the struggle. Pretty stupid behaviour, really, when you come to think about it, as I shall do very shortly. Low Frustration Tolerance will give way to Low Self-Esteem, and another wave of depression will move in to cover the Passmore psyche with low cloud and outbreaks of drizzle. Quite unnecessary. After all, it's only half an hour till the next train, and the Pullman Lounge is a very civilized place to wait in. It's rather like a brothel, or how I imagine brothels to be, but without the sex. You go up the stairs that lead to the table-service restaurant and the Superloo, and halfway along the passage to the latter there's a discreetly inconspicuous door with a bell-push and speaker grille in the wall beside it. When you press the bell-push, a female voice asks you if you have a first-class ticket, and if you say "Yes" the door springs open with a click and a buzz, and you're in. There's a nice-looking girl at the desk who smiles as you show your ticket and sign the Visitors' Book, and offers you complimentary coffee or tea. It's calm and hushed inside, air-conditioned, carpeted and comfortably furnished with armchairs and banquettes upholstered in soothing tones of blue and grey. There are newspapers, and telephones, and a photocopier. Down below, the hoi polloi waiting for trains must sit on their luggage, or on the floor (since there are no seats in the vast marbled concourse) or else patronize one of the fast-food outlets – Upper Crust, Casey Jones, The Hot Croissant, Pizza Hut, etc. – that cluster together in a junk-food theme park at one end of

I got so carried away by that bit of description that I discovered I'd missed the 5.10 as well. Or rather I discovered I'd left myself only two minutes in which to catch it, and I couldn't bear the thought of running down the ramp towards the same ticket-collector and having him shut the barrier in my face again, like some kind of dream repetition of the original trauma. So I may as well, while I wait for the 5.40, record why I was on such a short fuse in the first place.

I called in at Jake's office on my way to Euston. It's a small set of rooms over a tatty tee-shirt and souvenir shop in Carnaby Street. There was a new girl in the tiny reception office at the top of the stairs, tall and slim, in a very tight, very short black dress that barely covered her bum when she stood up. She introduced herself as Linda. After she'd shown me into Jake's room and shut the door, he said, "I know what you're thinking, and no, she isn't the one. Not," he added, with his cheeky chappie grin, "that I could swear she won't be, one day. Did you get a look at those legs?" "I could hardly avoid it, could I?" I said. "Given the dimensions of your office and her skirt." Jake laughed. "What's the news from Heartland?" I said. He stopped laughing. "Tubby," he said, leaning forward earnestly in his swivel chair, "you're going to have to find some acceptable way of writing Priscilla out of the series. Acceptable to everyone, I mean. I know you can, if you set your mind to it." "And if I can't?" I said. Jake spread his hands. "Then they'll get somebody else to do it." I felt a small, premonitory spasm of anxiety. "They can't do that without my agreement, can they?" "I'm afraid they can," said Jake, swivelling his chair to pull open a drawer, and avoiding my eye in the process. "I looked up the original contract." He took a file from the drawer and passed it to me across the desk. "Clause fourteen is the relevant one."

The contract for the first series had been drawn up a long time ago, when I was just another scriptwriter, with no particular clout. Clause fourteen said that if they asked me to write further series based on the same characters, and I declined, they could employ other writers to do the job, paying me a token royalty for the original concept. I can't recall giving this clause any special thought at the time, but I'm not surprised that I agreed to it. Getting the programme extended for another series was then my dearest ambition, and the idea that I might not want to write it myself would have seemed absurd. But the clause referred not just to a second series, but to "series", in the indefinite plural. Effectively I had signed away my copyright in the story and characters. I reproached Jake for not having spotted the danger and re-negotiated the clause in subsequent contracts. He said he didn't think Heartland would have played ball anyway. I don't agree. I think we could have twisted their arm between the second and the third series, they were so keen. Even now I can't believe that they would turn the whole show over to another writer, or writers. It's my baby. It's me. Nobody else could make it work as well.

Could they?

This is a dangerous train of thought, fraught with new possibilities for loss of self-esteem. Anyway, I'd better stop, or I'll miss the 5.40 as well.

✻　✻　✻　✻　✻　✻　✻　✻　✻　✻　✻　✻　✻　✻　✻　✻　✻

Friday 26th Feb., 8 p.m. Jake called this morning to say he'd received a note from Ollie Silvers, *"just summarizing the main points of our conversation with Tubby last Sunday, to avoid any misunderstanding."* This brings clause fourteen into operation, and means that I have twelve weeks in which to make up my mind whether to write Priscilla out of the script myself, or let someone else do the deed.

Aromatherapy with Dudley this afternoon. Dudley Neil-Hutchinson, to give his name both barrels. He looks a bit like a hippie Lytton Strachey – tall, spindly, with a long woolly beard that you'd think was attached to his granny glasses. He wears jeans and deck shoes and ethnic print shirts and waistcoats from the Oxfam shop. He tucks his beard into the waistcoats so that it doesn't tickle when he massages you. He practises at home in a modern three-bedroomed semi near the airport, triple-glazed to exclude the sound of aircraft taking off and landing. Sometimes, lying prone on the massage table, you feel a shadow pass over you and if you look up quickly enough you catch a glimpse of a huge plane swooping silently over the rooftops, so close you can pick out the white faces of passengers at the portholes. It's quite alarming at first. Dudley does two mornings a week at the Wellbeing, but I prefer to go to his house for treatment because I don't want Miss Wu to know I'm resorting to aromatherapy as well as acupuncture. She's so sensitive, she might take it as a personal vote of no confidence in her skills. I can just imagine bumping into her as I came out of a session with Dudley, and the silent, hurt look of reproach in her dark brown eyes. Miss Wu doesn't know about Alexandra, either. Alexandra knows about Miss Wu, but not about Dudley. I haven't told her, not because she'd feel threatened, but because she might be disappointed in me. She respects acupuncture, but I don't think she would have much time for aromatherapy.

It was June Mayfield who put me onto it. She works in Make-Up at Heartland, and sits in the wings during recordings of *The People Next Door*, ready to dart forward and titivate Debbie's hair when required, or powder the actors' noses if they get shiny under the lights. I was chatting to her in the canteen one day and she told me aromatherapy had changed her life, curing her of the migraines that had been the bane of her existence for years. She gave me Dudley's card, and I thought I'd give it a try. I'd just given up yoga, on account of my Internal Derangement of the Knee, so I had a vacant slot in my therapy schedule. I used to go once a fortnight to Miss Flynn, a seventy-five-year-old lady with elastic joints who teaches Pranayama yoga. It's not the sort where you stand on your head for hours or tie yourself in knots that have to be unravelled in Casualty. It's mostly about breathing and relaxation, but it does entail attempting the lotus position or at least the half-lotus, which Miss Flynn didn't think would be a good idea while I was having trouble with my knee, so I packed it in. To tell you the truth, I was never much good at yoga anyway. I could never manage the "slipped second" which is a vital part of it, when you're supposed to empty your mind and not think of anything at all. Miss Flynn tried to teach me a mental routine according to which you empty your mind first of thoughts about work, then of thoughts about family and friends, then of thoughts about yourself. Well, I could never get past first base. As soon as I silently pronounced the word "work" to myself, thoughts about script revisions and casting problems and audience figures would start swarming in my head. I would develop worries about work that I never had before.

Aromatherapy is easier. You just lie there and let the therapist massage you with what are called essential oils. The theory behind it is quite simple – perhaps too simple. Dudley explained it to me at my first session. "If you hurt yourself, what's your instinctive reaction? You rub the affected part, right?" I asked how you rub your mind. He said, "Ah, that's where the essential oils come in." Aromatherapists think that, through absorption into the skin, the oils enter the bloodstream and thus affect the brain. Also that the inhalation of the oils' distinctive aromas has a stimulating or calming effect on the nervous system, depending on which ones you use. There are uppers and downers in aromatherapy, or "high notes" and "bass notes" as they call them. According to Dudley, it's a very ancient form of medicine which was practised in China and Egypt yonks ago. But, like everything else, nowadays it's computerized. When I go to see Dudley I tell him my symptoms, and he writes them into his personally devised aromatherapy programme, called PHEW (no, I made that up, the filename is ATP), presses a key, and the computer comes up with a list of suggested essential oils – juniper, jasmine, peppermint or whatever. Then Dudley lets me sniff them and makes up a cocktail of the ones I like best, using a vegetable "carrier oil" as a base.

I didn't feel the same inhibition about discussing sexual matters with Dudley as I did last week with Miss Wu, so when he asked me how I'd been since the last treatment, I mentioned the non-ejaculation incident. He said that the ability to have sexual congress without ejaculating was highly prized by oriental mystics. I said they were welcome to it. He tapped away at his Apple Mac for a few moments and it came up with bergamot, ylang-ylang and rose otto. "Didn't you give me rose for depression, last time?" I said, with a hint of suspicion in my voice. "It's a very versatile oil," said Dudley suavely. "It's used against impotence and frigidity as well as depression. Also grief and the menopause." I asked him if that included the male menopause, and he laughed without answering.

✻ ✻ ✻ ✻ ✻ ✻ ✻ ✻ ✻ ✻ ✻ ✻ ✻ ✻ ✻ ✻ ✻

Saturday, 27th Feb. Well, it worked, up to a point. We made love last night and I came. I don't think Sally did, but she wasn't really in the mood, and seemed surprised when I suggested it. I can't say the earth moved for me, either, but at least I had an ejaculation. So the old essential oil of rose did the trick, as far as impotence is concerned. But not as far as depression, grief and the male menopause are concerned. I woke at 3.05 with my brain churning like a cement-mixer, anxieties like sharp pebbles in a general grey sludge of Dread, and spent the next few hours in a shallow dozing state, dropping off and waking again with the fleeting sensation of having been in a dream without being able to remember what it was. My dreams are like silvery fish: I grab at their tails, but they wriggle from my grasp, and shimmy down into the dark depths. I wake gasping for breath, my heart pounding, like a diver surfacing. Eventually I dropped a sleeping tablet and lapsed into a dreamless coma from which I woke, in an empty bed, at nine-thirty, sullen and dry-mouthed.

Sally had left a note to say she'd gone to Sainsbury's. I had some errands to do myself, so walked to the High Street. I was standing impatiently in line at the Post Office when I heard a woman's voice say at my shoulder, "Are you desperate?" I swivelled round, thinking she was addressing me, but it was a mother talking to her little boy. "Can't you wait till we get home?" she said. The little boy shook his head miserably and pressed his knees closer together.

Later. I was desperate enough to give old Kierkegaard another go, and had better luck this time. I dipped into *Either/Or*, because the title intrigued me. A socking great book, in two volumes, and very confusingly written, a dog's breakfast of essays, stories, letters etc., written by two fictitious characters called A and B, and edited by a third called Victor Eremitus, all aliases for Kierkegaard I presume. What particularly caught my eye was a short piece in the first volume called "The Unhappiest Man". As I read it, I felt like I did when I first saw the list of Kierkegaard's book titles, that he was speaking directly to my condition.

According to K., the unhappy man is "always absent to himself, never present to himself." My first reaction was: no, wrong, Søren old son – I never stop thinking about myself, that's the trouble. But then I thought, thinking about yourself isn't the same as being present to yourself. Sally is present to herself, because she takes herself for granted, she never doubts herself – or at least not for long. She *coincides* with herself. Whereas I'm like one of those cartoon characters in a cheap comic, the kind where the colour doesn't quite fit the outline of the drawing: there's a gap or overlap between the two, a kind of blur. That's me: Desperate Dan with his blue chin sticking out but not quite coinciding with his jawline.

Kierkegaard explains that the unhappy man is never present to himself because he's always living in the past or the future. He's always either hoping or remembering. Either he thinks things were better in the past or he hopes they'll be better in the future, but they're always bad *now*. That's ordinary common-or-garden unhappiness. But the unhappy man "in a stricter sense" isn't even present to himself in his remembering or his hoping. Kierkegaard gives the example of a man who looks back wistfully to the joys of childhood which in fact he never himself experienced (perhaps he was thinking of his own case). Likewise the "unhappy hoper" is never present to himself in his hoping, for reasons which were obscure to me until I came to this passage: "Unhappy individuals who hope never have the same pain as those who remember. Hoping individuals always have a more gratifying disappointment."

I know exactly what he means by "gratifying disappointment". I worry about making decisions because I'm trying to guard against things turning out badly. I *hope* they'll turn out well, but if they do turn out well I hardly notice it because I've made myself miserable imagining how they could turn out badly; and if they turn out badly in some unforeseen way (like clause fourteen in the Heartland contract) that only confirms my underlying belief that the worst misfortunes are unexpected. If you're an unhappy hoper you don't really believe things will get better in the future (because if you did you wouldn't be unhappy). Which means that when they *don't* get better it proves you were right all along. That's why your disappointment is gratifying. Neat, eh?

I also have a persistent feeling that things were better in the past – that I must have been happy once, otherwise I wouldn't know I was unhappy now, and somewhere along the way I lost it, I blew it, I let it go, though I can only recall that "it" in fleeting fragments, like watching the 1966 World Cup Final. It's possible, however, that I'm kidding myself, that really I was always miserable because I was always an unhappy hoper. Which paradoxically would make me an unhappy rememberer too.

How can you be both? Easy-peasy! That's precisely the definition of the unhappiest man:

> This is what it amounts to: on the one hand, he constantly hopes for something he should be remembering . . . On the other hand he constantly remembers something he should be hoping for . . . Consequently what he hopes for lies behind him and what he remembers lies before him . . . He is forever quite close to the goal and at the same moment at a distance from it; he now discovers that what it is that makes him unhappy, because now he has it, or because he is this way, is precisely what a few years ago would have made him happy if he had had it then, whereas then he was unhappy because he did not have it.

Oh yes, this guy has my number alright. The unhappiest man. Why then am I grinning all over my face as I read?

Sunday afternoon, 28th Feb. I didn't go to the studio today. I thought I would show Heartland that I resent the way they're treating me. Sally approved. I left a message on the office answerphone early this morning to say I wouldn't be coming in. I didn't give a reason, but Ollie and Hal will figure it out. It's the first time I've missed a recording since last April, when I had a stomach bug. Needless to say, I'm punishing myself more than I'm punishing them. Hal will be too busy to brood on my absence, and Ollie is not the brooding type. Whereas I have nothing to do except brood. The day has passed with excruciating slowness. I keep looking at the clock and working out what stage of rehearsal they will have reached. It's five past four now, and dark already. It's bitterly cold outside, with a thin coating of snow. Blizzards expected in other parts of the country, the papers say.

The posh Sundays are full of handwringing and breastbeating. The country seems to be going through some huge crisis of confidence, Internal Derangement of the National Psyche. The Gallup poll published last week showed eighty per cent of the electorate were dissatisfied with the Government's performance. According to another poll, more than forty per cent of young people think that Britain will become a worse country to live in over the next decade. Which means, presumably, they think that either Labour won't win the next election, or it won't make any difference if they do. We've become a nation of unhappy hopers.

And unhappy rememberers: I wasn't the only one, it seems, to feel that the death of Bobby Moore measured the extent of our decline. There are lots of nostalgic articles in the papers about him and the 1966 World Cup. Our losing the third Test in succession to India this week hasn't helped national morale, either. *India!* When I was a boy a Test series against India was always a dead boring prospect because it was bound to be a walkover for England.

It's half past five. Rehearsals will be over by now, and the cast will be tucking into their meal in the canteen before going off to Make-Up. Ron Deakin always has sausage, egg and chips. He swears he never eats fry-ups at home, but says that sausage, egg and chips go with the character of Pop Davis. He's quite superstitious about it – got into quite a panic one day, when they ran out of sausages in the kitchen. I wonder if he will be put off by my not being there as usual tonight. The actors like me to be around on recording day, they find it reassuring. I'm afraid I'm punishing them, as well as myself, by staying away.

The more I think about it, and I can think of nothing else, the worse I feel. I'm trying to resist deciding that I have made the wrong decision, but I can feel myself being drawn inexorably towards that conclusion as if by the gravitational force of a black hole. In short, I can feel myself getting into one of my "states". The state, *c'est moi*, as Amy might say. How am I going to get through the rest of the evening? I stare at the key marked HELP on my keyboard. If only it could.

✳ ✳ ✳ ✳ ✳ ✳ ✳ ✳ ✳ ✳ ✳ ✳ ✳ ✳ ✳ ✳

Monday morning, 1st March. At about 6.45 yesterday evening, just as Sally was laying the table for our evening meal, my nerve broke. I rushed out of the house, shouting an explanation to Sally without giving her time to tell me I was a fool, backed the Richmobile out of the garage, slithering and sliding all over the drive – I damn near dented the offside wing on the gatepost – and drove at imprudent speed into Rummidge, arriving at the studio just in time to take my seat for the recording.

It went brilliantly. A wonderful audience – sharp, appreciative, together. And the script wasn't bad, either, though I says it myself. The story-line is that the Springfields decide to put their house up for sale in order to get away from the Davises, but without telling the Davises because they feel guilty about it, and the Davises keep unknowingly sabotaging the plan by turning up or doing something outrageous just when the Springfields are showing potential buyers round the house. The audience loved it. I expect a lot of them want to move house themselves and can't because they have negative equity. Negative equity is when your mortgage is more than your house is worth. There's a lot of it about. It's a kind of internal derangement of the property market. Not funny, if you've got it, but it might make you see the funny side of Edward and Priscilla's dilemma. Or, to put it another way, watching their farcical trials and tribulations might make you feel better about your negative equity, especially as the episode ends with the Springfields reconciled to staying where they are. I often feel that sitcom has that kind of therapeutic social effect.

The cast felt the good vibrations coming from the audience and were in cracking form. There were hardly any re-takes. We wrapped at eight-thirty. Everybody was smiling afterwards. "Hallo, Tubby," said Ron Deakin, "we missed you at rehearsal today." I mumbled something about being tied up. Hal gave me a quizzical look, but said nothing. Isabel, the floor manager, told me I'd been well out of it, that the rehearsal had been full of snags and cock-ups. "But that's always the way," she said. "If the rehearsal runs like a train, you can be sure the recording will be a disaster." (Isabel is an unhappy hoper.) Ollie wasn't there: he'd phoned in to say the roads were too dodgy in his part of the world. Several members of the cast decided to stay overnight in Rummidge in view of the weather, so we all went to the bar. There was a genial, relaxed atmosphere, everybody basking in the sense of a job well done, cracking jokes, buying rounds. I felt a huge affection for them all. It's like an extended family, and in a way I'm the father of it. Without my scripts, they would never have come together.

Samantha Handy came into the bar, having tucked young Mark up in bed for the night at a nearby hotel, just as I was leaving. She gave me a nice smile, so I smiled back, pleased that she evidently didn't bear me a grudge from last week's conversation. "Oh, are you going already?" she said. "Breaking up the party?" "Got to," I said. "How's the script-writing going?" "I'm going to discuss my idea with an agent," she said. "I've got an appointment with Jake Endicott next week. He's *your* agent, isn't he? I mentioned that I knew you, I hope you don't mind." "No, of course not," I said, thinking to myself, *Cheeky bitch!* "Be careful what you wear," I said. She looked anxious. "Why? Has he got a thing about clothes?" "He's got a thing about good-looking young women," I said. "I'd advise a nice, long, baggy bin-liner." She laughed. Well, she can't say I didn't warn her. Jake will go ape when he sees those knockers. She has a pretty face, too, round and freckled, with a hint of a double chin that's like a trailer for the opulent curves straining at her blouse-front. She took my advice about asking Ollie if she could read some scripts and apparently he's given her a bundle to report on. A young woman to watch, in more ways than one.

I drove home slowly and deliberately on the icy, deserted roads. Sally was already asleep when I got in. Something about her posture in the bed, flat on her back, and the set of her mouth, told me that she had gone to bed displeased with me – whether for breaking my resolution to stay away from the recording, or for fastforwarding out of the house just as she was serving up supper, or for driving in dangerous conditions, or for all these things, I couldn't tell. I found out this morning it was something else. Apparently, after I told her I wouldn't be going to the studio as usual yesterday, she'd invited a couple of neighbours round for a drink in the evening. She swears she told me, so I suppose she must have done, though I haven't the faintest memory of it. Worrying. She had to phone the Websters again and cancel. Embarrassing, undoubtedly. They're Tory-voting zombies, but they ask us every year to their Christmas Eve drinks party, and we never ask them back. (On the rare occasions when we give a party I pore over the guest list for hours, agonizing over the choice of names, trying to arrive at a perfectly balanced crowd of scintillating and mutually compatible conversationalists. The Websters are not even considered for such gatherings, though excluding them doesn't of course prevent me from being in a state of anxiety bordering on hysteria as the party approaches, or from anaesthetizing myself with drink as soon as possible after it starts.) So yesterday evening would have been an opportunity to level up the scores a bit. Sally says now we'll have to ask them to dinner to make up. I hope that's just a threat. Anyway, I'm in the doghouse. All the euphoria of last night has evaporated. My knee is playing up this morning, and I've definitely pulled a muscle in my back.

* * * * * * * * * * * * * * * * *

Monday afternoon. Just back from physiotherapy. I told Roland about the back muscle, but not that I pulled it fighting with a bantam-weight Pakistani ticket-puncher. He assumed it was another tennis injury. In fact I haven't played this past week, partly because of the weather and partly because I haven't felt like getting together with my usual partners after what Rupert had told me about Joe and Jean. Roland gave me an old-fashioned back massage as well as Ultrasound on the knee. It's what physiotherapy was all about when he trained – he's good at it and he enjoys it. His hands are his eyes, he feels his way into the deepest core of your aches and pains, and gently but firmly eases away the inflammation. Dudley isn't a patch on him.

Roland's wife had read him something out of the paper over breakfast this morning, about new extracts from the Diana Squidgey tapes being published in Australia. I said I found it hard to believe these conversations were overheard accidentally. Roland didn't. It came out that he spends a lot of time at night listening to police messages on the VHF waveband of his Sony portable. "I listen for hours, sometimes," he said. "In bed, with the earphones on. There was a drug bust in Angleside last night. Quite exciting it was." So Roland suffers from insomnia too. It must be particularly horrible if you're blind, lying awake in the night, dark on dark.

One of the depressing things about depression is knowing that there are lots of people in the world with far more reason to feel depressed than you have, and finding that, so far from making you snap out of your depression, it only makes you despise yourself more and thus feel more depressed. The purest form of depression is when you can give absolutely no reason why you're depressed. As B says, in *Either/Or*, "A person in sorrow or distress knows why he sorrows or is distressed. If you ask a melancholic what it is that weighs down on him, he will reply, 'I don't know what it is, I can't explain it.' Therein lies melancholy's infinitude."

I'm beginning to get the hang of this peculiar book. The first part consists of the papers of A – jottings, essays like "The Unhappiest Man", and a journal called *The Seducer's Diary*, which is supposed to have been edited by A, but written by someone else called Johannes. A is a young intellectual layabout who suffers from depression, only he calls it melancholy, and makes a cult of it. In the *Diary* Johannes describes how he seduces a beautiful innocent girl called Cordelia, just to see if he can pull it off against all the odds, and then callously discards her when he succeeds:

> now it is over and I want never to see her again . . . Now all resistance is impossible, and only when it is there is it beautiful to love; once it is gone, love is only weakness and habit.

It's not clear whether we're supposed to think *The Seducer's Diary* is something A found, or that he made it up, or that it's really a disguised confession. It's riveting stuff, anyway, though there's no sex in it – no bonking, I mean. There's a lot about sexual feelings. This, for example:

Today my eyes have rested upon her for the first time. It is said that sleep can make an eyelid so heavy that it closes of its own accord; perhaps this glance of mine has a similar effect. Her eyes close, and yet obscure forces stir within her. She does not see that I am looking at her, she feels it, feels it through her whole body. Her eyes close and it is night, but inside her it is broad daylight.

Perhaps that's how Jake pulls the birds.

The second part of *Either/Or* consists of some inordinately long letters from B to A, attacking A's philosophy of life, and urging him to give up melancholy and get his act together. B seems to be a lawyer or a judge, and is happily married. He's a bit of a prig, actually, but a shrewd one. The bit I quoted just now about melancholy's infinitude is from his second letter, entitled "The Equilibrium between the Aesthetic and the Ethical in the Development of the Personality," but the book as a whole is about the *opposition* of the aesthetic and the ethical. A is the aesthete, B is the ethicist, if that's a word. (Yes, it is. Just looked it up.) A says: either/or, it doesn't matter what you choose, you will regret your choice whatever it is. "If you marry, you will regret it, if you do not marry you will regret it; if you marry or do not marry, you will regret both," and so on. That's why A is so interested in seduction (whether the seduction of Cordelia was real or imagined, A is clearly fascinated by the idea, which means so was old Søren), because to him marriage entails choice (which he would inevitably regret) whereas seduction makes someone else choose and leaves him free. By having Cordelia, Johannes proved to himself that she wasn't worth having, and is free to discard her and go back to his melancholy. "My melancholy is the most faithful mistress I have known," he says. "What wonder then that I love her in return?"

B says you must choose. To choose is to be ethical. He defends marriage. He attacks melancholy. "Melancholy is sin, really it is a sin as great as any, for it is the sin of not willing deeply and sincerely, and this is the mother to all sins." He is kind enough to add: "I gladly admit that melancholy is in a sense not a bad sign, for as a rule only the most gifted natures are afflicted with it." But B is in no doubt that the ethical life is superior to the aesthetic. "The person who lives ethically has seen himself, knows himself, permeates his whole concretion with his consciousness, does not allow vague thoughts to fuss around in him, nor tempting possibilities to distract him with their legerdemain . . . He knows himself." Or herself. Sally is the ethical type, whereas I'm the aesthetic type – except that I believe in marriage, so the cap doesn't quite fit. And where does Kierkegaard himself stand? Is he A or B, or both, or neither? Is he saying that you must choose between A's philosophy and B's, or that whichever you choose you will regret it?

Reading Kierkegaard is like flying through heavy cloud. Every now and again there's a break and you get a brief, brilliantly lit view of the ground, and then you're back in the swirling grey mist again, with not a fucking clue where you are.

Monday evening. According to an encylopaedia I've just looked up, Kierkegaard came to think that the aesthetic and the ethical are only stages on the way to full enlightenment, which is "religious". The ethical seems to be superior to the aesthetic, but in the end proves to be founded on nothing more substantial. Then you have to throw yourself on God's mercy. I don't much like the sound of that. But in making that "leap", man "finally chooses himself". A haunting, tantalizing phrase: how can you choose yourself when you already are yourself? It sounds like nonsense, yet I have an inkling of what it might mean.

Sally signalled that she is still pissed off with me by declining to watch *The People Next Door* tonight, claiming she was too busy. It's a Monday night ritual, when the show is on the box, that we sit down at nine o'clock and watch it together. It's a funny thing, but however familiar you are with a TV programme before it's transmitted, having written the script, attended rehearsals, watched the recording and seen a VHS tape of the final edited version, it's always different when you watch it being actually transmitted. Knowing that millions of other people are watching it at the same time, and *for the first time*, changes it somehow. It's too late to alter it or stop it, and that imparts an edge to the experience. It's a faint replica of what happens in the theatre when you do your show in front of an audience for the first time. Every Monday evening as the last commercial before the programme freezes and fades on the screen, and the familiar theme tune strikes up over the title sequence, I feel my pulse quickening. And absurdly I find myself willing the cast on as if they were performing live, mentally urging them to get the most out of their lines and sight gags, though rationally I know that everything, every syllable and pause, every nuance of voice and gesture, and the responses of the studio audience, are already fixed and unalterable.

Sally gave up reading my scripts in draft years ago – or perhaps I gave up showing them to her: it was six of one and half a dozen of the other. She never much liked the basic concept of *The People Next Door*, and didn't think it would catch on. When it was a runaway success she was pleased of course, for my sake, and for the sake of the lolly that started gushing through the letterbox as if we'd struck oil in the back garden. But, typically, it didn't shake her faith in her judgement in the least. Then she started to work so hard at her own job that she really had no time or energy to spare for reading scripts, so I stopped bothering her with them. In fact it's more useful to me to have her watch the programmes not knowing what's coming next. It gives me an idea of how the other 12,999,999 viewers are reacting, if I multiply her appreciation by a factor of about eight. When Sally gives a chuckle, you can bet they're falling off their chairs and wetting themselves all over the country. But tonight I had to sit through the show in glum silence, on my own.

* * * * * * * * * * * * * * * * *

Tuesday afternoon, 2nd March. To Alexandra today. She had a cold, and a stuffed-up nose which she kept blowing ineffectually like somebody learning to play the cornet. "Excuse me for mentioning it," I said, "but you'll give yourself sinus trouble if you blow your nose like that. I had a yoga teacher once who showed me how to clear my nose, one nostril at a time." I demonstrated, by pressing a finger against one side of my schnozzle, then against the other. Alexandra smiled weakly and thanked me for the advice. It's the one thing about yoga that's really stayed with me. How to blow your nose.

Alexandra asked me how I'd been in the last week. I told her about the kerfuffle over the future of *The People Next Door*. She asked me what I was going to do. "I don't know," I said. "All I know is that whatever I do, I'll regret it. If I write Priscilla out of the script, I'll regret it, if I let someone else do it, I'll regret it. I've been reading Kierkegaard," I added, thinking Alexandra would be impressed, but she didn't respond. Perhaps she didn't hear: she blew her nose just as I said "Kierkegaard."

"You're prejudging the issue," she said. "You're setting yourself up for failure."

"I'm just facing facts," I said. "My indecision is final, as the man said. Take last weekend." I told her about my vacillation over attending the recording session.

"But you did stick to a decision in the end," Alexandra observed. "You went to the studio. Do you regret it?"

"Yes, because it put me in the wrong with Sally."

"You didn't know at the time that she had invited those neighbours round."

"No, but I should have listened when she told me. And anyway I knew she would disapprove of my going to the studio for other reasons, like the road conditions – that's why I rushed out of the house before she had the chance to talk me out of it. If I *had* given her the chance, I would have finally got the message that the Websters were coming round."

"And in that case you would have stayed in?"

"Of course."

"And is that what you wish had happened?"

I thought for a moment. "No," I said.

We both laughed, rather despairingly.

Am I really in despair? No, nothing as dramatic as that. More like what B calls doubt. He makes a distinction between doubt and despair. Despair is better because at least it entails choice. "So then choose despair, since despair is itself a choice, for one can doubt without choosing to, but despair one cannot without choosing to do so. And when one despairs one chooses again, and what does one choose? One chooses oneself, not in one's immediacy, not as this contingent individual, one chooses oneself in one's eternal validity." Sounds impressive, but is it possible to choose despair and not want to top yourself? Could you just accept despair, live in it, be proud of it, rejoice in it?

B says there's one thing he agrees with A about: that if you're a poet you're bound to be miserable, because "poet-existence as such lies in the obscurity that results from despair's not being carried through, from the soul's constantly shivering in despair and the spirit's being unable to gain its true transparency." So it seems you can be shivering in despair without actually choosing it. Is this my state? Does it apply to script-writer-existence as well as poet-existence?

Philip Larkin knew all about this sort of despair. I just looked up "Mr Bleaney":

> But if he stood and watched the frigid wind
> Tousling the clouds, lay on the fusty bed
> Telling himself that this was home, and grinned,
> And shivered, without shaking off the dread
>
> That how we live measures our own nature,
> And at his age having no more to show
> Than one hired box should make him pretty sure
> He warranted no better, I don't know.

It's all there: "Shivered . . . dread . . . I don't know."

What made me think of Larkin was a report in the paper today that Andrew Motion's forthcoming biography will reveal him in an even worse light than the recent edition of his letters. I haven't read the *Letters* and I don't want to. I don't want to read the new biography, either. Larkin is my favourite modern poet (about the only one I can understand, actually) and I don't want to have the pleasure of reading him ruined. Apparently he used to end telephone conversations to Kingsley Amis by saying, "Fuck Oxfam." Admittedly, there are worse things than saying "Fuck Oxfam", for instance actually doing it, like the gunmen in Somalia who steal the aid intended for starving women and children, but still, what did he want to say a stupid thing like that for? I took out my charity cheque book and sent off fifty quid to OXFAM. I did it for Philip Larkin. Like Maureen used to collect indulgences and credit them to her dead granddad. She explained it to me one day, all about Purgatory and temporary punishment –

daftest stuff you ever heard in your life. Maureen Kavanagh. I wonder what happened to her. I wonder where she is now.

✳ ✳ ✳ ✳ ✳ ✳ ✳ ✳ ✳ ✳ ✳ ✳ ✳ ✳ ✳ ✳ ✳

Wednesday 3rd March, late. I met the squatter in the entryway tonight. This is how it happened.

Amy and I went to see *An Inspector Calls* at the National. Brilliant production on a stunning surrealist set, played without a break, like a perfectly remembered dream. I never rated Priestley before, but tonight he seemed as good as bloody Sophocles. Even Amy was swept away – she didn't attempt to recast the play once over supper. We ate in Ovations, a selection of starters – they're always better than the main courses. Amy had two and I had three. And a bottle of Sancerre between us. We had a lot to talk about besides the play: my trouble with Heartland and Amy's latest crisis over Zelda. Amy found a pill in Zelda's school blouse pocket when she was doing the laundry, and she was afraid it was either Ecstasy or a contraceptive. She couldn't decide which would be worse, but she didn't dare to ask the girl about it for fear of being accused of spying on her. She fished the pill, sealed inside an airmail envelope, out of her great swollen bladder of a handbag, and tipped it on to my side-plate for inspection. I said it looked like an Amplex tablet to me, and offered to suck it and see. I did, and it was. Amy was hugely relieved at first. Then she said, with a frown, "Why is she worried about bad breath? She must be kissing boys." I said, "Weren't you at her age?" She said, "Yes, but not with our tongues down each other's throats like they do now." "We used to," I said, "it was called French kissing." "Well, you can get AIDS from it nowadays," said Amy. I said I didn't think you could, though I don't really know.

Then I told her about clause fourteen. She said it was outrageous and I should sack Jake and get the Writers' Guild to challenge the contract. I said that changing my agent wouldn't solve the problem and that Jake's lawyer had already checked the contract and it was impregnable. Amy said, "*Merde.*" We kicked around various ideas for writing Priscilla out of the series, which became more and more facetious as the level of the wine fell in the bottle: Priscilla is reclaimed by a former husband whom she supposed to be dead, and whom she omitted to mention to Edward when they married; Priscilla has a sex-change operation; Priscilla is kidnapped by aliens from outer space . . . I still think the best solution is for Priscilla to die in the last episode of the present series, but Amy wasn't surprised that Ollie and Hal gave it the thumbs-down. "Not death, darling, *anything* but death." I said that was a rather strong reaction. "Oh God, you sound just like Karl," she said.

The remark gave me a rare glimpse of what passes between Amy and her analyst. She's usually rather secretive about their relationship. All I know is that she goes to his office every weekday morning at nine sharp, and he comes into the waiting room and says good morning, and she precedes him into the consulting room and lies down on the couch and he sits behind her and she talks for fifty minutes. You're not supposed to come with a prepared topic, but to say whatever comes into your head. I asked Amy once what happened if nothing worth saying came into your head, and she said you would be silent. Apparently she could in theory be completely silent for the whole fifty minutes and Karl would still collect his fee; though Amy being Amy, this has never actually happened.

It was about eleven when we came out of the theatre. I put Amy in a cab, and walked home to exercise the old knee joint. Roland says I should walk at least half an hour every day. I always enjoy crossing Waterloo Bridge, especially at night, with the buildings all floodlit: Big Ben and the Houses of Parliament to the west, the dome of St Paul's and the knife-sharp spires of other Wren churches to the east, with the red light on top of Canary Wharf winking on the horizon. London still feels like a great city, seen from Waterloo Bridge. Disillusionment sets in when you turn into the Strand and find that all the shop doorways have their quilted occupants, like mummies in a museum.

It didn't occur to me that my own chap would be in residence, perhaps because I'd only ever seen him from inside the flat, on the video screen, well after midnight. He was sitting against the wall of the entryway, with his legs and lower trunk inside his sleeping-bag, smoking a roll-up. I said, "Hey, out of it, you can't sleep here." He looked up at me, brushing a long forelock of lank ginger hair from his eyes. I should say he's about seventeen. Hard to tell. He had a faint smear of gingery bristle on his chin. "I wasn't asleep," he said.

"I've seen you sleeping here before," I said. "Hop it."

"Why?" he said. "I'm not doin' any harm." He drew his knees up inside the sleeping-bag, as if to let me pass without stepping over him.

"It's private property," I said.

"Property is theft," he said, with a sly sort of grin, as if he was trying me out.

"Oh ho," I said, covering my surprise with sarcasm, "a Marxist vagrant. What next?"

"It weren't Marx," he said, "it was proud one." Or that's what it sounded like.

"What proud one?" I said.

His eyes seemed to go out of focus momentarily, and he shook his head in a dogged sort of way. "I dunno, but it weren't Marx. I looked it up once."

"Anything wrong, sir?"

I turned round. Blow me if there weren't a couple of coppers standing there. They'd materialized as if in answer to an unspoken prayer. Except that I didn't want them now. Or not yet. Not at that precise moment. I surprised in myself a strange reluctance to hand the youth over to the power of the law. I don't suppose they would have done anything worse than move him on, but I didn't have time to work that out. It was a split-second decision. "It's alright, officer," I said, to the one who had spoken to me. "I know this young man." The young man himself had meanwhile scrambled to his feet and was busily rolling up his sleeping-bag.

"You live here, do you, sir?" said the policeman. I produced my keys in an over-eager demonstration of ownership. The two-way cell radio clipped to the chest of the other policeman began to squawk and crackle with some message about a burglar alarm in Lisle Street, and after a few more words with me the two of them walked away in step.

"Thanks," said the youth.

I looked at him, already regretting my decision. ("If you shop him you will regret it, if you don't shop him you will regret it, shop him or don't shop him, you will regret both . . .") I was strongly tempted to tell him to bugger off, sharpish, but, glancing up the street, I saw the two coppers eyeing me from the next corner. "I suppose you'd better come in for a few minutes," I said.

He looked at me suspiciously from under his hank of hair. "Yer not queer, are yer?" he said.

"Good God, no," I said. As we silently ascended in the lift, I realized why I hadn't taken advantage of the miraculous appearance of the two policemen to get rid of him. It was that little phrase, "*I looked it up*," that had thrown me momentarily off balance, and on to his side. Another looker-upper. It was as if I had encountered on my doorstep a younger, less privileged image of myself.

"Nice," he said approvingly, as I let him into the flat and switched on the lights. He went over to the window and looked down into the street. "Cor," he said. "You can hardly hear the traffic."

"It's double-glazed," I said. "Look, I only invited you here to stop the police hassling you. I'll give you a cup of tea, if you like –"

"Ta," he said, sitting down promptly on the sofa.

"– I'll give you a cup of tea, but that's it, understand? Then you're on your way, and I don't want to see you here again, ever. All right?" He nodded, rather less emphatically than I could have wished, and took a tin of rolling tobacco out of his pocket. "And I'd rather you didn't smoke, if you don't mind," I said.

He sighed, and shrugged, and put the tin back in the pocket of his anorak. He was wearing the regulation kit of the young West End vagrant: quilted anorak, blue jeans, Doc Martens, plus a grubby fawn knitted scarf so long it dangled to his ankles. "Mind if I take this off?" he said, shrugging off the anorak without waiting for my permission. "It's a bit warmer than I'm used to." Without the artificial padding of the anorak, he looked thin and frail in a threadbare jersey out at the elbows. "Don't use this place much, do yer?" he said. "Wherejer live the rest of the week?" I told him. "Oh, yeah, up north, ennit?" he said vaguely. "Wodjer need two places for?"

His inquisitiveness made me uneasy. To stem the flow of questions, I asked him some myself. His name is Grahame – with an "e", he informed me, as if this mute suffix was a rare and aristocratic distinction. He comes from Dagenham, and has the kind of background you might expect: broken home, absentee father, mother a boozer, truancy from school, in trouble with the law when he was twelve, taken into care, placed with foster parents, ran away, was put in a home, ran away from that, came Up West, as he calls the West End, drawn by the bright lights. Lives by begging, and the occasional casual job, handing out fliers in Leicester Square, washing cars in a Soho garage. I asked him why he didn't try and get a regular job, and he said solemnly, "I value my freedom." He's a queer mixture of naivety and streetwise sophistication, only half-educated, but with some surprising nuggets of information buried in that half. He saw a copy of Kierkegaard's *Repetition* that I bought second-hand in Charing Cross Road today, and picked it up, frowning at the spine. "Kierkegaard," he said, "the first existentialist." I laughed aloud in sheer astonishment. "What d'you know about existentialism?" I said. "Existence precedes essence," he said, as if reciting the beginning of a nursery rhyme. He wasn't reading from the dust jacket, because the book didn't have one. I think he's one of these people with a photographic memory. He'd seen the phrases somewhere and memorized them without having a clue what they mean. But it was astonishing that his eye had fallen on them in the first place. I asked him where he'd come across Kierkegaard's name before, and he said, in the Library. "I noticed it," he said, " 'cos of the funny spelling. The two 'a's'. Like '*Aarghhh!*' in a comic." He spends a lot of time in the Westminster Reference Library, just off Leicester Square, browsing through encyclopaedias. "If you just go in for the warm, they chuck you out after a while," he said. "But they can't if you're reading the books."

The longer the conversation went on, the more difficult it became to bring it to a close and turn him out into the cold street again. "Where will you sleep tonight?" I asked him. "I dunno," he said. "Can't I sleep downstairs?" "No," I said firmly. He sighed. "Pity, it's a nice little porch. Clean. No draughts to speak of. I 'spect I'll find somewhere."

"How much does the cheapest bed cost round here?" I asked.

He gave me a quick appraising glance. "Fifteen quid."

"I don't believe you."

"I'm not talking doss-houses," he said, with a certain indignation, "I'm not talking Sally Army. I'd rather sleep on the pavement than in one of them places, filthy old men coughing and farting all night and interfering with you in the toilets."

In the end I gave him the fifteen pounds, and escorted him out of the building. In the porch he thanked me nonchalantly, turned up his collar, and sloped off in the direction of Trafalgar Square. I very much doubt whether he will blow his windfall on a room for the night – it would keep him in food and tobacco for two or three days – but my conscience is salved. Or is it?

As I was going to bed, it occurred to me to try and solve the mystery of "proud one" by consulting the dictionary I keep in the flat. It has names of famous people in it, as well as words, and sure enough, there he was, though I'd never heard of him before: "*Proudhon, Pierre Joseph. 1809–65, French socialist, whose pamphlet* What is Property? *(1840) declared that property is theft.*" How about that?

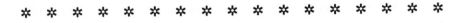

QUAINT TALES OF BRITISH RAIL NO. 167
(By "Intercitizen")

For some months past the escalator between the taxi drop underneath Euston station and the main concourse has been out of action. Before that, it was intermittently under repair. Large plywood screens were erected round it for weeks at a time, and passengers, or "customers" as British Rail calls us nowadays, struggling up the emergency staircase with our luggage, babies, pushchairs, elderly and infirm relatives etc., would hear from behind this barricade the banging and clattering of fitters wrestling with the machine's constipated intestines. Then the screen would be removed, the moving staircase would move again for a few days, and then it would break down again. Lately it has been left in this state, stricken in mid-cycle, no apparent effort being made to repair it. With typical British stoicism passengers have got accustomed to using it as if it were an ordinary solid staircase, though the steps are uncomfortably high for this purpose. There is a lift somewhere, but to use it you have to have a porter, and there are no porters to be found at the taxi drop.

Recently a printed notice appeared at the foot of this paralysed machine:

WELCOME NEWS
A New Escalator for Euston

We are sorry this escalator is out of use. It is life expired [*sic*]. An order has been placed for the manufacture and installation of a new escalator. It will be finished and ready for use by August 1993.

Intercity Retail Manager

Thursday evening, 4th March.
I had lunch with Jake today, at Groucho's. We saw off two bottles of Beaujolais Villages between us, which I enjoyed at the time but regretted later. I went straight to Euston by taxi and, having some time in hand, copied out the notice at the bottom of the broken escalator, swaying slightly on my feet and giggling to myself, attracting curious glances from passengers as they hurried past and hurled themselves at the steel assault course. "*It is life expired.*" I like it. It could be a new slogan for British Rail as privatization approaches, instead of "*We're Getting There.*"

I fell asleep in the train and woke feeling like shit just as it was pulling out of Rummidge Expo station. I could pick out the Richmobile in the car park, its pearly paintwork blanched by the arc-lights. I had to wait half an hour at Rummidge Central for a train back, and mooched about for a while in the shopping precinct above the station. Most of the plateglass windows were plastered with SALE notices, or exposed bare and dusty interiors, the shells of liquidated businesses. I bought an evening newspaper. "MAJOR TAKES SWING AT DOOM-MONGERS," said one headline. "900,000 WHITE-COLLAR WORKERS UNEMPLOYED," said another. Muzak piped soothingly from hidden speakers.

I descend to the subterranean gloom of the platforms to catch my train. It is reported running late. Waiting passengers sit hunched with hands in pockets on the wooden benches, their breath condensing in the chill damp air, gazing wistfully along the track to the mouth of a tunnel where a red signal light glows. An adenoidal voice apologizes for the delay, "which is due to operating difficulties." It is life expired.

Jake saw Samantha on Tuesday. "Smart kid," he said. "Thanks for pointing her in my direction." "I didn't," I said. "I only warned her about your deplorable morals." He laughed. "Don't worry, my boy, she's not my type. She has no ankles, have you noticed?" "Can't say I have," I said. "I never got that far down." "Legs are very important to me," Jake said. "Take the lovely Linda, for example." He was eloquent for some minutes on the subject of his new secretary's legs, hissing and flashing like scissor-blades in black nylon tights under her hanky-sized skirt as she walks in and out of his office. "I've got to have her," he said. "It's only a matter of time." We were well into the second bottle at this stage. I asked him if he didn't sometimes feel a qualm of guilt about his philandering.

JAKE: But of course. That's the point. That's the attraction. The attraction of the forbidden. Listen, I'll tell you a story. (JAKE *refills* TUBBY'S *glass and then his own.*) It happened last summer. I was sitting in the garden one Sunday afternoon browsing through the papers – Rhoda was indoors doing something in the kitchen – and the kids next door were playing in their garden in one of those inflatable paddling pools. It was a hot day. They had some friends or relatives visiting, so there were two boys and two girls of about the same age, four to six years old, I suppose. I couldn't see because of the hedge, but I could hear them alright. You know how water seems to excite kids – makes them even noisier than usual. There was a lot of shouting and shrieking and splashing from next door. I got a bit peeved about it, actually. We didn't have many weekends last summer when it was warm enough to sit out in the garden, and here was my precious sabbath being ruined. So I levered myself off the lounger and went over to the hedge intending to ask if they could lower the volume a bit. As I approached, I heard one of the little girls say, obviously to one of the little boys, "You're not allowed to pull our knickers down." She spoke in a very clear, posh voice, like a juvenile Samantha describing a rule in croquet. "You're not allowed to pull our knickers down." Well, I just curled up. I had to stuff a knuckle in my mouth to stop myself laughing aloud. The kid's remark was completely innocent of sexual meaning, of course. But for me it summed up the whole business. The world is full of desirable women and you're not allowed to pull their knickers down – unless you're married to them, and then there's no fun in it. But sometimes we get lucky and they let us. It's always the same, under the knickers, of course. The same old hole, I mean. But it's always different, too, because of the knickers. "You're not allowed to pull our knickers down." Says it all. (JAKE *drains glass*.)

✳, ✳ ✳ ✳ ✳ ✳ ✳ ✳ ✳ ✳ ✳ ✳ ✳ ✳ ✳ ✳

Friday evening 5th March. To the Wellbeing this afternoon for acupuncture. (Sings, to the opening bars of "Jealousy": "*Therapy! Nothing but therapy! It's never-ending, Not to mention what I'm spending . . .*") Actually I feel more positive this evening than I have lately, but I don't know whether this is because of the acupuncture or because I haven't had anything to drink. Miss Wu did her stuff with heat today instead of the usual needles. She puts little granules of what looks like incense on my skin at the pressure points, and applies a lighted taper to them, one at a time. They glow red-hot like cinders, and give off wisps of faintly perfumed smoke. I feel like a human joss-stick. The idea is that as the granules burn down, the heat increases and produces an effect like the stimulus of a needle, but she has to whip them off with a pair of tweezers before they actually burn me. I have to tell her precisely when the sensation of heat becomes painful, otherwise the smell of singed flesh mingles with the smell of incense. It's quite exciting.

Miss Wu asked me about the family. I was slightly abashed to discover that I had nothing new to report since my last visit. I have a vague memory that Sally spoke to Jane on the phone a few days ago, and relayed some news to me, but I didn't take it in at the time, and I was too embarrassed to ask Sally later what it was, because she's still pissed off with me for letting her down over the Websters. I'm afraid I've been a bit preoccupied lately. I've been reading a lot of Kierkegaard, and a biography of him by Walter Lowrie. Writing this journal takes up a lot of time, too. I don't know how long I'll be able to keep it going at this rate – I'm amazed by how much printout I've got already. Kierkegaard's journals in their complete, unedited form run to 10,000 pages apparently. I picked up a paperback selection of them in Charing Cross Road. There's a passage early on about him going to see his doctor which made me sit up. Kierkegaard asked the doctor if he thought his melancholy could be overcome by willpower. The doctor said he doubted it, and that it might be dangerous even to try. Kierkegaard resigned himself to living with his depression:

> From that instant my choice was made. That grievous malformation with its attendant sufferings (which undoubtedly would have caused most others to commit suicide, if they had enough spirit left to grasp the utter misery of that torture) is what I have regarded as the thorn in the flesh, my limitation, my cross . . .

The thorn in the flesh! How about that?

Søren Kierkegaard. Just the name on the title page has a peculiar, arresting effect. It's so strange, so extravagantly foreign-looking to an English eye – almost extra-terrestrial. That weird *o* with the slash through it, like the zero sign on a computer screen – it might belong to some synthetic language invented by a sci-fi writer. And the double *aa* in the surname is almost as exotic. There are no native English words with two consecutive a's, I think, and not many loan-words either. I've always been irritated by the nerds who put small ads in newspapers beginning with a meaningless row of *A's*, just to be sure of getting pole position in the column, like: "*AAAA Escort for sale, D Reg., 50,000 miles, £3000 o.n.o.*" It's cheating. There ought to be a rule against it, then people would have to use a bit of ingenuity. I just looked at the first page in the dictionary: *aa, aardvark, Aarhus, . . . Aa* is a Hawaiian word for a certain kind of volcanic rock, and an *aardvark* is a nocturnal mammal that eats termites – the name comes from obsolete Afrikaans, it says. *"Aardvark-grey Escort for sale"* would make an eye-catching ad. (I presume by night all aardvarks are grey.)

Once you start browsing in dictionaries, you never know where it will lead you. I noticed that *Aarhus*, the name of a port in Denmark, was given the alternative spelling of *Århus*. Further research revealed that this is the usual way the double *aa* is written in modern Danish, a single *a* with a little circle on top. So if Kierkegaard were alive today he would write his name as Kierkegård. More unsettling still was the discovery that all this time I've been pronouncing his name incorrectly. I thought it was something like Sor'n Key-erk-er-guard. Not at all. Apparently the *o* is pronounced like *eu* in the French *deux*, the *Kierk* is pronounced as *Kirg* with a hard *g*, the *aa* sounds like *awe* in English, and the *d* is mute. So the name sounds something like Seuren Kirgegor. I think I'll stick with the English pronunciation.

The *a* with the little circle on top reminds me of something, but I can't for the life of me remember what. Frustrating. It'll come back to me one day, when I'm not trying.

I've also been reading *Repetition*, subtitled *An Essay in Experimental Psychology*. A rum book. Well, they're all rum books. Each one is different, but the same themes and obsessions keep cropping up: courtship, seduction, indecision, guilt, depression, despair. *Repetition* has another pretend-author, Constantine Constantius, who is the friend and confidant of a nameless young man, and *he's* a bit like A in *Either/Or*. The young man falls in love with a girl who reciprocates his feelings and they become engaged. But instead of being made happy by this situation, the guy is immediately plunged into the deepest depression (Constantius calls it "melancholy", like Kierkegaard in his *Journals*). What triggers this reaction is a fragment of verse (the young man has ambitions to be a poet himself) which he finds himself repeating again and again:

> To my arm-chair there comes a dream
> From the springtime of youth
> A longing intense
> For thee, thou sun amongst women.

The young man is a classic case of the unhappiest man. Instead of living in the present, enjoying his engagement, he remembers the future; that is to say, he imagines himself looking back on his youthful love from the vantage point of disillusioned old age, like the speaker of the poem, and then there seems to be no point in getting married. "He was in love, deeply and sincerely in love, that was evident – and yet all at once, in one of the first days of his engagement, he was capable of recollecting his love. Substantially he was through with the whole relationship. Before he begins he has taken such a terrible stride that he has leapt over the whole of life." It's a wonderfully barmy and yet entirely plausible way of cheating yourself of happiness. Constantius sums it up: "He longs for the girl, he has to restrain himself by force from hanging around her the whole day, and yet at the very first instant he has become an old man with respect to the whole relationship . . . That he would become unhappy was clear enough, and that the girl would become unhappy was no less clear." He decides that for the girl's own good he must break off the engagement. But how can he do this without making her feel rejected?

Constantius advises him to pretend to have a mistress – to set up a shop-girl in an apartment and go through the motions of visiting her – so that his fiancée will despise him and break off the engagement herself. The young man accepts this advice, but at the last moment lacks the nerve to carry it out, and simply disappears from Copenhagen. After an interval he starts writing letters to Constantius, analysing his conduct and his feelings in relation to the girl. He's still completely obsessed with her, of course. He's become an unhappy rememberer. "What am I doing now? I begin all over again from the beginning, and from the wrong end. I shun every outward reminder of the whole thing, yet my soul, day and night, waking and sleeping, is incessantly employed with it." He identifies himself with Job. (I looked up Job in the Bible. I'd never actually read the Book of Job before. It's surprisingly readable – bloody brilliant, actually.) Like Job, the young man bewails his miserable condition ("My life has been brought to an impasse, I loathe existence, it is without savour, lacking salt and sense"), but whereas Job blames God, the young man doesn't believe in God, so he isn't sure whose fault it is: "How did I obtain an interest in this enterprise they call reality? Why should I have an interest in it? Is it not a voluntary concern? And if I am to be compelled to take part in it, where is the director?" The young man longs for some sudden transforming event or revelation, a "tempest" like the one that comes at the end of the Book of Job, when God really sticks it to Job and says in effect, "Can you do what I can do? If not, belt up," and Job submits and God rewards him by giving him twice as many sheep and camels and she-asses as he had before. "Job is blessed and has received everything double," says the young man. "This is what is called a repetition." Then he reads in a newspaper that the girl has married somebody else, and he writes to Constantius that the news has liberated him from his obsession: "I am again myself . . . The discord in my nature is resolved, I am again unified . . . is this not then a repetition? Did I not get everything doubly restored? Did I not get myself again, precisely in such a way that I must doubly feel its significance?" His last letter ends with a rapturous thankyou to the girl, and an ecstatic dedication of himself to the life of the mind:

> . . . first a libation to her who saved a soul which sat in the solitude of despair. Hail to feminine magnanimity! Long life to the high flight of thought, to moral danger in the service of the idea! Hail to the danger of battle! Hail to the solemn exultation of victory! Hail to the dance in the vortex of the infinite! Hail to the breaking wave which covers me in the abyss! Hail to the breaking wave which hurls me up above the stars!

Now if you know anything about Kierkegaard's life, and I know a bit by now, you don't need to be told that this story was very close to his own experience. Soon after he got engaged to Regine he started to have doubts about whether they could ever be happy together, because of his own temperament. So he broke off the engagement, even though he was still in love with the girl, and she was still in love with him and begged him not to break it off, as did her father. Kierkegaard went away to live in Berlin for a while, where he wrote *Either/Or*, which was a long, roundabout apology and explanation for his conduct towards Regine. He said later that it was written for her and that the "Seducer's Diary" in particular was meant to "help her push her boat from the shore", i.e., to sever her emotional attachment to him, by making her think that anyone capable of creating the character of Johannes must be something of a cold-blooded selfish bastard himself. You could say that Kierkegaard's writing "The Seducer's Diary" was like the young man in *Repetition* pretending to have a mistress. In fact, when he finished *Either/Or*, Kierkegaard immediately started work on *Repetition*, going over the same ground in a story that was much closer to his own experience. But when he came back to Copenhagen and discovered that Regine was already engaged to somebody else, was he overjoyed? Did he feel liberated and unified like the hero of *Repetition*? Did he hell. He was devastated. There's an entry in the Journals at this time which obviously describes his feelings:

> The most dreadful thing that can happen to a man is to become ridiculous in his own eyes in a matter of essential importance, to discover, for example, that the sum and substance of his sentiment is rubbish.

Obviously he'd been secretly hoping that his decision to break off the engagement would be miraculously reversed without his own volition, and that he would marry Regine after all. Even when he was sailing to Germany, on his way to Berlin, he noted in his journal: "Notwithstanding it is imprudent for my peace of mind, I cannot leave off thinking of the indescribable moment when I might return to her." *That* was the repetition he had in mind: he would get Regine twice. Like Job he would be blessed and receive everything double. He actually heard about her new engagement when he was working on *Repetition*, and scrapped the original ending of the story, in which the hero commits suicide because he cannot bear to think of the suffering he has caused his beloved.

So all that high-falutin' stuff about feminine magnanimity and the vortex of the infinite was an attempt to get over his disappointment at Regine's transference of her affections to someone else, an effort to see this as a triumph and vindication of his conduct, not an exposure of his folly. It didn't work. He never ceased to love her, or think of her, or write about her (directly or indirectly) for the rest of his life; and he left everything he owned to her in his will (there wasn't much left when he died, but it's the thought that counts, and in this case reveals). What a fool! But what an endearing, entirely human fool.

Repetition is a typically teasing, haunting Kierkegaard title. We normally think of repetition as inherently boring, something to be avoided if possible, as in "repetitive job". But in this book it's seen as something fantastically precious and desirable. One meaning of it is the restoration of what seems to be lost (e.g. Job's prosperity, the young man's faith in himself). But another sense is the enjoyment of what you have. It's the same as living-in-the-present, "it has the blessed certainty of the instant." It means being set free from the curse of unhappy hoping and unhappy remembering. "Hope is a charming maiden that slips through the fingers, recollection is a beautiful old woman but of no use at the instant, repetition is a beloved wife of whom one never tires."

It occurs to me that you could turn that last metaphor around: not repetition is a beloved wife, but a beloved wife (or beloved husband) is repetition. To appreciate the real value of marriage you have to discard the superficial idea of repetition as something boring and negative, and see it as, on the contrary, something liberating and positive – the secret of happiness, no less. That's why B, in *Either/Or*, begins his attack on A's aesthetic philosophy of life (and the melancholia which goes with it) by defending marriage, and urging A to marry. (This is getting quite exciting: I haven't thought as hard as this for years, if ever.)

Take sex, for instance. Married sex is the repetition of an act. The element of repetition outweighs any variation there may be between one occasion and another. However many postures you experiment with, however many erotic techniques and sex-toys and games and visual aids you might employ, the fact that you have the same partner means that every act is essentially (or do I mean existentially?) the same. And if our experience is anything to go by (mine and Sally's, I mean) most couples eventually settle on a certain pattern of love-making which suits them both, and repeat it over and over. How many sex acts are there in a long-lasting marriage? Thousands. Some will be more satisfying than others, but does anybody remember them all distinctly? No, they merge and blend in the memory. That's why philanderers like Jake think married sex is inherently boring. They insist upon variety in sex, and after a while the means of obtaining variety become more important than the act itself. For them the essence of sex is in the anticipation, the plotting, the planning, the desiring, the wooing, the secrecy, the deceptions, the assignations. You don't make assignations with your spouse. There's no need. Sex is just there, to enjoy when you want it; and if your partner doesn't feel like it for some reason, because they're tired or have a cold or want to stop up and watch something on the telly, well, that's no big deal, because there will be plenty of other opportunities. What's so wonderful about married sex (and especially middle-aged, post-menopausal sex, when the birth-control business is over and done with) is that you don't have to be thinking about it all the time. I suspect that Jake is thinking about it even while he's phoning clients and drawing up contracts; probably the only time he *isn't* thinking about sex is when he's actually having it (because orgasm is a kind of slipped second, it empties the mind of thought for an instant) but I bet as soon as he comes he's thinking about it again.

What applies to sex applies to everything else in marriage: work, recreation, meals, whatever. It's all repetition. The longer you live together, the less you change, and the more repetition there is in daily life. You know each other's minds, thoughts, habits: who sleeps on which side of the bed, who gets up first in the morning, who takes coffee and who takes tea at breakfast, who likes to read the news section of the paper first and who the review section, and so on. You need to speak to each other less and less. To an outsider it looks like boredom and alienation. It's a commonplace that you can always tell which couples in a restaurant are married to each other because they're eating in silence. But does this mean that they're unhappy with each other's company? Not at all. They're merely behaving as they do at home, as they do all the time. It's not that they have nothing to say to each other, but that it doesn't have to be said. Being happily married means that you don't have to *perform* marriage, you just live in it, like a fish lives in the sea. It's remarkable Kierkegaard intuitively understood that, even though he was never married himself, and threw away his best chance of having the experience.

Sally just came into my study to tell me she wants a separation. She says she told me earlier this evening, over supper, but I wasn't listening. I listened this time, but I still can't take it in.

✳ ✳ TWO ✳ ✳

✳ ✳   Brett Sutton   ✳ ✳

Statement of.......................... Michael Brett SUTTON
Age of Witness....................... Over 21
Occupation of witness............ Tennis Coach
Address .... 41 Upton Road, RUMMIDGE R27 9LP.

This statement, consisting of 5 pages, each signed by me, is true to the best of my knowledge and belief and I make it knowing that, if it is tendered in evidence, I shall be liable to prosecution if I have wilfully stated anything which I know to be false or do not believe to be true.
Dated the: 21st March 1993.

I first noticed Mr Passmore behaving strangely towards me about two weeks ago. I've been coaching his wife for some months, but I know him only slightly, as someone I would say hello to if we passed each other at the Club, nothing more. I've never coached him. Mrs Passmore told me he had a chronic knee injury which hadn't responded to surgery, and it handicaps him considerably as regards tennis. I've seen him playing occasionally, wearing a rigid brace, and I thought he managed pretty well, considering, but I imagine he finds it very frustrating not being able to move around the court properly. I think perhaps that's why he got this crazy idea into his head. If you're keen on sport, there's nothing worse than long-term injury. I know – I've been through it myself: cartilage problems, tendinitis, I've had them all. It really gets you down. The whole world looks grey, everything seems against you. You only have to get some crisis in your personal life and you flip. Mr Passmore doesn't look the athletic type, but I gather sport matters to him. Mrs Passmore told me that before his injury they used to play each other a lot, but now she doesn't like to because he can't bear her to win, but he complains if she doesn't try to. Actually I think she could beat him now even if he was fully fit: she's come on a lot, lately. I've been coaching her twice a week all through this winter.

The first time Mr Passmore behaved oddly towards me was in the Men's locker room at the Club, about two weeks ago, though I hardly registered it at the time. It's only in retrospect that it seems significant. I was stripping off my tennis gear before taking a shower, and I happened to look up and saw Mr Passmore, staring at me. He was fully dressed. As soon as he caught my eye, he looked away, and started fiddling with the key of his locker. I wouldn't have thought anything of it except that before he caught my eye he was fairly obviously staring at my private parts. I won't say it's never happened to me before, but it surprised me coming from Mr Passmore. I actually wondered whether I'd imagined it, it was all over so fast. Anyway, I soon forgot all about it.

A few days later I was coaching Mrs Passmore on one of the indoor courts, in the evening, and Mr Passmore turned up and sat watching us from behind the netting at the end of the hall. I presumed that he'd made an appointment to meet his wife at the Club, and was early. I smiled at him, but he didn't smile back. His being there seemed to bother Mrs Passmore. She started making mistakes in her play, mis-hitting the ball. Eventually she went over to Mr Passmore and spoke to him through the netting. I gathered that she was asking him to leave, but he just shook his head and smiled in a sneery sort of way. She came over to me then and said that she was sorry, but she'd have to stop the coaching session. She looked angry and upset. She insisted on paying me for the full session though she'd only had half-an-hour. She walked out of the court without a glance at Mr Passmore, who remained seated on the bench, hunched inside his overcoat, with his hands in the pockets. I felt a bit embarrassed, walking past him on my way out. I assumed they were having some kind of row. I didn't dream for a moment that it had anything to do with me.

A few days after that, the phone calls started. The phone would ring, I'd pick it up and say "Hallo?" and no one would reply. After a while there would be a click, as the caller put the receiver down. The calls came at all hours, sometimes in the middle of the night. I reported them to BT, but they said there was nothing they could do. They advised me to disconnect my bedside phone at night, so I did, and left the answerphone on downstairs. Next morning, there were two calls recorded, but no messages. One evening about nine o'clock I answered the phone and a high falsetto voice said, "Can I speak to Sally, please? This is her mother." I said I thought she must have the wrong number. She didn't seem to hear me, and asked again to speak to Sally, saying it was urgent. I said there was nobody called Sally at my address. I didn't make the connection with Mrs Passmore, even though we are on first-name terms. And although the voice sounded rather strange, it never crossed my mind that it was an impersonation.

A few nights after that I was woken in the middle of the night by a noise. You know what it's like when that happens: by the time you're fully awake, the noise has stopped and you have no idea where it came from, or whether the whole thing was a dream. I put on a tracksuit, because I always sleep in the nude, and went downstairs to check, but there was no sign of anyone trying to break in. I heard a car starting up in the street outside and went to the front door just in time to see a white car turning the corner at the end of the street. Well, it looked white under the street-lighting, but it could have been silver. I didn't have a good enough view to identify the make. The next morning I discovered that someone had been in the back garden. They'd got in by the side way and knocked over some panes of glass that were leaning up against the tool-shed – I'm in the middle of building a cold-frame. Three of the panes were broken. That must have been the noise I heard.

Two days later I got up in the morning and found my ladder leaning up against the wall of the house under my bedroom window. Someone had taken it from the space between the garage and the garden fence where I keep it. There was no sign of any attempt to break in, but I was alarmed. That was when I first reported the incidents to your station. Police Constable Roberts came round. He advised me to have a burglar-alarm system fitted. I was in the process of getting quotes when I lost my house keys. I keep them in my tennis bag usually during the day, because they're rather heavy in the pocket of my tracksuit, but last Friday they disappeared. I was beginning to get seriously worried, by now, that someone was trying to burgle my house. I thought I knew who it was too – a member of the Club's groundstaff. I'd rather not say who. I have a number of trophies at home, you see, and this person once asked me about them, and what they were worth. I made an arrangement with a locksmith to have the locks changed the next day.

That night – it was about three o'clock – I was woken by Nigel squeezing my arm and whispering in my ear, "I think there's someone in the room." He was shaking with fear. I turned on the bedside lamp, and there was Mr Passmore standing on the rug on my side of the bed, with a torch in one hand and a large pair of scissors in the other. I didn't like the look of the scissors – they were big, dangerous-looking things, like drapers' shears. As I said, I always sleep naked, and so does Nigel, and there was nothing within reach I could have used to defend us with. I tried to keep calm. I asked Mr Passmore what he thought he was doing. He didn't answer. He was staring at Nigel, completely gobsmacked. Nigel, who was nearest the door, jumped out of bed and ran downstairs to phone 999. Mr Passmore looked round the room in a dazed sort of way and said, "I seem to have made a mistake." I said, "I think you have." He said, "I was looking for my wife." I said, "Well, she's not here. She's never been here." Suddenly it all fell into place, and I realized what had been going on, in his head I mean. I couldn't help laughing, partly in relief, partly because he looked such a fool standing there with the scissors in his hand. I said, "What were you going to do with those, castrate me?" He said, "I was going to cut your ponytail off."

I don't want to press charges. To be perfectly honest I'd rather not have to give evidence in court which might be reported in the local press. It could have a damaging effect on my work. Some of the members of the Club are prejudiced, I'm afraid. I'm not ashamed of being gay, but I'm discreet about it. I live a fair distance from the Club, and nobody there knows anything about my private life. I don't think Mr Passmore will cause me any more trouble, and he's offered to pay for the broken panes of glass.

136

✳ ✳ Amy ✳ ✳

WELL, THE MOST AWFUL THING has happened. Laurence's wife wants a separation. He called me last night to tell me. I knew at once it must be something *catastrophique* because I've told him not to phone me at home unless it's terribly important. I have to go upstairs to my bedroom extension, and Zelda always wants to know afterwards who called and what it was about, and I wouldn't put it past her to listen in on the downstairs phone. We have a routine that Laurence phones me at the office in the lunch hour or I call him when he's at his flat. I know you think I should be more upfront with Zelda about my relationship with Laurence, but – No, I know you haven't *said* as much, Karl, but I can tell. Well, of course, if you insist, I must take your word, but I suppose it's possible that *subconsciously* you disapprove. I mean, if *I* can suppress things, I suppose it's possible you can, too, isn't it? Or are you sure you're absolutely completely totally superhumanly rational? Sorry, sorry. I'm very upset, I hardly slept a wink last night. No, he had no idea. He's utterly devastated. Apparently she just marched into his study on Friday evening and announced that she wanted a separation. Just like that. Said she just couldn't stand living with him any more, he was like a zombie, that was the word she used, a zombie. Well, he is often a little *distrait*, I have to admit, but writers often are, in my experience. I should have thought she'd be used to it by now, but evidently not. She said they didn't communicate, and they didn't have anything in common any more, and now that the children were grown up and had left home there was no point their going on living together.

Lorenzo spent the whole weekend trying to talk her out of it, but to no avail. Well, I think first he tried to argue that there was nothing

137

wrong with the marriage, that it was like any other marriage, something to do with repetition and Kierkegaard, I couldn't quite follow it, he was hardly coherent, poor dear. Yes, he's developed a thing about Kierkegaard lately, for some reason. Anyway, when that didn't work he changed tack and said he would turn over a new leaf and talk to her at meals and take an interest in her work and go away with her on Weekend Breaks and that sort of thing, but she said it was too late.

Sally. Her name's Sally. I've only met her a few times, mostly at parties given by Heartland, and she always struck me as rather guarded and self-contained. She likes to make one drink last the whole evening and stay cold sober while all around her are getting smashed. I think it confirms her sense of what a worthless load of layabouts we television folk are. Goodlooking in a rather *noli me tangere* way. High cheekbones, a strong chin. A bit like Patricia Hodge, but more athletic, more windbeaten. Oh. I keep forgetting that you never go to the theatre or watch television. What on earth *do* you do in your spare time? Oh, I might have guessed. Do you read Kierkegaard? He doesn't sound my cup of tea. Or Laurence's either, come to that. I wonder what he sees in him. No, Laurence asked her if there was anyone else, and she says there isn't. I asked him if it was conceivable that Sally suspected there was something between him and me, something more than what there actually is I mean, which is entirely innocent, as you know, but he said absolutely not. Well, she knows that we're good friends but I don't think she has any idea how often we see each other outside work and I wondered if someone had been gossiping or sending poison-pen letters, but Laurence said she didn't mention my name or accuse him of anything like that. Oh dear. *Quel cauchemar!*

I should have thought it was obvious. Laurence is my dearest friend, my dearest male friend anyway. I don't like to see him wretched. I know you're smiling cynically. Anyway, I don't mind admitting that my reasons for feeling upset are partly selfish. I was very happy with our relationship. It suited me. It was intimate without being . . . I don't know. All right, without being sexual. But no, I don't mean sexual, or not just sexual, I mean possessive or demanding or something. After all, our relationship was never sex*less*. There's always been an element of . . . of gallantry in Laurence's treatment of me. Yes, gallantry. But the fact that he's happily married – was happily married – and that that was understood by both of us, took all the potential tension out of the relationship. We could enjoy each other's company without wondering whether we wanted to go to bed together or whether we expected each other to want to, if you follow me. I enjoyed dressing up to go out with Laurence – dressing up to go out with a girlfriend is never quite the same – but I didn't have to think about *un*dressing for him afterwards. If you're a single woman and you go out with a man you've either got to insist tediously on going Dutch or you have an uneasy feeling that you're incurring some kind of erotic debt which may be called in at any moment.

No, I've no idea what his sex life was like with Sally. We never discussed it. Yes, I told him all about my experiences with Saul, but he never told me anything about him and Sally. I didn't ask. A kind of *pudeur* restrained me. *Pudeur*. After all, they were still married, it would have been an intrusion . . . Oh, all right, perhaps I didn't want to hear about it in case she turned out to be one of those women who have multiple orgasms as easy as shelling peas and can do the whole Kama Sutra standing on their heads. What's so funny about that? They do stand on their heads in the Kama Sutra? Oh well, you know what I mean. I've never pretended I don't feel inadequate about sex. I mean, why else am I here? But I was never jealous of Sally. She was welcome to that part of Laurence's life, and to that part of Laurence for that matter. I just didn't want to hear about it. Oh, am I using the past tense? Yes I am, aren't I. Well, I certainly don't think that our relationship is over, but I suppose I'm afraid it will change, in ways I can't predict. Unless they get back together, of course. I suggested to Laurence that they should see a marriage counsellor, but he just groaned and said, "They'll only say I need psychotherapy, and I'm having that already." I asked him how he knew that's what they would say, and he said, "From experience." It seems this isn't the first time Sally has been seriously pissed off with the marriage. Once she walked out of the house for a whole weekend, he didn't know where she'd gone, and came back just as he was phoning the police.

She didn't say a word for days because she'd got laryngitis, she'd been tramping all over the Malverns in pouring rain, but when she got her voice back she insisted on their going to marriage guidance. That's how Laurence started on psychotherapy. He never told me that before. I suppose there was no reason why he should, but it was a little disturbing to have it sprung on me now. I suppose one never does tell anybody *everything* about oneself. Except one's analyst of course . . .

Well, I saw Laurence yesterday evening, at his flat. He rang me at work to say he was coming up to town but he didn't want to eat out, so I knew I was in for a long, harrowing *tête à tête*. I stopped off at Fortnum's after work to pick up some quiche and salad. Laurence didn't eat much of it, but he drank quite a lot. He's very depressed. I mean, he was depressed before, but now he's really got something to be depressed about. Yes, I think he's quite conscious of the irony.

Things haven't improved *chez* Passmore. Sally has moved into the guest bedroom. She goes to work early in the morning and comes back late in the evening, so she doesn't have to talk to Laurence. She says she'll talk at the weekend, but she can't cope with his problems and do her own job at the same time. I think it's rather ominous that she says "*his* problems", not "their problems", don't you? Mind you, I understand how she feels about talking to Laurence in his present state. After four hours of it last night I was completely *fiinito*. I felt like a sponge that had been saturated and squeezed so often it had lost all its spring. And then, when I said I had to go home, he asked me to stay the night. He said it wasn't for sex, but just so he could hold me. He hasn't had any proper sleep since last Friday, and he does look quite hollow-eyed, poor sweet. He said, "I think it would help me to sleep if I could just hold you."

Well, of course it was out of the question. I mean, leaving aside whether I wanted to be held, and the risk of its developing into something else, I couldn't possibly stay out all night without warning. Zelda would've been worried sick, and if I'd phoned her with some improvised story she would have seen through it immediately, she always knows when I'm lying, it's one of her most irritating habits. Incidentally, it was Bad Breast time again this morning. Yes. We had a bitter row at breakfast, about muesli. Not *just* about muesli, of course. They didn't have her usual brand at Safeways the last time I went shopping so I bought another kind and this morning the old packet had run out so I put this other one on the table and she refused to touch it because it had added sugar. A *minuscule* quantity, and brown sugar too, the healthy sort, as I pointed out, but she refused to eat any of it, and as it's the only thing she ever has for breakfast, apart from coffee, she went off to school on an empty stomach, leaving me feeling incredibly guilty, exactly as she had intended, of course. Her parting shot was to say that I was trying to make her eat sugar because she's slim and I'm fat, "disgustingly fat" was the phrase she used, do you think that's true? No, I don't mean about my being disgustingly fat, I don't consider myself fat at all, even though I would like to lose a few pounds. I mean is it possible that I'm subconsciously jealous of Zelda's figure? Oh you always bat these questions back at me. I don't know. Perhaps I am a little bit. But I honestly didn't know there was any sugar in the bloody muesli.

Where was I? Oh yes, Laurence. Well, I had to say no, though I did feel badly about it, he looked so woeful, so pleading, like a dog that wants to come in out of the rain. I said, couldn't he take a sleeping pill, and he said he didn't want to because they made him so depressed when he woke up, and if he got any more depressed than he was already he was afraid he'd top himself. He smiled when he said that to show it was a joke, but it worried me. He did go and see his psychotherapist on Monday, but she doesn't seem to have been much help. That may be Laurence's fault, because when I asked him he couldn't remember anything she'd said. I'm not sure he took in anything *I* said last night, either. All he wants to do is pour out his version of things, not listen to any constructive advice. I nearly said to him, you should try analysis, darling, that's all I do, five days a week: pour out my version of things without getting any constructive advice. Just my little joke, Karl. Yes, of course I know that jokes are disguised forms of aggression . . .

Well, things have gone from bad to worse. Sally's moved out of the house, and Laurence is all on his own there. It's a five-bedroomed detached, in an upmarket residential area on the outskirts of Rummidge. I've never been there, but he showed me some photographs. It's what the estate agents call a modern house of character. I couldn't say what character. French farmhouse crossed with golf club, perhaps. Not my taste, but comfortable and substantial. Set well back from the road, at the end of a longish drive, with a lot of trees and shrubs round it. He said to me once, "It's so quiet there I could hear my hair growing, if I had any hair." Yes, he's bald. Didn't I ever mention it? He jokes about it, but I think it bothers him. Anyway, I don't like to think of him all on his own in that house, like a bead in a rattle.

I gathered that last weekend was rather fraught. Sally told him she was prepared to talk, but there had to be a time limit on their discussions, not more than two hours at a time, and only one session a day. It sounded like quite a sensible idea to me, but Laurence couldn't accept it. He says her college sent her on a management course recently and she's trying to treat their marital crisis as if it were an industrial dispute, with agendas and adjournments. He agreed to the condition, but when it came to the crunch, and the two hours were up, he wouldn't stop. Eventually she said that if he didn't stop harassing her she would move out of the house until he came to his senses. And he rather foolishly said, "All right, move out, see if I care," or words to that effect, so she did. She wouldn't tell him where she was going and she hasn't told him since.

Laurence is convinced that there is another man after all and that she staged this row so she could be with him. He thinks he knows who it is, too: the tennis coach at their sports club. It doesn't sound like Sally to me, but you can never tell. You remember I told you Saul swore blind there was nobody else when he asked me for a divorce, and then I discovered he'd been screwing Janine for months. Laurence says Sally started taking tennis lessons a few months ago and shortly afterwards she decided to colour her hair. No, it doesn't sound much to go on, but he's quite convinced and in his present mood there's no arguing with him. He isn't coming to London this week because he says he's too busy. I think he means too busy stalking the tennis coach. I don't like the sound of it at all, but I can't help feeling a guilty kind of relief that I won't have to do another four-hour counselling session tonight.

Laurence is taking up more and more of our time, isn't he? Can't you say something to get me off the subject? What about some free association? I used to enjoy that, we never seem to do it any more.

All right. Mother. My mother. In the kitchen at Highgate. The afternoon sun is shining through the frosted kitchen window, throwing a mottled pattern on the table, and over her arms and hands. She's wearing one of those old-fashioned floral print pinafores that crossed at the back and tied at the front. We're chopping vegetables together for a stew, or soup. I'm about thirteen, fourteen. I've just started my periods. She's telling me about the facts of life. About how easy it is to get pregnant, and how wary I must be of men and boys. Chopping up carrots as she speaks, as if she would like to cut off their willies . . . I wonder why I should think of that? I suppose it's because I'm worried about Zelda. Of course I've told her all about the facts of life, but should I make sure she's fixed up with contraception or will she take that as an encouragement to promiscuity? You don't think that's it? What then? Oh, go on, Karl, let yourself go for once, give me an interpretation. No, don't – I know, it's really about me and Laurence, isn't it? Oh God . . .

Well, Sally has got herself a lawyer now. Yes. Laurence had a letter from him asking if he'll instruct his own solicitor to enter into discussions about a separation settlement. Also with a proposal from Sally that they should agree to go to their sports club on alternate days, to avoid embarrassing encounters. Apparently Laurence has been going down there and watching Sally practising with the tennis coach. She says it puts her off her game. I should think it would. Of course this has only convinced him all the more that she has something to hide *re* the tennis coach. Laurence told his solicitor to tell Sally's that if she wanted to live apart from him she would have to do it on her own salary plus she could have back whatever she had contributed to their savings, which isn't very much of course compared to what Laurence has earned in recent years. I think it's a bad sign that they're quarrelling about money already, and using lawyers, that was when things became really nasty between Saul and me. Oh dear, I have a dreadful feeling of *déjà vu* about all this . . .

Well, things have gone from bad to worse. Laurence has had an injunction served on him to stop him going into the college where Sally works, or university I think it's called now, Volt University or Watt University – something electrical anyway. Her lawyer wrote back to say that she considered herself entitled to half their savings because she supported him for years by her teaching when he was trying to make it as a scriptwriter. Laurence went to the University in a towering rage and ambushed her outside her office and made a public scene. She told him that he was out of his mind. Well, I think perhaps he is, poor sweet. So Sally took out an injunction against him, and if he goes there again he could be arrested. In fact he's not even allowed to go within a one-mile radius of the place. That particularly annoys him because it means he can't try and follow her when she leaves work to find out where she's living. He's been keeping watch on the tennis coach's house, but so far no luck. He says it's only a matter of time before he catches them. I think he means *in flagrante*. Heaven knows what he thinks he's going to do if he does catch them. Laurence would hardly be a match for a tennis coach if it came to blows . . .

Well, it seems that Sally wasn't having an affair after all, not with the tennis coach anyway. Apparently he's gay. Yes. Well, I must admit I had a job not to laugh myself, when Laurence told me. I don't know exactly how he found out, he was a bit evasive on the phone, but he seemed quite certain. He sounded very low, too, poor sweet. As long as he suspected the tennis coach he had a target for his anger and resentment. You can't hate someone if you don't know who they are. Anyway, I suspect he's beginning to think that Sally may have been telling the truth after all, about why she wanted a separation – that she just couldn't bear living with him any more. It hasn't done anything for his self-esteem. I remember when I found out about Janine, I was a tiny bit secretly relieved as well as absolutely furious, because it meant that I needn't blame myself for the failure of the marriage. Or not entirely.

Another depressing development for Laurence is that his children know about the split now. I think that's a kind of Rubicon as far as he's concerned. As long as they didn't know, there was always the possibility that he and Sally might get back together again with no serious damage done, no embarrassment, no loss of face. When Sally walked out the last thing he said to her – he told me he ran down the drive after her car and banged on her window to make her wind it down – the last thing he said was, "Don't tell Jane and Adam." Of course they had to know sooner or later. Sally probably told them almost immediately, but Laurence has only just found out that they know. He's had phone calls from both of them. They're being very careful not to take sides, but the main thing that's struck him is that they don't seem to be terribly upset or even terribly surprised. It's obvious to me that Sally must have been confiding in them for some time and preparing them for what's happened. I think this is beginning to dawn on Laurence, too. "I feel as if I've been living in a dream," he said, "and I've just woken up. But what I've woken up to is a nightmare." Poor Lorenzo. Speaking of dreams, I had a very peculiar one last night . . .

Well, it's happened, I knew it would, I could see it coming: Laurence wants to sleep with me. Not just to hold me. For sex. The beast with two backs. It was one of Saul's expressions, don't pretend you've never heard it before, Karl. It's in Shakespeare somewhere. I can't remember which play, but I'm sure it's in Shakespeare. Well, it's no odder than most of the other available phrases. "Sleep with," for instance. I knew a girl once, called Muriel, who used to say she was sleeping with her boss when she meant that she had it off with him in the back of his Jaguar in Epping Forest during their lunch hour. I shouldn't think they got much sleep.

Laurence raised the subject over dinner last night. I suppose I should have been forewarned when he took me to Rules instead of our usual *trattoria*. And encouraged me to order the lobster. It was just as well we were eating early and the restaurant was half-empty, otherwise people would have been falling off their chairs trying to listen in. He said the only reason he hadn't tried to make love to me before was because he believed in fidelity in marriage, and I chipped in *tout de suite* to say that I quite understood and respected him for it. He said it was very generous of me to take that view but he felt he had been exploiting me in a way, enjoying my company without any commitment, and that now Sally had walked out on him there was no reason why we should inhibit ourselves any longer. I said that I didn't feel at all exploited, or inhibited for that matter. Not quite as bluntly as that, of course. I tried to explain that I valued our relationship precisely because there were no sexual strings to it, hence no tension, no anxiety, no jealousy. He looked very dejected and said, "Are you saying you don't love me?" and I said, "Darling, I haven't *allowed* myself to love you in that way." He said, "Well, now you can." And I said, "Supposing I allow myself to, and then Sally and you get together again, what then?" He said very gloomily that he couldn't imagine that could ever happen. Relations between them are getting worse. She's talking about a divorce now, because Laurence refuses to discuss financial arrangements for a voluntary separation, which is very silly of him. His solicitor told him Sally would get half their joint assets and up to a third of their joint income as maintenance in a divorce settlement. Laurence thinks that she shouldn't get anything at all, because she deserted him. The letters are flying back and forth between the lawyers. And now he wants to sleep with me.

So what should I do? Oh, I know you won't tell me, it's just a rhetorical question. Except a rhetorical question is when the answer is implied, isn't it? And I don't know the answer to this one. I told Laurence I would think about it, and I have, I've thought of little else since last night, but I don't know what to do, I really don't. I'm very fond of Laurence, and I'd like to help him through this crisis. I realize that he just wants to be comforted and I wish I was like one of those earth-motherly, heart-of-gold women in movies who give their bodies generously to nice men at the drop of a hat, but I'm not. Fortunately Laurence remains wonderfully *galant*. We went back to his flat after Rules began to fill up with the post-theatre crowd and talked some more, but there was no hanky-panky or any attempt at it. A strange thing happened when he saw me out, though. He always comes down in the lift with me and puts me in a taxi to go home. When we opened the street door of the building, there in the entryway was one of those young vagrants you see everywhere nowadays, in a sleeping- bag. We had to practically step over him to get into the street. Well, I just ignored him, it seemed the safest thing to do, but Laurence said *hallo* to him, as if there were nothing untoward about his being there, as if the man, or boy rather, was somebody he knew. While we stood on the pavement looking out for a taxi, I hissed at Laurence, "Who is that?" and he replied, "Grahame." As if he was a neighbour or something. Then a taxi came and I didn't have a chance to ask him anything more. I think I had a dream about it last night . . .

Well, I suppose the fact that I used that expression of Saul's, the beast with two backs, last time, and applied it to Laurence, could be significant – is that what you were getting at? That I'm afraid of having sex with Laurence because sex with Saul was such a disaster? But is that cowardice or good sense?

I know you think it's unnatural that I've never had sex with anyone since the divorce. No, I know you haven't said so explicitly – when did you ever say anything explicitly? But I can read between the lines. Well, for instance you referred to my relationship with Laurence as a sort of *mariage blanc*. Well, I'm virtually certain it was you who said it, not me. Anyway, I distinctly remember your suggesting that I was using my relationship with Laurence as a kind of alibi. And I said that we've become so close that having sex with anyone else would have seemed like infidelity. Which is true.

Zelda comes into it too, of course. If I decide to go to bed with Laurence, will she find out? Can I keep it from her? Should I keep it from her? Would knowing about it drive her into the arms of some lecherous spotty youth? You hinted once that I hadn't come to terms with the fact that sooner or later she's going to have sex. That as long as she was under-age I could rationalize my defence of her virginity as responsible parenthood, but that eventually she would become a young adult and decide to have sex with somebody and that there would be nothing I could do to prevent it and so I'd better accept it, but that I wouldn't be able to if I didn't have a satisfying sexual relationship of my own. So maybe this is a heaven-sent opportunity for me to become what you would consider a whole woman again, would you say?

Then at the back of my mind there's another consideration. The possibility of marriage. If Sally and Laurence divorce, it would be sort of logical for *us* to get hitched. No, I don't think so, otherwise he would have mentioned it when he was trying to seduce me the other night. That may be why he took me to Rules, actually, because the *padrona* at the Italian restaurant we usually go to is always singing the praises of matrimony, casting hints that Lorenzo ought to make an honest woman of me – she doesn't know he's married already. I think that secretly, or unconsciously, he still yearns to be reconciled with Sally. He complains bitterly about her behaviour, but I think if she agreed to give the marriage another try he'd scurry back to her with his tail wagging. I'm under no illusions about that. But if she's serious, if she really goes through with it, then I'm pretty sure he would want to marry again. I understand the way his mind works better than he does himself. He's the marrying type. And who would he marry but me?

I've been trying to imagine what it would be like. There might be some resistance from Zelda at first, but I think she would accept him eventually. It would be good for her to have an adult male in the house, good for both of us. A slightly rosy, soft-focus picture keeps coming into my mind of the three of us together in the kitchen, Laurence helping Zelda with her homework at the kitchen table, and me smiling benevolently from the Aga. We don't have an Aga, so I suppose that implies that I would want to move house. Whatever Sally got in a divorce settlement, Laurence would still be pretty well off. You know how it is once you start daydreaming, you think vaguely about the possibility of getting married again, and before you know where you are you're choosing the curtain material for your summer cottage in the Dordogne. But it has occurred to me that if Laurence were to pop the question one day, it would be as well to know already if we were, you know, physically compatible, don't you think? Or don't you?

I'm sure it wouldn't be a really bad experience, anyway. Laurence is very sweet and gentle. Saul was always so overbearing in bed. Do this, do that, do this faster, do that slower. He directed us as if we were making a porn movie. It wouldn't be like that with Laurence. He wouldn't expect me to do anything kinky – at least, I don't think he would. Yes, Karl, I know it's a subjective concept . . .

Well, did you see the story in *Public Interest*? The latest issue, it came out yesterday. No, I don't suppose you do, but everybody else I know reads it avidly. While pretending to despise it of course. It has a media gossip column called "O.C." It's short for "Off Camera." Somehow they got hold of the story of Laurence and the tennis coach. Yes. It seems that Laurence actually broke into the man's house in the middle of the night, hoping to surprise him in bed with Sally, and found him in bed with another man. Can you imagine? No, I had no idea until I read the rag myself. Harriet came into the office yesterday morning with the latest issue and laid it on the desk in front of me without a word, open at the "O.C." page. I practically *died* when I read it. Then I phoned Laurence but his agent had already told him. He says the story is essentially accurate, except that it has him holding a jemmy in his hand when in fact it was a pair of scissors. You may well ask. Apparently he was going to cut off the man's ponytail. Just as well the rag didn't get hold of *that* detail. The whole piece was cruelly mocking, needless to say. "Tubby Passmore, follically-challenged scribe of the Heartland sitcom 'The People Next Door', found himself recently in a situation funnier than anything he has invented . . ." That sort of thing. And there was a cartoon of him as Whatsisname, the Greek god who was married to Venus and found her in bed with Mars – Vulcan, that's the one. It was done in the style of an old painting, "after Titian", or Tintoretto, or somebody, it said underneath. With poor Lorenzo very fat and bald in a tunic and the tennis coach and his friend very naked, intertwined on the bed, and all of them looking very embarrassed. It was quite witty, actually, if you weren't personally involved. Laurence doesn't know how they got hold of the story. The tennis coach didn't press charges because he wants to keep his private life under wraps, so he obviously wasn't the source. Fortunately for him the piece doesn't give his name. But the police were involved, so probably one of them sold the story to *P.I.* Laurence is devastated. He feels the whole world is laughing at him. He daren't show his face in the Groucho or his tennis club or anywhere people know him. The cartoon seemed to cut particularly deep. He went off and looked up the story of Venus and Mars and Vulcan and discovered that Vulcan had a gammy leg. He seemed to think that was a diabolically clever touch, though I think it's just coincidence myself. Yes, Laurence has a bad knee, didn't I tell you before? He gets sudden piercing pains in the knee joint for no apparent reason. He's had surgery but it came back. I'm sure it's psychosomatic. I've asked him if he can remember any childhood trauma associated with his knee, but he says not. Which reminds me, the other day I remembered an accident that happened to me when I was a little girl . . .

Well, I've told Laurence I will. Sleep with him, of course. Yes. He's been in such depths of depression about the *Public Interest* story that I felt I must do something to cheer him up. No, of course it isn't my only motive. Yes, I probably had made my mind up already. Well, almost. The *P.I.* business just tipped the balance. So I'm taking two days off from work and we're making a long weekend of it. The weekend after next. Leaving Thursday evening, returning Monday afternoon. So I'll have to miss my sessions on the Friday and the Monday. Yes, I know I'll have to pay for them, Karl, I remember that little speech you made when I started. Well, if you detect an underlying note of hostility I daresay there is one. Considering I've hardly missed a session in three years, I should have thought you might have waived the fees on this occasion, after all it's a kind of emergency. To save Laurence's sanity. I expect he would pay the fees himself if I asked him, but you probably wouldn't approve of that, would you?

I don't know yet, Laurence is making the arrangements. I said anywhere, as long as it's abroad, and preferably warm. I felt we had to go away somewhere. *My* house is out of the question, of course, and it wouldn't feel right in his flat either, not the first time, anyway,. It's very small, and sometimes you feel the whole sordid West End is pressing against the walls and windows trying to get in: the restaurant smells, the traffic noise, the tourists and the dossers . . . Yes, I did ask him about that young vagrant. It seems he started camping out in Laurence's porch a few weeks ago. Laurence tried to get rid of him, but in a very Laurentian way ended up inviting him in for a cup of tea. Bad move. Then he gave him some money to find a bed for the night. *Very* bad move. Of course the youth came back soon afterwards, hoping for more *largesse*. Laurence claims he hasn't given him any, but he's certainly abandoned any attempt to get rid of him. I told him to get the police to move him on, but he wouldn't. "He isn't doing any harm," he said. "And he keeps the burglars away." Which I suppose is true, in a way. The flats are unoccupied most of the time. But I suspect Laurence lets him stay there because he's lonely. Laurence is lonely. I think he likes having somebody to greet as he goes in and out, somebody who doesn't read *Public Interest*. I had a dream last night about that cartoon, by the way. I was Venus, Saul was Mars and Laurence was Vulcan. What do you make of that?

Well, we're going to Tenerife, I'm afraid. Laurence went to a travel agent and said he wanted somewhere warm abroad but not long-haul and that's what they came up with. I wish I'd made the arrangements myself now. Laurence is not really up to it. Sally always used to book their holidays. The Canary Islands *sound* nice, the name I mean, but I've never heard a good word about them from anybody who's actually been there. Have you? *Been* there. No, I don't suppose you would. Harriet went to Gran Canaria once and said it was ghastly though she tried to deny it yesterday not to depress me. Perhaps Tenerife is nicer. Well, it's only a few days after all, and at least it will be warm.

I've told Zelda that I'm going on business – that Laurence is setting an episode of *TPND* in the Canaries, a story about a package holiday, and that we've got to cast some local people for it. It's a rather implausible alibi, actually. Not the idea of the Canaries as such, because they do film the occasional episode on location, and in fact Laurence is rather taken with the package holiday idea, imagining the

Springfields waking up in their hotel room on their first day, delighted at having escaped from the Davises for a fortnight, only to find them having breakfast on the next balcony, maybe he'll actually write it if there's another series – but that I would have to go there to cast it, especially at this stage, is unlikely, if you know anything about the business. Zelda accepted it with a suspicious lack of suspicion. I can't help feeling that she knows there's more to this trip than television, but I must say she's been as sweet as pie about it. She's been very helpful about advising me what clothes to take. It seems a queer reversal of roles, as if she's helping me plan my *trousseau*. I've arranged for Zelda to spend the weekend with her friend Serena, so that's put her in a good mood. And Serena's mother is a sensible woman so I don't have to worry about them getting up to mischief. All in all, I'm rather looking forward to the trip. I can do with a few days of *la dolce vita* in the sun.

Well, as a dirty weekend it was a disaster, to put it bluntly. It wasn't up to much as a holiday, either, at first. Have you ever been to Tenerife? No, you said, I remember. Well, given a choice between the Siberian salt mines and a four-star hotel in Playa de las Americas, I'd choose Siberia any day. Playa de las Americas is the name of the resort where we stayed. Laurence chose it from the travel agent's brochure because it's near the airport, and we were due to arrive late at night. Well, that seemed to make sense, but it turned out to be the most ghastly place you can imagine. *Playa* is the Spanish for beach, of course, but it doesn't have a beach, not what I'd call a beach. Just a strip of black mud. All the beaches in Tenerife are black, they look like photographic negatives. The whole island is essentially an enormous lump of coke, and the beaches are made of powdered coke. It's volcanic, you see. There's actually a huge great volcano in the middle of the island. Unfortunately it's not active, otherwise it might erupt and raze Playa de las Americas to the ground. Then it might be worth visiting, like Pompeii. Picturesque concrete ruins with tourists carbonized in the act of parading in wet tee-shirts and pouring *sangria*

down their throats.

Apparently only a few years ago it was just a tract of rocky barren shoreline, then some developers decided to build a resort there, and now it's Blackpool beside the Atlantic. There's a gaudy mainstreet called the Avenida Litoral that's always choked with traffic and lined with the most vulgar bars and cafés and discos you ever saw, emitting deafening music and flashing lights and greasy cooking smells all round the clock, and apart from that there's nothing except block after block of high-rise hotels and timeshare apartments. It's a concrete nightmare, with hardly any trees or grass.

We didn't realize how horrible it was immediately, because it was dark when we arrived, and the taxi from the airport took us by what seemed a suspiciously roundabout route to me, but on reflection perhaps the driver was trying to spare us the full impact of the Avenida Litoral on our very first evening. We didn't speak much during the drive, except to remark on how warm and humid the air was. There wasn't much else to talk about because we couldn't see anything until we reached the outskirts of Playa de las Americas, and then what we saw didn't excite comment: deserted building sites and immobile cranes and blank cliffs of apartment buildings with just a few windows lit up and *De Venta* signs outside, and then a long arterial road lined with hotels. Everything was made of ferro-concrete, bathed in a sickly low-wattage yellow light from the streetlamps, and everything looked as if it had been built, very cheaply, the week before last. I could sense Laurence slumping lower and lower in his corner of the back of the car. Both of us already knew we'd come to Pitsville, but we couldn't bring ourselves to admit it. A dreadful constraint had come over us since we landed: the conscious-ness of what we had come here to DO, and our anxiety that it should be a success, made us fearful of breathing a word of disappointment about the venue.

At least, I consoled myself, the hotel is bound to be all right. Four stars, Laurence had assured me. But four stars in Tenerife doesn't mean what it means in England. Four stars in Tenerife is your just-slightly-above-average package holiday hotel. I dread to think what a one-star hotel in Tenerife is like. My heart sank – and it was already somewhere near my knees – when we walked into the lobby and took in the vinyl-tiled floor and the plastic-covered sofas and the dusty rubber plants wilting under the fluorescent ceiling lights. Laurence checked in and we followed the porter up in the lift in silence. Our room was bare and functional, clean enough, but smelling strongly of disinfectant. There were twin beds. Laurence looked at them with dismay and told the porter he had ordered a double room. The porter said all the rooms in the hotel had twin beds. Laurence's shoulders slumped a few degrees lower. When the porter had gone he apologized dolefully and vowed vengeance on the travel agent when he got home. I said gamely that it didn't matter and opened the sliding windows to step out on to the little balcony. The swimming pool was spread out below – a random shape, like a blot in a Rorschach test, set among artificial rocks and palm trees. It was lit from under the water, and glowed a brilliant blue in the night. The pool was the only thing we had seen so far that was remotely romantic, but the effect was spoiled by the powerful public-baths odour of chlorine that rose from the water, and the thump of the bass notes from a disco still in deafening progress on the far side. I closed the shutters against the noise and the smell and turned on the air-conditioning. Laurence was dragging the beds together, making a frightful noise as the bed-legs squeaked on the tiled floor and revealing that the room wasn't quite as clean as it had first looked because there was dust behind and underneath the bedside cabinets, and discovering that the leads on the bedside lamps weren't long enough to stretch to the new positions, so we ended up putting the beds back where they were. I was secretly relieved because it made it easier to suggest that we went straight off to sleep. It was late and I was exhausted and I felt about as sexy as a sack of Brussels sprouts. I think Laurence felt much the same, because he agreed readily enough. We used the bathroom decorously, one after the other, and then kissed chastely and got into our respective beds. Immediately I could feel through the thin sheets that my mattress was plastic-covered. Can you believe it? I thought only babies and elderly incontinents were given plastic-covered mattresses. Not so – package tourists too. I can tell you're fidgeting, Karl – you want to know whether we DID IT in the end, or not, don't you? Well, you'll just have to be patient. This is my story and I'm going to tell it in my own way. Oh, is it? Already? Well, till tomorrow, then.

Well, what do you think has happened? You'll never guess. Sally has moved back into their house in Rummidge and announced that she's going to stay, living separate lives. Yes, that's what it's called, "separate lives", it's a recognized legal term. It means you share the marital home while divorce proceedings are going on, but you don't live together. Don't cohabit. Laurence got back home yesterday – he spent the night in his London flat – to find Sally waiting for him with a typewritten sheet of proposals about how they should share the house, who should have which bedroom, and what hours they should each have the use of the kitchen and what days use of the washing machine. Sally was very explicit about not doing Laurence's laundry. She'd already bagged the master bedroom with the *en suite* bathroom, and had a new lock fitted on the bedroom door. He found all his suits and shirts and things had been very carefully moved and neatly put away in the guestroom. He's absolutely furious, but his lawyer says there's nothing he can do about it. Sally chose her moment well. She'd asked if she could collect some clothes from the house last weekend, and he said yes, any time, because he'd be away, and she had her own keys to the house of course. But instead of taking her clothes away she moved back in, when he wasn't there to try and stop her. No, she doesn't know that he was in Tenerife with me. In fact, she *mustn't* know.

Oh yes, where was I? Well, nothing happened the first night, as I said, except that we slept in our separate beds – till quite late, in spite of the incontinents' mattresses, because we were both so tired. We ordered breakfast in our room. It wasn't encouraging: canned orange juice, limp cardboard-flavoured croissants, jam and marmalade in little plastic containers – the continuation of airline food by other means. We tried eating out on our little balcony, but were driven inside by the sun, which was already surprisingly hot. The balcony faced east and didn't have an awning or an umbrella. So we ate in the room with the shutters closed. Laurence re-read the *Evening*

Standard which he'd bought the day before in London. He offered to share it with me, but I felt his reading over breakfast at all was not quite *comme il faut*, in the circs. When I made a little joke about it, he frowned in a puzzled sort of way and said, "But I always read the paper over breakfast," as if it were a fundamental law of the universe. It's extraordinary how as soon as you have to share space with somebody, you begin to see them in a completely different light, and things about them irritate you which you never expected. It reminded me of my first months of married life. I remember how appalled I was by the way Saul used to leave the toilet, with streaks of shit in the bowl, as if nobody had ever explained to him what a toilet-brush was for, but of course it was years before I could bring myself to mention it. Sharing the toilet in Tenerife was a bit of a nightmare, too, as a matter of fact, but the less said about that the better.

We decided to spend our first morning lazing beside the – Oh, yes, you *would* want to know about that, wouldn't you? Well, the bathroom was windowless, as they usually are in modern hotels, and the extractor fan didn't seem to be working, at least it wasn't making any kind of noise, so I made sure I used the bathroom first after breakfast. It won't surprise you in the light of our previous discussions about toilet training that, how shall I put this, that when I manage to do number twos the stools are rather small, hard, dense little things. Are you sure you want me to go on? Well, the fact is that this Tenerife toilet simply couldn't cope with them. When I pulled the chain they danced about merrily in the water like little brown rubber balls, and refused to disappear. I kept pulling the chain and they just kept bobbing back to the surface. Talk about the return of the repressed. I got quite frantic. I just couldn't leave the bathroom until I got rid of them. I mean, it's not very pleasant to find someone else's turds floating in the toilet just as you're going to use it, and it certainly puts a damper on romance, wouldn't you say? I couldn't bring myself to apologize or explain to Laurence, or make a joke of it. You have to be married to somebody for at least five years to do that. What I really needed was a good bucket of water to slosh into the toilet bowl, but the only container in the bathroom was a waste-paper bin made of plastic latticework. Eventually I got rid of my little pellets by pushing them round the U-bend one by one with the toilet brush, but it's not an experience I would care to repeat.

Well, as I say, we decided to spend our first morning lazing beside the pool. But when we got down there, every lounger and every parasol was taken. People were sprawled all over the place, soaking up the skin cancer. Laurence is very fair-skinned and he has an extraordinary amount of hair on his torso which soaks up suntan lotion like blotting-paper but lets all the harmful rays through. I tan easily, but I've read so many bloodcurdling articles in women's magazines lately about the effect on your skin that now I'm terrified of exposing a single inch. The only bit of shade was a scruffy patch of grass right up against the wall of the hotel and miles from the poolside. We sat there uncomfortably on our towels for a while and I began to work up a grudge against the people who had claimed loungers by dumping their belongings on them and then buggered off for a late breakfast. I suggested to Laurence that we should requisition a pair of these unoccupied loungers, but he wouldn't. Men are such cowards about things like that. So I did it on my own. There were two loungers side by side under a palm tree with folded towels on them, so I just moved a towel from one lounger to the other and made myself comfortable. After about twenty minutes a woman came up and glared at me, but I pretended to be asleep and after a while she picked up both towels and went away, and Laurence came over rather sheepishly and took the other lounger.

This small victory put me in a good mood for a while, but it soon wore off. I'm not much of a swimmer and Laurence has to be careful because of his knee, and the pool which looked all right from the balcony was actually rather unpleasant to swim in, the wrong shape and overcrowded with boisterous children and reeking of chlorine. I read somewhere that it's not the chlorine itself that makes the smell but the chemical reaction with urine, so those kids must have been peeing in the water for all they were worth, and kept going back to the Coke machine to refuel. After we'd had our dip, there wasn't anything to do except read, and the loungers weren't really designed for reading, they were that cheap sort that you just can't adjust. The tubular steel frame bends upwards a bit at the end, but not enough to support your head at a comfortable reading height, so that you have to hold the book up in the air and after about five minutes your arms feel as if they're going to drop off. I'd brought A. S. Byatt's *Possession* with me, and Lorenzo had something by Kierkegaard, *Fear and Trembling* I think it was called, which didn't sound very appropriate to the occasion. You could tell what kind of people the other guests in the hotel were by what they were reading: Danielle Steel and Jeffrey Archer and the English tabloids which had arrived in the middle of the morning. Most of them looked to me like car workers from Luton but I didn't say so because Laurence has a thing about metropolitan snobbery.

Neither of us had brought swimming-towels from home, thinking that a four-star hotel would provide them, but this one didn't, and there was only one smallish bathtowel per person in the room, so we decided to go for a walk and do a little shopping. We needed sunhats, too, and rubber flip-flops, because the concrete round the pool was hot as hell by this time. So we got dressed again and out we went into the noonday sun, which was beating off the pavement and bouncing off the walls of the timeshare apartment buildings like laser beams. According to the hotel's streetplan we were only a couple of blocks from the sea, so we thought we'd walk in that direction and look for a beach shop, but there was no beach and no shop, just a low wall at the end of a cul-de-sac, and below it a narrow strip of what looked like wet cinders being churned by the sea. We turned round and walked back to the main road where there was a little shopping centre, built underground for some reason, a dismal tunnel of shops selling souvenir tat and tourist requisites. It seemed impossible to buy anything that hadn't got the word "Tenerife" blazoned on it, or a map of the island printed on it. Something in me rebelled against buying a towel I wouldn't be seen dead with once I got home, so we followed the main road into the centre of the town to see if we could find a wider selection. It turned out to be a walk of well over a mile, almost completely devoid of shade. At first it was boring, and then it got horrible. There was an especially horrible bit on the Avenida Litoral called the Veronicas, densely packed with bars and clubs and restaurants offering "*Paella* and chips" and "Beans on the toast".

Most of these places had disco music blaring into the street from the loudspeakers to attract customers, or else they were showing at maximum volume videos of old British sitcoms on wall-mounted television sets. It seemed to sum up the total vacuousness of Playa de las Americas as a holiday resort. Here were all these Brits, sitting on an extinct volcano in the middle of the sea two thousand miles from home, buying drinks so they could watch old episodes of *Porridge* and *Only Fools and Horses* and *It Ain't Half Hot, Mum.* "Did you ever see anything so pathetic?" I said to Laurence, and just then we came up to a café that was showing *The People Next Door.* It wasn't getting a very good audience rating, I'm afraid. In fact there were only four people in the place, a middle-aged couple looking like scalded giant crabs, and a pair of sulky young women with punk hairstyles. Of course, Laurence had to go in. I never knew a writer yet who could avert his eyes from a television screen when his own work is being shown. Laurence ordered a beer for himself and a g & t for me, and sat there mesmerized, with a fond smile on his face, like an infatuated parent watching a home movie of his infant son's first steps. I mean, nobody is more of a fan of Laurence's work than me, but I hadn't come all this way to sit in a bar and watch golden oldies from *The People Next Door.* There seemed to be only one thing to do, so I did it. I tossed back my g & t and ordered another one, a double. Laurence had another beer, and we shared a microwaved pizza, and then we had a brandy each with our coffee. Laurence suggested that we go back to the hotel for a *siesta.* In the taxi on the way back he put his arm round my shoulder, so I guessed what kind of a *siesta* he had in mind. Oh, is it time already? Till tomorrow then. Yes, of course I've heard of Scheherazade, what about her . . . ?

Well, it was lucky I was half-pissed, otherwise it would have been just too embarrassing for words. I mean, one either had to laugh or cry, and having a few drinks inside me, I laughed. I got the giggles as soon as I saw Laurence putting on his knee-support when we were preparing for our *siesta.* It's made of some spongy stretch fabric, like they use to make wet-suits, and it's bright red, with a hole in it for his kneecap to poke through. It looked particularly funny when he had nothing else on. He seemed rather surprised by my reaction. Apparently he always wears it when he and Sally have sex. When he put on an elasticated elbow bandage as well I nearly had hysterics. He explained that he'd had a recurrence of tennis elbow lately and didn't want to take any chances. I wondered if he was going to put on anything else, a pair of shin-pads perhaps, or a cycling helmet. Actually that wouldn't have been a bad idea, because the bed was so narrow he was in some danger of falling on the floor during foreplay. This involved a lot of licking and nuzzling on his part. I just closed my eyes and let him browse. It was quite nice, though ticklish, and I kept giggling when I think I was supposed to moan. Then it appeared he wanted me to straddle him while he lay on his back, because of his knee, and that he expected me to handle the trickiest bit of the proceedings myself, so to speak. I knew an actress once who told me that she had a recurrent dream of being on stage without knowing the play she was in, having to guess her lines and moves from what the other actors were saying and doing. I felt as if I was understudying Sally under a similar handicap. I don't know what she makes of the part, but I felt like a cross between a hooker and an orthopaedic nurse. However, I went through with it gamely, and jigged up and down a bit on top of him until he gave a groan and I rolled off. But it turned out that he was groaning because he couldn't come. "Perhaps you had a little too much to drink at lunch, darling," I said. "Perhaps," he said gloomily. "Was it all right for you?" Of course I said it was wonderful, though to be honest I've had more pleasure from a nice hot bath at the end of a long day, or a really top-class Belgian chocolate with a cup of freshly-ground Colombian coffee. Frankly.

Well, we slept for an hour or so after that, and then we showered and had a cup of tea on our balcony, which was in the shade by now, and read our books until it was time to go down and have a drink in the bar before dinner. We weren't talking to each other much because everything that came into our heads, my head anyway, was something we dared not say, about how awful the place was and what a disaster the whole trip was turning out to be, knowing there were three days still to go. We were on *demi-pension* terms at the hotel. They gave us little coupons when we checked in that you had to surrender as you went into the dining-room, a vast barrack of a place with about four hundred people shovelling food into themselves for all they were worth as if they were eating against the clock in some kind of TV gameshow. You helped yourself to *hors d'oeuvres* and desserts and they brought the main course to your table. There was a choice of chicken *chasseur* and fish fried in breadcrumbs. It was about BBC canteen standard, edible but dull. We had a bottle of red wine but I drank most of it because Laurence was girding himself to perform later. It didn't make for a very relaxing evening. We went out for a stroll and walked down to the shore again to watch the waves churning the wet cinders. Then there seemed nothing else to do except go to bed. It was either that or go back into town and what the Veronicas was like at night was all too easy to imagine. So we made love again and the same thing happened. He had an erection, but he couldn't, what's the word, emit, no matter how hard I jigged up and down. He was frightfully upset about it, though I said it didn't matter, in fact I was delighted, I never did like the sensation of slowly leaking into one's nightie afterwards. He said, "There must be something wrong with me." I said, "It's not you, it's this ghastly hotel and the dreadful place it's in, it's enough to make anyone impotent."

It was the first time I'd expressed my real feelings since we got there. He took it like a slap in the face. "I'm sorry," he said stiffly. "I did my best." "Of course you did, *chéri*," I said. "I'm not blaming you, it was the stupid travel agent. But why don't we move somewhere nicer?" "We can't," he said. "I paid in advance." He seemed to think we were under a contractual obligation to stay the full four nights. It took me quite a while to get him to see that we could well afford – at least *he* could – to forfeit the cost of the remaining two. It was as if the ghosts of his parents had risen up to forbid such a scandalous waste of money. "Anyway," he said, "there's only one five-star hotel in Playa de las Americas, and it's full. The travel agent tried it." "I should think it *is* full," I said. "Anybody who booked into a five-star hotel in Playa de las Americas would probably barricade themselves in their room and never come out. But I suppose there are five-star hotels in other places in Tenerife?" "How would we get there?" Laurence said. "Hire a car, my sweet," I said, thinking to myself, this is like talking to a child.

Well, by taking command of the arrangements, I got us out of that hellhole immediately after breakfast next morning. Laurence would have liked to sneak out of the hotel without telling them, but we had to check out to pay for some extras so I had the satisfaction of telling the reception staff why we were going, not that they cared. We hired an air-conditioned car from Avis and drove up the coast to the capital, Santa Cruz. You never saw such a barren, boring landscape in your life, like the surface of the moon in a heatwave. But Santa Cruz is quite a nice little town, slightly scruffy but civilized. There's one really classy hotel, with a pool in a beautiful shady garden, and a decent restaurant. Robert Maxwell had his last meal there, actually, before he threw himself off his yacht. If he had been in Playa de las Americas there wouldn't have been all that speculation about why he did it.

Well, we had a very pleasant weekend in Santa Cruz. The hotel gave us a huge high-ceilinged suite, with a marble bathroom with a window that opened, and a vast double bed in which we cuddled and slept like babies. We didn't do anything else in it. I said to Laurence, don't let's risk another *débâcle*, my dear, now that things are going so nicely, and he seemed happy to agree. The truth is that I had decided I wasn't going to marry Laurence even if he asked me, and that I didn't want a sexual relationship with him, or indeed anyone else. I decided I could do without sex, thankyou very much, for the rest of my life. I realized what a fool I'd been, going on and on analysing my relationship with Saul, wondering what went wrong, why I didn't satisfy him, when it was what satisfied *me* that was important, and putting my body at the disposal of another man after all these years wasn't going to do that. I hope Laurence and I can go back to our chaste, companionable relationship, but if we can't, *tant pis*.

So really, it wasn't such a disaster after all, my dirty weekend. I really think I see things more clearly than ever before, as a result of it. I see that there's nothing *wrong* with me. I can accept myself for what I am. I don't *need* sex. I don't *need* a man. And I don't need *you*, Karl, not any more. Yes. This is the end of the analysis. You told me I'd know. And I do. This is our last session, Karl. Yes. This is the big goodbye. I'm cured.

✳ ✳ Louise ✳ ✳

STELLA? . . . IT´S LOUISE . . . Hi! . . . Oh fine. How about you? . . . Oh. I *thought* you sounded depressed on the answerphone . . . Yeah, look I'm sorry I didn't get back to you before, but I've been so busy you wouldn't believe . . . Meetings meetings meetings . . . Yeah, it's the same movie, only now it's called *Switchback*. You know what they say about Hollywood, everything takes either five minutes or five years, and this baby looks like it's gonna be a five-year pain in the ass. Anyway, why are you in the pits? . . . Uh huh . . . Uh huh . . . I kinda guessed . . . Listen, sweetheart, you won't thank me for saying this right now, but honestly you're better off without him . . . Sure I never liked him, but was I right or was I right? Didn't I say, never trust a man who wears a gold cross round his neck? . . . He exploited you, honey . . . As soon as you'd like paid for his root-canal work, and the acting lessons, he dumped you . . . Well, of course you feel that way now, but you'll get over it, trust me, I've been there. Wait a minute, I got another call. Don't go away . . .

Hi. That was Nick, calling from New York, just to say hallo . . . Yeah, just for a few days. He's got this client who's opening a play off-Broadway. Say, Stella, you want me to take your mind off your troubles with this really weird thing that happened to me yesterday? . . . OK, kick off your shoes and put your feet up and lend me your ears . . .

It was about six o'clock yesterday evening. I'd just come in from a meeting at Global Artists, and showered and changed and was wondering whether to fix myself something to eat or call Sushi Express, when the phone rings and I hear this British voice saying, "Hallo, Louise, this is Laurence Passmore." Laurence Passmore?

Like the name means nothing to me, and I don't recognize the voice. So I say, "Oh yes?" in a neutral kinda way, and the guy gives a nervous little giggle and says, "I suppose this is what disc-jockeys call a blast from the past." "Do I know you?" I say, and there's like a pained silence for about a minute and then he says, "The people next door? Four years ago?" and the penny drops. This is the guy who created the original British version of *Who's Next Door?* Yeah. It's called *The People Next Door* over there. When I was working for Mediamax they bought the rights, and he came over from England as like a consultant on the pilot, and I was assigned to look after him. But like the name "Laurence" hadn't rung a bell. "Didn't you have a different name, then?" I asked him. "Tubby," he said. "Tubby Passmore, of course," I said. He came into sharper focus at once: fiftyish, balding, stocky build. He was a nice guy. Kinda shy, but nice. "I never liked that nickname, to tell you the truth," he said, "but I seem to be stuck with it." "Hey," I said, "Nice of you to call. What business brings you to L.A.?" "Well, I'm not here on business, actually," he said. Brits say "actually" an awful lot, have you noticed? "Vacation?" I said, thinking he must be on his way to Hawaii or somewhere. "A sort of vacation," he said, and then: "I was wondering whether you would be free for dinner this evening."

Well, ninety-nine times out of a hundred, it would have been outta the question. Nick and I were out every night last week. *Every night.* But as it happened Nick was away and I had nothing planned and I thought, what the hell, why not? I knew there would be nothing below the line on this date . . . Because once, when he was here before, I made a play for him and he backed off . . . Yeah . . . Well, I'd just split up with Jed and I was kinda lonely. So was he. But he turned me down, in the nicest possible way, because he loved his wife . . . Yeah, there are such men, Stella. In England there are anyway . . . Well, when I said yes to dinner he was like ecstatic. He said he was staying at the Beverly Wilshire and I thought to myself, anybody who is paying for himself at the Beverly Wilshire is my kind of date, and I was just wondering whether I had enough pull with the maître d' at Morton's to get us a table at short notice when he said, "I'd like to go to that fish restaurant down by the beach at Venice where we went before." Well,

I couldn't remember what restaurant he was talking about, and he couldn't remember the name, but he said he would recognize it if he saw it, so I did the decent thing and offered to drive us down there. Venice isn't my favourite place, but I figured maybe it was just as well I wasn't seen at Morton's with an obscure English TV writer – I mean it's not like this guy is Tom Stoppard or Christopher Hampton or anything.

So I put on something casual and drove down to Beverly Hills to pick up Tubby Passmore at the appointed time. He was hovering by the doors, so I didn't get out of the car, just honked and waved. It took him about ten minutes to notice me. He looked just as I remembered him, perhaps a few pounds heavier, with a big potato-shaped face and a fringe of baby-fine hair hanging down over the collar of his jacket. Nice smile. But I couldn't imagine why I'd ever wanted to get in the sack with him. He got into the car and I said "Welcome back to L.A." and stuck out my hand just as he made a lunge at my cheek, so there was a little confusion but we laughed it off. He said, almost accusingly, "You've changed your car," and I laughed and said, "I should think so. I must have had at least five cars since you were here . . ." No, it's a Mercedes. I traded in the BMW for a white Mercedes with red leather interior. It looks great. Just a minute, I got another call . . .

Fuckit fuckit fuckit . . . Sorry, just thinking aloud. That was Lou Renwick at Global Artists. Our star won't sign unless his buddy directs, and the buddy's last picture was a crock of shit. These people are such assholes. Never mind, I'm gonna hang in there. I have points in this one . . . Yeah, I optioned the book . . . Where was I? Oh, yeah, well, we drive out to Venice, and walk up and down by the beach, weaving between the joggers and surfers and roller-skaters and frisbee-throwers and dog-walkers, looking for this restaurant, and eventually he thinks he's found it, but it has the wrong name and it isn't even a regular fish restaurant but a Thai place. However when we ask inside they say they've only been in business for about a year, so we figure it probably is the right one. In fact the look of it stirs a faint memory in me too.

Tubby wanted to eat outside, though it was kinda cool and I was underdressed for *al fresco* dining . . . Oh, a sleeveless top, and that black cotton skirt I bought in your shop last year. With the gold buttons? That's the one. Tubby said there'd been a wonderful sunset when we ate in Venice before, but yesterday was overcast you remember, so there was no particular reason to sit outside, but he more or less insisted. The waiter asked if we'd like anything to drink and Tubby looked at me and said, "Whiskey sour, yes?" and I laughed and said I didn't drink cocktails any more, I'd just have a mineral water, and he looked strangely put out. "You *will* drink some wine?" he said anxiously, and I said maybe a glass. He ordered a bottle of Napa Valley Chardonnay, which struck me as a tad economical for a guy who was shacked up at the Beverly Wilshire, but I didn't say anything.

All the way out to Venice I'd been jabbering away about *Switchback* because my head was full of it and I guess I was like showing off a bit, letting him know I'm a pukka movie producer now, not just a TV executive. So when we'd ordered our food I figured it was time to let him have his turn. "So what's been happening to you, lately?" I said. Well, it was like the moment in a disaster movie when somebody casually opens a door in a ship and a million tons of seawater knocks them off their feet. He gave a sigh that was like almost a groan, and proceeded to pour out a tale of unrelieved woe. He said his wife wanted to divorce him and his TV company wanted to take his show away from him and he had a chronic knee injury that wouldn't heal. Seems his wife walked out without warning, and then walked right back in again two weeks later to share the house under some special arrangement called "separate lives". Like they not only have separate bedrooms but they have to take turns to use the kitchen and the washing machine. Apparently the British divorce courts are very strict on laundry. Yeah. If she knowingly washed his socks it could screw up her petition, he says. Not that there's any risk of that. They don't even speak to each other when they meet on the stairs. They send each other notes, like North and South Korea. No. He suspects there's somebody, but she says not, she just doesn't want to be married to him any more. Their kids are grown up . . . She's some kind of college professor. He said it just blew him away when she told him . . . Nearly thirty years – can you believe it? I didn't know there was anybody left in the entire world, outside of a Sunset Home, who'd been married to the same person for thirty years. What seemed to bug him more than anything was that all that time he'd never cheated on her once. "Not that I haven't been tempted," he said. "Well, you know that, Louise." And then he gave me this long, soulful look out of his pale blue, bloodshot eyes.

I tell you, I broke out in goosebumps all over, and it wasn't because of the breeze coming off the ocean. I suddenly realized what this date was all *about*. I realized that it was in this very restaurant that I had tried to seduce him all those years ago . . . Yeah! The whole thing came flooding back into my head, like a flashback sequence in an old *film noir*. We'd had a nice dinner and a bottle of wine and I'd snuck out to the Ladies' room between courses to do some blow . . . Yeah, I was doing drugs in those days . . . Always carried a stash in my handbag, Colombia's favourite cash crop . . . But Tubby wasn't into that sorta stuff. He thought when people offered him coke at a party they meant a drink. He thought being loaded meant having a lotta money. Even the idea of smoking pot freaked him out, so I never let on I was snorting the hard stuff. I wonder he never guessed, the way I used to laugh at his little English quips. Anyway, there I was, feeling high and horny, and there was this nice clean Englishman sitting opposite who obviously fancied me but was too decent or too timid to take the initiative, so I took it myself. Apparently I said I'd like to take him home and fuck his brains out . . . Yeah. He quoted the exact words to me. They were engraved on his memory. You see what I mean? This whole date was like a reprise of the one all those years ago. The Venice restaurant, the table outside, the Napa Valley Chardonnay . . . That was why he was so upset that I'd changed my car and the fish restaurant had turned into a Thai restaurant and I didn't drink whiskey sours any more. That was why he made us sit outside. He was trying to recreate the exact circumstances of that evening four years ago as far as possible in every detail. Every detail except one . . . Exactly! Now that his wife had walked out on him he wanted to take me up on my offer to fuck him. He'd flown all the way from England specifically for that purpose. It didn't seem to have occurred to him that my circumstances might have changed in the meantime, not to mention my mood. I guess in his head I was forever sitting at that table beside the ocean, gazing wistfully out to sea and waiting for him to reappear, released from his matrimonial vows, to sweep me into his arms. Wait a minute, I got another call . . .

Hi. How did we exist before Call Waiting? That was Gloria Fawn's agent. She passed on *Switchback*. So what's new, I don't suppose he even showed her the script. Well, fuck 'em . . . Oh yeah, so like I was saying, it really freaked me out to think that this guy had flown six thousand miles to change his mind about a proposition that was four years old. It was like you said to someone, pass the salt, and four years later he shows up with a salt cellar. Well, I figured I'd better set him straight as soon as possible, so when he tried to top up my wine glass I put my hand over it and said I was cutting down because I was trying to conceive and if I succeeded I'd have to give up completely . . . Yeah. I thought I'd better go for it. The old biological clock is ticking away. Nick is keen . . . Well, thanks, Stella. I'm relying on you for some chic maternity wear . . . Anyway, this announcement stopped Tubby Passmore in his tracks, but he still didn't get it. I think for a moment he thought I wanted to have a child by *him* . . . Well, you can laugh, but this guy is unreal, I'm telling you. So then I explained I was with Nick and he like crumpled in front of my eyes. I thought he was going to start crying into his shrimp and lemon-grass soup. I said to him, "What's the matter?" though I knew very well what was the matter, and he quoted Kierkegaard at me . . . Yeah, Kierkegaard the philosopher. Not Kierkegaard the smorgasbord. Heh heh. He said, "The most dreadful thing that can happen to a man is to become ridiculous in his own eyes in a matter of essential importance." Yeah. That was it. I wrote it down afterwards.

Well, as you can imagine, the evening never recovered. I ate all the food and he drank all the wine, and I did all the talking. I couldn't help feeling sorry for the guy, so I told him about Prozac. Believe it or not, he'd never heard of it. He shook his head and said he never took tranquillizers. "I had a bad experience with Valium, once," he said. Valium! I mean this guy is pharmaceutically in the Stone Age. I explained to him that Prozac wasn't a tranquillizer, or an ordinary anti-depressant, but an entirely new wonder-drug. I gave him a real sales pitch . . . Sure, honey, don't you? Doesn't everybody in Hollywood? . . . Well, Nick and I swear by it. Sure. We have a chart thumbtacked to the kitchen wall telling us when to take our little green and white capsules . . . Well, it changed my life . . . No, I wasn't depressed, you don't have to be depressed to take it. It does wonders for your self-confidence. Like I'd never have had the courage to resign from Mediamax without Prozac . . . Oh, yeah, I read that story in *Time* magazine but I never experienced anything like that . . . You should try it, really, Stella . . . Well, there is one side effect, I have to admit: it makes it harder to have an orgasm. But as you haven't got a lover at the moment, honey, what have you got to lose? No, of course not, Stella, but Prozac could tide you over . . . Well, fine, honey, we all have our own ways of coping with adversity . . . Oh, I drove him back to the Beverly Wilshire and he fell asleep in the car, either from booze or jet-lag or disappointment or a combination of all of them. The bell captain opened the door of the car, and I gave Tubby a kiss on the cheek, and pushed him out and watched him stumble into the lobby. I felt kinda sorry for him, but what could I do? . . . I don't know, I suppose he'll go back to London . . . Would you really? . . . Well, I don't know. I could ask him, if you like . . . Are you sure this is a good idea, Stella? . . . Well, if you say so. You realize he's not exactly England's answer to Warren Beatty, don't you? . . . Oh he's clean all right, you don't have to worry about that. I'll call him right now and tell him I've got this gorgeous unattached girlfriend who's dying to meet him . . . Speak to you soon.

✳ ✳ Ollie ✳ ✳

OH, HALLO GEORGE, how goes it in Current Affairs? Good good. Oh, surviving, just about. Thanks, I need one. Draught Bass, please. Oh, make it a pint. Ta. Yeah, one of those mornings. My secretary is off sick, our fax machine is on the blink, the BBC have snapped up a Canadian soap I had my eye on, and some cunt of a solicitor is suing us because he has the same name as the bent lawyer in that episode of *Motorway Patrol* – did you see it? No, the week before last. Ah, thank you, Gracie. And a packet of crisps, smoky bacon flavour. No, no, George, let me pay for the crisps. Well, if you insist. Thanks, Gracie. Cheers, George. Ah. I needed that. What? Oh, I suppose we'll buy him off with a few grand, it's cheaper in the long run. Shall we sit down? Over there, in the corner. I like to have my back to the wall in this place, less chance of being overheard. Yeah, but it doesn't mean they're not out to get you. Ha ha. Here we are. Have a crisp. If I could open the bloody packet. They should make something to open these plastic packets with, something like a cigar-cutter you could carry in your pocket, I've a good mind to patent it, you could make a fortune. Oops! See what I mean? Either it won't open at all or it splits down the middle and spills the whole shoot in your lap. Have one, anyway. I saw a bloke in a pub the other day, I swear to God he went ten rounds with a packet of Walton's Crisps. Broke a fingernail trying to tear the packet open, damn near broke a tooth trying to bite through it, finished up in desperation setting fire to it with his cigarette-lighter. I kid you not. I think he was trying to melt the corner of the packet but it went up in flames, whoosh, singed the bloke's eyebrows and stank the place out with the smell of burning chip fat. Honest. Now if we put that on television we wouldn't dare say Walton's Crisps, they'd be down on us like a ton of bricks, well fair enough I suppose, but it's coming to something if you have to check the name of every bloody solicitor in the country before a script can be cleared. Nice drop of beer, this.

Yeah, it's been one of those mornings all right. To top it all, I had a meeting with Tubby Passmore. A basket case if ever there was one. Well, he's giving me a lot of grief at the moment. I suppose you know about Debbie Radcliffe? Oh, I thought Dave Treece would've put you in the picture. Well, keep it under your hat, but she wants to leave *The People Next Door*. Yeah. You bet it's serious. Her contract runs out at the end of the current series, and she won't renew at any price, the stupid cow. I dunno, she says she wants to go back on the stage. Is she? Well, I wouldn't know, I never go to the theatre if I can help it. Can't stand it. It's like being strapped to your seat in front of a telly with only one channel. And you can't talk, you can't eat, you can't drink, you can't go out for a piss, you can't even cross your legs because there's no room. And they charge you twenty quid for the privilege. Anyway, she's adamant, so we've got to write her part out of the show. It's still getting great ratings, as you know. Absolutely. At least one more series, probably two or three. So we asked Tubby to rewrite the last episode or two of the present series so as to get rid of Priscilla, you know, Debbie's part, to make way for a new woman in Edward's life in the next series, see? We gave Tubby some ideas, but he wouldn't buy any of 'em. He said the only way was to literally kill her off. In a car accident or on the operating table or something. Yeah, unbelievable, isn't it? We'd have the whole fucking country crying its eyes out. Debbie's got to go in a way that leaves the viewers feeling good, stands to reason. I mean, nobody's pretending it's easy. But if there's one thing I've learned from twenty-seven years in television, it's that *there's always a solution*. I don't care what the problem is, whether it's scripts or casting or locations or budget, there's always a solution – if you think hard enough. The trouble is most people are too fucking idle to make the effort. Only they call it integrity. Tubby said he'd rather see the show come to an end than compromise the integrity of his characters. Did you ever hear such bullshit? This is sitcom we're talking about, not fucking Ibsen. I'm afraid he's getting delusions of grandeur, the latest is he wants to write a – Oh, well, fortunately we discovered that under our contract we can hire another writer to take over if Tubby declines to write another series. Yeah. Of course, we don't *want* to. We'd prefer Tubby to do the job himself. Oh, fuck his moral rights, George! The point is that he could do the job better than anybody else, if he would only make the effort. Well, it's a standoff at the moment. He has five weeks to come up with an acceptable idea to ease Debbie out of the show, or else we get another writer. I dunno, I'm not very hopeful. He doesn't seem to be living in the real world these days. His private life is in deep shit. You know his wife's left him? Yeah. First I knew about it was when he called me up one night, at home, very late. He sounded a bit pissed – you know, breathing heavily and long pauses between words. He said he had an idea for writing Debbie out of the show. "Suppose," he said, "suppose Priscilla just walks out on Edward without warning? Suppose she just tells him in the last episode that she doesn't want to stay married to him? There isn't any other man. She just doesn't love him any more. She doesn't even like him any more. She says living with him is like living with a zombie. So she's decided to leave him." I said to him, "Don't be ridiculous, Tubby. There has to be more motivation than that. Nobody will believe it." He said, "Won't they?" and put the phone down. Next thing I hear is that his wife has walked out on him. You saw that piece in *Public Interest*? Well, that was the point, wasn't it? There was no other man. The bloke was gay. Looks as if Tubby's wife walked out because, like he said, she just didn't want to be married to him any more. He's taken it very hard. Of course, anybody would. Will you have another? Same again? What was it, the Club red? Oh, the Saint Emilion, right. You think it's worth the extra, do you? No, no, you shall have the Saint Emilion, George. I don't know anything about wine, never pretended to. Small or large? I think I'll just have a half myself, work to do this afternoon. Oh, right. I'm going to get myself a pie, what about you? Chicken and mushroom, right.

There we are. One large glass of Saint Emilion. They'll call out when the pies are ready. We're nineteen. I was in a pub the other day where they give you playing-cards instead of these cloakroom tickets.

The girl at the bar calls out "Queen of Hearts" or "Ten of Spades" or whatever. Clever idea, I thought. I'm always losing these fiddly little things and forgetting my number. Your pie was one twenty-five by the way. Oh, ta. That's all the change I've got, I'll have to owe you the ten pee, alright? Cheers. Yes, well, he made an appointment to see me this morning. I thought perhaps he'd had a brilliant new idea about how to get rid of Debbie's part, but no such luck. Instead it turns out that he wants to try his hand at straight drama. Yeah. You won't believe this, George. He wants to do a series about a geezer called Kikkiguard. Oh, is that how you pronounce it? You've heard of him, then? Yeah, that's right, a Danish philosopher. What else do you know about him? Well, I didn't even know that much, till Tubby told me. I was gobsmacked, (a), that he was interested in the subject, and (b), that he thought we would be. I said to him, very slowly, "You want to write a drama series for Heartland Television about a Danish philosopher?" I mean, if he'd said it was about a Danish pastry it wouldn't have sounded any dafter. He just nodded his head. I managed not to laugh in his face. I've been through this before with comedy writers. They all get ideas above their station eventually. They want to do without a studio audience, or write about social problems. The other week Tubby had a reference to abortion in his script. I ask you – abortion in a sitcom! You have to either humour them or tell 'em to get stuffed. I still have hopes Tubby may see sense about *The People Next Door*, so I humoured him. I said, "OK, Tubby, pitch it to me. What's the story?"

Well, there was no story, to speak of. This, whatsisname, Kierkegaard bloke, was the son of a wealthy merchant in Copenhagen, we're in what, the Victorian period, early Victorian. The old man was a gloomy, guilt-ridden old bugger, who brought his children up accordingly. They were very strict Protestants. When he was a young man Kierkegaard kicked against the traces a bit. "They think he may have gone to a brothel once," Tubby said. "Just once?" I said. "He felt very guilty about it," Tubby said. "It was probably his only sexual experience. He got engaged to a girl called Regine later, but he broke it off." "Why?" I said. "He didn't think they'd be happy," he said. "He suffered a lot from depression, like his father." "I can see this

173

isn't going to be a comedy series, Tubby," I said. "No," he said, without cracking a smile. "It's a very sad story. After he broke off the engagement, nobody could understand why, he went off to Berlin for a while and wrote a book called *Either/Or*. He came back to Copenhagen, secretly hoping for a reconciliation with Regine, but found she'd got engaged to another man." He stopped and looked at me soulfully, as if this was the biggest tragedy in the history of the world. "I see," I said, after a while. "And what did he do then?" "He wrote a lot of books," Tubby said. "He was qualified to be a minister, but he didn't agree with making religion a kind of career. Luckily he'd inherited a substantial fortune from his father." "It sounds like the only bit of luck he did have," I said. Oh, did she say nineteen, George? Over here, my love, we're nineteen. One steak and kidney and one chicken and mushroom, that's it. Lovely. Thanks. That was quick. Microwaved of course. You want to be careful with your first bite, they can burn your bloody tongue these pies. They're hotter inside than they look. Mm, not bad. What's yours like? Good. So. Tubby Passmore, yes. I asked him if Kierkegaard was famous in his lifetime. "No," said Tubby. "His books were considered peculiar and obscure. He was ahead of his time. He was the founder of existentialism. He reacted against the all-encompassing idealism of Hegel." "This doesn't sound like the stuff of prime-time commercial television, Tubby," I said. "I would only glance at the books," he said. "The main emphasis would be on Kierkegaard's love for Regine. He was never able to forget her, even after she got married." "What happened?" I said. "Did they have an affair?" He looked quite shocked at the suggestion. "No, no," he said. "He saw her around Copenhagen – it was a small place in those days – but they never spoke. Once they came face to face in church and he thought she was going to say something, but she didn't, and neither did he. It would make a great scene," he said. "Tremendous emotion, without a word spoken. Just close-ups. And music, of course." Apparently that was the nearest they ever came to getting together again. When Kierkegaard asked the husband's permission to write to her, he refused. "But he always loved her," Tubby said. "He left her everything in his will, though there wasn't much left when he died." I asked him what he died of. "An infection of the lungs," he said. "But in my opinion it was really a broken heart. He had lost the will to live. Nobody really understood his suffering. When he was on his deathbed, his uncle said that there was nothing wrong with him that couldn't be cured by straightening his shoulders. He was only forty-eight when he died." I asked what else this geezer did apart from writing books. The answer was, nothing very much, except take carriage drives in the country. I said, "Where's your jeopardy, Tubby? Where's your suspense?" He looked rather taken aback. "This isn't a thriller," he said. "But you've got to have some kind of threat to your hero," I said. "Well," he said, "there was a time when a satirical magazine started to attack him. That caused him a lot of pain. They made fun of his trousers." "His trousers?" I said. I tell you George, I had a struggle to keep a straight face through all this. "Yes, they printed caricatures of him with one leg of his trousers shorter than the other." Well, as soon as he said "caricature" I remembered that cartoon in *Public Interest*, and it all clicked into place. Yeah, you got it in one. The guy's developed some sort of strange identification with this Kierkegaard bloke. It's all connected with his marital problems. But I didn't let on. I just recapped the story as he'd pitched it to me. "OK, Tubby, let me see if I've got this right," I said. "There's this Danish philosopher, nineteenth century, who gets engaged to a bird called Regine, breaks off the engagement for reasons nobody understands, she marries another guy, they never speak to each other again, he lives for another twenty-odd years writing books nobody understands, then he dies, and a hundred years later he's hailed as the father of existentialism. Do you really think there's a TV drama series there?" He thought for a moment, and then he said, "Perhaps it would be better as a one-off." "Much better," I said. "But of course, that's not my territory. You'd have to talk to Alec Woosnam about it." I thought that was a rather clever move, sending him off to bend Alec's ear about Kierkegaard. No, of course Alec won't buy it, do me a favour! But he'll string Tubby along if I ask him to. Get him to write a treatment, talk to people at Channel Four, go through the motions. If we indulge him on Kierkegaard, he just might play ball over Debbie's part in *The People Next Door*. No, he doesn't have a script editor. We had one on the first series, but we never felt the need after that. Tubby turns in his scripts direct to me and Hal, and we work on them together. I don't think he'd take kindly to having a script editor again. But it's a thought, George, definitely a thought. Another one? Well I shouldn't really, but this pie's given me a terrible thirst, must be oversalted. Oh, you might as well make it a pint. Ta.

* * Samantha * *

HETTY, DARLING, HOW ARE YOU? Omigod, I don't need to ask, do I? Poor you. Your jaw is swollen out like a pumpkin. I expect you're surprised to see me, but I phoned and your flatmate told me you were here, and as I was passing I thought I'd pop in even though it's not a proper visiting hour. I don't think they really mind, do they? Can't you talk at all? Oh dear, what a shame. I was looking forward to a nice chat. Well, you'll just have to nod and shake your head and use your eyes, darling, like a good television actress. I bought you some grapes, where shall I put them – on here? They've been washed, so you can help yourself. No? Can't eat *anything*? What a curse wisdom teeth are. Badly impacted was it? *Two* of them? No wonder you look so poorly. Mmm . . . these are rather delicious. No pips. You're sure that if I peeled one for you, you wouldn't . . . ? No? Oh well, all right. Does it hurt terribly? I suppose they pumped you full of painkillers. You *must* demand more as soon as they wear off. Hospitals are terribly mean about that, they think pain is improving. Well, I'm going to have to make all the conversational running, aren't I? Fortunately I've got lots to talk about. The fact is I just had the most bizarre weekend and I'm dying to tell somebody all about it who isn't connected with work. I've got a new job at Heartland, you see, a proper job. Script editor. I started last week. Basically it means you read the writer's first drafts and make comments and suggestions and generally act as a buffer between him and the producer or director. It's the first stepping-stone to writing or producing oneself. You know I've been chaperoning that little brat Mark Harrington in *The People Next Door*? Well now I'm working with the writer, Tubby Passmore. Well, you may pull a face, Hetty, but thirteen million people can't be wrong, not in television they can't. Tubby asked for me himself. I got to know him through the chaperoning – we would meet at rehearsals, in the canteen and so on. He was always perfectly pleasant, but rather shy. I had him down as a herbivore. I always say there are two kinds of men, the herbivores and the carnivores. It's something about the way they look at you. Because I've got these tits I get a lot of looks. I know you used to say at school that you'd kill for them, Hetty, but frankly I'd give anything for a figure like yours. No, honestly. Clothes hang so much better on a flat-chested figure. Not that you're *completely* flat, darling, but you know what I mean. Anyway, some men just run their eyes appreciatively over you as if you were a statue or something, those are the herbivores, they just want to browse, and others look at you as if they would like to tear your clothes off and sink their teeth into you, those are the carnivores. Jake Endicott is a carnivore. He's my agent. Tubby's agent too, as it happens. And Ollie Silvers, the producer of *The People Next Door* – he's another carnivore. When I talked to Tubby one day about my writing ambitions, he suggested I asked Ollie to give me some scripts to read and report on, you know, unsolicited ones, the slush-pile. So I went to see him wearing my cream linen suit without a blouse and all through the interview I could see he was trying to look down my front to see what I was wearing under the jacket, if anything. I walked out of his office with a pile of scripts. I can see you disapprove, Hetty, but I'm completely postfeminist about this, I'm afraid. I think it's a great mistake for women to make all this fuss about sexual harassment. It's like unilateral disarmament. In a man's world we've got to use all the wiles and weapons we've got. I don't think you should shake your head as hard as that, darling, your stitches might come undone. It may be different in the Civil Service, for all I know. Anyway, as I say, I thought Tubby was a confirmed herbivore. If we were sitting at the same table in the canteen or the bar, he would chat to me in a fatherly sort of way, but he never made a pass or anything approaching one. He's old enough to *be* my father, actually. On the corpulent side, as the name implies. Balding. A big egg-shaped head. He always reminds me of the pictures of Humpty Dumpty in a copy of *Alice in Wonderland* I had as a child. I cultivated him purely out of self-interest, I don't mind admitting. Goodness I must stop eating your grapes. Just one more then.

Well, as I was saying, Tubby always seemed completely immune to my feminine charms, in fact I was slightly piqued by his lack of interest, but then his attitude suddenly changed. It was after his marriage broke up – oh, I forgot to mention, his wife left him a month or two ago. There were lots of rumours – that she'd come out as a lesbian or gone to live in an ashram or that she found him in bed with her tennis coach. All wildly off the mark, as I found out later. We didn't see much of him for some weeks. But then he turned up at rehearsals one day, in London, a grotty place in Pimlico that Heartland use, and immediately made a set at me. Without any warning. I remember seeing him push through the swing doors and stand at the threshold looking round the room until he spotted me, and then he came straight over and plonked himself down beside me, hardly bothering to say hallo to Hal Lipkin, that's the director, or any of the cast. Deborah Radcliffe smiled at him but he walked straight past her without a glance, which didn't please her very much. I could see her looking daggers at us out of the corner of my eye. Tubby looked wrecked. Bloodshot eyes. Unshaven. Crumpled clothes. It turned out that he'd just flown in from L.A., and come straight to the rehearsal rooms from Heathrow. I said that it showed great devotion to duty and he stared at me as if he didn't understand what I was talking about, so I said, "I mean, attending rehearsals when you must be exhausted." He said, "Oh, bugger the rehearsals," and in the next breath asked me out to dinner that very evening. Well, I was supposed to be going to see a film with James, but I didn't let that stop me. I mean if a famous, well, famous in television terms, writer asks a nobody like me out to dinner, you go. If you don't want to stay a nobody all your life, you go. That's the way it works, darling, believe me. Incidentally, James thinks I spent this last weekend visiting my grandmother in Torquay, just remember that if you should happen to see him, won't you?

So Tubby took me to this little Italian restaurant in Soho, Gabrielli's. I'd never been there before, but he was obviously a regular. They received him with open arms as if he was a long-lost son

– all except the owner's wife, who was giving me the evil eye for some reason. Tubby was basking in all the attention until the woman came over to put some breadsticks on the table and said, looking at me, "Is this your daughter, then, Signor Passmore?" and Tubby went very red and said, no I wasn't, and then this woman said, "And 'ow is Signora Amy?" and Tubby went even redder and said he didn't know, he hadn't seen her for a while, and this interfering old bitch gave a smug sort of smile and disappeared into the kitchen. Tubby looked like Humpty Dumpty after he'd fallen off the wall. He muttered that he sometimes ate there with Amy Porteus, the casting director for *The People Next Door*. I've met her a couple of times. She's a dumpy little brunette, in her forties I should say, always slightly overdressed and reeking of perfume. I said in a bantering tone that he obviously wasn't in the habit of bringing young women there anyway, and he said dourly no, he wasn't, and asked if I would like a drink. I had a Campari and soda and he had just a mineral water. I told him about my idea for a soap, and he nodded his head and said it sounded interesting, but he didn't really seem to be attending. What darling, what don't you understand? Mime it. Oh! Not a soup, darling, a *soap*, you know like *Eastenders*, only what I have in mind is more like *Westenders*. I asked him if he'd been to L.A. on business, and he said, "Partly," but he didn't explain what the other part was. They served us quite a decent meal and we had a bottle of Chianti that was supposed to be very special but he drank hardly any of it, he said because of his jet-lag, he was afraid he might fall asleep. Over the dessert he steered the conversation rather clumsily towards sex. "You've no idea," he said, "how repressed we were about sex when I was young. Nice girls simply didn't. So nice boys couldn't, most of the time. The country was full of twenty-five-year-old virgins, many of them male. I suppose you find that difficult to credit. I suppose you wouldn't think twice about having sex with someone you liked, would you?" So I said – what? Oh, right, I'll speak more quietly. These beds are rather close together, aren't they? What's she in for? Mime it. Appendix? No. Hysterectomy? Really? Well mimed, darling. You know, there's the makings of a rather good parlour game here.

So I said it would depend on whether I really liked the person, and he looked at me soulfully and said, "Do you really like *me*, Samantha?" Well, I was a bit taken aback at the speed with which we'd reached this point. It was like being taken for a ride in one of those GTi's that look like sedate family saloons and do nought to sixty in about three seconds flat. So I laughed my tinkle-of-tiny-bells laugh and said it sounded like a leading question. He looked very despondent and said, "So you don't, then?" I said on the contrary I liked him very much but I thought he was exhausted and jet-lagged and didn't quite know what he was doing or saying and I didn't want to take advantage of him. Well he pondered that for a moment, frowning to himself, and I thought, you've blown it, Samantha, but to my relief his Humpty-Dumpty face broke into a smile, and he said, "You're absolutely right. What about some dessert? They do a rather good tiramisu here." He poured himself a full glass of wine, knocked it back as if making up for lost time, and ordered another bottle. He talked about football for the rest of the meal, which I can't say is my favourite conversational topic, but fortunately we'd nearly finished. He put me in a cab outside the restaurant, gave the driver a tenner for the fare, and kissed me on the cheek like an uncle. Ah, here comes the tea-trolley. Can you drink from a cup? Oh good. I was going to say that if you couldn't, I'd drink it for you. Shall I take your biscuits, then? Pity to waste them. Mmm, custard creams, my favourite. What a shame you can't have any.

So where was I? Oh yes, well a few days later I got a message to go and see Ollie Silvers at Heartland's London office. I spent a whole morning agonizing over what to wear, and what to leave off, but in the event it turned out to be quite unnecessary because he offered me the job straightaway. Hal Lipkin was with him. They sat at each end of a long sofa, and took turns to shoot remarks at me. "You may have noticed that Mr Passmore's been acting rather strangely lately," Ollie said. "His marriage is on the rocks," Hal said. "He's taken it very hard," said Ollie. "We're concerned about him," said Hal. "We're also concerned about the show," said Ollie. "We'd like to do another series," said Hal. "But a snag has cropped up," said Ollie. I can't tell you what the snag is, darling, because they swore me to secrecy. I know you don't mix with media journalists, but nevertheless. I shouldn't even have told you there *is* a problem. It's all terribly hush-hush. Basically they want Tubby to rewrite the last scripts of the present series to open the way for a new development of the story in the next series. Putting a new sit in the sitcom, you might say. "But Tubby doesn't seem to be able to concentrate his mind on the problem," said Hal. "So we think he needs a script editor," said Ollie. "A kind of minder-cum-dramaturge," said Hal. "Somebody to keep his nose to the grindstone and his arse to the typing chair," said Ollie. "We put it to Tubby," said Hal. "And he asked for you," said Ollie. They hadn't given me a chance to say a word all this time – I was just looking from one to the other like a spectator at Wimbledon. But now they paused as if inviting a response. I said I was flattered. "You should be," Ollie said. "We would have preferred somebody with more experience," said Hal. "But those reports you wrote for me were very sharp," said Ollie. "And you must know the show inside-out by now, watching rehearsals all this time," said Hal. I said, "Yes. I expect that's why Mr Passmore suggested me for the job." Ollie gave me a carnivorous leer and said, "Yes, I expect it is." He didn't know, of course, that Tubby had taken me out to dinner and propositioned me just a few days before.

Naturally I assumed that this new development was a rather more subtle second attempt at seduction on Tubby's part. So I wasn't surprised when almost the first thing he did when I started work was invite me to go away with him for a weekend. I called him from my new office, or rather from my new desk in the office I share with two other girls. We're all script editors – for some reason script editors nearly always *are* women. Like midwives. I said, "Hallo, this is Samantha, I suppose you know I'm your new script editor," and he said, "Yes, I'm very pleased you took the job." I didn't let on that I knew he'd asked for me. I said, "When shall we meet?" and he said, "Come to Copenhagen with me next weekend." I said, "What for?" and he said, "I've got to do some research." I said, "What has Copenhagen got to do with *The People Next Door*?" and he said, "Nothing. I'm writing a film about Kierkegaard, didn't Ollie tell you?" I said that no, Ollie hadn't made that entirely clear, but I was of course happy to help him in any way I could. He said he would book flights and hotel rooms and get back to me about the details. I noticed the plural "rooms" with approval. I mean, I understood what I was letting myself in for, but a girl has her pride. You needn't look at me like that, Hetty.

As soon as he was off the phone, I called Ollie and told him Tubby seemed to think I had been assigned to help him develop a film about Kierkegaard, not *The People Next Door*. You do know who Kierke-gaard is, don't you darling, or rather was? Of course you do, you did PPE at Oxford. Sorry. I have to admit he was just a name to me before the weekend, but now I know more about him than I really want to. Not the most obvious subject for a TV film, you must agree. By the way, in case you think I've got his name wrong, that's the way they pronounce it in Danish, Kierke*gawd*, as in "Oh my Gawd," which is what Ollie said when I told him Tubby wanted to take me to Copenhagen and why. I heard him sighing and muttering to himself, and the click of a lighter as he lit a cigar, and then he said, "Look, Samantha my love, go along with it, humour him, do the Kierkegaard bit, go through the motions, but just keep reminding him at every opportunity about *The People Next Door*, OK?" I said, OK.

Have you ever been to Copenhagen? Neither had I till this weekend. It's very nice, but just a little dull. Very clean, very quiet – hardly any traffic at all compared to London. Apparently they had the very first pedestrianized shopping precinct in Europe. It seems to sum the Danes up, somehow. They're terribly green and energy-conscious. We stayed at a luxury hotel but the heat was turned down to a point that was almost uncomfortable, and in the room there was a little card asking you to help conserve the earth's resources by cutting down on unnecessary laundry. The card is red on one side and green on the other, and if you leave it green side up they only change your sheets every third day, and they don't change the towels at all unless you leave them on the bathroom floor. Which is all very sensible and responsible but just a teeny bit of a downer. I mean, I'm as green as the next woman at home, for instance I always buy my shampoo in biodegradable bottles, but one of the pleasures of staying in a luxury hotel is sleeping in crisp new sheets every night and using a fresh towel every time you take a shower. I'm afraid I left my card red side up all through the weekend and avoided the chambermaid's eye if I met her in the corridor.

We flew from Heathrow on Friday evening – Club Class, nothing but the best my dear, a hot meal with real knives and forks and as much booze as you could down in the two hours. I drank rather a lot of champagne and probably talked too much in consequence, at least the woman in the row in front kept turning round to glare at me, but Tubby seemed quite amused. By the time we got to the hotel, though, I was beginning to feel rather tired and I asked if he'd mind if I went straight to bed. He looked a bit disappointed, but then said gallantly, no, not at all, it was a good idea, he'd do the same and then we'd be fresh for the morning. So we parted very decorously in the corridor outside my room, under the eyes of the porter. I fell into bed and passed out.

The next day was bright and sunny, ideal for exploring Copenhagen on foot. Tubby had never been there before either. He wanted to get the feel of the place, and also look for possible locations. There's no shortage of well-preserved eighteenth- and early-nineteenth-century buildings, but the problem is modern traffic signs and street furniture. And there's a picturesque dock called Nyhavn, with genuine old ships moored in it, but the genuine old buildings overlooking it have been converted into trendy restaurants and a tourist hotel. "We'll probably end up shooting the film somewhere else entirely," Tubby said, "somewhere on the Baltic or the Black Sea." We had a smorgasbord lunch at a place on the Nyhavn and then went to the City Museum where they have a Kierkegaard room.

Tubby was very excited about this in anticipation, but it turned out to be a bit of an anticlimax, at least I thought so. A smallish room for a museum, about thirty feet by fifteen, with a few sticks of furniture and half a dozen glass cases displaying bits and pieces connected with Kierkegaard – his pipes, his magnifying glass, some pictures and old books. You wouldn't have given them a second glance in an antique shop, but Tubby pored over them as if they were sacred relics. He was especially interested in a portrait of Kierkegaard's fiancée, Regine. He was engaged to her for about a year and then broke it off, but regretted it ever after according to Tubby. The portrait was a small oil painting of a young woman in a low-cut green dress with a dark green shawl round her shoulders. He stared at the picture for about five minutes without blinking. "She looks like you," he said eventually. "Do you think so?" I said. She had dark brown eyes and hair to match, so I suppose he meant she had big tits. Actually, to be fair, there was something about the mouth and chin that was not unlike me. She also looked as if she was quite fun – there was a suspicion of a smile on her lips and a twinkle in her eye. Which was more than you could say for Kierkegaard, to judge from the drawing of him that was in the same case: a skinny, crooked, long-nosed old fogey in a stovepipe hat and carrying a furled umbrella like a gun under his arm. Tubby said it was a caricature done for a newspaper when Kierkegaard was in his forties, and pointed out another drawing done by a friend when he was a young man where he looked quite handsome, but somehow you didn't believe in it as much as in the caricature. The crooked back was because he suffered from curvature of the spine. He used to prefer to write standing up at a high desk, which was one of the pieces of furniture in the room. Tubby stood at it himself for a moment, making some notes in a reporter's notebook he'd brought with him, and a little German girl who had come into the room with her parents stared at him as he was writing and said to her father, *"Ist das Herr Kierkegaard?"* I laughed, because anyone who looked less like Kierkegaard would be hard to imagine. Tubby heard me laugh and looked round. "What is it?" he asked. When I explained, he blushed with pleasure. He's absolutely obsessed with Kierkegaard, especially his relationship with this girl Regine. There was another piece of furniture in the room, at the opposite end to the desk, a sort of cupboard about five feet high. Tubby found out from the museum brochure that Kierkegaard had it made especially to keep his mementos of Regine in. Apparently she pleaded with him not to break off their engagement, and said she would be glad to be allowed to spend the rest of her life with him even if she had to live in a little cupboard, the silly cow. "That's why it hasn't got any shelves inside," Tubby said. "So she would just fit inside." I swear his eyes filled with tears as he read it out of the brochure.

We had dinner that evening in the hotel restaurant: plain cuisine but excellent ingredients, mostly fish, beautifully cooked. I had baked turbot. Am I boring you, darling? Oh, good, I just thought I saw your eyes close for a moment. Well all through the meal I kept trying to turn the conversation on to the topic of *The People Next Door* and he kept dragging it back to Kierkegaard and Regine. I really began to get thoroughly sick of the subject. I was also hankering to see a bit of Copenhagen nightlife after dinner. I mean it has the reputation of being a very liberated city, with lots of sex shops and video parlours and live sex shows and suchlike. I hadn't seen a trace of anything like that so far, but I presumed they must be somewhere. I wanted to do a little research of my own, for my *Westenders* project. But when I threw out some hints to this effect, Tubby seemed strangely slow on the uptake, almost as if he didn't *want* to understand me. I thought perhaps he had plans for a private live sex show with just the two of us, but no. At about ten-fifteen he yawned and said it had been a long day and perhaps it was time to turn in. Well I was astonished – and, I have to admit, a little piqued. I mean it wasn't that I positively fancied him, but I expected him to show a little more evidence of fancying me. I couldn't believe that he had brought me all the way to Copenhagen just to talk about Kierkegaard.

The next morning was Sunday, and Tubby insisted we went to church, because that was what Kierkegaard would have done. He was very religious apparently, in an eccentric sort of way. So we went to this incredibly dreary Lutheran service, all in Danish of course, which made it even more boring than chapel at school, if you can believe that. And after lunch we went to see Kierkegaard's tomb. He's buried in a cemetery about two miles from the city centre. His name actually means "churchyard" in Danish, so as Tubby observed we were visiting Kierkegaard in the *kierkegaard*, which was about the only joke of the afternoon. It was quite a nice place, with flower beds and trees planted to make avenues, and according to the guidebook the Copenhagen people use it like a park in fine weather and have picnics there and everything, but the afternoon we were there it was raining. We had some trouble locating the grave, and when we did find it it was a bit of a let-down, like the room in the museum. It's a little patch of ground enclosed by an iron railing, with a monument to Kierkegaard's father in the middle and two stone tablets propped up against it with the names of his wife and children including Søren carved on them. That's Kierkegaard's first name, Søren, with one of those funny crossed-out Danish os. But you probably knew that already, didn't you? Sorry, darling. We stood in the rain for a few minutes in respectful silence. Tubby took his hat off, and the rain ran off his bald pate and down his face and off the end of his nose and chin. We didn't have an umbrella, and I soon began to feel rather damp and uncomfortable, but Tubby insisted on looking for Regine's grave. He'd read somewhere that she was buried in the same churchyard. There was a kind of index to all the graves on a noticeboard near the entrance, but Tubby couldn't remember Regine's married name so he had to look through columns and columns until he came to a Regine Schlegel. "That's her!" he cried, and charged off to look for the plot – 58D or whatever it was – only he couldn't find it. The plots are not very well marked, and there was nobody around to ask because it was Sunday and pouring with rain, and I was getting more and more fed up squelching about in sopping wet clothes and shoes with water dripping off the trees and running down the back of my neck and I said I wanted to go back to the hotel, and he said rather crossly, all right, go, and gave me some money to take a taxi, so I did. I had a long hot bath and used *two* clean towels and threw them both on the floor and had tea from room service and a miniature bottle of cherry brandy from the minibar, and began to feel in a better humour. Tubby came back about two hours later, soaked to the skin. And despondent because he hadn't managed to find Regine's grave and there wouldn't be time to go back the next morning and ask somebody because we had to catch an early plane.

The evening followed the same pattern as before: dinner in the hotel restaurant followed by a proposal from Tubby that we retire early – to our own rooms. I couldn't believe it. I began to wonder if there was something wrong with me, like bad breath, but I checked as I was getting ready for bed and it was sweet and fresh. Then I took off all my clothes and looked at myself in the mirror and I couldn't see anything wrong there either, in fact I thought to myself that if I were a man I wouldn't be able to keep my hands off me, if you follow. I was beginning to feel rather randy, to be honest, out of sheer frustration, and not a *bit* sleepy, so I decided to watch an adult movie on the hotel's in-house video channel. I got a half-bottle of champagne out of the minibar and sat me down in front of the telly in my dressing-gown and tuned in. *Well*, my dear, what a surprise I got! I don't know if you've ever watched one of those movies in a British hotel. No? Well, you haven't missed anything, believe me. I used to watch them occasionally when I stayed at the Rummidge Post House on the chaperoning job, just for a giggle. One of my duties was to make sure the little Harrington brat couldn't watch them. The hotel reception used to put a bar on the set in his room, much to his disgust. In fact, those films have nothing more explicit in them than many pro-grammes you see on network television, indeed less so, the only difference being that the so-called adult movies consist *entirely* of sex scenes, and look incredibly cheap, and are incredibly badly acted and have incredibly silly story lines. And they're extremely short and full of clumsy jump-cuts because all the really raunchy bits have been censored for hotel distribution. Well I was hoping that the Danish ones might be a bit more daring, but I wasn't prepared for hard-core pornography, which was what I got. I switched on in the middle of the film and there were two men and a girl naked on a bed together. Both the men had absolutely enormous erections and one was being sucked off voraciously by the girl, as if her life depended on it, while the other one was doing her from behind, you know, doggy-fashion. I couldn't believe my –

What? Oh. I'm sorry, but I wasn't talking to you. Well, I can't help it if your hearing is unusually good. If you don't want to eavesdrop on other people's private conversations, why don't you put those earphones on and listen to the radio?

Hmmph! What a cheek. I mean, I'm sorry about her hysterectomy and everything, but she didn't have to be so stroppy. I wasn't talking all that loud, was I? Oh, all right, Hetty, I'll move my chair nearer to the bed and murmur in your ear, is that better? So there were these three people in the film sucking and fucking away like mad and after about ten minutes they all had the most tremendous orgasms – no really, they did, Hetty, honestly. At least the men did, because they pulled their willies out to show the semen squirting all over the place. The girl rubbed it into her cheeks as if it was skincare lotion. Are you feeling all right, darling? You're looking a little pale. The time? It's . . . good heavens, half past three. I must go soon, but I'll just finish the story. Well the film went on in the same style. The next scene showed two naked girls, one black and one white, taking turns to lick each other, but they weren't real lesbians because the two men from the previous scene peeped through the window at them and came in and it turned into another orgy. Well, I don't mind telling you that by this time I was quite wet with excitement and one big hot flush from head to toe. I've never felt so randy in my entire life. I was *beside* myself. I would have fucked *anybody* at that moment, never mind the nice clean English scriptwriter in the next room who had, I thought, brought me to Copenhagen specifically for that purpose. It could only be shyness, I decided, that was holding him back. I should phone him up and tell him about the amazing video I had found on the hotel telly and invite him to come and watch it with me. I reckoned that a few minutes' exposure to the movie, sitting next to me in my dressing-gown with not a stitch on underneath, would soon see off his shyness. I should perhaps explain that I had polished off the half-bottle of champers by this time and was feeling pretty reckless as well as randy. He took quite a time to answer the phone, so I said I hoped I hadn't woken him up. He said, no, he had been watching television and had just turned down the volume before picking up the phone. Only he hadn't turned it down quite enough. I recognized the tinkly disco music and faint moaning and groaning in the background. There's not very much dialogue in these films. Not much work for a script editor, I should think. I giggled and said, "I think you must be watching the same movie as me." He mumbled something, sounding terribly embarrassed, and I said, "Wouldn't it be more fun if we watched it together? Why don't you come along to my room?" There was a silence and then he said, "I don't think that would be a good idea," and I said, "Why not?" and he said, "I just don't." Well, we sparred like that for a while, and then I got impatient and said, "For God's sake, what's the matter with you? Last week in that Italian restaurant you made it very obvious that you fancied me, and now that I'm practically throwing myself at you, you hang back. What did you bring me here for if you don't want to sleep with me?" There was another pause and then he said, "You're quite right, that was why I asked you to come, but when I got here I found I couldn't do it." I asked him why not. He said, "Because of Kierkegaard." I thought this was terribly funny and said, "We won't tell him." He said, "No, I'm serious. Perhaps on Friday evening, if you hadn't been so tired . . ." "You mean pissed," I said. "Well, whatever," he said. "But as I started to explore Copenhagen and think about Kierke-gaard, and especially when we went to the room in the museum, it was as if I felt his presence, like a spirit or a good angel, saying, 'Don't exploit this young girl.' He had a thing about young girls, you see." "But I'm dying to be exploited," I said. "Come and exploit me, in any position you like. Look at the screen, now. Would you like that? I'll do it with you." I won't tell you what it was, darling, you might be shocked. "You don't know what you're saying," he said. "You'd regret it in the morning." "No I wouldn't," I said. "Anyway, why are you watching this filthy movie if you're so virtuous? Would Kierke-gaard approve of that?" "Probably not," he said, "but I'm not doing any harm to anyone else." "Tubby," I said, putting on my most seductive voice, "I want you. I need you. Now. Come. Take me." He gave a sort of groan and said, "I can't. I've just taken a towel from the bathroom." It was a second or two before the penny dropped. I said, "Well, I hope you leave it on the floor so the next guest doesn't get it," and slammed the phone down in a temper. I turned off the telly, swallowed a sleeping tablet and a miniature of scotch and passed out. When I woke up the next morning I saw the funny side of it, but Tubby couldn't face me. He left a message at Reception with my air ticket, saying that he'd gone back to the cemetery to look for Regine's grave and would be returning by a later plane. So what do you think of that for a story? Oh, I forgot, you can't speak. Never mind, I've got to dash anyway. Oh, dear, I've eaten all your grapes. Listen, I'll come back tomorrow and bring you some more. No? You think you'll be out by then? Really? Well, I'll give you a ring at home, then. Goodbye, darling. I *have* enjoyed our chat.

✳ ✳ Sally ✳ ✳

BEFORE WE START, Dr Marples, I'd like to establish the agenda of this meeting, so there's no misunderstanding. I agreed to see you because I want Tubby to accept that our marriage is over. I'd like to help you to help him to come to terms with that fact. I'm not interested in trying to negotiate a reconciliation. I hope that's quite clear. That's why I said in my letter that I would only meet you on my own. We're beyond marriage counselling now, well beyond it. Quite sure. Yes, we tried it before – didn't Tubby tell you? About four or five years ago. I can't remember her name. It was somebody in Relate. After a few weeks with both of us, she recommended that Tubby should have psychotherapy for his depression. He told you about *that*, I presume? Yes, Dr Wilson. Well, he saw him for about six months, and he seemed better for a while. Our relationship improved, we didn't bother to go back to Relate. But within a year he was worse than ever. I decided that he would never be any different, and that I'd better organize my life so that I was less affected by his moods. I threw myself into work. God knows there was no shortage of things to do. Teaching, research, administration – committees, working parties, syllabus design and suchlike. My colleagues complain about the paperwork in higher education these days, but I rather enjoy mastering it. I have to face the fact that I'm never going to do earth-shaking research, I started too late, but I'm good at admin. My field is psycholinguistics, language acquisition in young children. I have published the odd paper. Oh does he? Well, he doesn't understand a word of it, so he's easily impressed. He's not really an intellectual, Tubby. I mean, he has a wonderful ear for speech, obviously, but he can't think abstractly about it. It's all intuitive with him.

So I threw myself into work. I didn't consider divorce at that stage. I was brought up very conventionally, my father was a C of E vicar, and for me there's always been a certain stigma attached to divorce. It's an admission of failure in a way, and I don't like to fail at anything I set out to do. I knew that to other people – friends, relatives, even our children – our marriage must have seemed very successful. It had lasted so long without any visible upsets, and our standard of living soared with Tubby's success. We had the big house in Hollywell, the flat in London, the two cars, holidays in luxury hotels, and so on. The children were through university and happily settled in adult life. I think most people we knew envied us. It would have been galling – it *has* been galling these last few weeks – to admit that the outward appearance was an illusion. I suppose too I shrank from the bitterness and anger that seem inseparable from divorce. We'd seen a fair amount of it among our friends. I thought, if I occupied myself fully at work, I could put up with Tubby's moodiness at home. I used to bring work home as well, as extra protection. It was a wall I could retreat behind. I thought that as long as we enjoyed doing *some* things together, like tennis, and golf, and were still having sex regularly, that would be enough to sustain the marriage. Yes, I read an article once that made a great impression on me, saying that marriage breakdown in the fifties – I mean between couples in their fifties, not the nineteen-fifties – was nearly always associated with one partner's loss of interest in sex. So I worked hard at that. Well, if he didn't initiate it, I did. After sport was always a good time, when we were both feeling good from the exercise. I thought that sport and sex and a comfortable lifestyle would be enough to get us through the Difficult Fifties – that's what the article was called, it comes back to me now, "The Difficult Fifties."

Well, I was wrong. It wasn't enough. Tubby's knee injury didn't help, of course. It separated us as regards sport – he couldn't compete with me any more – and it put a damper on sex. He wouldn't risk it for weeks, months, after the operation, and even then he always seemed more concerned about protecting his knee than having a good time. Then when it became apparent that the operation hadn't been a success, he fell into a deeper depression than ever. This past year he's been impossible to live with, completely wrapped up in himself, not listening to a word anybody says to him. Well, I suppose he must listen to his agent and his producer and so on, he could hardly function otherwise, but he didn't listen to what *I* was saying to him. You've no idea how infuriating it is when you've been talking to someone for minutes on end, and they've been nodding and making phatic noises, and then you realize they haven't taken in a single word you've said. You feel such a fool. It's as if you were teaching a class while writing on the blackboard and then you turn round to find that they've all quietly left the room and you've been talking to yourself for you don't know how long. The last straw was when I told him Jane had rung up to tell us she was pregnant – Jane's our daughter – and that she and her partner were going to get married, and he just grunted, "Oh yes? Good," and went on reading bloody Kierkegaard. And, you'd hardly credit this, even when I keyed myself up to tell him that I'd had enough and wanted to separate he didn't listen to what I was saying at first.

Oh, I'm afraid I can't take this Kierkegaard thing seriously. I told you, Tubby's not an intellectual. It's just a fad, something to impress other people with. Perhaps me. Perhaps himself. A device to dignify his petty little depressions as existentialist *Angst*. No, I've not read any myself, but I know roughly what he's about. My father used to quote him occasionally in his sermons. Not any more, but of course we had to when we were children, every Sunday, morning and evening. I think that's why I find Tubby's obsession with Kierkegaard rather absurd. Tubby had a totally secular upbringing, knows absolutely nothing about religion, whereas I've been all through it and out the other side. It was painful, I can tell you. For years I concealed it from my father, that I no longer believed. I think it broke his heart when I finally came clean. Perhaps I waited too long to tell him what I really felt, as I did with Tubby about our marriage.

Well, I could say that it was none of your business, couldn't I? But no, there isn't anyone else. I suppose Tubby's been unloading his paranoid fantasies on you. You know about his ridiculous suspicion of my tennis coach? Poor man, I haven't been able to look him in the eye since, let alone have any lessons. I really don't know why Tubby went berserk with jealousy. Well, yes I do, it was because he just couldn't accept that the problem in our marriage was himself. It had to be somebody else's fault, mine, or some phantom lover of mine. It would have been so much better for all concerned if he could have faced facts calmly. All I wanted was an amicable separation and a reasonable financial settlement. It was all his fault that it's escalated into a battle, with lawyers and injunctions and separate lives in the house and so on. He could still avoid a lot of unnecessary pain and expense by simply agreeing to the divorce, and making a fair settlement. No, he's not. He's at his London flat, I suppose. I don't know, I haven't seen him in the last few weeks. The bills keep coming in for the house, for gas and electricity and so on, and I forward them to him but he doesn't pay them, so I've had to pay some myself to avoid having the services turned off, which isn't fair. He very meanly drew out most of the money in our joint bank account the day after I left the house, and all the deposit accounts are in his name only, so I'm having to meet all my expenses out of my monthly salary, including lawyers' fees. I'm really having a struggle to make ends meet.

No, I don't hate him, in spite of the way he's behaved. I feel sorry for him. But there's nothing I can do for him any more. He must work out his own salvation. I have to study my own needs. I'm not a hard-hearted woman. Tubby pretends that I am, but I'm not. It hasn't been easy for me, all this stuff with lawyers and so on. But having screwed myself up to take this step, I've got to see it through. This is my last chance to forge an independent life for myself. I'm just young enough to do it, I think. A few years younger than Tubby, yes.

It was such a long time ago. We were two different people, really. I was doing teaching practice in a Junior School in Leeds and he turned up there one day with a theatre group that toured schools. Five young people, would-be actors who couldn't get Equity cards, had formed a company on a shoestring and were going around the country in an old Dormobile, towing a trailer full of props. They did stripped-down versions of Shakespeare for secondary schools and dramatized fairy-tales for juniors. They weren't very good, to be honest, but they made up in enthusiasm for what they lacked in technique. After they'd done their show in the school hall and the kids had gone home, we invited them into the staff-room for tea and biscuits. I thought they were terribly bohemian and adventurous. My own life had been so respectable and sheltered in comparison. I did English at Royal Holloway, a women's college of London University marooned in the Surrey stockbroker belt. My parents insisted on my going to a single-sex college if I wasn't going to live at home, and I failed my Oxbridge entrance exams, so it was Royal Holloway or Leeds University. I was determined to get away from home, but I came back to do my PGCE in Leeds, to save money. I chose junior-school teaching – not many graduates did – because I didn't fancy trying to control the roughs and toughs in the state comprehensives that were replacing the kind of grammar school I had gone to myself. In those days I wore pastel twin-sets and pleated skirts to mid-calf and sensible shoes and hardly any make-up. These young actors wore scruffy dark sweaters with holes in them, and had long greasy hair and smoked a lot. There were three boys and two girls and they all slept together in the Dormobile most of the time, Tubby told me, to save money. One night he parked it on top of a hill and didn't put the handbrake on properly, and it slowly trundled down the hill until it ran up against a police station. He told the story in such a droll way, he made me laugh aloud. That's what first attracted me to him, I think – the way he could make me laugh spontaneously, joyously. Laughing at home tended to be politely restrained or – amongst us children – mocking and sarcastic. With Tubby, I laughed before I realized I was laughing. If I were to try and put into a nutshell what has been wrong with our marriage for the last few years – why I didn't get anything out of it, any happiness, any glad-to-be-alive feeling – I'd say it was because he didn't make me laugh any more. Ironic, really, isn't it, when you think that every week he makes millions of people laugh at his television show. Not me, I'm afraid. I find it totally unfunny.

Anyway, that first day, he rather cheekily asked for my phone number and I rather recklessly gave it to him. I met him several times while he and his friends were in the Leeds area, in the evenings in pubs. Pubs! I had hardly ever been in a pub before I met Tubby. I didn't invite him home. I knew my parents wouldn't approve of him, though they would never admit why – because he was unkempt and under-educated and had a Cockney accent. I suppose you know he left school at sixteen? Well he did, with just a couple of O-Levels. He went to grammar school after the Eleven-Plus but never fitted in, was always bottom of the class. I don't know – a combination of temperament, bad teaching and lack of support at home, I suppose. His parents were working-class – very decent, but not very education-conscious. Anyway, Tubby left school as soon as he could, and went to work as an office-boy for a theatrical impresario, that's how he got interested in the stage. After National Service he went to drama school and tried to make it as an actor. That was when I met him. He played all the comic parts in the Dormobile troupe's repertory, and wrote the scripts for their fairy-tale adaptations. He discovered in due course that he was better at writing than acting. We kept in touch after the troupe left Yorkshire. That summer I went up to Edinburgh, where they were doing a show in the Festival – the Fringe, of course – and distributed fliers and programmes, without telling my parents what I was up to. Then, much against their wishes, I applied for my first teaching job in London, knowing Tubby was based there. The Dormobile company had gone bust, and he was scraping a living as a temporary office worker, writing jokes for stand-up comedians in his spare time. We started to go steady. Eventually I had to bring him home one weekend to meet the family. I knew it would be sticky, and it was.

My father had a living in an inner suburb of Leeds which had been going down in the world for decades. The church was huge, neo-gothic, blackened redbrick. I can't remember it ever being full. It had been built on the top of a hill by the wealthy manufacturers and merchants who originally lived in the big stone villas that surrounded it, overlooking their factories and warehouses and the streets of terraced workers' cottages at the bottom of the hill. There were still a few professional middle-class owner-occupiers when my father took over the parish, but most of the big houses were converted into flats or occupied by extended Asian families in the nineteen-fifties. My father was an earnest, well-meaning man, who read the *Guardian* when it was still called the *Manchester Guardian*, and did his best to make the

Church responsive to the needs of the inner city, but the inner city never seemed to be very interested apart from weddings and christenings and funerals. My mother supported him loyally, scrimping and saving to bring up her children in a respectable middle-class style on my father's inadequate stipend. There were four of us, two boys and two girls. I was the second oldest. We all went to local single-sex grammar schools, but we grew up in a kind of cultural bubble, insulated from the lives of our peers. We had no television, partly because Father disapproved of it, but also because we couldn't afford it. Going to the cinema was such a rare treat that the intensity of the experience used to upset me, and I rather dreaded the prospect as a child. We had a gramophone, but only classical records. We all learned to play musical instruments, though none of us had any real talent, and sometimes the whole family would sit down together and stumble through a piece of chamber music, making a noise that started the neighbourhood dogs howling. We were teetotal – again, as much from economy as principle. And we were very argumentative. The main family recreation was scoring points off each other in conversation, especially at meals.

Tubby was completely flummoxed by this. He wasn't used to family meals in any case. He very rarely sat down at the same table with his mother and father and brother, except for Sunday lunch and other high days and holidays. When he lived at home, he and his father and his brother would eat separately, at different times from each other, and from Mrs Passmore. When they came in in the evening, from work or school, she would ask them what they wanted, and then she would cook it and wait on them at table, as if she was running a café, while they ate with a newspaper or a book propped up against the salt cellar. I couldn't believe it when I first visited his home.

He found our domestic life equally bizarre, "as archaic as the *Forsyte Saga*," he said to me once: sitting down *en famille* two or three times a day, with grace before and after meals, cloth napkins which you had to replace in your own special napkin-ring at the end of each meal so as to save laundry, and proper cutlery, however worn and tarnished, soup spoons for soup and fish knives and forks for fish, and so on. Our food was pretty horrible, and there was never enough of it when it was nice, but it was served with due ceremony and decorum. Poor Tubby was completely adrift that first weekend. He started eating before everyone else was served, he used his dessert spoon for his soup and his soup spoon for dessert and committed all kinds of other *faux pas* that had my younger brother and sister sniggering up their sleeves. But what really stunned him was the cut-and-thrust of mealtime conversation. It wasn't that there was any real debate. Father thought he was encouraging us to think for ourselves, but in fact there were very strict limits to what it was permissible to say. You couldn't have argued against the existence of God, for instance, or the truth of Christianity or the indissolubility of marriage. We children very soon cottoned on to these constraints, and domestic conversation became more of a point-scoring game, the aim being to discredit one of your siblings in the eyes of the rest of the family. If you misused a word, for instance, or made some error of fact, the others would be down on you at once like a ton of bricks. Tubby couldn't cope with this at all. Of course, he used it much later in *The People Next Door*. The Springfields and the Davises are based essentially on my family and his, *mutatis mutandis*. The Springfields are totally secular, but that mixture of highmindedness and disputatiousness, their un-acknowledged snobbery and prejudice, all go back to Tubby's first impression of my family, while the Davises are a more rumbustious, somewhat sentimentalized version of his own, with bits of his Uncle Bert and Aunt Molly added. I suppose that's why I never cared for the programme. It stirs too many painful memories. Our wedding was particularly gruesome, with the two sets of totally incompatible relatives grinding and grating against each other.

Why did I marry him? I thought I was in love with him. Well, perhaps I was. What is love, except thinking you're in it? I was longing to rebel against my parents without knowing how to do it. Marrying Tubby was a way of asserting my independence. And we were both desperate for sex – I mean just the normal appetites of youth – but I wasn't rebellious enough to think of having it outside marriage. And then Tubby did have an undeniable charm in those days. He had faith in himself, in his gift, and he made me share that faith. But most of all, he was fun to be with. He made me laugh.

✳ ✳ THREE ✳ ✳

TUESDAY, 25th May. The plane trees outside my window are in leaf: rather listless, anaemic leaf, with no visible blossom, not like the creamy phallic candles of the chestnuts outside my study in Hollywell. There aren't any squirrels scampering about in these branches, either, but that's hardly surprising. I should be grateful – I *am* grateful – that trees grow here at all, considering the pollution in central London. There's a narrow, featureless short cut between Brewer Street and Regent Street called Air Street that always makes me smile when I clock the nameplate. I smile rather than laugh because it's invariably choked with traffic pumping carcinogenic exhaust fumes into the atmosphere, and you wouldn't want to open your mouth if you could help it. Air Street. I don't know how it got the name, but you could make a fortune selling bottled air round here.

Now that I'm living permanently in the flat I find it claustrophobic. I miss the clean-smelling air of Hollywell, I miss the squirrels playing tag in the garden, I miss the daytime hush of those suburban streets where the loudest noise at this time of year is the burr of a distant lawnmower, or the *pock pock* of a game of tennis. But I couldn't stand the strain of sharing the house with Sally any longer. Passing her in stony-faced silence on the stairs or in the hall; exchanging curt accusing little notes (*"If you must leave the laundry to soak, please remove it before it is my turn to use the utility room." "As I bought the last bottle of Rinse-Aid for the dishwasher perhaps you would like to replace it next time"*); hiding when she opened the front door to a neighbour or tradesman so that we wouldn't be obliged to speak to each other in front of them; picking up the phone to make a call and dropping it like a hot brick because Sally was already using it, and then being tempted to press the monitor button and listen in . . . Whoever dreamed up that "separate lives" lark had a sadistic streak – or a warped sense of humour. When I described it to Jake he said, "You know, there's a great idea for a sitcom there." I haven't spoken to him since.

It feels strange, writing this journal again. There's quite a gap in it. After Sally dropped her bombshell that evening (what exactly is, or was, a bombshell, incidentally? And how do you drop one without blowing yourself up? Is it a grenade, or a mortar shell, or was it a primitive kind of aerial bomb that they lobbed out of the open cockpits of the old biplanes? The dictionary isn't much help) – after Sally burst into my study that Friday evening, and announced that she wanted a separation, I was too upset to be able to write anything, even a journal, for weeks. I was beside myself with jealousy and rage and self-pity. (Now *there's* a good cliché for you, "beside myself": as if you're so full of negative feelings that you shake your mind loose from your body, severing the connections between them, and the one is unable to voice the pain of the other.) All I could think of was how to get even with Sally: by being obstructive over money; by trying to track down and expose the lover I was sure she must have; and by having an affair with somebody myself. Why did I think that this last would bother her, I wonder? In any case, even if I'd succeeded I wouldn't have been able to let Sally know, because then she could have sued for a quick divorce on the grounds of adultery. If I try and untwist the tangled and frazzled wires of my motivation at that time, I would have to say that I was trying to make up for lost philandering.

What was most painful about Sally's UDI was of course her rejection of me as a person, and the implied judgement that our thirty years together, or a good many of them, had been worthless, meaningless, as far as she was concerned. After she walked out of the house I sat on the floor of the living-room with all our family photograph albums, which I hadn't looked at for years, spread out around me, and turned the pages with tears streaming down my cheeks. The unbearable poignancy of those snaps! Sally and the children grinning into the lens from deckchairs, pushchairs, swings, sandcastles, paddling pools, swimming pools, bicycle saddles, pony saddles, the decks of cross-Channel ferries and the patios of French *gîtes*. The kids gradually getting taller and stronger from year to year, Sally getting a little thinner in the face and greyer in the hair, but always looking healthy and happy. Yes, happy. Surely the camera couldn't lie? I snivelled and wiped away my tears and blew my nose, peering intently at the brightly coloured Kodak prints to see if I could discern in Sally's face any sign of the disaffection to come. But her eyes were too small, I couldn't see into the eyes, which is the only place where a person can't disguise what they're thinking. Perhaps it had all been an illusion, our "happy marriage", a smile for the camera.

Once you begin to doubt your marriage, you begin to doubt your grasp of reality. I thought I knew Sally – suddenly I found I didn't. So perhaps I didn't know myself. Perhaps I didn't know anything. This was such a vertiginous conclusion that I sheered away from it, and took refuge in anger. I demonized Sally. The breakup of our marriage was all her fault. Whatever truth there might be in her complaints about my self-centredness, moodiness, abstractedness, etc. etc. (and admittedly my inattention to the news about Jane's pregnancy was an embarrassing lapse) they didn't amount to grounds for leaving me. There had to be another reason, viz., another man. There were plenty of examples of adultery in our circle of acquaintance to support the hypothesis. And our lifestyle since the children left home would have made it very easy for Sally to maintain another relationship, with me being in London for two days a week, and her professional life a closed book as far as I was concerned. What particularly angered me was that I hadn't taken advantage of the situation myself. "Anger" isn't quite the word, though. Chagrin, or as Amy would say, *chagrin*, is better – it has the teeth-grinding, bottled-up, you'll-be-sorry-for-this quality of resentment that had me in its grip. I was chagrined at the thought of all the women I might so easily have had in the course of my professional life, especially in recent years, if I hadn't resolved to be faithful to Sally: actresses and production assistants and publicity girls and secretaries – all susceptible to the *mana* of a successful writer. Freud said, so Amy told me once, that all writers are driven by three ambitions: fame, money and the love of women (or men, I presume, as the case might be, though I don't think Freud took much account of women writers, or gay ones). I admit to pursuing the first two ambitions, but scrupulously abstained from the third on principle. And what was my reward? To be put out to grass when I had served my turn, when my sexual powers were on the wane.

That last thought threw me into a panic. How many years did I have left to make up for lost opportunities in the past? I recalled what I had written in my journal a few weeks earlier: *"You won't know it is your last fuck while you're having it, and by the time you find out you probably won't be able to remember what it was like."* I tried to remember when Sally and I last made love, and couldn't. I looked back through the journal and found it logged under Saturday, 27th February. There wasn't any detail, except that Sally had seemed surprised when I took the initiative, and complied rather listlessly. Reading that fuelled my suspicions. I leafed back further to the conversation with the boys at the tennis club: *"You want to watch your Missus, Tubby . . . Good at other games, too, I'm told . . . He's certainly got the tackle . . ."* The solution to the mystery burst inside my head like a flare. Brett Sutton, of course! The tennis lessons, the new sports clothes, the sudden decision to dye her hair . . . It all fitted together. My head became a blue-movie house, flickering with lurid images of Sally naked on the couch in the Club's First Aid room, throwing back her head in ecstasy as Brett Sutton shafted her with his enormous cock.

I discovered I was mistaken about Brett Sutton. But the need to have sex myself, as soon as possible – for revenge, for compensation, for reassurance – became an all-consuming preoccupation. Naturally I thought first of Amy. For some years our relationship had had all the marks of an affair – the secrecy and regularity of our meetings, the discreet restaurant meals, the covert telephone calls, the exchange of confidences – everything except the act of intercourse. I had refrained from crossing that threshold out of misplaced loyalty to Sally. Now there was no moral reason to hold back. So I argued to myself at the time, the immediate post-bombshell time. What I didn't consider was (*a*) whether I really desired Amy and (*b*) whether she desired me. We discovered in Tenerife that the answer to both questions was "no".

Wednesday 26th May. Letters from Jane and Adam this morning. I didn't feel like opening them – just recognizing the handwriting on the envelopes turned my stomach over – but I couldn't settle to anything until I did. Both were short notes asking how I am and inviting me to visit. I suspect some kindly collusion: the coincidence of receiving them on the same day is too blatant.

I saw each of them separately after Sally walked out of the house, but before she moved back. Adam and I had lunch in London one day, and then I went down to spend a weekend in Swanage with Jane and Gus. Both were uncomfortable occasions. For the lunch with Adam I chose a restaurant I'd never been to before, so I wouldn't be recognized. It turned out to be full, with tables much too close together, so Adam and I couldn't speak freely even if we'd wanted to, and had to communicate in a kind of elliptical code. If anyone *was* eavesdropping they probably thought we were discussing a rather unsuccessful dinner party rather than the break-up of a thirty-year-old marriage. I preferred that, though, to the weekend in Swanage, when Gus kept tactfully leaving Jane and me on our own to have the kind of heart-to-heart conversation neither of us really wanted, because we'd never had one before and didn't know how to do it. Jane's relationship to me has always been a humorously scolding one, getting at me for environmentally unsound forms of consumption, like bottled mineral water, coloured paperclips, and hardwood bookshelves, or for sexist jokes in *The People Next Door*. It was a game we played, partly for the entertainment of others. We didn't seem to have a routine for talking intimately.

On the Sunday afternoon Jane and I took their dog for a walk along the crescent-shaped beach, exchanging desultory observations about the weather, the tide, the windsurfers in the bay. The baby is due in October, apparently. I asked her how she was feeling as regards the pregnancy, and she said she was over the morning-sickness period thank God; but that topic fizzled out too, perhaps because it was uncomfortably connected in both our minds with the terminal row between Sally and me. Then on the way back, when we were nearly at the cottage, Jane said abruptly, "Why don't you just give Mummy what she wants? You'd still have plenty to live on, wouldn't you?" I said it was a matter of principle. I didn't accept that Sally could walk out on me just because she found me difficult to live with, and still expect me to support her in the style of life to which she'd become accustomed. Jane said, "You mean, she was being paid to put up with your moods?" I said, "No, of course not." But in a way I suppose Jane was right, though I wouldn't have put it quite like that. She's a shrewd girl, Jane. She said, "I think your making all that money from *The People Next Door* had a bad effect on both of you. You seemed to worry more than when you were hard up. And Mummy became jealous." I had never thought before that Sally might be jealous of my success.

Although both Jane and Adam tried to be impartial, I felt that privately they were both on Sally's "side", so I didn't seek them out again after those two meetings. Also I was plotting to take Amy to Tenerife and afraid they might find out and tell Sally.

Tenerife was certainly a disastrous choice, but really the whole enterprise was doomed before it began. While I had kept Amy under wraps, as it were, never attempting any contact more intimate than a friendly kiss or cuddle, I invested her with a certain glamour, the glamour of the forbidden, the self-denied. Once I had her naked on a bed she was just a plump little lady with rather hairy legs which I hadn't noticed before because she always wore stockings or tights. She also had a body distinctly lacking in muscle tone. I couldn't help comparing her physique unfavourably with Sally's, and reflecting that something seemed to have gone seriously wrong with my strategy. What on earth was I doing in this shitty hotel room in this godawful resort with a woman consider-ably less desirable than the estranged wife I was trying to get even with? It was hardly surprising that Tenerife was an erotic disaster. As soon as I got back – indeed, even before – I began to thumb through my mental backlist of female acquaintance in search of a likely partner younger and more attractive than Amy. I came up with Louise.

Within days I was airborne again, en route for Los Angeles. Another fiasco. Indeed, a double fiasco, if you count the blind date with Stella which Louise fixed up for me after she shattered my hopes. Some hopes. I knew, really, even as I booked my flight to L.A. (open ticket, Business Class; it cost the earth but I wanted to arrive in good shape) that the likelihood of Louise still being unattached and available after all those years was remote in the extreme, and simply suppressed the knowledge because I couldn't bear the thought of failure. It was like Kierkegaard going back to Copenhagen a year after breaking off his engagement, fondly imagining Regine would still be unattached and grieving for him, and then discovering that she was engaged to Schlegel. The attraction of Louise was precisely that she was someone I could have had in the past, and had foolishly, perversely, denied myself. It was the lure of Repetition, the idea of having Louise offer herself to me again, making possession doubly sweet, that impelled me to travel all those thousands of miles.

Stella, on the other hand, was just a potential one-night stand as far as I was concerned. I had a day and a night to kill before the next available flight back to London, so when Louise called me the morning after our outing to Venice to say that she had a friend who was dying to meet me, I agreed. I met her in the lobby of the Beverly Wilshire and took her to dinner in the hotel's ludicrously expensive restaurant. She seemed quite attractive at first sight, blonde and slim and groomed to a high polish. I blinked in the glitter and dazzle of her teeth, hair-lacquer, nail-varnish and costume jewellery. But her smiles lasted just a fraction of a second longer than seemed quite natural, and her facial skin had a tightness under the pancake make-up that suggested it had been lifted. She didn't beat about the bush, saying over our pre-dinner Margaritas, "Louise tells me we have a lot in common: we've both been betrayed and we both want to get laid, right?" I laughed uneasily, and asked her what she did for a living. It turned out that she owns a boutique on Rodeo Drive where Louise shops sometimes. When we were seated she startled me by asking if I had been tested for HIV. I said no, it hadn't seemed necessary, because I had always been faithful to my wife. "So Louise told me," Stella said. "What about your wife? Has she been faithful to you?" I said I now believed that she had been, and asked her what she would like to eat. "I'll have a Caesar salad and *fiilet mignon*, very rare. You don't mind my asking you these questions, Tubby?" "Oh no," I said politely. "Only in my experience it's best to get these things outa the way at the beginning. Then we can both relax. How about since your wife walked out? You been with anybody else?" "Just once," I said. "A very old friend." "You used a condom, of course?" "Oh yes, of course," I lied. Actually Amy had used a diaphragm. I think Stella could tell I was lying. "You have some with you?" she said, when they had brought us the Caesar salad. "Well, not *on* me," I said. "I meant, in your room." "Well, there may be some in the minibar," I quipped, "it seems to have everything else." "It doesn't matter, I have some in my purse," Stella said without cracking a smile. When she started talking about latex gloves and dental dams over the *fiilet mignon*, I panicked. If she was so concerned about safe sex, I thought to myself, she must have reason to be. For the first time in my life I simulated acute internal derangement of the knee, writhing about in my seat in, though I says it myself, a very convincing impression of unbearable pain. The guests at neighbouring tables were quite concerned. The maître d' flashed a signal to the waiters and two of them carried me out into the lobby. I apologized to Stella, excused myself and retired to bed alone. Stella asked me to call her the next day, but the next day I was on the first plane out of LAX to Heathrow.

It was somewhere over the polar icecap that Samantha rose before my inward eye like a vision of sexual promise. Why hadn't I thought of her before? She was young, desirable, and had gone out of her way to cultivate my acquaintance. Furthermore she exuded health and hygiene, and was extremely smart. You couldn't imagine Samantha taking any risks with unsafe sex. Yes, she was obviously my best chance of proving to myself I was still a man. I could hardly wait to land in Heathrow. Red-eyed, soiled and unshaven, I jumped into a cab and went straight to the studio, where I knew I would find Samantha at rehearsal.

It wasn't surprising that my first clumsy attempt at seduction failed, especially with Signora Gabrielli doing her best to fuck it up. But when, a few days later, Ollie suggested assigning a script editor to work with me I saw my opportunity and insisted on Samantha. She understood very well what a favour I had done her, and was clearly prepared to pay for it in time-honoured showbiz style. My fatal mistake, fatal from the philandering point of view I mean, was to stage the seduction in Copenhagen, trying to kill two birds with one stone: combining a little Kierkegaard research with the long-desired, long-frustrated illicit fuck, in a luxury hotel far, but not inconveniently far, from anywhere we were likely to be recognized. I should have known that the two missions wouldn't mix. I should have reckoned with the effect of walking the pavements that Kierkegaard walked a century and a half ago, seeing the actual streets, squares and buildings that were just names in print before, Nytorv, Nørregade, the Borgerdyd-skole, and examining the poignant, homely mementos of S.K. in the Bymuseum: his pipes, his purse, his magnifying glass and the case Regine made for it; the cruel caricature in the *Corsair*; and the portrait of Regine, bonny, buxom and with a smile just about to part her full lips, obviously painted in her happy days before Kierkegaard broke off their engagement. And then to stand at Kierkegaard's very desk and write on it! I had the most extraordinary feeling that he was present somehow in the room, hovering at my shoulder.

In consequence I found myself curiously and embarrassingly reluctant to pursue the amorous objective of the trip, and when the beautiful Samantha shamelessly offered me all the delights of her sumptuous body, I couldn't take advantage of it. Something held me back, and it wasn't the fear of impotence, or of aggravating my knee injury. Call it conscience. Call it Kierkegaard. They have become one and the same thing. I think Kierkegaard is the thin man inside me that has been struggling to get out, and in Copenhagen he finally did.

Kierkegaard says somewhere in the *Journals* that when he discovered that Regine was engaged to Schlegel, and realized that he had lost her irrevocably, "my feeling was this: either you throw yourself into wild dissipation, or into religiousness absolute." My frantic, idiotic sexual odyssey after Sally walked out, trying desperately to get laid in turn by Amy, Louise, Stella and Samantha, was my attempt at wild dissipation. But when it failed, religion wasn't a viable alternative for me. All I could do by way of relief was wank, and write. Actually, it was all Kierkegaard could do for quite a time – write. (Perhaps he wanked too, it wouldn't entirely surprise me.) It's only the late books, the ones he published under his own name, that can be described as "absolutely religious", and frankly I find them a turn-off. The titles alone are a turn-off: most of them are called *Edifying Discourses*. The so-called pseudonymous works, especially the ones he wrote immediately after the break-up with Regine, under the names of Victor Eremitus, Constantine Constantius, Johannes de Silentio and other quaint aliases, are very different, and much more interesting: a kind of effort to come to terms with his experience, to accept the consequences of his own choices, by approaching the material obliquely, indirectly, though fictions, concealed behind masks. It was the same impulse that made me write the monologues, I suppose. Dramatic monologues, I think they're called, because they're addressed to somebody whose lines are just implied. I remember that much from Fifth-Form English. We had to learn one by Browning, off by heart. "My Last Duchess":

> That's my last duchess, painted on the wall
> Looking as if she were alive. I call
> That piece a wonder now . . .

The Duke is a crazy jealous husband who, it turns out, has murdered his wife. I would never have murdered Sally, of course, but there were times when I came close to hitting her.

It was Alexandra's idea, in a way, though she had no notion of the torrent of words her suggestion would release, or the form they would take. I went to see her in a state of dull despair about a week after I got back from Copenhagen. I had renounced dissipation, but I still felt depressed. It was like the economy. The day I returned from Denmark (on the last plane – it took me hours to find Regine's grave, a flat tombstone rather pathetically overgrown with vegetation, but after all her true monument is Kierkegaard's works) the Government announced that the recession was officially over, but nobody could tell the difference. Production might be rising at the rate of 0.2 per cent, but there were still millions of people unemployed and hundreds of thousands trapped in negative equity.

I holed up in my flat. I didn't want to go out in case I was recognized. I lived in terror of meeting someone I knew. (Anyone except Grahame, of course. When I feel unbearably lonely I invite him in for a cup of tea or cocoa and a chat. He's always there in the evenings from about nine o'clock onwards, and sometimes during the day too. He's become a kind of sitting tenant.) I felt sure that all my friends and acquaintances were thinking and talking about me all the time, laughing and sniggering over the cartoon in *Public Interest*. When I went up to Rummidge to see Alexandra I travelled standard class and wore my Ray-Bans, hoping the ticket collectors wouldn't recognize me. I was sure they read *Public Interest* too.

I asked Alexandra about Prozac. She looked surprised. "I thought you were opposed to drug therapy," she said. "This is supposed to be something entirely new," I said. "Non-addictive. No side-effects. In the States even people who aren't depressed take it, because it makes them feel so good." Alexandra knew all about Prozac, of course, and gave me a technical explanation of how it's supposed to work, all about neurotransmitters and serotonin re-uptake inhibitors. I couldn't really follow it. I said I was already a bit slow on the re-uptake, and hardly needed any more inhibiting in that line, but apparently that wasn't what it meant at all. Alexandra views Prozac with some suspicion. "It's not true that there are no side-effects," she said. "Even advocates admit that it inhibits the patient's capacity to achieve orgasm." "Well, I'm already suffering the side-effect," I said, "so I might as well take the drug." Alexandra laughed, baring her big teeth in the widest grin I have ever drawn from her. She hastily straightened her features. "There are unconfirmed reports of more serious side-effects," she said. "Patients hallucinating, trying to mutilate themselves. There's even a murderer who's claiming that he killed under the influence of Prozac." "My friend didn't mention anything like that," I said. "She told me it makes you feel better than well." Alexandra looked at me in silence for a moment with her big brown gentle eyes. "I'll put you on Prozac if you really want me to," she said. "But you must understand what's entailed. I'm not talking about side-effects, now, I'm talking about *effects*. These new SRI drugs change people's personalities. They act on the mind like plastic surgery acts on the body. Prozac may give you back your self-esteem, but it won't be the same self." I thought for a moment. "What else do you suggest?" I said.

Alexandra suggested that I should write down exactly what I thought other people were saying and thinking about me, privately or to each other. I recognized the strategy, of course. She believed that it was not the *actuality* of other people's opinions, but my *fear* of what these opinions might be, that was making me wretched. Once I focused on the question – *what do other people really think of me?* – and made myself answer it explicitly, then instead of projecting my lack of self-esteem onto others, and allowing it to rebound upon myself, I would be forced to acknowledge that other people didn't really loathe and despise me, but respected and sympathized with and even liked me. It didn't quite work out like that, though.

Being the sort of writer I am, I couldn't just summarize other people's views of me, I had to let them speak their thoughts in their own voices. And what they said wasn't very flattering. "You've been very hard on yourself," Alexandra said, when she finally saw what I'd written. It took me some weeks – I got a bit carried away – and I only sent the stuff to her last week, quite a bulky package. I went up to Rummidge yesterday for her verdict. "They're very funny, very acute," she said, leafing through the sheaves of A4 with a reminiscent smile playing over her pale, unpainted lips, "but you've been very hard on yourself." I shrugged and said I had tried to see myself truthfully from other people's points of view. "But you must have made up a lot of these things." Not all that much, I said.

I had to use my imagination a bit, of course. I never saw Brett Sutton's statement to the police, for instance, but I had to make one myself, and they gave me a copy to take home, so I knew what the format was like, and it wasn't hard to guess what Brett Sutton's version of events would have been. And although Amy was always very secretive about her sessions with Karl Kiss, I knew she would have been giving him daily bulletins about developments in our relationship following Sally's bombshell, and I've had plenty of opportunity to study the way she thinks and talks. Most of the things she says to Karl in the monologue she said to me at one time or another, like remembering her mother slicing carrots in the kitchen while telling her the facts of life, or dreaming of the cartoon in *Public Interest* with me as Vulcan and Saul as Mars. The bit about her sewage-disposal problems in the Playa de las Americas hotel was an extrapolation from listening to her endlessly cranking the handle of the toilet when she was in the bathroom. The ending is a little too neat, perhaps, but I couldn't resist it. Amy did return to England in a bouncy, self-assertive mood, saying that she was going to give Karl his "*congé*", but the last I heard she was back in analysis again. I don't see much of Amy, actually, these days. We tried meeting again for a meal once or twice, but we couldn't seem to get back onto the old friendly footing. Embarrassing memories of Tenerife kept getting in the way.

Whether Louise actually described our reunion to Stella in such detail, I have no idea, but whatever she told her would have been on the phone. Louise may have given up smoking and drinking and drugs (apart from Prozac), but she's completely addicted to the telephone. She had her dinky Japanese portable beside her plate at the Venice restaurant all through our meal, and kept interrupting my heartbroken confidences to take and make calls about her movie. Ollie wasn't difficult. I must have been trapped with him in a bar a hundred times. I did take a few liberties with Samantha. She mentioned – I can't remember the context now – that she had a friend who was suffering from impacted wisdom teeth, but the hospital visit was all my invention. I just liked the idea of this helpless, speechless captive auditor unable to stem the flow of Samantha's loud recapitulation of our would-be dirty weekend in Copenhagen. She's a smart babe, Samantha, but sensitivity is not her strong point.

The hardest one to write was Sally's. I didn't show it to Alexandra because she might have thought I was taking a liberty, writing her into it. I know she invited Sally to come and see her, because she asked if I had any objection (I said no). And I believe Sally agreed, but Alexandra never told me what she said, so I assumed it was discouraging. It was almost physically painful, reliving the bust-up through Sally's eyes. That's why the monologue changes halfway from being one side of a conversation with Alexandra to being a stream of reminiscence about our courtship. But that was painful too, reliving those days of hope and promise and laughter. The most chilling thing that Sally said to me in the course of that long hellish weekend of argument and pleading and recrimination before she walked out, the moment when I knew, really knew, in my heart, that I'd lost her, was when she said: "You don't make me laugh any more."

✶ ✶ ✶ ✶ ✶ ✶ ✶ ✶ ✶ ✶ ✶ ✶ ✶ ✶ ✶ ✶ ✶ ✶

Thursday 27th May, 10 a.m. It took me all day to write yesterday's entry. I worked without a break, except for five minutes when I nipped out to Pret A Manger for a prawn and avocado sandwich, which I ate at the table as I went on writing. There was a lot to catch up on.

I finished at about seven, feeling tired, hungry and thirsty. My knee was giving me gyp too: sitting in one position for long periods is bad for it. (What is "gyp", I wonder? Dictionary says "*probably a contraction of* gee up", which doesn't sound very probable to me. More likely something to do with Egypt, as in "gyppy tummy", a bit of army slang from the days of the Empire.) I went out to stretch my legs and refuel. It was a fine warm evening. The young swarmed round Leicester Square tube station as they always do at that time of day, whatever the season. They bubble up from the subway like some irrepressible underground spring, spill out on to the pavement, and stand around outside the Hippodrome in their flimsy casual clothes looking eager and expectant. What are they hoping for? I don't think most of them could tell you if you asked them. Some adventure, some encounter, some miraculous transformation of their ordinary lives. A few, of course, are waiting for a date. I see their faces light up as they spot their boyfriend or girlfriend approaching. They embrace, oblivious to the fat baldy in the leather jacket sauntering past with his hands in his pockets, and move off, arms round each other's waists, to some restaurant or cinema or bar throbbing with amplified rock music. I used to meet Sally on this corner when we were courting. Now I buy a *Standard* to read over my Chinese meal in Lisle Street.

The trouble with eating alone, well one of the troubles anyway, is that you tend to order too much and eat too fast. When I came back from the restaurant, bloated and belching, it was only 8.30, and still light. But Grahame was already settling himself down for the night on the porch. I invited him in to watch the second half of the European Cup Final between AC Milan and Marseille. Marseille won 1–0. A good game, though it's hard to work up much passion about a match with no British club involved. I remember when Manchester United won the European Cup with George Best in the side. Delirious. I asked Grahame if he remembered, but of course he wasn't even born then.

Grahame is lucky to still be occupying the porch. Herr Bohl, the Swiss businessman who owns flat number 5 and resides there occasionally, took exception to his presence and proposed to call the police and have him ejected. I appealed to Bohl to let him stay on the grounds that he keeps the porch beautifully clean and deters passers-by from tossing their rubbish into it and drunks from using it as a nocturnal urinal, which they used to do frequently and copiously. This cunning appeal to the Swiss obsession with hygiene paid off. Herr Bohl had to admit that the porch smelled considerably sweeter since Grahame's occupancy, and withdrew his threat to call the police.

It helped my case that Grahame himself always looks clean and doesn't smell at all. This puzzled me for a long time until one day I ventured to ask him how he managed it. He smiled slyly and told me he would let me into a secret. The next day he led me to a place on Trafalgar Square, just a door in the wall with an electronic lock on it that I must have passed scores of times without noticing it. Grahame tapped out a sequence of numbers on the keypad and the lock buzzed and opened. Inside was an underground labyrinth of rooms providing food, games, showers and a launderette. It's a kind of refuge for homeless young people. There are even dressing-gowns provided so that if you've only got one set of clothes you can sit and wait while they're being washed and dried. It reminded me a bit of the Pullman Lounge at Euston Station. I sent a donation to the charity that runs it the other day. Knowing it's there makes me feel slightly less guilty about knowing that Grahame is sleeping in the porch. The rich man in his castle, the poor man at his gate . . .

Actually, there's no reason why I should feel guilty at all. Grahame has chosen to live on the street. Out of a pretty lousy set of options, admittedly, but it's probably the best life he's ever had – certainly the most independent. "I am the master of my fate," he said to me solemnly one day. It was one of these phrases he had seen somewhere and memorized, without knowing who said it. I looked it up in my dictionary of quotations. It comes from a poem by W. E. Henley:

> It matters not how strait the gate,
> How charged with punishments the scroll,
> I am the master of my fate:
> I am the captain of my soul.

I wish I was.

11.15. Jake just rang. I listened to him leave a message on the answerphone without picking up the receiver or returning his call. He was trying to lure me to lunch at Groucho's. He's getting jittery because we're approaching the deadline after which Heartland can exercise their right to employ another writer. Well, let them. I'm much more interested in Søren and Regine than in Priscilla and Edward these days, but I know Ollie Silvers has no intention of making a programme about Kierkegaard, however much work I do on *The People Next Door*, so why should I bother?

Grahame was quite impressed when he found out I was a TV scriptwriter, but when I mentioned the name of the show he said, "Oh, that," in a distinctly sniffy tone. I thought this was a bit cheeky, especially as he was swigging my tea and stuffing himself with carrot cake from Pret A Manger at the time. "It's all right, I suppose," he said, "if you like that sort of thing." I pressed him to explain why he obviously didn't like it himself. "Well, it ain't real, is it?" he said. "I mean, every week there's some great row in one of the houses, but it's always sorted out by the end of the programme, and everybody's sweet as pie again. Nothing ever changes. Nobody ever gets really hurt. Nobody hits anybody. None of the kids ever run away." "Alice ran away once," I pointed out. "Yeah, for about ten minutes," he said. He meant ten minutes of screen time, but I didn't quibble. I took his point.

2.15 p.m. I went out for a pub lunch and when I came back there was a message from Samantha on the answerphone: she's had an idea for solving the Debbie–Priscilla problem that she wants to discuss with me. She said she would be back at her desk by three, which seems to imply a rather leisurely lunch, but gave me time to leave a message on *her* answerphone, asking her to put the idea on paper and mail it to me. I only communicate by answerphone or letter nowadays. This allows me to control the agenda of all discussions and avoid the dreaded question, *"How are you?"* Sometimes if I'm feeling particularly lonely I call my bank's Phoneline service and check the balances in my various accounts with the girl whose recorded voice guides you through the digitally coded procedure. She sounds rather nice, and she doesn't ask how you are. Though if you make a mistake she says, *"I'm sorry, there appears to be a problem."* Too true, darling, I tell her.

"Only when I write do I feel well. Then I forget all of life's vexations, all its sufferings, then I am wrapped in thought and am happy." – Kierkegaard's journal, 1847. While I was writing the monologues I was – not happy exactly, but occupied, absorbed, interested. It was like working on a script. I had a task to perform, and I got some satisfaction in performing it. Now that I've finished the task, and brought my journal more or less up to date, I feel restless, nervous, ill-at-ease, unable to settle to anything. I have no aim or objective, apart from making it as difficult as possible for Sally to get her hands on my money, and my heart isn't really in that any more. I've got to go up to Rummidge to see my lawyer tomorrow. I could instruct him to throw in the towel, settle the divorce as quickly as possible and give Sally what she wants. But would that make me feel any better? No. It's another either/or situation. It doesn't matter what I do, I'm bound to regret it. *If you divorce you'll regret it, if you don't divorce you'll regret it. Divorce or don't divorce, you'll regret both.*

Perhaps I still hope that Sally and I will get together again, that I can have my old life back, that everything will be as it used to be. Perhaps, in spite of all my tantrums and tears and plots for revenge – or because of them – I haven't truly despaired of our marriage. B says to A: "In order truly to despair one must really want to, but when one truly wills despair one is truly beyond it; when one has truly chosen despair one has truly chosen what despair chooses, namely oneself in one's eternal validity." I suppose you could say I chose myself when I declined Alexandra's offer to put me on Prozac, but it didn't feel like an act of existential self-affirmation at the time. More like a captured criminal holding out his wrists for the handcuffs.

5.30. I suddenly thought that as I'm going up to Rummidge tomorrow, I might as well try to fit some therapy in. I made a couple of phone calls. Roland was fully booked, but Dudley was able to give me an appointment in the afternoon. I didn't try Miss Wu. I haven't seen her since that Friday when Sally dropped her bombshell. I haven't felt like it. Nothing to do with Miss Wu. Association of ideas: acupuncture and my life falling apart.

9.30. I ate at an Indian restaurant this evening and came home at about nine, spicing the metropolitan pollution with explosive, aromatic farts. Grahame said a man had rung my doorbell. From his description I guessed it was Jake. "Friend of yours, is he?" Grahame enquired. "Sort of," I said. "He asked me if I'd seen you lately. Didn't give a very flattering description." Naturally I asked what it was. "Fattish, bald, round-shouldered." The last epithet shook me a bit. I've never thought of myself as particularly round-shouldered. It must be the effect of depression. How you feel is how you look. I don't think it was only his childhood accident that made Kierkegaard's spine curve. "What did you tell him?" I asked. "I didn't tell him nothing," said Grahame. "Good," I said. "You did well."

✳ ✳ ✳ ✳ ✳ ✳ ✳ ✳ ✳ ✳ ✳ ✳ ✳ ✳ ✳ ✳ ✳

Friday 28th May. 7.45 p.m. Just returned from Rummidge. I drove, simply to give the Richmobile a run: I keep it in a lock-up garage near King's Cross, and hardly ever use it these days. Not that there was much pleasure to be had on the M1 today. It had broken out in a rash of cones, like scarlet fever, and contraflow between Junctions 9 and 11 was causing a five-mile tailback. Apparently a car towing a caravan had contraflowed into a lorry. So I was late for my appointment with Dennis Shorthouse. He specializes in divorce and family litigation for my solicitors, Dobson McKitterick. I never had any dealings with him until the bust-up with Sally. He's tall, grey-haired, with a spare frame and a lined, beaky face, and rarely moves from behind his large, eerily tidy desk. Just as some doctors keep themselves preternaturally clean and neat as if to ward off infection, so Shorthouse seems to use his desk as some kind of *cordon sanitaire* to keep his clients' misery at a safe distance. It has an in-tray and an out-tray, both always empty, a spotless blotter and a digital clock, subtly angled towards the client's chair like a taxi-meter, so you can see how much his advice is costing you.

He'd had a letter from Sally's solicitors, threatening to sue for divorce on the grounds of unreasonable behaviour. "As you know, adultery and unreasonable behaviour are the only grounds for an immediate divorce," he said. I asked him what constituted unreasonable behaviour. "A very good question," he said, joining his fingertips and leaning forward across the desk. He launched into a long disquisition, but I'm afraid my mind wandered and I suddenly became aware that he had fallen silent and was looking expectantly at me. "I'm sorry, would you just repeat that, please?" I said. His smile became a trifle forced. "Repeat how much?" he said. "Just the last bit," I said, not having a clue how long he had been speaking. "I asked you, what kind of unreasonable behaviour Mrs Passmore was likely to complain of, if she were under oath." I thought for a moment.

"Would my not listening when she was talking to me count?" I said. "It might," he said. "It would depend on the judge." I got the impression that if Shorthouse were judging me himself, I wouldn't stand much chance. "Have you ever physically assaulted your wife?" he said. "Good God, no," I said. "What about drunkenness, verbal abuse, jealous rages, false accusations, that sort of thing?" "Only since she walked out on me," I said. "I didn't hear you say that," he said. He paused for a moment before summing up: "I don't think Mrs Passmore will risk lodging an unreasonable behaviour petition. She won't qualify for legal aid, and if she were to lose the costs could be considerable. Also she would be back to square one as regards the divorce. She's threatening this to bring pressure on you to co-operate. I don't think you need worry." Shorthouse smirked, obviously pleased with his analysis. "You mean she won't get a divorce?" I said. "Oh, she'll get it eventually, of course, on grounds of irretrievable breakdown of the marriage. It's a question of how long you want to make her wait." "And how much I want to pay you to delay things?" I said. "Quite so," he said, glancing at the clock. I told him to carry on delaying.

Then I went to see Dudley. Drawing up outside his house I thought wistfully of all the previous occasions on which I had visited him with nothing more serious to complain of than a general, ill-defined malaise. A wide-bodied jet thundered overhead as I rang the doorbell, making me cringe and cover my ears. Dudley told me it was a new scheduled service to New York. "Be useful to you, won't it, in your line of work?" he remarked, "You won't have to go from Heathrow any more." Dudley has a rather exaggerated notion of the glamour of a TV scriptwriter's life. I told him I was living in London now, anyway, and the reason. "I don't suppose you have an essential oil for marital breakdown, do you?" I said. "I can give you something for stress," he offered. I asked him if he could do anything about my knee, which had been playing up badly on the M1. He tapped away on his computer and said he would try lavender, which was allegedly good for aches and pains *and* stress. He took a little phial out of his big, brass-bound case of essential oils, and invited me to smell it.

I don't think Dudley can have ever used lavender on me before, because sniffing it triggered the most extraordinarily vivid memory – of Maureen Kavanagh, my first girlfriend. She's been flitting in and out of my consciousness ever since I started this journal, like a figure glimpsed indistinctly at the edge of a distant wood, moving between the trees, gliding in and out of the shadows. The smell of lavender drew her out into the open – the lavender and Kierkegaard. I made a note some weeks ago that the symbol for the double *aa* in modern Danish, the single *a* with a little circle on top, reminded me of something I couldn't pin down at the time. Well, it was Maureen's handwriting. She used to dot her *i*s that way, with a little circle instead of a point, like a trail of bubbles above the lines of her big round handwriting. I don't know where she got the idea from. We used to write to each other even though we saw each other every morning at the tram stop, just for the thrill of having private letters. I used to write her rather passionate love-letters and she would send back shy little notes of disappointing banality: "I did homework after tea, then I helped Mum with her ironing. Did you listen in to Tony Hancock? We were in fits." She used mauve stationery from Woolworths that was scented with lavender. That whiff from Dudley's phial brought it all back – not just her handwriting, but Maureen in all her specificity. Maureen. My first love. My first breast.

There was a letter from Samantha in the mailbox when I got in, with her idea for writing Debbie's part out of *The People Next Door* : in the last episode Priscilla is knocked off her bike by a lorry and killed instantly, but returns as a ghost, which only Edward can see, and urges him to find another partner. Not exactly original, but it has possibilities. You have to admit, the girl is smart. In another mood, I might have tinkered with it. But all I can think about at the moment is Maureen. I feel an irresistible urge coming over me to write about her.

Maureen

A MEMOIR

I FIRST BECAME AWARE of Maureen Kavanagh's existence when I was fifteen, though nearly a year passed before I managed to speak to her and discover her name. I used to see her every weekday morning, as I waited for the tram which took me on the first stage of my tedious three-leg journey to school. That was Lambeth Merchants', a direct-grant grammar school to which, pushed by a well-intentioned junior-school head, I unluckily gained admission at the Eleven-Plus. I say unluckily because I believe now that I would have been happier, and therefore have learned more, at some less prestigious and pretentious establishment. I had the innate intelligence, but not the social and cultural back-up, to benefit from the education on offer at Lambeth Merchants'. It was an ancient foundation that took obsessive pride in its history and tradition. It accepted fee-paying pupils as well as the cream of the 11-Plus, and modelled itself on the classic English public school, with "Houses" (though there were no boarders), a chapel, a school song with words in Latin, and numerous arcane rituals and privileges. The buildings were sooty neo-gothic redbrick, turreted and crenellated, with stained-glass windows in the chapel and the main assembly hall. The teachers wore gowns. I never fitted in and never did well academically, languishing at the bottom of my class for most of my school career. My Mum and Dad were unable to help me with my homework, and indulged my tendency to skimp it. I spent most evenings listening to comedy shows on the radio (my classics are *ITMA, Much Binding in the Marsh, Take It From Here*, and *The Goon Show*, not the *Aeneid* and *David Copperfield*) or playing football and cricket in the street with my mates from the local secondary modern. Sport was encouraged at Lambeth Merchants' – they even gave "caps" for representing the school – but the winter game was rugby, which I loathed, and school cricket was played with a pomp and circumstance that I found tedious. The only success I enjoyed at school was as a comic actor in the annual play. Otherwise I was made to feel stupid and uncouth. I became the class clown, and perennial butt of the masters' sarcasm. I was caned frequently. I looked forward to leaving school as soon as I had taken the O-Level examinations I did not expect to pass.

Maureen went to the Sacred Heart convent school in Greenwich, also courtesy of the Eleven-Plus. She had an equally awkward journey from Hatchford where we both lived, but in the opposite direction. Hatchford was, I suppose, a desirable outer suburb of London when it was first built at the end of the nineteenth century, just where the Thames plain meets the first Surrey hills, but was almost part of the decaying inner city by the time we were born. Maureen lived at the top of one of the hills, in the lower half of a huge Victorian villa that had been divided into flats. Her family inhabited the basement and ground floor. We lived in a little terraced house in Albert Street, one of the streets off the main road at the bottom of the hill, where the trams ran. My dad was a tram-driver.

It was a hard job. He had to stand for eight hours or more at the controls, on a platform open to the elements on one side, and a certain amount of brute force was needed to apply the brakes. In the winter he came home from work chilled and haggard, and crouched over the coal fire in the living-room, hardly able to speak till he had thawed out. There was a more modern type of tram, streamlined and fully enclosed, which I saw occasionally in other parts of London, but my Dad always worked on the old clapped-out pre-war trams, open at each end, that screeched and rattled and groaned as they lurched from stop to stop. Those red, double-decker trams, with a single headlamp that glowed in the fog like a bleary eye, with their clanging bells, their brass fittings and wooden seats polished by the friction of innumerable hands and bums, their top decks reeking of cigarette-smoke and sick, their muffled grey-faced drivers and chirpy, mittened clippies, are inseparably linked with my memories of childhood and adolescence.

Every weekday I caught my first tram at Hatchford Five Ways on my way to school. I used to wait not at the stop itself but on the corner just before it, outside a flower shop, from which I could sight my tram as soon as it appeared around a distant curve in the main road, swaying on the rails like a galleon at sea. By moving my angle of vision about thirty degrees I could also look up the long straight incline of Beecher's Road. Maureen always appeared at the top at the same time, at five minutes to eight, and took three minutes to reach the bottom. She passed me, crossed the road, and walked a few yards to wait for a tram going in the opposite direction to mine. I watched her boldly when she was distant, covertly as she approached me, while ostensibly looking out for my tram. After she had passed, I would saunter to my stop, and watch her as she waited, with her back turned to me, on the other side of the road. Sometimes, just as she came up to the corner, I would risk turning my head in feigned boredom or impatience at the non-appearance of the tram, and glance at her as if by accident. Usually she had her eyes lowered, but on one occasion she was looking straight at me and our eyes met. She blushed crimson and looked quickly down at the pavement as she passed. I don't think I breathed for five minutes afterwards.

This went on for months. Perhaps a year. I didn't know who she was, or anything about her, except that I was in love with her. She was beautiful. I suppose a less impressionable, or more blasé, observer might have described her as "pretty" or "nice-looking" rather than beautiful, judging her to be a little too short in the neck, or a little too thick in the waist, to qualify for the highest accolade, but to me she was beautiful. Even in her school uniform – a pudding-bowl hat, a gabardine raincoat and pleated pinafore dress, all in a dead, depressing shade of navy blue – she was beautiful. She wore the hat at a jaunty angle, or perhaps it was the natural springiness of her auburn hair that pushed it to the back of her head, the rim framing her heart-shaped, heart-stopping face: big, dark brown eyes, a small, neat nose, generous mouth, dimpled chin. How can you describe beauty in words? It's hopeless, like shuffling bits of an Identikit picture around. Her hair was long and wavy, drawn over her ears and gathered by a clasp at the back of her neck into a kind of loose mane that fell halfway down her back. She wore her raincoat unbuttoned, flapping open at the front, with the sleeves turned back to expose the cuffs of her white blouse, and the belt knotted behind. I discovered later that she and her schoolfriends spent endless hours contriving such tiny modifications of the uniform, trying to outwit the nuns' repressive regulations. She carried her books in a kind of shopping-bag, which gave her a womanly, grown-up look, and made my big leather satchel seem childish in comparison.

I thought of her last thing at night, before I fell asleep, and when I woke in the morning. If, as very rarely happened, she was late appearing at the top of Beecher's Road, I would let my tram go by without boarding it, and take the consequences of being late for school (two strokes of the cane) rather than forfeit my daily sight of her. It was the purest, most selfless romantic devotion. It was Dante and Beatrice in a suburban key. Nobody knew my secret, and torture wouldn't have dragged it from me. I was going through the usual hormonal storm of adolescence at the time, swamped and buffeted by bodily changes and sensations I could neither control nor put a name to – erections and nocturnal emissions and sprouting body hair and the rest of it. There was no sex education at Lambeth Merchants', and my Mum and Dad, with the deep repressive puritanism of the respectable working class, never discussed the subject. Of course the usual smutty jokes and boasts circulated in the school playground and were illustrated on the walls of the school bogs, but it was difficult to elicit basic information from those who appeared to know without betraying a humiliating ignorance. One day a boy I trusted told me the facts of life as we walked back from an illicit lunchtime visit to the local chip-shop – "when your dick gets stiff you poke it in the girl's slit and come off in her" – but this act, though inflaming to contemplate, seemed ugly and unclean, not something I wanted to associate with the angel who descended daily from the top of Beecher's Road to receive my dumb adoration.

Of course I longed to speak to her, and thought continually about possible ways of getting into conversation with her. The simplest method, I told myself, would be to smile and say hallo one morning, as she passed. After all, we were not total strangers – it was a quite normal thing to do to somebody you met regularly in the street, even if you didn't know their name. The worst that could happen was that she would ignore me, and walk straight past without responding to my greeting. Ah, but that worst was chilling to contemplate. What would I do the *next* morning? And every morning after that? As long as I didn't accost her, she couldn't rebuff me, and my love was safe even if unrequited. I spent many hours fantasizing about more dramatic and irresistible ways of making her acquaintance – for example, pulling her back from certain death as she was about to step under the wheels of a tram, or defending her from attack by some ruffian bent on robbery or rape. But she always showed admirable caution and common sense when crossing the road, and the pavements of Hatchford at eight o'clock in the morning were rather short of ruffians (this, after all, was 1951, when the word "mugging" was unknown, and even at night unaccompanied women felt safe in well-lit London streets).

The event that finally brought us together was less heroic than these imaginary scenarios, but it seemed almost miraculous to me at the time, as if some sympathetic deity, aware of my tongue-tied longing to make the girl's acquaintance, had finally lost patience, plucked her into the air and flung her to the ground at my feet. She was late appearing at the top of Beecher's Road that day, and I could see that she was hurrying down the hill. Every now and then she would break into a run – that rather endearing kind of running that girls do, moving their legs mainly from the knees, throwing out their heels at an angle behind them – and then, encumbered by her heavy bag of books, she would slow to a brisk walking pace for an interval. In this flustered and flurried state she seemed more than usually beautiful. Her hat was off her head, retained by the narrow elastic strap round her throat, her long mane swung to and fro, and the energy of her stride made her bosom move about thrillingly beneath her white blouse and pinafore dress. I kept her in my direct line of vision longer than usual, as long as I dared; but eventually, to avoid giving the impression of staring rudely, I had to avert my eyes and go through the pretence of looking along the main road for my tram – which was in fact, by this time, quite near.

I heard a cry and suddenly there she was, sprawled at my feet, her books scattered all over the pavement. Breaking into a run again, she had caught the toe of her shoe on the edge of an uneven paving-stone, tripped, and fallen, dropping her bag as she broke her fall. She was up on her feet in an instant, before I could lend her a supporting hand, but I was able to help her pick up her books, and to speak to her. "Are you alright?" "Mmm," she mumbled, sucking a grazed knuckle. "Stupid." This last epithet was clearly addressed to herself, or possibly to the paving-stone, not to me. She was blushing furiously. My tram passed, its wheels grating and squealing in the grooved tracks as it took the corner. "That's your tram," she said. "It doesn't matter," I replied, filled with rapture at the implication of this remark – that she had been observing my movements as closely as I had been observing hers over the past months. I carefully gathered up a number of foolscap sheets that had fallen out of a folder, covered with large round handwriting, the *i*s topped with little circles instead of dots, and handed them to her. "Thanks," she muttered, stuffing them into her bag, and hurried away, limping slightly.

She was just in time to catch her usual tram – I saw her emerge from the top of the stairs on to the upper deck as it passed me moments later. My own tram had gone without me, but I didn't care. *I had actually spoken to her!* I had almost touched her. I kicked myself for not having been quick enough to help her get up from the ground – but never mind: a contact had been made, words had been exchanged, and I had done her a small service by picking up her books and papers. From now on I would be able to smile and say hallo every morning when she passed me. As I contemplated this exciting prospect, something shiny caught my eye in the gutter: it was the clip on a Biro pen, which had obviously fallen out of her bag. I pounced on it exultantly and stowed it away in an inside pocket, next to my heart.

Ballpoint pens were still something of a novelty in those days, and absurdly expensive, so I knew the girl would be pleased to have it restored to her. I slept with it under my pillow that night (it leaked and left blue stains on the sheet and pillowcase, for which I was bitterly berated by my mother, and clipped round the ear by my father) and took up my usual position outside the florist's shop the next morning five minutes earlier than usual, to be sure of not missing the pen's owner. She was indeed a little early herself in making her appearance at the top of Beecher's Road, and descended the incline slowly, with a kind of self-conscious deliberation, carefully placing each foot in front of the other, looking down at the pavement – not, I was sure, just to avoid tripping up again, but because she knew I was observing her, waiting for her. They were tense, highly charged minutes that ticked by as she walked down the hill towards me. It was like that wonderful shot at the end of *The Third Man*, when Harry Lime's girlfriend walks towards Holly Martins along the avenue in the frozen cemetery, except that she walks right past him without a glance, and this girl was not going to, because I had a flawless pretext to stop her and talk to her.

As she approached me she affected interest in a flight of starlings wheeling and swooping in the sky above the Co-op bakery, but when she was a few yards away she glanced at me and gave me a shy smile of recognition. "Erm, I think you dropped this yesterday," I blurted out, whipping the Biro from my pocket and holding it out to her. Her face lit up with pleasure. "Oh, thanks ever so much," she said, stopping and taking the pen. "I thought I'd lost it. I came back here yesterday afternoon and looked, but I couldn't find it." "No, well, I had it," I said, and we both laughed inanely. When she laughed, the tip of her nose twitched and wrinkled up like a rabbit's. "Well, thanks again," she said, moving on. "If I'd known where you lived, I'd have brought it round," I said, desperately trying to detain her. "That's alright," she said, walking backwards, "As long as I've got it back. I daren't tell my Mum I'd lost it." She treated me to another delicious nose-wrinkling smile, turned her back on me and disappeared round the corner. I still didn't know her name.

It wasn't long before I found out, though. Every morning after her providential dive at my feet I smiled and said hallo as she passed, and she blushed and smiled and said hallo back. Soon I added to my greeting some carefully rehearsed remark about the weather or enquiry about the functioning of the ballpoint pen or complaint about the lateness of my tram which invited a reply on her part, and one day she lingered at the corner outside the florist's for a few moments' proper conversation. I asked her what her name was. "Maureen." "Mine's Laurence." "Turn me over," she said, and giggled at my blank look. "Don't you know the story of Saint Laurence?" I shook my head. "He was martyred by being slowly roasted on a gridiron," she said. "He said, 'Turn me over, this side is done.'" "When was that?" I asked, wincing sympathetically. "I dunno exactly," she said. "Roman times, I think."

This grotesque and slightly sick anecdote, related as if there was nothing the least disturbing about it, was the first indication I had that Maureen was a Catholic, confirmed the following day when she told me the name of her school. I had noticed the heart embroidered with red and gold thread on her blazer badge, but without realizing its religious significance. "It means the Sacred Heart of Jesus," she said, making a little reflex inclination of her head as she pronounced the Holy Name. These pious allusions to gridirons and hearts, with their incongruous associations of kitchens and offal, made me slightly uneasy, reminding me of Mrs Turner's threats to wash me in the Blood of the Lamb in infancy, but didn't deter me from seeking to make Maureen my girlfriend.

I had never had a girlfriend before, and was uncertain of how to start, but I knew that courting couples often went to the cinema together, because I had queued with them outside the local Odeon, and observed them necking in the back rows. One day, as Maureen lingered outside the florist's, I summoned up the courage to ask her if she would go to the pictures with me the following weekend. She blushed and looked at once excited and apprehensive. "I dunno. I'd have to ask my Mum and Dad," she said.

The next morning she appeared at the top of Beecher's Road accompanied by an enormous man, at least six foot tall and, it seemed to me, as wide as our house. I knew it must be Maureen's father, who she had told me was foreman at a local building firm, and viewed his approach with alarm. I was afraid not so much of physical assault as of a humiliating public scene. So, obviously, was Maureen, for I could see she was dragging her feet and hanging her head sulkily. As they drew nearer, I fixed my gaze on the long perspective of the main road, with its shining tram-tracks receding to infinity, and hoped against hope that Mr Kavanagh was just escorting Maureen, and would ignore me if I made no attempt to greet her. No such luck. A huge shape in a navy-blue donkey-jacket loomed over me.

"Are you the young blackguard who's been pesterin' my daughter?" he demanded in a thick Irish accent.

"Eh?" I said, stalling. I glanced at Maureen, but she avoided my eye. She was red in the face and looked as if she had been crying. "Dad!" she murmured plaintively. The young overalled assistant arranging flowers in buckets outside the florist's paused in her labours to enjoy the drama.

Mr Kavanagh poked me in the chest with a huge forefinger, horny and calloused and hard as a policeman's truncheon. "My daughter's a respectable girl. I won't have her talkin' to strange fellas on street corners, understand?"

I nodded.

"Mind you do, then. Off you go to school." This last remark was addressed to Maureen, who slouched off with one despairing, apologetic glance at me. Mr Kavanagh's attention seemed caught by my school blazer, a gaudy crimson garment with silver buttons, which I loathed, and he screwed up his eyes at the elaborate coat of arms with its Latin motto on the breast pocket. "What's this school that you go to?" I told him, and he seemed impressed in spite of himself. "Mind you behave yourself, or I'll report you to your headmaster," he said. He turned on his heel and walked back up the hill. I stayed where I was, looking along the main road until my tram came in sight, and my pulse rate returned to normal.

Of course this incident only drew Maureen and me closer together. We became a pair of star-crossed lovers, defying her father's ban on further contact. We continued to exchange a few words every morning, though I now prudently stationed myself just round the corner, out of sight of anyone surveying the Five Ways from the top of Beecher's Road. In due course Maureen persuaded her mother to let me call at their house one Saturday afternoon when her father was out, working overtime, so that she could see for herself I wasn't the kind of street-corner lout they had imagined when she first asked if she could go to the pictures with me. "Wear your school blazer," Maureen advised, shrewdly. So, to the astonishment of my own parents and disgust of my mates, I missed a home game at Charlton and put on the blazer I never normally wore at weekends and walked up the long hill to Maureen's house. Mrs Kavanagh gave me a cup of tea and a slice of home-made soda bread in her big, dark, chaotic basement kitchen, and burped a baby over her shoulder as she assessed me. She was a handsome woman in her forties grown stout from childbearing. She had her daughter's long hair, but it was going grey, and piled up in an untidy knot at the back of her head. Like her husband she spoke with an Irish brogue, though Maureen and her siblings had the same South London accent as myself. Maureen was the eldest child, and the apple of her parents' eye. Her scholarship to the Sacred Heart convent was the subject of particular pride, and the fact that I was a grammar-school boy was obviously a mark in my favour. Against me was the fact that I was a *boy*, and non-Catholic, therefore an inherent threat to Maureen's virtue. "You look like a decent sort of lad," said Mrs Kavanagh, "but her father thinks Maureen is too young to be gallivanting about with boys, and so do I. She has her homework to do." "Not every night, Mum," Maureen protested. "You already have the Youth Club on Sundays," said Mrs Kavanagh, "That's quite enough socializing at your age."

I asked if I could join the youth club.

"It's the parish youth club," said Mrs Kavanagh. "You have to be a Catholic."

"No you don't, Mum," Maureen said. "Father Jerome said non-Catholics can join if they're interested in the Church." Maureen looked at me and blushed.

"I'm very interested," I said, quickly.

"Is that so?" Mrs Kavanagh looked at me sceptically, but she knew she had been out-manoeuvred. "Well, if Father Jerome says it's alright, I suppose it's alright."

Needless to say, I had no genuine interest in Catholicism, or indeed in religion of any kind. My parents were not churchgoers, and observed the Sabbath only to the extent of forbidding me and my brother to play in the street on Sundays. Lambeth Merchants' was nominally C of E, but the prayers and hymns at morning assembly, and occasional services in the chapel, seemed part of the school's ceaseless celebration of its own heritage rather than the expression of any moral or theological idea. That some people, like Maureen and her family, should voluntarily submit themselves to such boredom every Sunday morning, when they could be enjoying a long lie-in instead, was incomprehensible to me. Nevertheless I was prepared to feign a polite interest in her religion, if that was the price of being allowed to keep Maureen company.

The following Sunday evening I turned up, by arrangement with Maureen, outside the local Roman Catholic church, a squat redbrick building with a larger-than-lifesize statue of the Virgin Mary outside. She had her arms extended, and a carved inscription on the plinth said: "I AM THE IMMACULATE CONCEPTION." A service was going on inside, and I lurked in the porch, listening to the unfamiliar hymns and droning prayers, my nostrils tickled by a strong sweet smell which I guessed must be incense. Suddenly there was a clamour of high-pitched bells, and I peeped through the doorway, looking down the aisle to the altar. It was quite a sight, ablaze with dozens of tall, thin lighted candles. The priest, dressed in a heavy embroidered robe of white and gold, was holding up something that flashed and glinted with reflected light, a white disc in a glass case, with golden rays sticking out all round it like a sunburst. He held the base of the thing wrapped in an embroidered scarf he had round his shoulders, as if it was too hot to touch, or radioactive. All the people, and there were a surprising number of them, were kneeling with their heads bowed. Maureen explained to me in due course that the white disc was a consecrated host, and that they believed it was the real body and blood of Jesus, but to me the whole business seemed more pagan than Christian. The singing sounded queer too. Instead of the rousing hymns I was used to at school ("To be a Pilgrim" was my favourite) they were singing slow, dirge-like anthems that I couldn't comprehend because they were in Latin, never my best subject. I had to admit, though, that there was a kind of atmosphere about the service that you didn't get in the school chapel.

What I liked about Catholics from the beginning was that there was nothing holier-than-thou about them. When the congregation came pouring out of the church, they might have been coming out of the pictures, or even a pub, the way they greeted each other and joked and chatted and offered each other cigarettes. Maureen came out accompanied by her mother, their heads covered with scarves. Mrs Kavanagh began talking to another woman in a hat. Maureen spotted me, and came over, smiling. "You found the way, then?" she greeted me. "What if your Dad sees us talking?" I asked nervously. "Oh, he never comes to Benediction," she said, untying her headscarf and shaking out her hair. "Thank the Lord." The paradoxical nature of this remark didn't strike me, and in any case my attention was fully absorbed by her hair. I had never seen it unrestrained before, fanned out in shining waves over her shoulders. She seemed more beautiful than ever. Conscious of my gaze, she blushed, and said she must introduce me to Father Jerome. Mrs Kavanagh seemed to have disappeared.

Father Jerome was the younger of the two priests who ran the parish, though he wasn't exactly young. He didn't look at all like our school chaplain or any other clergyman I had encountered. He didn't even resemble himself on the altar – for it was he who had presided over the service just finished. He was a gaunt, grizzled Dubliner, with nicotine-stained fingers and a shaving cut on his chin which he seemed to have staunched with a fragment of toilet-paper. He wore a long black cassock that reached to his scuffed shoes, with deep pockets in which he kept the materials for rolling his own cigarettes. One of these he lit with a pyrotechnic display of flame and sparks. "So you want to join our youth club, do you, young fella?" he said, brushing glowing wisps of tobacco from his cassock. "Yes please, sir," I said. "Then you'd better learn to call me Father instead of sir." "Yes, sir – Father, I mean," I stammered. Father Jerome grinned, revealing a disconcerting gap in his stained and uneven teeth. He asked me a few more questions about where I lived and where I went to school. The name of Lambeth Merchants' had its usual effect, and I became a probationary member of the Immaculate Conception parish youth club.

One of the first things Maureen had to do was to explain the name of her church. I presumed that it referred to Mary's being a virgin when she had Jesus, but no, apparently it meant that Mary herself was conceived "without the stain of original sin." I found the language of Catholicism very strange, especially the way they used words in their devotions, like "virgin", "conceived", "womb", that would have been regarded as bordering on the indecent in ordinary conversation, certainly in my home. I could hardly believe my ears when Maureen told me that she had to go to Mass on New Year's Day because it was the Feast of the Circumcision. "The feast of *what?*" "The Circumcision." "Whose circumcision?" "Our Lord's, of course. When he was a baby. Our Lady and Saint Joseph took him to the Temple and he was circumcised. It was like the Jewish baptism." I laughed incredulously. "D'you know what circumcision *is?*" Maureen blushed and giggled, wrinkling up her nose. " 'Course." "What is it, then?" "I'm not going to say." "You don't really know." "Yes I do." "I bet you don't." I persisted in my prurient interrogation until she blurted out that it meant "snipping off a bit of skin from the end of the baby's widdler," by which time my own widdler was standing up inside my grey flannel trousers like a relay-runner's baton. We were walking home from the youth club Sunday social at the time, and fortunately I was wearing a raincoat.

The youth club met twice a week in the Infants' School attached to the church: on Wednesdays for games, mainly ping-pong, and on Sundays for a "social". This consisted of dancing to gramophone records and partaking of sandwiches and orange squash or tea prepared by teams of girls working to a roster. The boys were required to stack the infants' desks at the sides of the room at the beginning of the evening, and replace them in rows at the end. We had the use of two classrooms normally divided by a folding partition wall. The floor was made of worn, unpolished wood blocks, the walls were covered with infantile paintings and educational charts, and the lighting was bleakly utilitarian. The gramophone was a single-speaker portable, and the records a collection of scratchy 78s. But to me, just emerging from the chrysalis of boyhood, the youth club was a site of exciting and sophisticated pleasures.

I learned to dance from a matronly lady of the parish who came in on games nights (when Maureen was seldom allowed out by her parents) and gave free lessons. I discovered that I was surprisingly good at it. "Hold your partner firmly!" was Mrs Gaynor's constant injunction, one I was glad to follow, especially when Maureen was my partner on Sunday nights. I danced mostly with her, needless to say, but club protocol forbade exclusive pairing, and I was a rather popular choice in "ladies' invitation" sets because of my nifty footwork. It was of course ballroom dancing – quickstep, foxtrot and waltz – with a few old-time dances thrown in for variety. We danced to strict-tempo music by Victor Sylvester, diversified with popular hits by Nat King Cole, Frankie Laine, Guy Mitchell and other vocalists of the day. Pee Wee Hunt's "Twelfth Street Rag" was a great favourite, but jiving was not allowed – it was expressly forbidden by Father Jerome – and the solo twisting, ducking and swaying that passes for dancing nowadays was still in the womb of time, awaiting its birth in the sixties. When, nowadays, I put my head inside a discothèque or nightclub patronized by young people, I'm struck by the contrast between the eroticism of the ambience – the dim, lurid lighting, the orgasmic throb of the music, the tight-fitting, provocative clothes – and the tactile impoverishment of the actual dancing. I suppose they have so much physical contact afterwards that they don't miss it on the dance floor, but for us it was the other way round. Dancing meant that, even in a church youth club, you were actually allowed to hold a girl in your arms in public, perhaps a girl you'd never even met before you asked her to dance, feel her thighs brush against yours under her rustling petticoats, sense the warmth of her bosom against your chest, inhale the scent behind her ears or the smell of shampoo from her freshly washed hair as it tickled your cheek. Of course you had to pretend that this wasn't the point of it, you had to chat about the weather or the music or whatever while you steered your partner around the floor, but the licence for physical sensation was considerable. Imagine a cocktail party where all the guests are masturbating while ostensibly preoccupied with sipping white wine and discussing the latest books and plays, and you have some idea what dancing was like for adolescents in the early nineteen-fifties.

Admittedly, Father Jerome did his best to damp down the fires of lust, insisting on opening the evening's proceedings with a tedious recitation of the "Hail Mary" ten times in succession, something he referred to as "a mystery of the holy rosary" – it was certainly a mystery to me what anybody got out of the droning gabble of words. And he hung about afterwards, eyeing the dancing couples to make sure everything was decent and above board. There was actually a clause in the club rules – it was known as Rule Five, and was the subject of mildly risqué humour among the members – that there must always be light visible between dancing couples; but it was not rigidly enforced or observed. Anyway, Father Jerome usually left (it was rumoured to drink whisky and play whist with some cronies in the presbytery) well before the last waltz, when we would turn out some of the lights, and the bolder spirits would dance cheek-to-cheek, or at least chest-to-chest. Naturally I always ensured that Maureen was my partner then. She was not an exceptionally good dancer, and when I saw her partnered by other boys she sometimes looked positively clumsy, which I didn't mind at all. She was responsive to my firm lead, and laughed with delight when I whirled her round and round at the end of a record, making her skirts swirl. She had two outfits for the Sunday-night socials: a black taffeta skirt worn with various blouses, and a white frock covered with pink roses that fitted her tightly round her bosom, which was shapely and well-developed for her age.

I was soon accepted by the other members of the club, especially after I joined its football team, which played on Sunday afternoons against other South London parishes, some with similarly bizarre names to ours, so you would get scorelines like, "Immaculate Conception 2, Precious Blood 1" or "Perpetual Succour 3, Forty Martyrs nil." I played at inside right, to such good effect that we won the league championship that season. I was top scorer, with twenty-six goals. The manager of a rival team found out that I wasn't a Catholic and made an official complaint that I shouldn't have been allowed to play in the league. For a while it looked as if the trophy might be taken away from us, but after we threatened to pull out of the league we were allowed to keep it.

We played on bumpy, sloping pitches in public parks, travelling by tram or bus, and changing in damp cheerless huts with a toilet and cold-water handbasin if we were lucky, but never baths or showers. The mud caked on my knees on the way home, and sitting in the bath later I would slowly straighten my legs in the water and pretend my knees were two volcanic islands sinking into the sea. When they had disappeared my engorged penis would rear up from the steaming, murky water like a wicked sea-serpent, as I thought about Maureen who would be washing her hair at the same time in preparation for the Sunday-evening social. She had told me she usually did this while taking a bath, because it was difficult to rinse her long hair while bending over a sink. I imagined her sitting in the warm, sudsy water, filling an enamel jug from the tap, pouring it over her head and making the long tresses stick to the curve of her breasts, like a picture of a mermaid I had seen once.

Maureen and some of the other girls from the youth club used to come to the Sunday-afternoon football matches to support us. When I scored a goal, I would look for her on the sidelines as I trotted back to the centre circle with the modest, self-contained demeanour I imitated from Charlie Vaughan, the Charlton Athletic centre-forward, and receive her adoring smile. I remember one goal in particular I scored with a spectacular flying header, I think it was a match against Our Lady of Perpetual Succour, Brickley, the neighbouring parish, and therefore something of a local derby. The goal was a pure fluke, actually, because I was never a great header of the ball. It was two-all in the last minutes of the game when I collected the ball from a clearance by our goalkeeper, beat a couple of opposing players and passed the ball out to our right-winger. His name was Jenkins – Jenksy, we called him: a small, prematurely wizened, stooped-shouldered boy, who smoked a Woodbine not only before and after every match, but also at half-time, and had been known to beg a drag of a spectator's cigarette during a lull in the game itself. In spite of appearances, he was surprisingly fast, especially going downhill, as he was on this occasion. He scuttled down the wing towards the corner-flag and crossed the ball, as he usually did, without looking, anxious to get rid of it before the opposing left-back caught up and crunched into him. I came pounding into the penalty area just as the ball came across in front of me at about waist height. I launched myself into the air and by lucky chance caught it smack in the middle of my forehead. It went into the net like a rocket before the goalie could move. The fact that the goal *had* a net (not many pitches we played on ran to such refinements) made it all the more satisfying. The opposing players gaped at me. My team-mates pulled me to my feet and clapped me on the back. Maureen and the other girls from Immaculate Conception were jumping up and down on the sidelines, cheering like mad. I don't think I have ever experienced a moment of such pure exultation in my life since. It was that night, after walking Maureen home from the youth club social, that I touched her breast for the first time, outside her blouse.

That would have been about a year after I first spoke to her. We advanced in physical intimacy slowly, and by infinitesimal degrees, for several reasons: my inexperience, Maureen's innocence, her parents' suspicious surveillance. Mr and Mrs Kavanagh were very strict, even by the standards of those days. They couldn't stop us meeting at the youth club, and they could hardly object to my escorting her home afterwards, but they forbade her to go out with me alone, to the pictures or anywhere else. On Saturday evenings she was required to babysit while they went to an Irish Club in Peckham, but she wasn't allowed to have me in the house while they were out, and she wasn't allowed to visit me at home. We continued to meet every morning at the tram stop, of course (except that it was a bus stop, now: the London trams were being phased out, and the tracks ripped up and tarmacked over – my Dad was given a desk job in the depot, and didn't complain) and we left our respective houses early to have more time to chat. I used to hand Maureen love letters to read on her way to school – she told me never to post them because her parents would have been sure to intercept one sooner or later. I asked her to post hers to me because it seemed grown-up to be receiving private correspondence, especially in mauve envelopes smelling of lavender, driving my young brother frantic with frustrated curiosity. There was little danger that my parents would pry into their contents, which were in any case totally innocuous. The letters were written on mauve lavender-scented notepaper in a big round hand, with the little circles over the *is*. On reflection, I think she got the idea from the advertisements for Biro pens. She used to get told off for it at school. Apart from the brief morning encounters at the tram stop, we could only meet in the context of youth-club activities – the socials, the games nights, the football matches, and occasional rambles in the Kent and Surrey green belt in the summer months.

Perhaps these restrictions helped to keep us devoted to each other for so long. We never had time to become bored with each other's company, and in defying Maureen's parents' disapproval we felt as if we were enacting some deeply romantic drama. Nat King Cole said it all for us in "Too Young", rolling the vowels round in his mouth like boiled sweets, to a background of syrupy strings and plangent piano chords:

> They try to tell us we're too young,
> Too young to really be in love.
> They say that love's a word,
> A word we've only heard
> But can't begin to know the meaning of.
> And yet we're not too young to know,
> This love will last though years may go . . .

It was our favourite tune, and I would always make sure that Maureen was my partner when somebody put it on the turntable.

Almost the only time we had alone together was when I walked her home from the youth-club socials on Sunday nights. At first, awkward and unsure of how to comport myself in this novel situation, I used to slouch along with my hands in my pockets, a yard apart from Maureen. But one cold night, to my intense delight, she drew close to me as if for warmth, and slipped her arm through mine. I swelled with the pride of possession. Now she was truly my girlfriend. She chattered on my arm like a canary in a cage – about the people at the youth club, about her schoolfriends and teachers, about her family, with its huge network of relations in Ireland and even America.

Maureen was always brimming over with news, gossip, anecdotes, whenever we met. It was trivial stuff, but enchanting to me. I tried to forget about my own school when I was out of it, and my family seemed less interesting than Maureen's, so I was content to let her make most of the conversational running. But occasionally she would question me about my parents and my early life, and she loved me to tell her how for so long I used to look out for her every morning at the corner of Hatchford Five Ways without ever daring to speak to her.

Even after she took my arm on the way home from the youth club, weeks passed before I ventured to kiss her goodnight outside her house. It was a clumsy, botched kiss, half on her mouth, half on her cheek, which took her by surprise, but it was returned with warmth. She broke away immediately with a murmured "Goodnight," and ran up the steps to her front door; but the next morning at the tram stop there was a dazed glow in her eyes, a new softness in her smile, and I knew that the kiss had been as momentous for her as for me.

I had to learn to kiss as I had learned to dance. In our male-dominated household there was almost a taboo on touching of any kind, whereas in Maureen's family, she told me, it was customary for all the children, even the boys, to kiss their parents goodnight. That was a very different matter from kissing me, of course, but it explained how naturally Maureen lifted her face to mine, how comfortable and relaxed she felt in my arms. Oh the rapture of those first embraces! What is it about kissing in adolescence? I suppose it gives you an intuitive sense of what sex will be like, the girl's lips and mouth being like the secret inside flesh of her body: pink, wet, tender. Certainly what we used to call French kissing, pushing your tongues into each other's mouths, is a kind of mimic intercourse. But it was a long time before Maureen and I went as far as that. For many months it seemed quite intoxicating enough to simply kiss, clasped in each other's arms, lips to lips, eyes closed, holding our breath for minutes at a time.

We used to do it in the shadows of the basement area of Maureen's house, putting up with the smell from the nearby dustbins for the sake of privacy. We stood there in all weathers. If it was raining, Maureen would hold her umbrella over both of us as we embraced. In cold weather I would undo the toggles of my duffelcoat (a proud new acquisition for weekend wear) and open the front of her raincoat to create a kind of tent in which to draw her close. One night I found the rose-patterned dress had a button missing at the back and slid my hand through the gap and felt her bare skin between her shoulder-blades. She shuddered and opened her lips a little more as she pressed them against mine. Weeks later I found my way through the front of her blouse, and caressed her stomach over a slippery satin slip. So it went on. Inch by inch I extended my exploration of her body, virgin territory in every sense of the word. Maureen was tender and yielding in my arms, wanting to be loved, loving to be caressed, but quite without sexual self-consciousness. She must have often felt my erect penis through our clothing as we embraced, but she never remarked on it, nor gave any sign of being embarrassed by it. Perhaps she thought mature widdlers were permanently hard as bones. Erections were more of a problem for me. When we had to part (it was dangerous to linger in the area for more than ten or fifteen minutes, for Mr Kavanagh knew when the youth-club socials ended and would sometimes come out on to the front porch to look down the road, while we cowered, half-frightened, half-amused, just underneath him) I would wait till Maureen had run up the steps and let herself into the house before walking off stiffly and bent slightly forward, like a man on stilts.

I suppose Maureen must have experienced her own symptoms of sexual arousal, but I doubt whether she recognized them as such. She had a naturally pure mind, pure without being prudish. Dirty jokes left her looking genuinely blank. She talked about wanting to get married and have children when she grew up, but she didn't seem to connect this with sexuality. Yet she loved to be kissed and cuddled. She purred in my arms like a kitten. Such sensuality and innocence could hardly co-exist nowadays, I believe, when teenagers are exposed to so much sexual information and imagery. Never mind the soft-porn videos and magazines available from any High Street video store or newsagent – your average 15-certificate movie contains scenes and language that would have had half the audience ejaculating into their trousers forty years ago, and have sent the makers and distributors to gaol. No wonder kids today want to have sex as soon as they're able. I wonder if they even bother with kissing at all, now, before they get their kit off and jump into bed.

I was less pure-minded than Maureen, but not much more knowing. Though I indulged in vague fantasies of having sex with her, especially just before falling asleep, and had frequent wet dreams in consequence, I had no intention of seducing her, and would certainly have made a terrible hash of it if I had tried. I set my sights no higher than getting to feel her naked breasts. But that was a kind of seduction when I accomplished it.

I had got as far as cupping one breast gently, inside her blouse, as we kissed, feeling the stitching of her brassière like Braille on my fingertips, when her Catholic conscience kicked in. In retrospect, it's surprising that it hadn't done so before. The trigger was a "retreat" at her school – a funny name, it seemed for me, for the event as she described it, three days of sermons, devotions and periods of compulsory silence, though the military associations were appropriate enough to its immediate effect on our relationship. It was a Dunkirk of the flesh. The visiting priest running the retreat (Maureen described him as big and grey-bearded, like pictures of God the Father, with piercing eyes that seemed to look right into your soul) had addressed the Fifth-Form girls in the presence of a grimly nodding Mother Superior on the subject of Holy Purity, and frightened them all silly with the awful consequences of desecrating their Temples of the Holy Ghost, as he designated their bodies. "If any girl here," he thundered, and Maureen claimed that he looked especially at her as he spoke, "should cause a boy to commit a sin of impurity in thought, word or deed, by the way she dresses or behaves, she is as guilty of that sin as he. More guilty, because the male of our species is less able to control licentious desires than the female." Afterwards the girls had to go to confession to him, and he winkled out of them the details of such liberties as they had allowed boys to take with their Temples of the Holy Ghost. It seems very obvious to me now that he was a dirty old man who got his kicks out of prying into the sexual feelings and experiences of vulnerable adolescent girls, and making them cry. He certainly made Maureen cry. So did I, when she told me I mustn't touch her "there" any more.

If there was one element of the Catholic religion above all others that made me determined to remain a Protestant, or an atheist (I wasn't quite sure what I really believed), it was Confession. From time to time Maureen made efforts to interest me in her faith, and I knew without having to be told that her dearest wish was to be the agent of my conversion. I thought it prudent to put in the occasional appearance at Benediction on Sunday evenings, to keep her happy and justify my membership of the youth club, but I steered clear of Mass after giving it a couple of tries. It was mostly in Latin (a subject that made my life particularly miserable at school until I was allowed to drop it and substitute Art) mumbled inaudibly by a priest with his back turned, and seemed to bore the rest of the congregation almost as much as it bored me, since many of them were saying their rosaries while it went on – though, God knows, the Rosary was even more boring, and unfortunately was an official part of Benediction. No wonder Catholics burst out of the church in such high spirits after these services, talking and laughing and breaking out packets of cigarettes: it was sheer relief from the almost unendurable boredom inside. The only exception was the Midnight Mass at Christmas, which was jollied up by carol-singing and the excitement of staying out late. Other aspects of the Catholic religion, like the startlingly realistic paintings and sculptures of the Crucifixion inside the church, the terraces of guttering votive candles, not eating meat on Fridays, giving up sweets for Lent, praying to Saint Anthony if you lost something, and acquiring "indulgences" as a kind of insurance policy for the afterlife, seemed merely quaintly superstitious. But Confession was in a different class.

One day when we were in the church on our own for some reason – I think Maureen was lighting a candle for some "intention" or other, perhaps my conversion – I peeped into one of the cupboard-like confessionals built against the side of the church. On one side was a door with the priest's name on it; on the other side a curtain. I drew back the curtain and saw the padded kneeler and the small square of wire mesh, like a flattened meat-cover, through which you whispered your sins to the priest. The mere idea made my flesh creep. Ironic, really, considering how dependent I became on psychotherapy later in life, but in adolescence nothing is more repugnant than the idea of sharing your most secret and shaming thoughts with a grown-up.

Maureen tried to rid me of my prejudice. Religious Instruction was her best subject at school. She had got to the convent and held her own there by conscientious hard work rather than natural brilliance, and the rote-learning of R.I. suited her abilities. "It's not the priest you're telling, it's God." "Why not just tell God, then, in a prayer?" "Because it wouldn't be a sacrament." Out of my theological depth, I grunted sceptically. "Anyway," Maureen went on, "the priest doesn't know who you are. It's dark." "Suppose he recognizes your voice?" I said. Maureen conceded that she usually avoided going to Father Jerome for that very reason, but insisted that even if the priest did recognize your voice he wasn't allowed to let on, and he would never under any circumstances reveal what you confessed to anybody else, because of the seal of confession. "Even if you'd committed murder?" Even then, she assured me, though there was a catch: "He wouldn't give you absolution unless you promised to give yourself up." And what was absolution, I enquired, pronouncing it "ablution" by mistake and making Maureen giggle, before she launched into a long rigmarole about forgiveness and grace and penance and purgatory and temporal punishment, that made about as much sense to me as if she had recited the rules of contract bridge. I asked her once, early in our relationship, what sins she confessed herself and not surprisingly she wouldn't tell me. But she did tell me about her Confession on the school retreat, and how the priest had said it was a sin for me to touch her as I had been doing and that I mustn't do it any more and that to avoid "the occasion of sin" we mustn't go down into the area and cuddle when I saw her home but just shake hands or perhaps exchange a single chaste kiss.

Dismayed by this turn of events, I concentrated all my resources on reversing it. I protested, I argued, I wheedled; I was eloquent, I was pathetic, I was cunning. And of course, in the end, I won. The boy always does win such struggles, if the girl can't bear to risk losing him, and Maureen couldn't. No doubt she had given me her heart because I was the first to ask for it. But I was also quite good-looking at that stage of my life. I hadn't yet acquired the nickname Tubby, and I still had my hair – rather gorgeous blond hair, as a matter of fact, which I combed back in a billowing wave petrified with Brylcreem. Also I was the best dancer in the youth club and star of the football team. Such things matter to young girls more than exam results and career prospects. We both took our O-Level exams that year. Maureen achieved five lowish passes, enough to proceed to the sixth form; I failed everything except English Literature and Art, and left school to work in the office of a big theatrical impresario in the West End, having responded to an advertisement in the *Evening Standard*. I was only a glorified office-boy, to tell the truth, franking mail, taking it to the Post Office, fetching sandwiches for the staff, and so on, but something of the glamour of the business rubbed off on me. Famous actors and actresses passed through our dingy office above a Shaftesbury Avenue theatre on the way to the boss's inner sanctum, and they would smile and say a word to me as I took their coats or fetched them cups of coffee. I quickly picked up the language of show business and responded to its febrile excitements, the highs and lows of hits and flops. I suppose Maureen recognized that I was maturing rapidly in this sophisticated milieu, and in danger of growing away from her. I was sometimes given complimentary tickets to shows, but there was no hope that Mr and Mrs Kavanagh would let her go to them with me. We no longer met every morning at the tram stop, because I now took a Southern Electric train from Hatchford Station to Charing Cross. Our meetings on Sundays and our walks home from the youth-club socials therefore became all the more precious. She could not deny me her kisses for long. I coaxed her into the shadows at the bottom of the area steps and slowly I inched my way back to the state of intimacy that had existed before.

I don't know what compact she made with God or her conscience – I thought it prudent not to enquire. I knew that she went to confession once a month, and to communion every week, and that her parents would get suspicious if she deviated from this routine; and I knew, because she had explained it to me once, that you couldn't get absolution for a sin unless you promised not to do it again, and that to swallow the consecrated host in a state of sin was another sin, worse than the first. There was some kind of distinction between big sins and little sins she may have used as a loophole. Big sins were called mortal sins. I can't remember what the little ones were called, but you could go to communion without being absolved of them. I'm very much afraid, though, that the poor girl thought breast-touching was a mortal sin, and believed she was in serious danger of going to hell if she should die without warning.

Her air and expression subtly altered in that period, though I was probably the only one to register the change. She lost some of her usual exuberance. There was a kind of abstractedness in her eyes, a wanness about her smile. Even her complexion suffered: her skin lost its glow, a rash of pimples occasionally broke out round her mouth. But most significant of all, she allowed me more freedoms than before, as if she had abandoned all hope of being good, or as she would have put it, in a state of grace, and further defence of her modesty was therefore pointless. When, one warm September night, I unbuttoned her blouse, and unfastened, with infinite care and delicacy, like a burglar picking a lock, the hook and eye that fastened her brassière, I encountered no resistance, nor did she utter a word of protest. She just stood there in the dark, beside the dustbins, passive and trembling very slightly, like a lamb brought to the sacrifice. She wasn't wearing a slip. Holding my breath I gently released a breast, the left one, from its cup. It rolled into my palm like a ripe fruit. God! I've never felt a sensation like it, before or since, like the first feel of Maureen's young breast – so soft, so smooth, so tender, so firm, so elastic, so mysteriously gravity-defying. I lifted the breast a centimetre, and weighed it in my cupped palm, then gently lowered my hand again until it just fitted the shape without supporting it. That her breast should still hang there, proud and firm, seemed as miraculous a phenomenon as the Earth itself floating in space. I took the weight again and gently squeezed the breast as it lolled in my palm like a naked cherub. I don't know how long we stood there in the dark, not speaking, hardly breathing, until she murmured, "I must go," put her hands behind her back to do up the fastener of her brassière, and vanished up the steps.

From that night onwards our kissing sessions invariably incorporated my touching her breasts under her clothing. It was the climax of the ritual, like the priest raising the glittering monstrance aloft at Benediction. I learned the contours of her breasts so well that I could have moulded them in plaster blindfolded. They were almost perfect hemispheres, tipped with small pointed nipples that hardened under my touch like tiny erections. How I longed to see them as well as touch them, and to suck and nuzzle them and bury my head in the warm valley between them! I was also beginning to harbour designs on the lower half of her anatomy, and to dwell licentiously on the possibility of getting my hands inside her knickers. Obviously none of this could be decently accomplished standing up in the dank basement area. Somehow or other I must contrive to be alone with her indoors somewhere. I was racking my brains for some such stratagem, when I suffered a sudden and unexpected setback. As I was seeing her home one night, she came to a halt under a lamp-post at some distance from her house and said, looking at me earnestly and twisting her hair in her fingers, that the kissing, and everything that went with it, had to stop. It was all because of the youth-club Nativity play.

The idea of the play had come from Bede Harrington, the chairman of the club committee. I had never heard of anyone called Bede before, and when I first met him I asked him in all innocence if his name was spelled B-e-a-d, as in rosary. He obviously thought I was taking the piss and informed me stiffly that Bede was the name of an ancient British saint, a monk known as the Venerable Bede. Bede Harrington himself enjoyed a fair amount of veneration in the parish, especially from the adult members. He was a year or two older than me and Maureen, and had had a brilliant academic career at St Aloysius's, the local Catholic grammar school. At the time of which I write he was Head Boy, in the third-year Sixth, and had just obtained a place at Oxford to study – or, as he liked to say, showing off his inside knowledge, "read" – English the following year. He was tall, with a long, thin, white face, its pallor heightened by his heavy horn-rimmed glasses, and by the coarse black hair that seemed to part in the wrong place, since it was always sticking up in the air or falling over his eyes. In spite of his intellectual achievements, Bede Harrington lacked the accomplishments most highly valued in the youth club. He didn't dance and he didn't play football, or indeed do any other sport. He had always been excused games at school because of his shortsightedness, and he claimed simply not to be interested in dancing. I believe he was in fact very interested in the opportunities it offered to get into physical contact with girls, but knew that, with his gangly, ill-co-ordinated limbs and enormous feet, he probably wouldn't be much good at it, and couldn't bear to look ridiculous while he was learning. Bede Harrington had to excel at whatever he did. So he made his mark on the youth club by getting himself elected as chairman of the committee and bossing everybody else around. He edited a club Newsletter, a smudgy, cyclostyled document written largely by himself, and forced upon the reluctant membership occasional events of an intellectual nature, like debates and quizzes, at which he could shine. During the Sunday-night socials he was to be seen in deep conference with Father Jerome, or frowning over the club's catering accounts, or sitting alone on a tilted chair, with his hands in his pockets and his long legs stretched out, surveying the shuffling, rotating throng with a faint, superior smile, like a school-master indulging the childish pastimes of his charges. There was a wistful longing in his eyes, though, and it sometimes seemed to me that they lingered with particular covetousness on Maureen, as she swayed in my arms to the music.

The Nativity play was a typical piece of Bede Harrington self-promotion. Not only did he write the script himself; he directed it, acted in it, designed it, selected the recorded music for it, and did almost everything else to do with it except sew the costumes, a task delegated to his adoring mother and hapless sisters. The play was to be performed in the Infants' school on three evenings in the week before Christmas, and again at a local old people's home run by nuns, for one night only, on January 6th, the feast of the Epiphany –

248

"Twelfth Night", as he pedantically informed us at the first auditions.

These took place on a Wednesday club night early in November. I went along to keep a proprietorial eye on Maureen. Bede Harrington had taken her aside the previous Sunday evening while I was dancing with somebody else, and extracted a promise from her to read for the part of the Virgin Mary. She was flattered and excited at the prospect, and since I was unable to persuade her to withdraw, I thought I had better join her. Bede looked surprised and not very pleased to see me at the auditions. "I didn't think this was your sort of thing," he said. "And, to be perfectly honest, I'm not sure it would be quite right to have a non-Catholic in the parish Nativity play. I'd have to ask Father Jerome."

It came as no surprise that Bede had reserved the part of Joseph for himself. I daresay he would have doubled as the Angel Gabriel, and played all three Kings as well, if it had been practicable. Maureen was quickly confirmed in the part of Mary. I flipped through a copy of the cyclostyled script in search of a suitable part for myself. "What about Herod?" I said. "Surely you don't have to be a Catholic to play him?"

"You can have a go if you like," Bede said grudgingly.

I did the scene where Herod realizes that the Three Kings are not going to return to tell him where they found the infant Messiah, as he had hypocritically asked them to do, pretending he wanted to pay homage himself, and ruthlessly orders the massacre of every male child under two in the region of Bethlehem. As I mentioned earlier, acting was about the only thing I was any good at, at school. I gave a terrific audition. I out-Heroded Herod, to coin a phrase. When I finished the other aspirant actors spontaneously applauded, and Bede could hardly avoid giving me the part. Maureen looked at me adoringly: not only was I the best dancer and top scorer in the club, I was also obviously the star actor too. She herself was not, to be honest, much of an actress. Her voice was too small, her body-language too timid, to communicate across the footlights. (A figure of speech, of course: we had no footlights. All we had in the way of stage lighting was a battery of desk lamps with coloured bulbs.) But her part mainly required her to look meek and serenely beautiful, which she was able to do without speaking or moving about much.

I quite enjoyed the first weeks of rehearsals. I particularly enjoyed teasing Bede Harrington and undermining his authority. I quarrelled with his direction, offered suggestions for improving his script, continually improvised new business, and blinded him with theatrical science, throwing around technical terms I had picked up from work, and with which he was unfamiliar, like "block", "dry" and "up-stage". I said the title of his play, *The Fruit of the Womb* (an allusion to the "Hail Mary") reminded me of "Fruit of the Loom" on the label inside my vests, provoking such mirth that he was obliged to change it to *The Story of Christmas*. I clowned outrageously, reading the part of Herod in a variety of funny voices, impersonations of Tony Hancock and Bluebottle and Father Jerome, and causing the rest of the cast to collapse in hysterics. Bede, needless to say, responded to these antics with ill grace, and threatened to expel me at one point, but I backed down and apologized. I didn't want to be fired from the show. Not only was it rather fun, but it afforded me many extra opportunities to meet Maureen, and see her home, which Mr and Mrs Kavanagh could not possibly veto. And I certainly didn't want to leave her unprotected in Bede Harrington's directorial power. I had noticed that, in his role as Joseph, he took every opportunity to put a supporting arm round Mary's shoulder on the journey to Bethlehem and during the Flight into Egypt. By watching his performance very intently, with a faint, sardonic smile on my face, I was confident that I deprived him of any thrill from these physical contacts; and afterwards, when I walked Maureen home, I enjoyed my own sensual pleasures all the more.

Then Bede succumbed, rather late in life, to chicken pox, and was off sick for two weeks. He sent a message that we should carry on rehearsing under the direction of a boy called Peter Marello, who was playing the Chief Shepherd. But Peter was also captain of the football team and a good mate of mine. He deferred readily to my judgement in matters theatrical, as did the other members of the cast, and I became in effect the acting director. I thought I improved the show no end, but Bede wasn't best pleased when he returned, spotted with fading pustules and pockmarks, to see the result.

I had cut out the tedious recitation of the whole of T.S. Eliot's "The Journey of the Magi" which Bede had put into the mouth of one of the Three Kings, and written two big new scenes for Herod, based on memories of Sunday-School bible stories and Scripture lessons at school. One had Herod dying horribly, eaten up by worms – this promised to be a wonderful Grand-Guignol spectacle, involving the use of Heinz tinned spaghetti in tomato sauce as a prop. The other was a kind of flash-forward to the beheading of John the Baptist by Herod at the behest of Salomé. I had persuaded a girl called Josie, in principle, to do the dance of the seven veils in a body-stocking; she was a cheerful peroxide-assisted blonde who worked in Woolworths, wore bright red lipstick, and had a reputation for being a good sport, or rather vulgar, according to your point of view. Unfortunately it appeared that I had muddled up three different Herods in the New Testament, so Bede deleted these "excrescences", as he called them, without my being able to put up much of a fight. Even so, I think it is safe to say that the character of Herod figured more prominently in our nativity play than in any version since the Wakefield cycle.

We were now well into December, and Father Jerome, who had left us very much to our own devices up till then, requested to see a run-through. It was perhaps just as well that Salomé's dance of the seven veils had been cut, because even without it our play was insufficiently reverent for Father Jerome's taste. To do Bede Harrington justice, he had tried to get away from the usual series of pious tableaux, and to write something more modern, or as we would learn to say in another decade, "relevant". After the Annunciation, for example, Mary suffered from her Nazarene neighbours something of the prejudice experienced by unmarried mothers in modern Britain, and the difficulty of finding room in the inn at Bethlehem was obliquely linked to the contemporary housing shortage. Father Jerome insisted on the removal of all such unscriptural material. But it was the spirit of the whole production which really disturbed him. It was too profane. "It's more like a pantomime than a Nativity play," he said, baring his fangs in a mirthless grin. "Herod, for instance, puts the Holy Family in the shade entirely." Bede looked at me reproachfully, but his long face lengthened even more as Father Jerome went on: "That's not Laurence's fault. He's a fine actor, giving his best. The trouble is with the rest of youse. There's not half enough spirituality. Just consider what this play is *about*. The Word made Flesh. God Himself come down from heaven as a helpless babby, to dwell amongst men. Tink of what it meant to Mary to be singled out to be the Mother of God – " here he looked searchingly at Maureen, who blushed deeply and lowered her eyes. "Tink what it meant to Saint Joseph, responsible for the safety of the Mother of God, and her infant Son. Tink what it meant to the shepherds, poor hopeless fellas whose lives were little better than the beasts they looked after, when the Angel of the Lord appeared to them saying, 'I bring you tidings of great joy, that shall be to all people, for this day is born to you a saviour, which is Christ the Lord.' You have got to *become* those people. It's not enough to *play* your parts. You've got to *pray* your parts. You should begin every rehearsal with a prayer."

Father Jerome went on for some time in this vein. It was in its way a remarkable speech, worthy of Stanislavsky. He completely transformed the atmosphere of our rehearsals, which he regularly attended from that day on. The cast approached their parts with a new seriousness and dedication. Father Jerome had convinced them that they must draw on their own spiritual life for inspiration, and if they didn't have a spiritual life they had better acquire one. This of course was very bad news for me, as regards my relationship with Maureen. After his public homily, I noticed that the priest drew her aside and engaged her in earnest conversation. There was something ominously suggestive of a penitent in her posture as she sat beside him, her eyes lowered, hands joined in her lap, nodding silently as she listened. Sure enough, on our way home that evening, she stopped me at the corner of her street and said, "It's late, Laurence. I'd better go straight in. Let's say goodnight." "But we can't kiss properly here," I said. She was silent for a moment, twisting and untwisting a strand of hair round her finger. "I don't think we should kiss any more," she said. "Not like we usually do. Not while I'm Our Lady."

Perhaps Father Jerome had observed that Maureen and I were very close. Maybe he suspected that I was leading her astray in the Temple of the Holy Ghost department. I don't know, but he certainly did the business on her conscience that evening. He told her what an extraordinary privilege it was for any young girl to portray the Mother of God. He reminded her that her own name was an Irish form of "Mary". He said how pleased and proud her parents must be that she had been chosen for the part, and how she must strive to be worthy of it, in thought, word and deed. As Maureen relayed his words in a mumbled paraphrase I tried to laugh off their effect, without success. Then I attempted rational persuasion, holding her hands and looking earnestly into her eyes, also in vain. Then I tried sulking. "Good-night, then," I said, plunging my hands into my raincoat pockets. "You can kiss me once," said Maureen miserably, her lifted face blue under the streetlamp. "Just once? Under Rule Five?" I sneered. "Don't," she said, her lip trembling, her eyes filling with tears. "Oh, grow up, Maureen," I said, and turned on my heel and walked away.

I spent a miserable, restless night, and next morning I was late for work because instead of catching my usual train I stood at the corner of Hatchford Five Ways and waited for Maureen. I could see her figure stiffen with sudden self-consciousness, even a hundred yards away, as she recognized me. Of course she had spent a wretched night too – her face was pale and her eyelids swollen. We were reconciled almost before my words of apology were out, and she went off to school with a buoyant step and a smile on her face.

I was confident that, as before, I would gradually overcome her scruples. I was wrong. It was no longer just a private matter of conscience for Maureen. She was convinced that to go on necking with me while portraying the Virgin Mary would be a kind of sacrilege, which might bring the wrath of God down not only upon herself but upon the play itself and everyone concerned in it. She still loved me, it caused her real anguish to deny me her embraces, but she was determined to remain pure for the duration of the production. Indeed, she made a kind of vow to that effect, after going to Confession (to old Father Malachi, the parish priest) and Communion, the weekend after Father Jerome's intervention.

If I'd had any sense or tact, I would have resigned myself to the situation, and bided my time. But I was young, and arrogant and selfish. I didn't relish the prospect of a chaste Christmas and New Year, a season when it seemed to me one was entitled to expect a greater, not a lesser, degree of sensual licence. The 6th of January seemed a long way off. I suggested a compromise: no necking until after the first run of the play was over, but a relaxation of the rule between Christmas Eve and New Year's Eve, inclusive. Maureen shook her head. "Don't," she murmured, "Please don't bargain with me." "Well, when then?" I insisted brutally. "How soon after the last performance are we going to get back to normal?" "I don't know," she said, "I'm not sure it *was* normal." "Are you trying to tell me we're never going to?" I demanded. Then she burst into tears, and I sighed and apologized and we made it up, for a while, until I couldn't resist nagging her again.

All this time the play was in the throes of final rehearsals, so we were forced constantly into each other's company. But tempers were short and nerves frayed all round, so I don't think anyone in the cast noticed that Maureen and I were going through a sticky patch except perhaps Josie, who had a small part as the Innkeeper's wife. I had long been aware that Josie fancied me from the regularity with which she asked me to dance in Ladies' Invitations, and I was aware, too, that she was jealous of Maureen's starring role in *The Story of Christmas*. Apart from Herod, Josie's was the only really unsympathetic character in the play; we were drawn together in rehearsals by this circumstance, and by a shared indifference to the religiosity which had overtaken the production, and deprived it of most of its fun. When the rest of the cast solemnly recited the rosary at the beginning of every rehearsal, led by Father Jerome or Bede Harrington, I would catch her eye and try to make her giggle. I flattered her performance at rehearsals and coached her in her lines. At the Sunday-night socials I asked her to dance more frequently than before.

Maureen observed all this, of course. The dumb pain I saw in her eyes gave me an occasional pang of remorse, but didn't alter my cruel design, to bring pressure on her virtue by arousing her jealousy. Perhaps subconsciously I wanted our relationship to end. I was trying to crush something in myself as well as in her. I called it childishness, stupidity, naivety, in my own mind, but I might have called it innocence. The world of the parish youth club, which had seemed so enchanting when Maureen first introduced me to it, now seemed . . . well, parochial, especially in comparison with the world I encountered at work. From office gossip about affairs between actors and actresses, casting-couches and theatrical parties, I picked up a lurid and exciting notion of adult sexual behaviour against which Maureen's convent-girl scruples about letting me fondle her tits (as they were coarsely referred to in the office) seemed simply absurd. I ached to lose my virginity, and it obviously wasn't going to be with Maureen, unless and until I married her, a possibility as remote as flying to the moon. In any case, I had observed what married life on a low income was like in my own home, and it didn't appeal to me. I aspired to a freer, more expansive lifestyle, though I had no idea what form it might take.

The crisis came on the night of the last performance of the Nativity play before Christmas. It was a full house. The show had enjoyed great word-of-mouth in the parish, and there had even been a review, short but favourable, in the local newspaper. The review was unsigned and I would have suspected Bede Harrington of having written it himself if the writer hadn't been particularly complimentary about my own performance. I think the backstage struggle of wills between myself and Maureen actually imparted a special intensity to our performances. My Herod was more muted than in the early days of rehearsals, but more authentically cruel. I felt a thrilling *frisson*, a kind of collective shudder, run through the audience as I gave orders for the Massacre of the Innocents. And there was a tragic quality in Maureen's Virgin Mary, even in the Annunciation scene – "as if," said the anonymous reviewer, "she saw prophetically the Seven Swords of Sorrow that would pierce her heart in the years to come." (Come to think of it, perhaps Father Jerome wrote that review.)

We didn't have a cast party, exactly, at the end of the three-night run, but there was a sort of celebration with cocoa and chocolate biscuits and crisps organized by Peter Marello's girlfriend Anne, our stage manager, when we had taken off our costumes and washed off our make-up and dismantled the set and stored it away for the final performance at Epiphany. Father Jerome blessed and congratulated us and departed. We were exhausted, but jubilant, and reluctant to break up the collective euphoria by going home. Even Maureen was happy. Her parents and her brothers and sisters had come back to see the show a second time, and she had heard her father shouting "Bravo!" from the back of the hall when we took our curtain call. I had discouraged my own parents from coming, but my Mum had attended the first night and pronounced it "very nice though a bit loud" (she meant the music, especially the "Ride of the Valkyries" which accompanied the Flight into Egypt) and my brother, who had accompanied her, looked at me the next morning almost with respect. Bede Harrington, his head quite turned by success, was full of grandiose plans to write a Passion Play for the following Easter. It was to be in blank verse, I seem to remember, with speaking parts for the various instruments of the Crucifixion – the Cross, the Nails, the Crown of Thorns, etc. In magnanimous mood, he offered me the part of Scourge without the formality of an audition. I said I would think about it.

The conversation turned to our various plans for Christmas, and I chose this moment to announce that my boss had given me four complimentary tickets for his production of *The Babes in the Wood* at the Prince of Wales on Boxing Day. These were really intended for me to take my family, but some imp put it into my head to impress the company with a casually generous gesture, and to put Maureen to the test at the same time. I asked Peter and Anne if they would like to go with Maureen and me. They accepted readily, but Maureen, as I had anticipated, said that her parents wouldn't let her. "What, not even at Christmas?" I said. She looked at me, pleading with her eyes not to be publicly humiliated. "You know what they're like," she said. "Pity," I said, aware that Josie was listening intently. "Anyone else interested?" "Ooh, I'll go, I love pantos," Josie said promptly. She added, "You don't mind, do you, Maureen?" "No, I don't mind," Maureen whispered. Her expression was stricken. I might as well have taken the dagger I wore on my belt as Herod, and plunged it into her heart.

There was an awkward pause for a moment, which I covered by recalling a near-disaster with a sagging backcloth in the crib scene of our play, and we were soon engaged in a noisy and hilarious recapitulation of the entire performance. Maureen didn't contribute, and when I looked round for her, she had disappeared. She had left without saying goodnight to anyone. I walked home alone, moodily kicking an empty tobacco tin ahead of me. I did not feel very pleased with myself, but I managed somehow to blame Maureen for "spoiling Christmas". I didn't join her at Midnight Mass as I had intended. Christmas Day at home passed in the usual claustrophobic stupor. I went through with the Boxing Day excursion to the pantomime, pretending to my parents that I only had a single ticket, and meeting Josie, Peter and Anne at Charing Cross station. Josie was dressed like a tart and had drenched herself in cheap scent. She daringly asked for gin and orange at the interval, nearly bankrupting me in the process, and laughed raucously at all the blue jokes in the show, much to the embarrassment of Peter and Anne. Afterwards I saw Josie home to her family's council flat, and embraced her in a dark space under the communal stairs to which she led me without preliminaries. She thrust her tongue halfway down my throat and clamped one of my hands firmly onto one of her breasts, which was encased in a wired, sharply pointed brassière. I had little doubt that she would have allowed me to go further, but had no inclination to do so. Her perfume did not entirely mask the smell of stale perspiration from her armpits, and I was already tired of her vacuous chatter and strident laugh.

The next day I received a letter from Maureen, posted on Christmas Eve, saying she thought it would be best if we didn't see each other for a while, apart from the last performance of the play. It was written in her round, girlish hand on the usual mauve notepaper smelling of lavender, but the *i*s were all dotted normally, not with the little bubbly circles. I didn't reply to the letter, but I sent one to Bede Harrington saying I couldn't make the last performance of the play, and recommending that he ask Peter Marello to double as Herod. I never went to the youth club again, and I dropped out of the football team. I missed the exercise, and it was probably from that time that my waistline began to expand, especially as I was acquiring a taste for beer. I became friendly with a young man called Nigel who worked in the box-office of the theatre over which our office was located, and he introduced me to a number of Soho pubs. We spent a lot of time together, and it was months before I realised that he was homosexually inclined. The girls in the office assumed that I must be too, so I made little headway with them. I didn't lose my virginity, in fact, until I was in the Army, doing National Service, and that was a quick and sordid business with a tipsy WRAC, up against the wall of a lorry park.

I saw Maureen occasionally in the months that followed the production of the Nativity play, in the street, or getting on and off a bus, but I didn't speak to her. If she saw me, she didn't show it. She looked increasingly girlish and unsophisticated to my eyes, in her eternal navy-blue raincoat and her unchanging hairstyle. Once, just after I received my National Service papers, we came face to face in a chemist's shop – I was going in as she was going out. We exchanged a few awkward words. I asked her about school. She said she was thinking of going in for nursing. She asked me about work. I told her I had just been called up, and that I hoped to be sent abroad and to see a bit of life.

In the event I was trained as a clerk and posted to a part of North Germany where beetroot fields stretched to the horizon and it was so cold in winter that I cried once on guard duty and the tears froze on my cheeks. The only escape I found from terminal boredom was through acting in and writing scripts for revues, pantomimes, drag shows and other home-made entertainments on the base. When I got back to civvy street I was determined to make my career in some branch of show business. I got a place in one of the less prestigious London drama schools, with a small scholarship which I supplemented by working in a pub at nights. I didn't see Maureen around Hatchford when I went back to visit Mum and Dad. I ran into Peter Marello once and he told me that she had left home to train as a nurse. That was about thirty-five years ago. I haven't seen or heard of her since.

Sunday 6th June. It took me a whole week to write that, doing practically nothing else. I printed off the last few pages at ten o'clock last night, and went out to stretch my legs and buy the Sunday papers. Men were unloading them from a van onto the pavement outside Leicester Square tube station, like fishermen selling their catch on the quayside, ripping open the bales of different sections – news, sport, business, arts – and hastily assembling the papers on the spot as the punters thrust out their money. It always gives me a kick to buy tomorrow's papers today, the illusion of getting a peep at the future. In fact, what I've been doing is catching up on the news of the past week. Nothing much has changed in the big wide world. Eleven people were killed when the Bosnian Serbs lobbed mortar shells into a football stadium in Sarajevo. Twenty-five UN soldiers were killed in an ambush by General Aidid's troops in Somalia. John Major has the lowest popularity rating of any British Prime Minister since polling began. I'm beginning to feel almost sorry for him. I wonder whether it isn't a cunning Tory plot to capture the low self-esteem vote.

I didn't buy any papers last week because I didn't want to be distracted from the task in hand. I hardly listened to the radio or watched television, either. I made an exception of the England – Norway match last Wednesday, and regretted it. What humiliation. Beaten 2–0 by a bunch of part-timers, and probably knocked out of the World Cup in consequence. They should declare a day of national mourning and send Graham Taylor to the salt mines. (He'd probably organize his chain-gang into a 3–5–2 formation, and have

259

them all banging into each other like the England team.) It spoiled my concentration on the memoir for at least half a day, that result.

I don't think I've ever done anything quite like it before. Perhaps I'm turning into a book writer. There's no "you" in it, I notice. Instead of telling the story as I might to a friend or somebody in a pub, my usual way, I was trying to recover the truth of the original experience for myself, struggling to find the words that would do maximum justice to it. I revised it a lot. I'm used to that, of course – scriptwriting is mostly rewriting – but in response to the input of other people. This time I was the only reader, the only critic, and I revised as I went along. And I did something I haven't done since I bought my first electric typewriter – wrote the first drafts of each section in longhand. Somehow it seems more natural to try and recover the past with a pen in your hand than with your fingers poised over a keyboard. The pen is like a tool, a cutting or digging tool, slicing down through the roots, probing the rockbed of memory. Of course I used a bit of licence in the dialogue. It all happened forty years ago and I didn't take any notes. But I'm pretty sure that I've been true to the emotions, and that's the important thing. I can't leave the piece alone, though: I keep picking up the printed-out sheets, re-reading them, tinkering and revising, when what I should be doing is tidying up the flat.

The kitchen looks like a tip, heaped with soiled plates and empty takeaway food containers, there's a pile of unopened mail on the coffee table, and the answerphone has stopped receiving messages because the tape is full. Grahame was quite disgusted by the state of the place when he came in to watch the England match. He has higher standards of housekeeping than me – sometimes he borrows my dustpan and brush to sweep his little square of marbled floor in the porch. I fear his days of occupation may be numbered, though. The two American academics in number 4 are over for the summer vacation, and they entertain a lot. Understandably they object to having a resident bum in the entryway over whom their arriving and departing guests must step. They told me in the lift yesterday that they were going to complain to the police. I tried to persuade them that Grahame was no ordinary bum, but without making much impression. He doesn't help his cause by referring to them contemptuously as "them yank poofters"

What reading and re-reading the memoir leaves me with is an overwhelming sense of loss. Not just the loss of Maureen's love, but the loss of innocence – hers and my own. In the past, whenever I thought of her – and it wasn't very often – it was with a kind of fond, wry, inner smile: nice kid, first girlfriend, how naive we both were, water under the bridge, that sort of thing. Going back over the history of our relationship in detail, I realized *for the first time* what an appalling thing I had done all those years ago. I broke a young girl's heart, callously, selfishly, wantonly.

I'm well aware, of course, that I wouldn't feel this way about it if I hadn't recently discovered Kierkegaard. It's really a very Kierkegaardian story. It has resemblances to "The Seducer's Diary", and resemblances to K's own relationship with Regine. Maureen – Regine: the names almost rhyme.

Regine put up more of a fight than Maureen, though. When K sent back her ring, she rushed straight round to his lodgings, and, finding him not at home, left a note begging him not to desert her, "in the name of Christ and by the memory of your deceased father." That was an inspired touch, the deceased father. Søren was convinced that, like so many of his siblings, he would die before his father – there seemed to be a curse on the family that way. So when the old man popped off first Søren thought he had in some mystical sense died *for* him. He dated his religious conversion from that time. So Regine's note really shook him. But he went on nevertheless pretending to be cold and cynical, breaking the girl's heart, perversely convinced that he "could be happier in unhappiness without her than with her." I just looked up his record of their last interview:

> I tried to talk her round. She asked me, Will you never marry? I replied, Well, in about ten years, when I have sowed my wild oats, I must have a pretty young miss to rejuvenate me. – A necessary cruelty. She said, Forgive me for what I have done to you. I replied, It is rather I that should pray for your forgiveness. She said, Kiss me. That I did, but without passion. Merciful God!

That "Kiss me" was Regine's last throw. When it didn't work, she gave up.

Reading that, I recalled again Maureen lifting her unhappy face to me, blue under the streetlamp's bleak light, and saying, "You can kiss me once," and my walking away. Did I ever embrace her after that, or did I continue to spurn the offer of a single chaste goodnight kiss? I didn't keep her last letter, and I can't remember what she said exactly, but the words were pretty banal, I'm sure. They always were. It wasn't anything she said, it was her presence that I remember: the swing of her hair, the shine in her eyes, the way she wrinkled up her nose when she smiled . . . I wish I had a photograph of her to hand. I used to carry a picture of her around in my wallet, a black-and-white holiday snap taken in Ireland when she was fifteen, leaning against a drystone wall, smiling and squinting into the sun, the breeze plastering her cotton skirt to her legs. The photo got creased and dog-eared from constant handling, and after we split up I threw it away. I remember how easily it tore in my fingers, the paper having lost all its gloss and spring, and seeing the scattered fragments of her image at the bottom of the wastepaper basket. The only other photographs I have of her are in a shoebox somewhere in the loft at home in Hollywell, along with other juvenile souvenirs. There aren't very many of them, because neither of us owned a camera in those days. There are a few snaps taken by other members of the youth club on rambles, and a group photo of the cast of the Nativity play. If I could be sure of picking a time when Sally is out, I've a good mind to drive up to Hollywell tomorrow and have a look for them.

6.30 p.m. Shortly after I had typed that last sentence, and switched off the computer, and as I was rolling up my sleeves preparatory to starting on the washing-up, I had an idea: instead of searching my attic for photographs of Maureen, why not try to find Maureen herself? The more I think about it, and I've thought of little else all afternoon, the more I'm taken with it. It's slightly scary, because I've no idea how she will react if I manage to trace her, but that's what makes it exciting. I've no idea where she is, or what's happened to her since we last met in the chemist's shop in Hatchford. She could be living abroad, for all I know. Well, that's no problem, I'd travel to New Zealand if necessary. She could be dead. I don't think I could bear that, but I have to admit it's possible. Cancer. A road accident. Any number of things. Somehow, though, I'm sure she's still alive. Married, probably. Well, certainly, a girl like Maureen, how could she not be married? She married a doctor, I expect, like most good-looking nurses, and stayed married to him, being a devout Catholic. Unless she stopped believing, of course. It does happen. Or she might be widowed.

Hey, I must be careful not to indulge in wishful fantasies here. She's probably a very respectable, rather dull, happily married woman, stout and grey-haired, living in a comfortable suburban house with curtains that match the loose covers on the three-piece suite, mainly interested in her grandchildren, and looking forward to getting her OAP railpass so she can visit them more often. She probably hasn't given me a thought for decades, and wouldn't know me from Adam if I turned up on her doorstep. Nevertheless that's what I'm going to do, turn up on her doorstep. If I can find it.

✻ ✻ ✻ ✻ ✻ ✻ ✻ ✻ ✻ ✻ ✻ ✻ ✻ ✻ ✻ ✻ ✻

Monday 7th June. 4.30 p.m. Whew! I'm exhausted, drained, and my knee aches. I've been back to Hatchford today. Hatchford Mon Amour.

I took the train from Charing Cross just after nine this morning. I was travelling against the rush hour, breasting waves of commuters with pallid Monday-morning faces who surged across the station concourse and swirled around the islanded Tie Rack, Knickerbox and Sockshop before being sucked down the plughole of the Underground. My train was almost empty for its return journey to the suburbs. Southern Electric the trains used to be called, Network Southeast they're called now, but nothing essential has changed on this line, except that the graffiti on the inside of the carriages are more abundant and colourful nowadays, due to the development of the felt-tip pen. *Vorsprung durch Technik.* I took my seat in the second coach from the front because that's the most convenient one for the exit at Hatchford, shuffled a clear space for my feet amid the litter on the floor, and inhaled the familiar smell of dust and hair-oil from the upholstery. A porter came down the platform, slamming the doors shut hard enough to make the teeth rattle in your head, and then the electric motor whined and ticked under the floor as the driver switched on the power. The train moved off with a jerk and rumbled over Hungerford Bridge, the Thames glittering in the sun through the trelliswork of girders; then lurched through the points between Waterloo East and London Bridge. From there the line is straight for miles, and the train rushed at rooftop level past workshops and warehouses and lock-up garages and scrap-merchants' yards and school playgrounds and streets of terraced houses, overlooked by the occasional tower block of council flats. It was never a scenic route.

It was years since I last travelled along this line, and decades since I alighted at Hatchford. In 1962 Dad had a bit of luck – the only bit of luck he had in his life, actually, apart from meeting Mum: £20,000 on the pools, Littlewoods' Three Draws. That was a lot of money in those days, enough for him to retire early from London Transport and buy a little bungalow at Middleton-on-Sea, near Bognor. After he and Mum moved there, I never had any need or inclination to return to Hatchford. It was eerie going back today, a dreamlike mixture of the familiar and the unfamiliar. At first I was struck by how little had changed around the Five Ways. There are different shopfronts and a new road layout – the florist's on the corner has turned into a video rental shop, the Co-op bakery is a DIY superstore, and the road is marked like a complicated board-game, with arrows and cross-hatching and mini-roundabouts – but the contours of the streets and buildings are essentially as I remember them. The sociology of the place has changed though. The little streets of terraced houses off the main road are now largely occupied by Caribbean and Asian families, as I discovered when I went to have a look at our old house in Albert Street.

The sash widows had been ripped out and replaced with sealed aluminium units, and a small glazed porch had been stuck over the front door, but otherwise it was the same house, greyish-yellowish brick, with a slate roof and a front garden a yard deep. There's still a big chip out of the stone window ledge at the front, where a piece of shrapnel hit it in the war. I knocked on the door and a grey-haired Caribbean man opened it a suspicious crack. I explained that I had once lived there and asked if I could come in and look around for a moment. He looked doubtful, as if he suspected me of being a snooper or a con-man, as well he might; but a young woman, who addressed him as Dad, appeared at his shoulder, wiping her hands on an apron, and kindly invited me to step in. What struck me first, apart from the spicy cooking smells lingering on the air, was the narrowness and darkness of the hall and staircase when the front door was closed: I'd forgotten the absence of light inside a terraced house. But the wall between the front and back parlours had been knocked down to make a bright and pleasantly proportioned living-room. Why hadn't we done that? We spent most of our lives crammed into the back room, where it was hardly possible to move without banging into each other or the furniture. The answer, of course, was the ingrained habit of always keeping something – whether it was a suit, a tea-service, or a room – "for best".

The extended living-room was cheerfully if gaudily decorated in yellows and purples and greens. The TV was on, and two small children, twin girls aged about three, were sitting on the floor in front of it, sucking their thumbs and watching a cartoon programme. The two fireplaces had been boarded up and the mantelpieces ripped out, and there were central-heating radiators under the front and rear windows. The room bore so little resemblance to what I remembered that I was unable to populate it with memories. I peered out at the small patch of ground we used to dignify with the name, "back garden". It had been largely paved over and partly covered by a lean-to extension of transparent fibreglass. There was a bright red barbecue on wheels, and a carousel for drying washing instead of the sagging rope that used to run diagonally from end to end, propped up by a cleft stick. The young woman told me her husband drove a Routemaster bus, and I seized gratefully on this thread of continuity with the past. "My Dad used to drive a tram," I told her. But I had to explain what a tram was. They didn't offer to show me the bedrooms, and I didn't ask. I pressed a pound coin into the hands of each twin, thanked their mother and grandfather, and left.

I walked back to the Five Ways and then began to climb Beecher's Road. It was quickly apparent that a certain amount of yuppification had taken place on the higher levels of Hatchford, probably in the property boom of the eighties. The big houses that had been divided up into rented flats in my childhood had in many cases reverted to single ownership, and been smartened up in the process, with brass fittings on the front doors, hanging flower-baskets in the porches, and potted shrubs in the basement areas. Through front windows I glimpsed the signs of AB lifestyles: ethnic rugs and modern prints on the walls, well-stocked black ash bookshelves, angular lampstands, state-of-the-art hi-fi systems. I wondered if the same fate would have overtaken 94 Treglowan Road, where Maureen's family used to live. First left at the top of Beecher's Road, then first right and right again. Was it the exertion of the climb or nervous expectation that made my heart beat faster as I approached the last corner? It was highly unlikely that Maureen's parents, even if they were alive, would still be living there; and even if they were it would be a chance in a million if she happened to be visiting them today. So I told myself, trying to calm my pulse. But I was not prepared for the shock I received when I turned the corner.

One side of the road, the side on which Maureen's house had stood, had been demolished and cleared, and in its place a small estate of new detached houses had been built. They were flimsy, meanly-proportioned brick boxes – so narrow they looked like sawn-off semis – with leaded windows and fake beams stuck on the facades, and they were laid out along a curving cul-de-sac called Treglowan Close. There was not a single visible trace of the monumental Victorian villa in which the Kavanaghs had lived, not a brick, not a stone, not a tree. I calculated that the entrance to the estate passed directly over the site of the house. The basement area where we had kissed, where I had touched Maureen's breasts, had been filled in, levelled off, and sealed under a coating of tarmac. I felt robbed, disoriented and quite irrationally angry.

The Church of the Immaculate Conception, on the other hand,

was still standing. Indeed, it had hardly changed at all. The statue of the Virgin Mary still stood on her pedestal in the forecourt signalling a wide. Inside there were the same dark stained pews, confessionals like massive wardrobes against the wall, votive candles dripping stalactites of wax. There was something new, though: up at what Philip Larkin called the holy end, in front of the carved and pinnacled altar that I remembered blazing with candlelight at Benediction, was a plain stone table, and there were no rails at the bottom of the altar steps. A middle-aged lady in an apron was hoovering the carpet on the altar. She switched off the machine and looked enquiringly at me as I hovered nearby. I asked if Father Jerome was still attached to the church. She had heard his name mentioned by some of the older parishioners, but thought he must have left long before she came to Hatchford herself. She had an idea that he had been sent to Africa by his order to work in the missions. And Father Malachi, I presumed, was dead. She nodded, and pointed to a plaque on the wall in his memory. She said the present parish priest was Father Dominic, and that I might find him in the presbytery. I remembered that presbytery meant the house where the priests lived, the first one around the corner from the church. A thirty-something man in a pullover and jeans opened the door when I rang the bell. I asked if Father Dominic was in. He said, "That's me, come in." He led me into a cluttered living-room, where a computer screen glowed green on a desk in the corner. "Do you understand spreadsheets?" he said. I confessed I didn't. "I'm trying to computerize the parish accounts," he said, "but really I need Windows to do it properly. How can I help you?"

When I said I was trying to trace someone who had lived in the parish forty years ago, he shook his head doubtfully. "The order who had the parish in those days were pretty hopeless at paperwork. If they had any files on parishioners, they must have taken them with them when they pulled out. All that's left by way of an archive are the registers of Baptisms, First Communions, Confirmations and Marriages."

I asked if I could see the marriage register, and he led me round to the back of the church, into a small room behind the altar that smelled of incense and furniture-polish, and took a large oblong leather-

267

bound book out of a cupboard. I started with the year in which I last saw Maureen and worked forward. It didn't take me very long to find her name. On 16th May 1959 Maureen Teresa Kavanagh of 94 Treglowan Road married Bede Ignatius Harrington of 103 Hatchford Rise. "Bugger me!" I exclaimed thoughtlessly, and apologized for my unseemly language. Father Dominic didn't seem bothered. I asked him if the Harrington family still lived in the parish. "It doesn't ring a bell," he said. "I'd have to check my database." We returned to the presbytery and he searched for the name on his computer without success. There weren't any Kavanaghs in the parish either. "Annie Mahoney might know something," he said. "She used to be the housekeeper in the presbytery in those days. I look after myself – can't afford a housekeeper. She lives in the next house but one. You'll have to shout, she's pretty deaf." I thanked him and asked if I could make a contribution to the parish software fund, which he received gratefully.

Annie Mahoney was a bent, withered little old lady in a bright green tracksuit and Reebok trainers with Velcro fastenings. She explained to me that because of the arthritis in her fingers she couldn't manage buttons and laces any more. She lived alone and obviously welcomed company and the chance of a chat. At first she thought I was the man from the Town Hall come to review her entitlement to a Home Help, but when that misunderstanding was cleared up she brought her mind to bear on my enquiry about the Kavanagh family. It was a tantalizing interview. She remembered the family. "Such a giant of a man, Mr Kavanagh, you could never forget him if you saw him only once, and his wife was a nice woman and they had five beautiful children, especially the oldest, I forget her name now." "Maureen," I prompted. "That's it, Maureen," she said. She remembered Maureen's wedding, which had been a posh one by the standards of the parish, with the groom and best man in tail-coats, and two Rolls-Royces to ferry the guests to the reception. "I think Dr Harrington paid for the cars, he was always a man to do things properly," Annie reminisced. "He died about ten years ago, God rest his soul. Heart, they said." She didn't know anything about Bede's and Maureen's married life however, where they lived or what Bede did for a living. "Maureen became a teacher, I think," she hazarded. I said I thought she wanted to be a nurse. "Oh yes, a nurse, that was it," said Annie. "She would have made a lovely nurse. Such a sweet-natured girl. I remember her as Our Lady in a Nativity play the youth club put on one Christmas, with her hair spread out over her shoulders, beautiful she looked." I couldn't resist asking Annie if she remembered the Herod in the same production, but she didn't.

I checked out the Harringtons' former house, a large villa set back from the main road with, as I recalled, a rather impressive entrance – two gateposts with stone globes the size of footballs on top. It belongs to a dental practice now. The gateposts have been removed and the front garden tarmacked over to make a parking lot for the partners and their patients. I went inside and asked the receptionist if she had any information about the previous owners, but she was unable or unwilling to help. I was tired and hungry and not a little melancholy by this time, so I caught the next train back to Charing Cross.

So Bede Harrington is my Schlegel. Well, well. I always thought he had his eye on Maureen, but I'm a bit surprised that she chose to marry him. Could you *love* Bede Harrington? (Without *being* Bede Harrington, I mean.) I can't flatter myself that it was on the rebound from me, though. Judging by the date of the wedding, it took him several years to persuade her, or to pluck up the courage to pop the question – so he must have had some attraction for her. I can't deny that I feel absurdly, pointlessly jealous. And keener than ever to trace her. But where do I go from here?

7.06 p.m. After devising various ingenious plans (e.g., find out which local estate agent handled the sale of 103 Hatchford Rise to the dentists, and see if I could get an address for Mrs Harrington Snr. out of them) I thought of a simpler expedient to try first: if Bede and Maureen still lived in London, they would probably be in the phone book, and Harrington wasn't such a common name. Sure enough, there were only two B. I. Harringtons. One of them, with an address in SW19, had OBE after his name, which I thought was just the sort of thing Bede would show off about if he had the chance, so I tried that number first. I recognized his voice instantly. Our conversation went more or less like this:

BEDE: Harrington.

ME: Is that the Bede Harrington who used to live in Hatchford?

BEDE: (*guardedly*) I did live there once, yes.

ME: You married Maureen Kavanagh?

BEDE: Yes. Who is this?

ME: Herod.

BEDE: I beg your pardon?

ME: Laurence Passmore.

BEDE: I'm sorry, I don't . . . Parsons, did you say?

ME: Passmore. You remember. The youth club. The Nativity play. I was Herod.
(*Pause*)

BEDE: Good God.

ME: How are you, then?

BEDE: All right.

ME: How's Maureen?

BEDE: She's all right, I think.

ME: Could I speak to her?

BEDE: She's not here.

ME: Ah. When will she be back?

BEDE: I don't precisely know. She's abroad.

ME: Oh – where?

BEDE: Spain, I should think, by now.

ME: I see . . . Is there any way I could get in touch with her?

BEDE: Not really, no.

ME: On holiday, is she?

BEDE: Not exactly. What is it you want?

ME: I'd just like to see her again . . . (*racking brains for a pretext*) . . . I'm writing something about those days.

BEDE: Are you a writer?

ME: Yes.

BEDE: What kind of writer?

ME: Television mostly. You may know a programme called *The People Next Door*?

BEDE: Never heard of it, I'm afraid.

ME: Oh.

BEDE: I don't watch much television. Look, I'm in the middle of cooking my dinner –

ME: Oh, sorry. I –
BEDE: If you leave me your number, I'll tell Maureen when she gets back.

I gave him my address and phone number. Before he rang off, I asked him what he got his OBE for. He said, "I presume for my work on the National Curriculum." It seems he's a fairly high-up civil servant in the Department of Education.

I'm very stirred up by this conversation, excited and at the same time frustrated. I'm amazed how much progress I've made in tracing Maureen in a single day, yet she's still tantalizingly out of reach. I wish now I'd pressed Bede for more details as to where she is and what she's doing. I don't like the idea of just waiting, indefinitely, for a phone call from her, not knowing how long it might be – days? weeks? months? – or whether Bede will even pass her my message when she gets back from wherever she is. "Spain by now . . . not exactly a holiday" – what the fuck does that mean? Is she on some kind of educational coach tour? Or a cruise?

9.35 p.m. I rang Bede again, apologized for disturbing him, and asked if we could meet. When he asked me what for, I elaborated my alibi about writing something set in Hatchford in the early fifties. He was less abrupt and suspicious than before – indeed his speech was slightly slurred, as if he'd had a bit too much to drink with his dinner. I said I lived quite near Whitehall, and asked if I could give him lunch one day this week. He said he retired at the end of last year, but I could visit him at home if I liked. SW19 turns out to be Wimbledon. Eagerly I suggested tomorrow morning, and much to my delight, he agreed. Before he rang off, I managed to slip in a question about Maureen: "On a sort of tour, is she?" "No," he said, "a pilgrimage."
Still a devout Catholic, then. Oh well.

✳ ✳ ✳ ✳ ✳ ✳ ✳ ✳ ✳ ✳ ✳ ✳ ✳ ✳ ✳ ✳ ✳

Tuesday 8th June. 2.30 p.m. I travelled by Network Southeast again this morning, but this time from Waterloo, and in a cleaner, smarter train than yesterday, appropriate to my more upmarket destination.

Bede and Maureen live in one of the leafy residential streets near the All England Club. It's entirely typical of Bede that he has never watched a tennis match in all his years in Wimbledon, and regards the Championships as merely an annual traffic nuisance. I've been to Wimbledon myself a few times in recent years as a guest of Heartland, (they host parties in one of the hospitality marquees, with champagne and strawberries and free tickets to the Centre Court) and it gave me a funny feeling to realize that I must have passed within a hundred yards of Maureen on those occasions without knowing it. I might well have driven past her in the street.

The house is quite an ordinary large inter-war semi, with a long back garden. They moved there early in their married life, Bede said, and extended it, building on top of the garage, and out at the back, and converting the loft, to accommodate their growing family, instead of moving. They have four children, all grown-up and flown the nest now, it appeared. Bede was on his own in the house, which had an unnaturally clean and tidy look, as if most of the rooms hadn't been disturbed since the last visit of the cleaning-lady. I peeped into some of them when I went upstairs to use the loo. I noticed that there were twin beds in the master bedroom, which gave me a silly satisfaction. Aha, no sex any more, I said to myself. Not necessarily true, of course.

Bede hasn't changed much except that his coarse unruly hair has turned quite white, and his cheeks are sunken. He still wears horn-rimmed glasses with lenses like bottle ends. But apparently I've changed a lot. Although I arrived at the time appointed, he greeted me uncertainly when he opened the front door. "You've put on weight," he said, when I identified myself. "And lost most of my hair," I said. "Yes, you had rather a lot of hair, didn't you," he said. He led me into the sitting-room (where, I was amused to note, the curtains matched the loose covers) and invited me rather stiffly to sit down. He was dressed like a man who has spent most of his life in a suit and doesn't know quite what to wear in retirement. He was wearing a tweed sports jacket with leather patches, and a checked shirt with a woollen tie, grey worsted trousers and dark brown brogues – rather heavy clothes for the time of year, even though it was a cool, blustery day.

"I owe you an apology," he said, in his familiar pompous way. "I was speaking to my daughter on the telephone this morning and she informs me that your programme – what is it called? – is one of the most popular on television."

"*The People Next Door.* Does your daughter watch it?" I asked.

"She watches everything, indiscriminately," he said. "We didn't have a television when the children were growing up – I thought it would interfere with their homework. The effect on Teresa was that she became completely addicted as soon as she left home and was able to get a set for herself. I have come to the conclusion," he went on, "that all effort to control other people's lives is completely futile."

"Including government?" I asked.

"Especially government," he said. He seemed to regard his career in the civil service as a failure, in spite of the OBE. "The educational system of this country is in a much worse state now than when I joined the Department," he said. "That isn't my fault, but I was unable to prevent it. When I think of all the hours I spent on committees, working-parties, writing reports, writing memoranda . . . all completely futile. I envy you, Passmore. I wish I'd been a writer. Or at least a don. I could have done a postgraduate degree after I got my First, but I took the Civil Service exam instead. It seemed the safer bet at the time, and I wanted to get married, you know."

I suggested that now he was retired he would have plenty of leisure to write.

"Yes, I always used to think that is what I would do in my retirement. I used to write a lot when I was young – poems, essays . . ."

"Plays," I said.

"Quite so." Bede allowed himself a wintry reminiscent smile. "But the creative juices dry up if they're not kept in circulation. I tried to write something the other day, something rather personal about . . . bereavement. It came out like a White Paper."

He left me for a few minutes to make some coffee in the kitchen, and I prowled round the room in search of clues to Maureen's existence. There were a number of fairly recent family photographs on display – graduations and weddings and one of Bede and Maureen together outside Buckingham Palace with Bede in morning dress – in which she appeared as a proud, smiling, matronly woman, her hair grey and cut short, but with the same sweet heart-shaped face I remembered. I stared greedily at these images, trying to reconstruct from them the missing years of her life (missing for me, I mean). Propped up on the mantelpiece was a brightly coloured picture postcard of St Jean Pied-de-Port in the French Pyrenees. On the other side was a brief message from Maureen to Bede: "Dear Bede: Am taking a rest here for a few days before tackling the mountains. All right except for blisters. Love, Maureen." I would have recognized the round, girlish hand anywhere, even though there were dots instead of bubbles over the *i*s. The card was postmarked about three weeks ago. Hearing Bede in the hall, I hastily replaced the card and scuttled back to my seat.

"So, how's Maureen?" I said, as he came in with a tray. "What has she been doing with herself while you were climbing the ladder in the DES?"

"She was a qualified nurse when I married her," he said, pushing down the plunger in the cafetière with both hands, like a man detonating dynamite. "We started a family almost immediately, and she gave up work to look after the children. She went back to nursing when our youngest started junior school, and became a sister in charge of a ward, but it's frightfully hard work, you know. She gave it up when we no longer needed the money. She does a lot of voluntary work, for the Church and so on."

"You both still go to church, then?" I said.

"Yes," he said curtly. "Milk? Sugar?" The coffee was grey and insipid, the digestive biscuits damp. Bede asked me some technical questions about writing for television. After a while, I pulled the conversation back to Maureen. "What's this pilgrimage she's on then?"

He stirred restively in his seat, and looked out of the window, where a boisterous wind was blowing, shaking the trees and sending blossom through the air like snowflakes. "It's to Santiago de

274

Compostela," he said, "in north-west Spain. It's a very ancient pilgrimage, goes back to the Middle Ages. St James the Apostle is supposed to be buried there. 'Santiago' is Spanish for St James, of course. 'St Jacques' in French. Maureen read about the pilgrimage route somewhere, a library book I think. Decided she wanted to do it."

"On foot," I said.

"Yes, on foot." Bede looked at me. "How did you know?"

I confessed to having peeped at her card.

"It's absurd of course," he said. "A woman of her age. Quite absurd." He took off his spectacles and massaged his brow as if he had a headache. His eyes looked naked and vulnerable without the glasses.

"How far is it?" I asked.

"Depends on where you start." He replaced his spectacles. "There are several different starting-points, all in France. Maureen started from Le Puy, in the Auvergne. Santiago is about a thousand miles from there, I believe."

I whistled softly. "Is she an experienced walker?"

"Not in the least," Bede said. "A stroll across Wimbledon Common on Sunday afternoon was her idea of a long walk. The whole idea is completely mad. I'm surprised she got as far as the Pyrenees, to be honest, without injuring herself. Or being raped, or murdered."

He told me that when Maureen first proposed doing the pilgrimage he offered to accompany her if they went by car, but she insisted on doing it the hard way, on foot, like the mediaeval pilgrims. It was apparent that they'd had a major row about it. In the end she went off defiantly on her own, about two months ago, with a rucksack and a bedroll, and he's only had two cards from her since, the latest being the one I had just seen. Bede is obviously worried sick as well as angry, and feeling not a little foolish, but there's nothing he can do except sit tight and hope she gets to Santiago safely. I found the story fascinating and, I must admit, derived a certain amount of *Schadenfreude* from Bede's plight. Nevertheless it seemed a surprisingly quixotic adventure for Maureen to undertake. I said something to this effect.

"Yes, well, she's been under a lot of stress, lately. We both have," Bede said. "We lost our son Damien last November, you see."

I blurted out some words of commiseration, and asked about the circumstances. Bede went to a bureau and took a framed photograph from one of the drawers. It was a colour snap of a young man, healthy and handsome, dressed in T-shirt and shorts, smiling at the camera, leaning against the front mudguard of a Land Rover, with a background of blue sky and brownish scrub. "He was killed in Angola," Bede said. "You may have read about it in the newspapers. He was working for a Catholic aid organization there, distributing relief supplies to refugees. Nobody knows exactly what happened, but it seems that some maverick unit of rebel soldiers stopped the truck he was in, and demanded that he hand over the food and medicine to them. He refused, and they pulled him and his African driver out of the truck and shot them. Damien was only twenty-five."

"How awful," I said, inadequately.

"Not much sense to be made of it, is there?" said Bede, turning his head to gaze out of the window again. "He loved Africa, you know, loved his work, was totally dedicated . . . We had his body flown back. There was a Requiem Mass. Lots of people came, people we had never even met. People from the charity. Friends of his from university. He was very popular. The priest who gave the address, some sort of chaplain to the charity, said Damien was a modern martyr." He stopped, lost in thought, and I couldn't think of anything to say, so we were silent for a moment.

"You think your faith is going to be a consolation at times like these," he resumed. "But when it happens, you find it isn't. Nothing is. Our GP persuaded us to see some busybody he called a Grief Counsellor. Stupid woman said we mustn't feel guilty. I said, why should I feel guilty? She said, because you're alive and he isn't. I never heard such rubbish. I think Damien was a fool. He should have given those brutes the damned food and driven away and never stopped until he was out of the whole bloody continent."

His gills were white with anger as he remembered. I asked him how Maureen had taken the tragedy.

"Hard. Damien was her favourite child. She was devastated. That's why she's gone off on this absurd pilgrimage."

"You mean, as a kind of therapy?" I said.

"It's as good a word as any, I suppose," said Bede.

I said I thought I had better be going. He said, "But we haven't talked much about the old days at Hatchford." I said perhaps another time. He nodded. "All right. Give me a ring. You know," he went on, "I never much liked you, Passmore. I used to think you were up to no good with Maureen at the youth club."

"You were absolutely right," I said, and wrung another thin smile from him.

"But I'm glad you came this morning," he continued. "I'm a bit lonely, to tell you the truth."

"Does Maureen ever talk about me?" I asked.

"No," he said. "Never." He spoke without malice or satisfaction, merely as if stating a matter of fact. While we were waiting for my taxi to come, he asked me if I had any children. I said two, one married, the other living with a partner. "Ah yes, they do that nowadays, don't they?" he said. "Even ours do. Think nothing of it. Not like it was in our youth, eh?"

"No indeed," I said.

"And your wife, what does she do?"

"She's a lecturer in one of the new universities," I said. "In Education. As a matter of fact, she spends a lot of her time counselling teachers who are having nervous breakdowns over the National Curriculum."

"I'm not surprised," said Bede. "It's a total shambles. I'd like to meet your wife."

"I'm afraid she's just left me," I said.

"Has she? Then that makes two of us," said Bede, in a characteristically clumsy effort at humour. At which point the doorbell rang, and I was driven off to Wimbledon station by an annoyingly loquacious driver. I didn't want to make small talk about the weather or the

277

prospects for the tennis. I wanted to think about the fascinating revelations of the morning.

A plan is forming in my mind, an idea so daft and exciting that I dare not even write it down yet.

✳   ✳   ✳   ✳   ✳   ✳   ✳   ✳   ✳   ✳   ✳   ✳   ✳   ✳   ✳   ✳

Friday 11th June. Well, I've made up my mind. I'm going after Maureen. I'm going to try and track her down on the road to Santiago de Compostela. I've spent the last three days making the necessary arrangements – booking the car ferry, getting a green card, buying guidebooks, maps, travellers cheques, etc. I ripped through the backlog of mail and phone messages, and dealt with the most urgent ones. There was a series from Dennis Shorthouse reporting that Sally has made a court application for a maintenance order to meet the running costs of the house, and asking with mounting urgency for instructions. I phoned him and told him I wouldn't obstruct divorce proceedings any longer, and would agree to appropriate maintenance and a reasonable financial settlement. He asked me what I meant by reasonable. I said, let her keep the house and I'll keep the flat, and the rest of the assets can be divided fifty-fifty. He said, "That's not reasonable, that's generous. The house is worth considerably more than the flat." I said I just didn't want to be bothered with it any more. I told him I was going abroad for a few weeks. I don't know how long it will take me to track down Maureen, or what I will do if I find her. I just know I have to look for her. I can't stand the thought of spending the summer cooped up in this flat, taking calls from people I'm trying to avoid in case it's her.

I haven't told Bede about my plan, in case he gets the wrong idea, though what the right idea would be I've really no idea. I mean I don't really know what I want from Maureen. Not her love back, obviously – it's too late for a Repetition. (Though I can't stop myself from going over every bit of evidence that her marriage to Bede has grown cold – if it was ever warm – like the single beds, their row over her pilgrimage, the rather cool "Dear Bede" postcard, etc. etc.) But if not love, then what? Forgiveness, perhaps. Absolution. I want to know

278

that she forgives me for betraying her all those years ago in front of the Nativity play cast. A trivial act in itself, but with enormous consequences. You could say that it determined the shape of the rest of my life. You could say it was the source of my middle-aged *Angst*. I made a choice without knowing it was a choice. Or rather (which is worse) I pretended that it was Maureen's choice, not mine, that we split up. It seems to me now that I never recovered from the effect of that bad faith. It explains why I can never make a decision without immediately regretting it.

I must try that on Alexandra next time I see her, though I'm not sure she'll be pleased. I seem to have abandoned cognitive therapy in favour of the old-fashioned analytical kind, finding the source of my troubles in a long-repressed memory. It would be a consolation, anyway, to share that memory with Maureen, to find out how she feels about it now. The fact that she is nursing a fresh grief of her own makes me all the more anxious to find her and make my peace with her.

Also in my mailjam was a draft script by Samantha filling out her idea for a kind of *The People Next Door*-meets-*Truly, Madly, Deeply*-meets-*Ghost* episode to end the present series. It wasn't at all bad, but I saw at once what needed doing to it. She had Priscilla's ghost appearing to Edward after the funeral. What must happen is that Priscilla appears to Edward immediately after her fatal accident, before anyone knows about it. He doesn't think she is a ghost at first, because she tries to break it to him gently. Then she walks through a wall – the party wall – into the Davises' house and back again, and the realization sinks in that she's dead. It's sad, but it isn't tragic, because Priscilla is still there, in a sense. There's even a kind of comedy in the scene. It's very thin ice, but I think it would work. Anyway, I did a quick rewrite and sent it back to Samantha with instructions to try it on Ollie.

Then I called Jake and listened meekly to ten minutes' bitter recrimination for not returning his calls before I was able to tell him about my work on Samantha's draft script. "It's too late, Tubby," he said flatly. "Clause fourteen applied weeks ago." "Have they hired another writer, then?" I asked, bracing myself for a positive reply.

"They must have," he said. "They need an agreed script for the last episode by the end of the month at the latest." I heard the creaking of his swivel chair as he rocked himself in it, thinking. "I suppose if they really went for this ghost idea, there might just be time," he said. "Where will you be the next two weeks?"

Then I had to break it to him that I was going abroad tomorrow for an indeterminate time and couldn't give any phone or fax numbers where he could contact me. I held the phone away from my ear like they do in old comedy films while he swore. "Why d'you have to take a holiday now, for fuck's sake?" I heard him exclaim. "It's not a holiday," I said, "it's a pilgrimage," and put the phone down quickly while he was still speechless.

It's extraordinary what a difference this quest for Maureen has made to my state of mind. I don't seem to have any difficulty in making decisions any more. I no longer feel like the unhappiest man. Perhaps I never was – I had a look at that essay again the other day and I don't think I got it quite right before. But I'm certainly present to myself when I'm remembering Maureen, or hoping to find her – never more so.

I'd just finished typing that sentence when I noticed a regularly blinking light reflected in my windows – it was dark, about ten o'clock, but I hadn't drawn the curtains. Squinting down into the street I saw the roof of a police car parked right outside the building with its blue revolving light flashing. I switched on the video monitor in the hall and there was Grahame, rolling up his sleeping-bag in the porch under the surveillance of a couple of policemen. I went downstairs. The more senior of the two policemen explained that they were moving Grahame on. "Were you the gentleman who made the complaint?" he asked. I said I wasn't. Grahame looked at me and said, "C'n I come up?" I said, "Alright. For a few minutes." The cops looked at me in astonishment. "I hope you know what you're doing, sir," said the senior one disapprovingly. "I wouldn't let this toerag into *my* house, I can tell you." "I ain't no toerag," said Grahame indignantly. The policeman eyeballed him fiercely. "Don't give me any of your lip, toerag," he hissed. "And don't let me catch you kipping in this doorway again. Understand?" He looked coldly at me. "I could have you for obstructing an officer in the performance of his duties," he said, "but I'll overlook it this time."

I took Grahame upstairs and gave him a cup of tea. "You're going to have to find another place, Grahame," I said. "I can't protect you any longer. I'm going abroad, probably for a few weeks."

He looked at me slyly from under his lank forelock. "Let me stay 'ere," he said. "I'll look after the place for you while you're away. Like a caretaker."

I laughed at his cheek. "It doesn't need a caretaker."

"You're wrong," he said. "There's all sorts of villains round 'ere. You might be burgled while you're away."

"I wasn't burgled before, when the flat was empty most of the time."

"I don't mean *live* 'ere," Grahame said, "just sleep. On the floor – not in your bed. I'd keep the place nice and clean." He looked around. "Sight cleaner 'n it is now."

"I expect you would, Grahame," I said. "Thanks, but no thanks."

He sighed and shook his head. "I just hope you don't regret it," he said.

"Well," I said, "if the worst comes to the worst – I'm insured."

I saw him out of the building. A light drizzle was falling. I felt a bit of a heel as he turned up his collar and shouldered his bedroll – but what could I do? I'd be crazy to give him the key to my flat. I might come back and find he'd turned it into a dosshouse for philosophical vagrants like himself. I thrust a couple of notes into his hand, and told him to get himself a room for the night. "Ta," he said, and sloped off into the warm wet night. I never met anybody who could accept favours with such nonchalance. I have a feeling I shan't see him again.

Thursday 17th June. I didn't get away as soon as I had planned. Shorthouse phoned me to say that he would feel happier if I waited a few days while he sorted out the details of a settlement with the other side. So I've hung about impatiently this week, filling in the time by reading everything I could find in the Charing Cross Road bookshops about the pilgrimage to Santiago. I went up to Rummidge this morning to sign the papers, and came back by the next train. This evening, as I was packing, I got an unexpected call from Sally. It was the first time we had spoken for weeks. "I just wanted to say," she said, in a carefully neutral tone of voice, "that I think you've been very generous." "That's alright," I said. "I'm sorry it's been such an unpleasant business," she said, "I'm afraid I was partly to blame." "Yes, well, these things are always painful," I said, "it doesn't bring out the best in people, divorce." "Well, I just wanted to say thankyou," said Sally, and rang off. I felt rather uneasy, speaking to her. Knowing my mind as I do, it wouldn't take much to make me start regretting my decision. I want to be out of here, away from it all, on the road. I'm off tomorrow morning. Santiago, here I come.

* * FOUR * *

SEPTEMBER 21st. I've come to the conclusion that the essential difference between book-writing and script-writing isn't that the latter is mostly dialogue – it's a question of tense. A script is all in the present tense. Not literally, but ontologically. (How about that, then? Comes of reading all those books about Kierkegaard.) What I mean is, in drama or film, everything is happening *now*. That's why stage directions are always in the present tense. Even when one character is telling another character about something that happened in the past, the *telling* is happening in the present, as far as the audience is concerned. Whereas, when you write something in a book, it all belongs to the past; even if you write, *"I am writing, I am writing,"* over and over again, the act of writing is finished with, out of sight, by the time somebody reads the result.

A journal is halfway between the two forms. It's like talking silently to yourself. It's a mixture of monologue and autobiography. You can write a lot of stuff in the present tense, like: *"The plane trees outside my window are in leaf . . ."* But really that's just a fancier way of saying, *"I am writing, I am writing . . ."* It's not getting you anywhere, it's not telling a story. As soon as you start to tell a story in writing, whether it's a fictional story or the story of your life, it's natural to use the past tense, because you're describing things that have already happened. The special thing about a journal is that the writer doesn't know where his story is going, he doesn't know how it ends; so it seems to exist in a kind of continuous present, even though the individual incidents may be described in the past tense. Novels are written after the fact, or they pretend to be. The novelist may not have known how his story would end when he began it, but it always *looks* as if he did to the reader. The past tense of the opening sentence implies that the story about to be told has already happened. I know that there are novels written entirely in the present tense, but there's something queer about them, they're experimental, the present tense doesn't seem natural to the medium. They read like scripts. A present-tense autobiography would be even queerer. Autobiography is always written after the fact. It's a past-tense form. Like my memoir of Maureen. Like this piece I've just finished writing.

I kept a journal of sorts on my travels, but my laptop packed up in the mountains of León, and I didn't have the time or opportunity to get it repaired, so I started keeping a handwritten diary. I've printed out my disks, and laboriously typed up the diary, but put together they made a very rough and rambling account of what happened to me. Conditions often weren't ideal for writing, and sometimes at the end of the day I was too tired or had imbibed too much *vino* to do more than make a few allusive notes. So I've written it out in a more coherent, cohesive narrative, knowing, so to speak, how the story ended. For I do feel I've reached the end of something. And, hopefully, a new beginning.

I drove from London to St-Jean-Pied-de-Port in two days. No sweat. The only problem was holding the Richmobile under the speed limit on the autoroute. The cruise control came in handy. So did the air-conditioning – the road was shimmering in the heat on the flat marshlands south of Bordeaux. When I climbed into the foothills of the Pyrenees the weather turned cooler, and it was raining when I reached St Jean Pied-de-Port (St John at the Foot of the Pass). It's a pleasant little market-cum-resort town of red gabled roofs and rushing brooks, nestling in a lumpy patchwork quilt of fields in various shades of green. There's a hotel with a restaurant that has two Michelin rosettes where I was lucky enough to get a room. I was told that a little later in the season I wouldn't have stood a chance without a reservation. There were already lots of hairy-kneed walkers in the town, wandering about disconsolately in wet cagoules, or mellowing out in the cafés while they waited for the weather to improve. You could tell which ones were pilgrims on their way to Santiago because they had scallop shells attached to their rucksacks.

The scallop shell, or *coquille* (hence, *coquilles St Jaques*, which they did extremely well at my hotel) is the traditional symbol of the pilgrimage to Santiago, for reasons that, like most things associated with this saint, remain obscure. One legend has it that a man rescued from drowning by St James's intervention was dragged from the sea covered in scallop shells. More probably it was just a brilliant piece of mediaeval marketing: pilgrims returning from Santiago wanted souvenirs, and scallop shells were plentiful on the shores of Galicia. They were a nice little earner for the city, especially as the Archbishop of Santiago was empowered to excommunicate anybody who sold them to pilgrims outside it. Nowadays, though, pilgrims wear the *coquille* on their way to Santiago as well as on the way home.

I was surprised by how many of them there were, even in St Jean Pied-de-Port. I had imagined Maureen as a solitary eccentric, retracing an ancient trail forgotten by the modern world. Not so. The pilgrimage has enjoyed a big revival lately, encouraged by a powerful consortium of interests: the Catholic Church, the Spanish Tourist Board and the Council of Europe, which adopted the Camino de Santiago as a European Heritage Trail a few years ago. Tens of thousands hit the road every summer, following the blue and yellow *coquille* signs erected by the Council of Europe. I met a German couple in a bar one evening who had walked all the way from Arles, the most southerly of the four traditional routes. They had a sort of passport issued by some society of St James which they'd had stamped at various stopping-points along the route. When they got to Santiago, they told me, they would present their passports at the Cathedral and receive their "*compostelas*", certificates of completion like the pilgrims of old used to get. I wondered whether Maureen had obtained such a passport. If so, it might help me to trace her. The Germans directed me to the local passport-stamper, advising me not to arrive outside her house by car. Genuine pilgrims must walk, or cycle, or ride horseback.

I walked up the narrow cobbled hill to the house, but I didn't pretend to be a pilgrim. Instead I pretended (in a mixture of pidgin English, fractured French and sign-language) to be Bede Harrington, trying to trace his wife who was urgently required back at in England. A lady who was a dead ringer for Mary Whitehouse opened the door, frowning as if she was fit to kill another pilgrim knocking on her door late in the evening, but when I told my story she became interested and co-operative. To my delight she had stamped Maureen's passport and remembered her well: *"une femme très gentille"*, but suffering from badly blistered feet. I asked her where she thought Maureen might have got to by now, and she frowned and shrugged, *"Ça dépend . . ."* It depended, obviously, on how many kilometres Maureen could walk per day. It's about 800 kilometres from St Jean Pied-de-Port to Santiago. A young and fit walker might average 30 kilometres a day, but Maureen would be lucky to do half as well as that. I got the map out in my hotel room and calculated that she might be anywhere between Logroño and Villafranca, a distance of 300 kilometres, and that was guessing in the dark. She might have rested somewhere for a week to let her blisters heal and be way behind schedule. She might have used public transport for part of the way, in which case she could have already arrived in Santiago – though knowing Maureen I doubted if she would bend the rules. I imagined her gritting her teeth and walking on through the pain barrier.

The next day I crossed the Pyrenees. I put the automatic shift in "Slow" to avoid excessive gear changes on the twisty road and breezed effortlessly to the top of the Val Carlos pass, overtaking several pilgrims slogging their way up the hill bowed under their backpacks. The weather had turned fine and the scenery was spectacular: mountains green to their peaks, valleys smiling in the sunshine, caramel-coloured cows with clinking bells, flocks of mountain sheep, vultures hang-gliding at eye level. Val Carlos, my guidebook informed me, means valley of Charles or Charlemagne, and on the Spanish side of the mountain is Roncesvalles, where there was a famous battle between Charlemagne's army and the Saracens, as recorded in the *Song of Roland*. Only they weren't Saracens at all, in reality, but Basques from Pamplona, narked because Charlemagne's boys had knocked their city about a bit. Nothing associated with the

Camino is quite what it claims to be. The shrine of Santiago itself seems to be a complete con, seeing there's no evidence the Apostle is actually buried there. The story goes that, after the death of Jesus, James went to Spain to convert the natives. He didn't seem to have much success because he returned to Palestine with only two disciples, and promptly had his head chopped off by Herod (I don't know which one). The two disciples were told in a dream to take the saint's remains back to Spain, which they did in a stone boat (yes, stone), which was miraculously wafted through the Mediterranean and the Straits of Gibraltar, up the west coast of the Iberian peninsula, and beached on the shores of Galicia. Some centuries later a local hermit saw a star twinkling above a hillock which, when excavated, revealed the remains of the saint and his disciples – or so it was claimed. They could have been anybody's bones, of course. But Christian Spain badly needed some relics and a shrine to boost its campaign to drive out the Moors. That's how St James became the patron saint of Spain, and *"Santiago!"* the Spanish battle-cry. According to another legend, he appeared in person at the crucial battle of Clavijo in 834 to rally the wilting Christian army, and personally slew seventy thousand Moors. The archdiocese of Santiago had the face to lay a special tax on the rest of Spain as a thankyou to St James, though in fact there is no evidence that the battle of Clavijo ever took place, with or without his intervention. In churches all along the Camino you see statues of *"Santiago Matamoros"*, St James the Moorslayer, depicting him as a warrior on horseback, wielding his sword and trampling the corpses of swarthy, thick-lipped infidels. They could become an embarrassment if Political Correctness ever gets a hold on Spain.

I found it hard to understand why millions of people had walked halfway across Europe in times past, often under conditions of appalling discomfort and danger, to visit the dubious shrine of this dubious saint, and even harder to understand why they were still doing so, albeit in smaller numbers. I got a sort of answer to the latter question at the Augustinian abbey of Roncesvalles, which has been offering hospitality to pilgrims since the Middle Ages. It looks fantastic from a distance, a cluster of grey stone buildings tucked into a fold in the green foothills, with the sun gleaming on its roof – only when you get close do you see that the roof is made of corrugated zinc, and the buildings are mostly undistinguished. A man in black trousers and a red cardigan watched me get out of my car and, observing the GB plates, greeted me in English. He turned out to be the monk on pilgrim duty. I did my Bede Harrington act, and he asked me to follow him to a little office. He had no memory of Maureen, but he said that if she had presented her passport at the monastery she would have been asked to complete a questionnaire. Sure enough he found it in a filing cabinet, completed in Maureen's big round hand four weeks earlier. "*Name*: Maureen Harrington. *Age*: 57. *Nationality*: British. *Religion*: Catholic. *Motives for journey (tick one or more)*: *1. Religious   2. Spiritual   3. Recreational   4. Cultural   5. Sporting.*" I noticed with interest that Maureen had only ticked one: "Spiritual."

The monk, who introduced himself to me as Don Andreas, showed me round the monastery. He said apologetically that I couldn't stay in the *refugio* because I was travelling by car, but when I saw the bleak, breeze-block dormitory, with its naked lightbulbs and rough wood-and-wire bunks, this seemed a deprivation I could bear. It was empty: the day's quota of pilgrims hadn't yet arrived. I found a little hotel in the nearby village with creaking floorboards and paper-thin walls, but it was clean and comfortable enough. I went back to the monastery because Don Andreas had invited me to attend the pilgrim mass which was held at six every evening. It seemed churlish to decline, and anyway I liked the idea of doing something Maureen would certainly have done a few weeks earlier. I thought it might help me to get inside her head, and track her down by some kind of telepathic radar.

I hadn't attended a Catholic service since we split up, and the pilgrim mass didn't bear much resemblance to anything I remembered from the repertory of the Immaculate Conception in the old days. There were several priests saying the mass at the same time and they stood in a semi-circle behind a plain table-style altar (like the one

I had noticed recently in the Hatchford church) facing the congregation in an island of light amid the general gloom of the huge chapel, so you could see all the business with the gold-plated goblets and plates quite clearly. The congregation were a motley crew of all ages, shapes and sizes, casually dressed in sweaters and shorts, sandals and trainers. It was obvious that most of them were not Catholics, and had even less of a clue about what was going on than I did. Perhaps they thought they had to attend the service if they were getting a free bed for the night, like dossers in a Sally Army hostel; or perhaps they got a genuine spiritual kick out of hearing the mutter of the liturgy echoing round the pillars and vaults of the ancient church, as it had for centuries. Only a handful went to communion, but at the end everyone was invited to go up to the altar steps to receive a blessing, pronounced in three languages – Spanish, French and English. To my surprise everybody in the pews stepped forward, and I rather sheepishly joined them. I even crossed myself at the blessing, a long-forgotten action I had copied from Maureen at Benediction years ago. I sent up a silent prayer To Whom It May Concern that I would find her.

I spent the next two weeks cruising up and down the roads of northern Spain, staring at every pilgrim I passed who remotely resembled Maureen, sometimes drifting dangerously into the middle of the road as I looked back over my shoulder to scrutinize the face of some walker with a likely-looking rear aspect. Pilgrims were always easy to identify – they invariably displayed the *coquille*, and usually carried a long staff or stick. But the further I went, the more of them there were on the roads, and I didn't have much to go on by way of distinctive features. Mme Whitehouse had recalled that Maureen was shouldering a backpack with a rolled polystyrene mat on top, but she couldn't remember the colours of either of these items. All the time I was tormented by the thought that I might be overtaking Maureen without knowing it – while she was resting her feet in some church or café, or while she was walking those parts of the Camino that veer off the modern road system and became a track or footpath impassable to four-wheeled traffic (certainly to my decadently low-slung vehicle). I stopped at every church I spotted – and there are an awful lot of them in this part of Spain, a legacy of the mediaeval pilgrimage. I checked out every *refugio* I could find – the hostels that offer free, very basic shelter to pilgrims all along the route. Most of them were so basic – stone-floored stables virtually – that I couldn't imagine Maureen would have slept in them; but I thought I might encounter in this way somebody who had met Maureen on the road.

I met all sorts of pilgrims. The most numerous were young Spaniards for whom the pilgrimage was obviously an impeccable excuse to get out of the parental home and meet other young Spaniards of the opposite sex. The *refugios* are unsegregated. I'm not suggesting any hanky-panky goes on (there's not enough privacy, anyway), but I sometimes seemed to catch in them of an evening a whiff of that puppyish flirtatiousness I remembered from the Immaculate Conception youth club. Then there were the more sophisticated young backpackers from other countries, bronzed and muscular, attracted by the buzz on the international grapevine that Santiago was a really cool trip, with great scenery, cheap wine and free space to spread your bedroll. There were cycling clubs from France and the Low Countries in matching T-shirts and bollock-hugging lycra shorts – a group much despised and resented by everybody else because they had back-up trucks to transport their luggage from stage to stage – and solo cyclists pedalling pannier-festooned mountain bikes at 78 r.p.m. There were couples and pairs of friends with a common interest in walking, or Spanish history, or Romanesque architecture, who were doing the Camino in easy instalments, year by year. For all these groups, it seemed to me, the pilgrimage was primarily an alternative and adventurous kind of holiday.

Then there were the pilgrims with more particular and personal motives: a young sponsored cyclist raising money for a cancer ward; a Dutch artist aiming to get to Santiago to mark his fortieth birthday; a sixty-year-old Belgian who was doing the pilgrimage as the first act of his retirement; a redundant factory worker from Nancy contemplating his future. People at turning-points in their lives – looking for peace, or enlightenment, or just an escape from the daily rat-race.

The pilgrims in this category were the ones who had travelled furthest, often walking all the way from their homes in northern Europe, camping on the way. Some had been on the road for months. Their faces were sunburned, their clothes weather-stained, and they had a kind of reserve or remoteness about them, as if they had acquired the habit of solitude on the long lonely miles, and found the sometimes boisterous and hearty company of other pilgrims unwelcome. Their eyes had a distant look, as though focused on Santiago. A few were Catholics, but most had no particular religious beliefs. Some had begun the pilgrimage in a light-hearted experimental mood and become deeply obsessed with it. Others were probably a little mad when they started. Heterogeneous as they were, it was this group of pilgrims who interested me most, because I thought they were most likely to have met Maureen on the road.

I described her as best I could, but drew a complete blank until I had got as far as Cebrero, a little village high up in the mountains of León, only a hundred and fifty kilometres from Santiago. It's a curious place, halfway between a folk village and a shrine. The dwellings are of antique design, circular stone-walled huts with conical thatched roofs, and peasants still live in them, probably subsidized by the Spanish government. The church contains relics of some gruesome mediaeval miracle, when the communion bread and wine turned into real flesh and blood, and the place is also said to be associated with the legend of the Holy Grail. It was certainly a crucial stage in my own quest. In the bar-cum-café next to the church, a homely place of bare boards and refectory tables, I got into conversation with an elderly Dutch cyclist who claimed he had met an English pilgrim called Maureen in a *refugio* near León a week before. She had a bad leg and had told him she was going to rest in León for a few days before continuing her journey. I had been in León recently, but I jumped into the Richmobile and headed back there, intending to check out every hotel in the city.

I was driving eastwards along the N120 between Astorga and Orbigo, a busy arterial road, when I saw her, walking towards me at the edge of the road – a plump, solitary woman in baggy cotton trousers and a broadbrimmed straw hat. It was only a glimpse, and I was doing seventy miles an hour at the time. I trod on the brakes, provoking an enraged bellow from a huge petrol tanker on my tail. With heavy traffic in both directions on the two-lane road, it was impossible to stop until, after a kilometre or two, I came to a drive-in café with a dirt carpark. I did a three-point turn in a cloud of dust and raced back down the road, wondering if I had hallucinated the figure of Maureen. But no, there she was, plodding along ahead of me on the other side of the road – or there was somebody, largely concealed by a backpack, rolled bedmat and straw hat. I slowed down, provoking more indignant hooting from the cars behind me, and turned to look at the woman's face as I passed. It was Maureen alright. Hearing the noise of the car horns, she threw a casual glance in my direction, but I was concealed behind the Richmobile's dark-tinted glass, and unable to stop. A few hundred yards further on I pulled off the road where the verge was broad enough to park, got out of the car, and crossed the tarmac. There was an incline at this point, and Maureen was walking downhill towards me. She walked slowly, with a limp, grasping a staff which she plonked down on the road in front of her at every second step. Nevertheless her gait was unmistakable, even at a distance. It was as if forty years had been pinched out of my existence, and I was back in Hatchford, outside the florist's shop on the corner of the Five Ways, watching her walk down Beecher's Road towards me in her school uniform.

If I had scripted the meeting I would have chosen a more romantic setting – the interior of some cool dark old church, perhaps, or a country road with wildflowers blowing in the breeze along its margins, where the bleating of sheep was the loudest noise. There would certainly have been background music (perhaps an instrumental arrangement of "Too Young"). As it was, we met on the edge of an ugly main road in one of the least attractive bits of Castile, deafened by the noise of tyres and engines, choked by exhaust fumes, and buffeted by gusts of gritty air displaced by passing juggernauts. As she approached I began to walk towards her, and she took notice of me for the first time. She slowed, hesitated, and stopped, as if she feared my intentions. I laughed, smiled, and held out my arms in what was supposed to be a reassuring gesture. She looked at me with alarm, clearly thinking I was some kind of homicidal maniac or rapist, and drew back, lifting her staff as if prepared to use it for self-defence. I stopped, and spoke:

"Maureen! It's all right! It's me, Laurence."

She started. "What?" she said. "Laurence who?"

"Laurence Passmore. Don't you recognize me?"

I was disappointed that she obviously didn't – didn't seem even to remember my name. But as she reasonably explained later, she hadn't given me a thought for donkey's years, whereas I had been thinking of almost nothing else except her for weeks. While I had been scouring north-west Spain, hoping to run into her at every turn of the road, my sudden apparition on the N120 was to her as bizarre and surprising as if I had parachuted out of the sky, or popped up through a hole in the ground.

I shouted above the howl and whine of traffic, "We used to go around together, years ago. In Hatchford."

Maureen's expression changed and the fear went from her eyes. She squinted at me, as if she were short-sighted, or dazzled by the sun, and took a step forward. "Is it really you? *Laurence Passmore?* What on earth are you doing here?"

"I've been looking for you."

"Why?" she said, and a look of anxiety returned to her face. "There's nothing wrong at home, is there?"

"No, nothing wrong," I reassured her. "Bede's worried about you, but he's OK."

"Bede? When did you see Bede?"

"Just the other day. I was trying to trace you."

"What for?" she said. We were now face to face.

"It's a long story," I said. "Get in the car, and I'll tell you." I gestured to my sleek silver pet, crouched on the opposite verge. She gave it a momentary glance, and shook her head.

"I'm doing a pilgrimage," she said.

"I know."

"I don't go in cars."

"Make an exception today," I said. "You look as if you could do with a lift."

In truth she looked a wreck. As we parleyed, I was mentally coming to terms with the sad fact that Maureen was no longer the Maureen of my memories and fantasies. She had reached that point in a woman's life when her looks begin irretrievably to desert her. Sally hasn't quite reached it, and Amy is still several years on the right side of it. Both of them, anyway, are resisting the ageing process with everything short of plastic surgery, but Maureen seemed to have surrendered without putting up much of a fight. There were crowsfeet at the corners of her eyes, and bags under them. Her cheeks, once so plump and smooth, were slack jowls; her neck was creased like an old garment; and her figure had gone soft and shapeless, with no perceptible waistline between the cushiony mounds of her bosom and the broad beam of her hips. The general effect had not been improved by the weeks and months she had spent on the road: her nose was sunburnt and peeling, her hair lank and unkempt, her knuckles grubby and her nails broken. Her clothes were dusty and sweat-stained. I must admit that her appearance was a shock for which the posed and retouched photographs in Bede's living-room had not prepared me. I daresay the years have been even harder on me, but Maureen hadn't been nurturing any illusions to the contrary.

As she hesitated, leaning forward in her scuffed trainers to balance the weight of her backpack, I noticed that she had placed some lumps of sponge rubber under the shoulder straps to protect her collarbone from chafing. For some reason this seemed the most pathetic detail of all in her general appearance. I felt an overwhelming rush of tenderness towards her, a desire to look after her and rescue her from this daft, self-lacerating ordeal. "Just to the next village," I said, "Somewhere we can get a cold drink." The sun was basting my bald pate and I could feel sweat trickling down my torso inside my shirt. I added coaxingly, "The car's air-conditioned."

Maureen laughed, wrinkling her sunburned nose in the way I remembered so well. "It had better be," she said. "I'm sure I stink to high heaven."

She sighed and stretched out luxuriously in the front seat of the

296

Richmobile as we moved off down the highway with the silent speed of an electric train. "Well, this is very swish," she said, looking round the interior of the car. "What make is it?" I told her. "We have a Volvo, at home," she said. "Bede says they're very safe."

"Safety isn't everything," I said.

"No, it isn't," she said, with a little giggle.

"This is a dream come true, you, know," I said. "I've been fantasizing for months about driving you in this car."

"Have you?" She gave me a shy, puzzled smile. I didn't tell her that in my fantasies she was still in her teens.

A few kilometres further on we found a bar with some chairs and tables outside in the shade of an old oak, away from the jabber of television and the hiss of the coffee machine. Over a beer and a *citron pressé* we had the first of many conversations that slowly filled in the information gap of thirty-five years. The first thing Maureen wanted to know, naturally enough, was why I had sought her out. I gave her a condensed account of what I have already written in these pages: that my life was in a mess, personally and professionally, that I had been suddenly reminded of our relationship and how shabbily I had treated her at the end of it, and had become consumed with a desire to see her again. "To get absolution," I said.

Maureen blushed under her sunburn. "Goodness me, Laurence, you don't have to ask for that. It was nearly forty years ago. We were children, practically."

"But it must have hurt, at the time."

"Oh, yes, of course. I cried myself to sleep for ages –"

"There you are, then."

"But young girls are always doing that. You were the first boy I cried over, but not the last." She laughed. "You look surprised."

"You mean, Bede?" I said.

"Oh no, not *Bede*." She screwed up her face in a humorous grimace. "Can you imagine anybody crying over Bede? No, there were others, before him. A wildly handsome registrar I was hopelessly in love with, like every other student nurse at the hospital. I doubt if he even knew my name. And after I qualified there was a houseman I had an affair with."

"You mean . . . in the full sense of the word?" I stared incredulously.

"I slept with him, if that's what you mean. I don't know why I'm telling you all these intimate details, but somehow the older you get, the less you care what people know, don't you find? It's the same with your body. In hospital it's always the young patients who are most embarrassed about being washed and bedpanned and so on. The old ones couldn't give a damn."

"But what about your religion? When you had the affair."

"Oh, I knew I was committing a mortal sin. But I did it anyway, because I loved him. I thought he would marry me, you see. He said he would. But he changed his mind, or perhaps he was lying. So after I got over it I married Bede instead."

"Did you sleep with him first?" The question sounded crude as I formulated it, but curiosity overcame good manners.

Maureen rocked with laughter. "Good heavens, no! Bede would have been shocked at the very idea."

I pondered these surprising revelations in silence for a few moments. "So you haven't been bearing a grudge against me all this time?" I said at length.

"Of course not! Honestly, I haven't given you a thought for . . . I don't know how many years."

I think she was trying to reassure me, but I was hurt, I have to admit. "You haven't followed my career, then?" I said.

"No, should I have done? Are you terribly famous?"

"Not famous, exactly. But I've had some success as a TV writer. Do you ever watch *The People Next Door*?"

"Is that a comedy programme – the kind where you can hear a lot of people laughing but you can't see them?"

"It's a sitcom, yes."

"We tend to avoid those, I'm afraid. But now I know you write for it . . ."

"I write all of it. It was my idea. I'm known as Tubby Passmore," I said, desperate to strike some spark of recognition.

"Are you really?" Maureen laughed and wrinkled her nose. "Tubby!"

"But I'd rather you called me Laurence," I said, regretting the revelation. "It reminds me of the old days."

But from then on she called me Tubby. She seemed delighted with the name and said she couldn't get it out of her head. "I try to say 'Laurence', but 'Tubby' comes out of my mouth instead," she said.

The day we met, Maureen was aiming to get to Astorga. She refused to let me drive her there from the café, but, admitting that her leg was painful, agreed to let me take her backpack on ahead. She was planning to spend the night at the local *refugio*, uninvitingly described in the pilgrim's guidebook as an "unequipped sports hall". Maureen pulled a face. "That means no showers." I said I would be bitterly disappointed if she wouldn't be my guest for dinner on this red-letter day, and she could shower in my hotel room. She accepted the offer with good grace, and we arranged to meet in the porch of the Cathedral. I drove to Astorga and checked into a hotel, booking an extra room for Maureen in the hope of persuading her to take it. (She did.) While I waited for Maureen I did the tourist bit in Astorga. It has a cathedral which is Gothic inside and baroque outside (I was just about able to tell the difference by this time) and a Bishop's Palace like a fairy-tale castle built by Gaudí, who designed that weird unfinished cathedral-sized church in Barcelona with spires like enormous loofahs. Astorga also boasts a lot of relics, including a chip off the True Cross and a bit of a banner from the mythical battle of Clavijo.

Maureen turned up at the Cathedral about three hours after we had parted, smiling and saying that, without the weight of her backpack, the walk had been like a Sunday-afternoon stroll. I asked to see her leg and didn't much like what I saw under the grimy bandage. The calf was bruised and discoloured and the ankle joint swollen. "I think you should show that to a doctor," I said. Maureen said she had seen a doctor in León. He had diagnosed strained ligaments, recommended rest, and given her some ointment which had helped a little. She had rested the leg for four days, but it was still troubling her. "You need more like four months," I said. "I know a bit about this sort of injury. It won't go away unless you pack in the pilgrimage."

"I'm not going to give up now," she said. "Not after getting this far."

I knew her well enough not to waste breath trying to persuade her to drop out and go home. Instead I devised a plan to help her get to Santiago as comfortably as possible with honour. Each day I would drive with her pack to an agreed rendezvous, and book us into some modest inn or b. & b. Maureen had no principled objection to such accommodation. She had treated herself to it occasionally, and the *refugios* were, she said, becoming increasingly crowded and unpleasant the nearer she got to Santiago. But her funds were low, and she hadn't wanted to ring up Bede and ask him to send her more money. She agreed to let me pay for our rooms on the understanding that she would repay her share when we got back to England, and kept scrupulous note of our expenses.

We inched our way to Santiago in very short stages. Even without her backpack, Maureen wasn't capable of walking more than ten to twelve kilometres a day without discomfort, and it took her up to four hours to cover even that modest distance. Usually, after arranging our accommodation, I would walk back along the Camino eastwards to meet her, and keep her company on the home stretch. It pleased me that my knee stood up well to this exercise, even when the going was steep and rugged. In fact, I realized that I hadn't felt a single twinge in it since I got to St Jean Pied-de-Port. "It's St James," Maureen said, when I remarked on this. "It's a well-known phenomenon. He helps you. I'd never have got this far without him. I remember when I was climbing the pass through the Pyrenees, soaked to the skin and utterly exhausted, feeling I couldn't go any further and would just roll into a ditch and die, I felt a force like a hand in the small of the back pushing me on, and before I knew where I was, I found myself at the top."

I wasn't sure how serious she was. When I asked her if she believed St James was really buried in Santiago, she shrugged and said, "I don't know. We'll never know for sure, one way or the other." I said, "Doesn't it bother you that millions of people may have been coming here for centuries all because of a misprint?" I was showing off a bit of knowledge gleaned from one of my guidebooks: apparently the original association of St James with Spain all goes back to a scribe who wrote mistakenly that the Apostle's patch was "Hispaniam" instead of "Hierusalem" (i.e., Jerusalem.) "No," she said. "I think he's around the place somewhere. With so many people walking to Santiago to pay him homage, he could hardly stay away, could he?" But there was a twinkle in her eye as she spoke of these things, as if it were a private joke or tease, designed to scandalize Protestant sceptics like me.

There was nothing frivolous about her commitment to the pilgrimage, however. *"It's absurd, quite absurd,"* I remembered Bede saying, but the word had a Kierkegaardian resonance for me which he didn't intend. In the mediaeval town of Villafranca there's a church dedicated to St James with a porch known as the *Puerta del Perdón*, the Doorway of Pardon, and according to tradition if a pilgrim was ill and made it as far as this door, he could turn back and go home with all the graces and blessings of a fully completed pilgrimage. I pointed out this loophole to Maureen when we got to Villafranca, and pressed her to take advantage of it. She laughed at first, but became quite annoyed when I persisted. After that I never attempted to dissuade her from trying to get to Santiago.

To tell the truth, I would have been almost as disappointed as Maureen herself if she had failed to make it. The pilgrimage, even in the bastardized, motorized form in which I was doing it, had begun to lay its spell upon me. I sensed, if only fragmentarily, what Maureen had experienced more deeply and intensely in the course of her long march from Le Puy. "You seem to drop out of time. You pay no attention to the news. The images you see on television in bars and cafés, of politicians and car bombs and bicycle races, don't hold your attention for more than a few seconds. All that matters are the basics: feeding yourself, not getting dehydrated, healing your blisters, getting to the next stopping-place before it gets too hot, or too cold, or too wet. Surviving. At first you think you'll go mad with loneliness and fatigue, but after a while you resent the presence of other people, you would rather walk on your own, be alone with your own thoughts, and the pain in your feet."

"You wish I wasn't here, then?" I said.

"Oh no, I was almost at the end of my tether when you turned up, Tubby. I'd never have got this far without you."

I frowned, like Ryan Giggs when he's made a goal with a perfect cross. But Maureen wiped the frown off my face when she added, "It was like a miracle. St James again."

In due course she talked about the death of Damien, and how it had led to her making the pilgrimage. "It's a terrible thing when a child dies before its parents. It seems against nature. You can't help thinking of all the things he will never experience, like marriage, having children, grandchildren. Fortunately I think Damien knew love. That's a consolation. He had a girlfriend in Africa, she worked for the same organization. She looked very nice in photographs. She wrote us a beautiful letter after he was killed. I hope they had sex. I should think they would have done, wouldn't you?"

I said yes, undoubtedly.

"When he was a student at Cambridge he brought a girl home once, not the same one, and he asked if they could sleep together in his room. I said no, not in my house. But I would've let him, if I'd known how short his life was going to be."

I said she mustn't blame herself for actions that were perfectly reasonable at the time.

"Oh, I don't blame myself," she said. "It's Bede who does that, though he denies it. He thinks he should have tried harder to persuade Damien not to make his career in relief work. Damien did VSO, you see, after graduating. He was going to go back to Cambridge afterwards and do a PhD. But he decided to stay in Africa. He loved the people. He loved the work. He had a full life, a very intense life, though it was short. And he did a lot of good. I kept telling myself that, after he was killed. It didn't help Bede, though. He became terribly depressed. When he retired he just moped around the house all day, staring into space. I couldn't stand it. I decided I had to get away somewhere on my own. I read an article about the pilgrimage in a magazine, and it seemed just what I needed. Something quite challenging and clearly defined, something that would occupy your whole self, body and soul, for two or three months. I read a book about the history of it, and was completely fascinated. Literally millions of pilgrims went along this road, when the only way of doing it was on foot or on horseback. They must have got something tremendous out of it, I thought to myself, or people wouldn't have kept on going. I got myself a guide to the route from the Confraternity of St James, and a rucksack and sleeping-bag and the rest of the kit from the camping shop in Wimbledon High Street. The family thought I was mad, of course, and tried to talk me out of it. Other people presumed I was doing it as a sponsored walk for charity. I said, no, I've done things for others all my life, this is for me. I've been a nurse, I'm a Samaritan, I'm –"

"Are you really?" I interjected. "A Samaritan? Bede didn't mention it."

"Bede never really approved," said Maureen. "He thought all that misery would leak out of the phone and infect me."

"I bet you're good at it," I said.

"Well, I've only lost one client in six years," she said. "I mean, only one actually topped himself. Not a bad record. Mind you, I found I was less sympathetic after Damien was killed. I didn't have the same patience with some of the callers, their problems seemed so much more trivial than mine. Do you know what our busiest day of the year is?"

"Christmas Day?"

"No, Christmas is second. Number one is St Valentine's Day. Makes you think, doesn't it?"

In our slow, looping dawdle along the Camino we were frequently overtaken by younger, fitter, or fresher walkers. The nearer we got to Santiago, the more of them there were. The annual climax of the pilgrimage, the feast of St James on 25th July, was only a couple of weeks away, and everybody was anxious to get there in good time. Sometimes, from a high point on the road, you could look down on the Camino ribboning for miles ahead, with pilgrims in ones and twos and larger clusters strung out along it like beads as far as the horizon, just as it must have looked in the Middle Ages.

At Cebrero we ran into a British television unit making a

documentary about the pilgrimage. They were ambushing pilgrims outside the little church and asking them about their motives. Maureen refused point-blank to take part. The director, a big blond chap in shorts and tee-shirt, tried to persuade her to change her mind. "We desperately need an older woman who speaks English," he said. "We're up to here in young Spaniards and Belgian cyclists. You'd be perfect." "No thank you," Maureen said. "I don't want to be on television." The director looked hurt: people in the media can never understand that the rest of the world doesn't have the same priorities as themselves. He turned to me as a second-best alternative. "I'm not a true pilgrim," I said.

"Ah! Who is a true pilgrim?" he said, his eyes lighting up.

"Someone for whom it's an existential act of self-definition," I said. "A leap into the absurd, in Kierkegaard's sense. I mean, what could be –"

"Stop!" cried the director "Don't say any more. I want to film this. Go and get David, Linda," he added to a freckled, sandy-haired young woman clutching a clipboard. David, it appeared, was the writer-presenter of the programme, but he couldn't be found. "He's probably sulking because he had to actually *walk* a bit this morning," muttered the director, who was also confusingly called David. "I'll have to do the interview myself."

So they set up the camera, and after the usual delay while the director decided where to set up the shot, and the cameraman and his focus-puller fiddled about with lenses and filters and reflectors, and the sound man was satisfied about the level of background noise, and the production assistant had stopped people walking in and out of shot behind me, I delivered my existentialist interpretation of the pilgrimage to camera. (Maureen by this time had got bored and wandered off to look at the church.) I described the three stages in personal development according to Kierkegaard – the aesthetic, the ethical and the religious – and suggested that there were three corresponding types of pilgrim. (I had been thinking about this on the road.) The aesthetic type was mainly concerned with having a good time, enjoying the picturesque and cultural pleasures of the Camino. The ethical type saw the pilgrimage as essentially a test of stamina and self-discipline. He (or she) had a strict notion of what was correct pilgrim behaviour (no staying in hotels, for instance) and was very competitive with others on the road. The true pilgrim was the religious pilgrim, religious in the Kierkegaardian sense. To Kierkegaard, Christianity was "absurd": if it were entirely rational, there would be no merit in believing it. The whole point was that you chose to believe without rational compulsion – you made a leap into the void and in the process chose yourself. Walking a thousand miles to the shrine of Santiago without knowing whether there was anybody actually buried there was such a leap. The aesthetic pilgrim didn't pretend to be a true pilgrim. The ethical pilgrim was always worrying whether he *was* a true pilgrim. The true pilgrim just did it.

"Cut! Great. Thanks very much," said the director. "Get him to sign a release, Linda."

Linda smiled at me, with pen poised over her clip board. "You'll get twenty-five pounds if we use it," she said "What's your name, please?"

"Laurence Passmore," I said.

The sound man looked up sharply from his equipment. "Not Tubby Passmore?" I nodded, he slapped his thigh. "I knew I'd seen you somewhere before. It was in the Heartland canteen, a couple of years ago. Hey, David!" he called to the director, who was walking away in search of another victim, "Guess who this is – Tubby Passmore, the writer. *The People Next Door*." He turned back to me: "Great show, I never miss it when I'm at home."

The director turned round slowly. "Oh no," he said, and mimed shooting himself in the head with his forefinger. "So you were just taking the piss?" He laughed ruefully. "We really fell for it."

"I wasn't taking the piss," I said. But I don't think he believed me.

The days passed in a slow, regular rhythm. We rose early, so that Maureen could set off in the cool of the early morning. She usually arrived at our rendezvous around noon. After a long, leisurely Spanish lunch we retired for a siesta and slept through the heat of the afternoon, coming to life again in the evening, when we would take the air with the natives, snacking in *tapas* bars and sampling the local *vino*. I can't describe how at ease I felt in Maureen's company, how quickly we seemed to resume our old familiarity. Although we talked a lot, we were often content to be together in a companionable silence, as if we were enjoying the sunset years of a long happy life together. Other people certainly assumed we were a married couple, or at least a couple; and the hotel staff always looked mildly surprised that we were occupying separate rooms.

One night, after she had been talking at some length about Damien, apparently in good spirits, even laughing as she recalled some childish misadventure he had had, I heard her weeping in the room next to mine, through the thin partition wall of the no-star hotel where we were staying. I tapped on her door and, finding it unlocked, went in. A street-lamp outside the window shed a dim illumination into the room through the curtains. Maureen was a humped shape that stirred and rearranged itself on the bed against one wall. "Is that you, Tubby?" she said.

"I thought I heard you crying," I said. I groped my way across the room, stumbled over a chair beside the bed, and sat down on it. "Are you alright?"

"It was talking about Damien," she said. "I keep thinking I've got over it, and then I find I haven't." She began to cry again. I felt for her hand and held it. She squeezed it gratefully.

"I could hug you, if that would help," I said.

"No, I'm alright," she said.

"I'd like to. I'd like to very much," I said.

"I don't think it would be a good idea, Tubby."

"I'm not suggesting we do anything else," I said. "Just a cuddle. It'll help you go to sleep."

I lay down beside her on the bed, outside the blanket and sheet, and put my arm round her waist. She turned over on to her side, with her back to me, and I curled myself around her soft ample bottom. She stopped crying, and her breathing became regular. We both fell asleep.

I woke, I didn't know how many hours later. The night air had

306

grown cool, and my feet were chilled. I sat up and rubbed them. Maureen stirred. "What is it?" she said.

"Nothing. Just a bit cold. Can I come under the bedclothes?"

She didn't say no, so I lifted the sheet and blanket and snuggled up to her. She was wearing a thin, sleeveless cotton nightgown. A pleasant warm odour, like the smell of fresh-baked bread, rose from her body. Not surprisingly, I had an erection.

"I think perhaps you'd better go back to your own bed," Maureen said.

"Why?"

"You might get a nasty shock if you stay here," she said.

"What do you mean?" She was lying on her back and I was massaging her stomach very gently through her nightgown with my finger-tips – it was something Sally liked me to do when she was pregnant. My head was pillowed on one of Maureen's big round breasts. Very slowly, holding my breath, I moved my hand up to cup the other one, just as I had done all those years ago, in the damp dark basement area of 94 Treglowan Road.

But it wasn't there.

"I did warn you," Maureen said.

It was a shock, of course, like climbing the stairs in the dark and finding there is one step fewer than you expected. I pulled my hand away in a reflex action, but put it back again almost immediately on the plateau of skin and bone. I could trace the erratic line of a scar, like the diagram of a constellation, through the thin fabric of the nightgown.

"I don't mind," I said.

"Yes you do," she said.

"No I don't," I said, and I unbuttoned the front of her nightdress and kissed the puckered flesh where her breast had been.

"Oh Tubby," she said, "that's the nicest thing anybody ever did to me."

"Would you like to make love?" I said.

"No."

"Bede will never know." I seemed to hear the echo of another conversation from the past.

"It wouldn't be right," she said. "Not on a pilgrimage."

I said I took her point, kissed her, and got out of the bed. She sat up, put her arms round me and kissed me again, very warmly on the lips. "Thanks Tubby, you're a darling," she said.

I went back to my room and lay awake for some time. I won't say that the problems and disappointments of my life seemed trivial beside Maureen's, but they certainly seemed smaller. Not only had she lost a beloved son – she had lost a breast, the part of a woman's body which defines her sexual identity perhaps more obviously than any other. And although Maureen herself would certainly have said that the former loss was the greater, it was the latter which affected me more, perhaps because I had never known Damien, but I had known that breast, known it and loved it – and written about it. My memoir had turned into an elegy.

I walked the whole of the last stage of the pilgrimage with Maureen. I put a few overnight things in her rucksack, and we shared carrying it. I left the car in Labacolla, a hamlet about twelve kilometres outside Santiago, near the airport, where the pilgrims of old used to wash themselves in preparation for their arrival at the shrine. The name literally means, "wash your bottom", and the bottoms of the mediaeval pilgrims probably needed a good scrub by the time they got there.

It was a warm, sunny morning. The first part of the route was through a wood and across some fields with pleasant open country to our left and the grumble of traffic from the main road to our right. Then we came to a village, at the far end of which is the Monte del Gozo, the "Mount of Joy", where pilgrims get their first view of Santiago. In olden times there used to be a race to the top, amongst each group, to be the first to see the long-desired goal. It's a bit of an anticlimax nowdays, because the hill has been almost entirely covered with a huge amphitheatre, and from this distance Santiago looks like any other modern city, ringed by motorways, industrial estates and tower blocks. If you look very hard, or have very good eyes, you can just make out the spires of the Cathedral.

Nevertheless, I was very glad I walked into Santiago. I was able to share something of Maureen's excitement and elation as she reached the finishing line of her marathon; I even felt a modicum of excitement and elation myself. You notice much more on foot than you do in a car, and the slowness of walking itself creates a kind of dramatic tension, delaying the consummation of your journey. Trudging through the ugly modern outskirts of the city only heightens the pleasure and relief of reaching its beautiful old heart, with its crooked, shady streets, odd angles and irregular rooflines. You turn a corner and there, suddenly, you are, in the immense Plaza del Obradoiro, looking up at the twin spires of the great Cathedral.

We arrived on the 24th July, and Santiago was bursting at the seams. The four-day *fiiesta* was already in progress, with marching bands, huge walking effigies on stilts, and itinerant musicians roving through the streets and squares. The pukka pilgrims like Maureen were swamped by hundreds and thousands of visitors, both secular tourists and pious Catholics, who had arrived by plane or train or bus or car. We were told the crowds were particularly big because it was a Holy Year, when the feast of St James falls on a Sunday, and the blessings and indulgences attached to the shrine are especially potent. I suggested to Maureen that we ought to see about getting accommodation without delay, but she was impatient to visit the Cathedral. I indulged her. It seemed unlikely that we would find anywhere to stay in the old town anyway, and I was resigned to going back to Labacolla for the night.

The Cathedral is a bit of a dog's breakfast architecturally but, as we say in television, it works. The elaborately decorated façade is eighteenth-century baroque, with a grand staircase between the two towers and spires. Behind it is the portico of the earlier romanesque building, the Portico de la Gloria, carved by a mediaeval genius called Maestro Matteo. It depicts in amazing, often humorous, detail, some two hundred figures, including Jesus, Adam and Eve, Matthew, Mark, Luke and John, twenty-four old codgers with musical instruments from the Book of Revelations, and a selection of the saved and the damned at the Last Judgement. St James has pride of place, sitting on top of a pillar just under the feet of Jesus. It's the custom for visitors to the Cathedral to kneel at the foot of the pillar, and place their fingers in the hollow spaces, like the holes in a knuckleduster, that have been worn into the marble through centuries of homage. There was a long line of people, many of them local to judge by their clothes and complexions, waiting to perform this ritual. Clocking Maureen, with her staff and rucksack and sunfaded clothes, as a genuine pilgrim, the people at the front of the line fell back respectfully and gestured her forward. She blushed under her tan and shook her head. "Go on," I urged her. "This is your big scene. Go for it." So she stepped forward and fell onto her knees and, with one palm pressed against the pillar, fitted the fingers of the other hand into the holes, and prayed for a moment with her eyes closed.

On the other side of the pillar, at the foot, Maestro Matteo has carved a bust of himself, and it's the custom to knock your head against his to acquire something of his wisdom. This was more my kind of mumbo-jumbo, and I duly banged my forehead against the marble brow. I observed some confusion between the two rituals. Every now and again somebody would bang their head against the pillar under the statue of St James as they put their fingers in the holes, and then everybody in the line behind them would follow suit. I was tempted to try slapping my buttocks like a Bavarian folkdancer as I paid homage, just to see if it caught on, but I didn't have the nerve.

We joined another line of people taking their turn to embrace the statue of St James on the high altar. The holy end of the Cathedral is an over-the-top fantasy in marble and gold leaf and carved painted wood. St James Matamoros, dressed and mounted like a Renaissance cavalry officer, charges with sword drawn above the canopy, which is supported by four gigantic, trumpet-blowing angels. St James the Apostle, swathed in jewel-encrusted silver and gold plate, presides over the altar looking more like a pagan idol than a Christian saint, especially as, seen from the main body of the church, he seems to have grown an extra pair of arms. These belong to the people who, standing on a little platform behind the altar, embrace him and, if they are pilgrims, pray for those who helped them on their way – the traditional "hug for St James". Beneath the altar is a crypt with the small silver coffin containing the remains of the saint – or not, as the case may be.

"Wasn't it wonderful?" Maureen said, as we came out of the Cathedral, into the bright sunlight of the square with its milling crowds. I agreed that it was; but I couldn't help contrasting the pomp and circumstance of this shrine with the small, austerely furnished room in the Copenhagen Bymuseum, its half-dozen cabinets containing a few homely objects, books and pictures, and the modest monument in the Assistens Kirkegård. I wondered whether, if Kierkegaard had been a Catholic, they would have made him a saint by now, and built a basilica over his grave. He would make a good patron saint of neurotics.

"Now we really ought to see about finding somewhere to stay," I said.

"Don't worry about it," Maureen said. "First I must get my *compostela*." We were directed to a little office off a square at the back of the Cathedral. Outside, a group of bronzed, elated-looking young Germans in *Lederhosen* and boots were photographing each other, triumphantly waving their pieces of paper at the camera. Maureen lined up inside and submitted her creased, stained passport to a young priest in a black suit seated behind a desk. He admired the number of stamps she had collected, and shook her hand as he passed over her certificate.

"*Now* can we see about a hotel?" I said, as we came out of the office.

"Well, actually," Maureen said, with a slightly embarrassed laugh, "I've reserved a room at the Reyes Catolicos. I did it before I left England."

The Hostal de los Reyes Catolicos is a magnificent Renaissance building which flanks the Plaza del Obradoiro on the left-hand side as you face the Cathedral. Originally the *refugio* to end all *refugios*, founded by King Ferdinand and Queen Isabella for the reception and care of pilgrims, it's now a five-star *parador*, one of the grandest hotels in Spain or indeed anywhere else.

"Fantastic! Why didn't you tell me?" I exclaimed.

"Well, there's a little problem. It's just the one room, and I booked it in the name of Mr and Mrs Harrington. I thought Bede might fly over and join me. But he was so mean about the pilgrimage that I never told him."

"Well then," I said, "I'll just have to impersonate Bede. It won't be the first time."

"You don't mind sharing then?"

"Not a bit."

"I asked for twin beds, anyway," said Maureen. "Bede prefers them."

"Pity," I said, and enjoyed her blushes.

As we approached the hotel a gleaming limousine pattered over the cobbles to pick up a smartly dressed elderly couple standing outside the entrance. The liveried, white-gloved doorman pocketed a tip, shut the car door and waved the driver on. He eyed us disapprovingly.

"My *compostela* entitles me to a free meal here," Maureen murmured. "But I'm told they give you rather nasty food and make you eat it in a grotty little room off the kitchens."

The doorkeeper evidently thought that this must be our reason for approaching the hotel, for he said something rather dismissive in Spanish and gestured us towards the back of the building. It was an understandable presumption, I suppose, given our somewhat scruffy appearance, but we took some satisfaction in putting him in his place. "We have a reservation," said Maureen, sweeping regally past the man, and pushing through the swing doors. A porter ran after us into the lobby. I gave him the rucksack to hold, while I went up to the reception desk. "Mr and Mrs Harrington," I said boldly. The clerk was suavely courteous. Funnily enough, he looked rather like Bede, tall, stooped and scholarly, with white hair and thick glasses. He checked his computer, and gave me a registration card to fill in. Maureen had booked for three nights, and paid a substantial deposit.

"How could you be sure you would get here, at exactly the right time?" I marvelled, as we followed the porter, who was trying with some difficulty to carry our rucksack as if it were a suitcase, to the room.

"I had faith," she said simply.

The Hostal is laid out in four exquisite quadrangles, with cloisters, fllowerbeds and fountains, each dedicated to one of the evangelists. Our room was off Matthew. It was large and luxurious, the single beds the size of small doubles. Samantha would have loved it. There were sixteen fluffy white towels of different sizes in the marble-lined bathroom, and no nonsense about getting a red card if you wanted them changed. Maureen cooed with delight at the array of taps, nozzles, adjustable mirrors and built-in hair dryer, and announced her intention of taking a bath and washing her hair immediately. At the bottom of her rucksack, folded flat as a parachute inside a plastic bag, was a clean cotton dress which she had been saving for this moment. She gave it to the hotel's housekeeper to be ironed, and I took a cab back to Labacolla to pick up my car, which contained a linen suit I hadn't previously worn on the trip.

So we didn't disgrace the hotel's elegant dining-room that evening. The food was amazingly expensive, but very good. Afterwards we went out into the square and squeezed into the vast crowd waiting to watch the fireworks. This is easily the most popular event of the *fiesta*. Spaniards love noise, and with this display they seemed determined to make up for their exclusion from World War Two. The climactic setpiece resembled an air raid on the Cathedral, with the whole structure apparently on fire, statues and stonework silhouetted against the flames, and cannonades of rockets exploding deafeningly overhead. I couldn't see what it had to do with St James, but the crowd loved it. There was a huge collective sigh as the vast stage faded to black, and a burst of cheering and clapping when the street-lights came on. The crowd began to disperse. We went back to the Reyes Catolicos. The doorman greeted us with a smile.

"Goodnight Señor, Señora," he said, as he held open the door.

We took turns to use the bathroom. When I came out, Maureen was already in bed. I stooped to give her a goodnight kiss. She put her arms round my neck and drew me down beside her. "What a day," she said.

"It's a pity sex isn't allowed on pilgrimages," I said.

"I'm not on a pilgrimage any more," she said. "I've arrived."

We made love in the missionary position. I came – no problem. No problem with the knee, either. "I'll never knock St James again," I said, afterwards.

"What d'you mean?" Maureen murmured drowsily. She seemed to have had a good time too.

"Never mind." I said.

When I woke next morning, Maureen wasn't there. She had left a note to say that she'd gone to the Cathedral early, to bag a seat for the great High Mass of St James; but she came back while I was having breakfast to say the church was already crammed full, so we watched the mass on television instead. It's a state occasion, broadcast live on the national network. I don't think Maureen missed much by not being there. Most of the congregation looked stupefied by the heat and the tedium of waiting. The high point of the service is the swinging of the *botafumeiro*, a gigantic censer, about the size of a sputnik, which is swung high into the roof of the cathedral, trailing clouds of holy smoke, by a team of six burly men pulling on an elaborate tackle of ropes and pulleys. If it ever broke loose at this mass it could wipe out the Spanish Royal Family and a large number of the country's cardinals and bishops.

We took a stroll round the old town, had lunch, and retired to our room for a siesta. We made love before we napped, and again that night. Maureen was as eager as me. "It's like giving up sweets for Lent," she said. "When Easter comes, you make a bit of a pig of yourself."

In her case Lent had lasted for five years, ever since her mastectomy. She said Bede hadn't been able to adjust to it. "He didn't mean to be unkind. He was wonderfully supportive when the tumour was diagnosed, and while I was in hospital, but when I came home I made the mistake of showing him the scar. I'll never forget the expression on his face. He couldn't get the image out of his head, I'm afraid. I tried keeping my prosthetic bra on in bed, but it made no difference. About six months afterwards he suggested we changed our double bed for two singles. He pretended it was because he needed a special mattress for his back, but I knew he meant that our sexual life was over."

"But that's terrible!" I said. "Why don't you leave him and marry me?"

"Don't be ridiculous," she said.

"I'm perfectly serious," I said. And I was.

That conversation took place on the edge of a cliff overlooking the Atlantic ocean. It was our third evening since arriving in Santiago, and our last together in Spain. The next day Maureen was flying back to London, with a ticket purchased months ago; after seeing her off at the airport I would drive the Richmobile to Santander to catch the ferry to England.

We had driven out of Santiago that afternoon, after a particularly passionate siesta, in search of a little peace and quiet – even Maureen had had enough of the crowds and clamour of the streets by now. We found ourselves on a road signposted to Finisterre and just kept going. I must have heard the name a thousand times on the radio in shipping forecasts and gale warnings without knowing that it was in Spain or twigging that it means "end of the world" in Latin. It was a long way – further than it looked on the map. The rolling wooded hills of the country around Santiago gave way to a more rugged, heath-like terrain of windblown grass broken by great slabs of grey rock and the occasional stubborn, slanting tree. As we approached the tip of the peninsula the land seemed to tilt upwards like a ramp, beyond which we could see nothing but sky. You really felt as if you were coming to the end of the world; the end of something, anyway. We parked the car beside a lighthouse, followed a path round to the other side of the building, and there was the ocean spread out beneath us, calm and blue, shading almost imperceptibly into the sky at the hazy horizon. We sat down on a warm, flat rock, amid coarse grass and wildflowers, and watched the sun, like a huge communion wafer behind a thin veil of cloud, slowly decline towards the wrinkled surface of the sea.

"No," said Maureen, "I couldn't leave poor old Bede. What would he do without me? He'd crack up completely."

"But you have a right to happiness," I said. "Not to mention me."

"You'll be alright, Tubby," she smiled.

"I like your confidence. I'm a notorious neurotic."

315

"You seem very sane to me."

"That's because of being with you again."

"It's been wonderful," she said. "But it's like the whole pilgrimage, a kind of kink in time, when the ordinary rules of life don't apply. When I go home, I'll be married to Bede again."

"A loveless marriage!"

"Sexless, perhaps, but not loveless," she said. "And I did marry him, after all, for better or for worse."

"Haven't you ever thought of leaving him?"

"No, never. It's the way I was brought up, I suppose. Divorce just wasn't thinkable for Catholics. I know that it's caused a lot of misery for a lot of people, but it's worked for me. It simplifies things."

"One less decision to make."

"Exactly."

We were quiet for a while. Maureen plucked and chewed a stalk of grass. "Have you thought of trying to get back together with your wife?" she said.

"There's no point. Her mind is made up."

I had of course told Maureen all about the break-up with Sally, in the course of our conversations over the past few weeks, and she had listened with a keen and sympathetic interest, but without making any judgements.

"When did you last see her?" Maureen asked. I worked it out: it was about three months. "You may have changed in that time, more than you know," Maureen said. "You told me yourself you were a little bit off your head in the spring." I admitted that that was true. "And Sally may have changed too," Maureen went on. "She may be waiting for an approach by you."

"That hasn't been the tenor of her lawyer's letters," I said.

"You can't go by them," Maureen said. "Lawyers are paid to bluster."

"True," I conceded. I recalled Sally's rather surprising phone call, just before I left London. If I hadn't been in such a hurry to be off, I might have interpreted her tone as conciliatory.

We sat and talked until the sun set, and then we had supper at a restaurant on the beach that looked as if it had been built out of driftwood, where we chose our fish from a sea-water tank and they grilled it for us over charcoal. Nothing we had tasted at the Reyes Catolicos could touch it. We drove home in the dark, and somewhere in the middle of the heathland I stopped the car and doused the lights and we got out to look at the stars. There was not an artificial light for miles, and hardly any pollution in the atmosphere. The Milky Way stretched across the sky from east to west like a pale, glimmering canopy of light. I had never seen it so clearly. "Gosh!" Maureen exhaled. "How wonderful. I suppose it looked like this everywhere in the olden days."

"The ancient Greeks thought it was the way to heaven," I said.

"I'm not surprised."

"Some scholars think that there was a sort of pilgrimage here long before Christianity: people following the Milky Way as far as they could go."

"Goodness, how do you know all these things, Tubby?"

"I look them up. It's a habit."

We got back into the car and I drove back fast to Santiago, saying little, concentrating on the road unwinding in my headlights. Back in the Reyes Catolicos, we fell asleep quickly in each other's arms, too tired, or too sad, to make love.

I had plenty of time on the ferry to ponder Maureen's advice, and by the time we docked in Portsmouth I had determined to give it a shot. I phoned Sally just to check that she would be in, and drove straight to Hollywell without stopping. The crunch of my tyres on the gravel of the drive brought Sally to the front door. She offered me her cheek to kiss. "You look well," she said.

"I've been in Spain," I said. "Walking."

"Walking! What about the knee?"

"It seems to be better, at last," I said.

"Wonderful. Come in and tell me all about it. I'll make a cup of tea."

It felt good to be home – I still thought of it as home. I looked round the kitchen with pride and pleasure in its sleek lines and smart colour scheme. Sally looked in good shape too. She was wearing a red linen dress with a long slit skirt that showed an occasional flash of tanned leg as she moved about the kitchen. "You're looking well yourself," I said.

"Thank you, I am. Have you come to pick up some of your things?"

"No," I said, my throat suddenly dry. I coughed and cleared it. "I've come to have a talk, actually. I've been thinking, Sal, perhaps we should have a go at getting back together. What d'you say?"

Sally looked dismayed. That's the only word to describe her face: dismayed. "No, Tubby," she said.

"I don't mean straight away. We could go on with separate living arrangements in the house for a while. Separate bedrooms, anyway. See how it goes."

"I'm afraid it's impossible, Tubby."

"Why?" I said, though I knew the answer before she spoke.

"There's someone else."

"You said there wasn't."

"Well, there wasn't, then. But now there is."

"Who is he?"

"Somebody at work. You don't know him."

"So you've known him for some time, then?"

"Yes. But we didn't . . . we weren't . . ."

Sally for once seemed at a loss for words. "We haven't been lovers till – till quite recently," she said at last. "Before that it was just a friendship."

"You didn't tell me about it, though," I said.

"You didn't tell me about Amy," she said.

"How did you know about Amy?" I said. My head was spinning.

"Oh, Tubby, everybody knows about you and Amy!"

"It was platonic," I said. "At least it was until you walked out."

"I know," she said. "When I met her I knew it must be."

"This chap at work," I said. "Is he married?"

"Divorced."

"I see."

"We'll probably get married. I expect that will make a difference to

318

the divorce settlement. You probably won't have to give me so much money." She gave me a wan smile.

"Oh, fuck the money," I said, and walked out of the house for ever.

It was a nasty shock, of course – to have my carefully prepared offer of reconciliation brushed aside, rendered redundant, cut off at the knees, shoved back down my throat almost before I'd uttered it. But driving back down the M1 through dwarf forests of cones, I began to see a positive side to the reversal. It was obvious that Sally had begun to lean towards this other bloke years ago, whatever the exact nature of their relationship. It wasn't, as I had thought ever since Brett Sutton turned out to be innocent, that she'd left me simply because she would rather be lonely than married to me. I found that curiously reassuring. It restored my self-esteem.

The day's shocks weren't over though. When I got back to London and let myself into the flat, I found it completely empty. It had been stripped bare. There was nothing movable left in it, down to the light bulbs and the curtain rails. The chairs, tables, bed, carpets, crockery and cutlery, clothes and household linen – all gone. The only thing that was left, very neatly placed in the middle of the bare concrete floor, was my computer. It was a thoughtful touch on Grahame's part: I had explained to him once how precious the contents of my hard disk were, and he didn't know that I had deposited a box of back-up files with my bank before I left for Spain. I don't know how he and his friends got in, because they hadn't damaged the door and had carefully locked it behind them when they left. Perhaps Grahame had taken an impression of my keys one day when he was in the flat and I was in the loo – I used to keep a spare set hanging in the kitchen. Or perhaps he just borrowed them once without my noticing. Apparently they arrived one morning in a removal van and had the cheek to ask the police for special permission to park outside the building while they moved the contents of my flat to some spurious new address.

When I stepped into the flat and looked round, after half a minute of mouth-open astonishment, I laughed. I laughed till the tears rolled down my cheeks and I had to lean against the wall and finally sit down on the floor. The laughter was a touch hysterical, no doubt, but it was genuine.

If this was a television script, I would probably end it there, with the final credits scrolling over the empty flat, and yours truly sprawled in one corner, his back against the wall, weeping with laughter. But that happened several weeks ago, and I want to bring this story up to date, up to the moment of writing, so that I can carry on with my journal. I've been very busy working on *The People Next Door*. Ollie and Hal really loved my rewrite of Samantha's script for the final episode of the last series. It went down a treat with the studio audience too, apparently. (I wasn't there, it was recorded on 25th July, the feast of St James.) And Debbie was so taken with playing Priscilla as a ghost that she changed her mind and signed up for a whole new series based on the idea. I'm writing the scripts, but Samantha will get a prominent credit, which is only fair. She's become Heartland's number one script-doctor in a very short time. I had a bet with Jake at lunch today that she'll have Ollie's job before two years are out.

Jake wasn't very sympathetic about my burglary. He said I was insane to have ever trusted Grahame, and pointed out that if I'd let him use the flat as his love-nest while I was away, Grahame and his mates wouldn't have dared to loot it. But I was able to refurnish the flat quite quickly – the insurance company were very fair – and I never liked the original furnishings much anyway. Sally chose them. It's been like starting a new life from scratch, replacing everything in the flat. It's too small to live in permanently, though. I'm thinking of moving out to the suburbs, Wimbledon to be precise. I see quite a lot of Maureen and Bede these days. It would be nice to be near them, and I thought I might try to join the local tennis club – I always did fancy wearing that dark green blazer. I went up to Hollywell the other day to empty my locker at the old Club. A slightly melancholy occasion, brightened by the circumstance that I ran into Joe Wellington and challenged him to a game of singles for a tenner. I beat the shit out of him, 6–0, 6–0, rushing the net after every serve and scampering back to the baseline when he tried to lob me. "What about your knee?" he gasped afterwards. "Just pay up with a smile,

Joe," I said. "Reason not the knee." I don't think he recognized the quote.

I have my eye on a nice little house up the hill from the All England Club. I shan't give up the flat, though. It's useful for business to have a base in the West End; and every now and then Maureen and I have a siesta here. I don't ask her how she squares it with her conscience – I've got more sense. My own conscience is quite clear. The three of us are the best of friends. We're going off together for a little autumn break, actually. To Copenhagen. It was my idea. You could call it a pilgrimage.